D0873753

WHAT A DUCHESS DOES

LORDS AND UNDEFEATED LADIES BOOK 3

JUDITH LYNNE

JUDITH LYNNE

Copyright © 2020 by Judith Lynne. 3rd ed.

All rights reserved.

No part of this book may be reproduced in any form or by any electronic or mechanical means, including information storage and retrieval systems, without written permission from the author, except for the use of brief quotations in a book review.

This is a work of fiction and as such its characters, events, words, and places are the product of the author's imagination. However, its story is set in 1813 when a duke in Britain is a person of great importance. Therefore the fictional duke in this fictional story encounters fictional versions of the real Prince Regent and the less well known but equally real Warren Hastings. With the exception of these historical personages reinvented as fictional ones for fictional purposes, any resemblance to persons living or dead is coincidental. As with some of the characters, the narrator's version of events may be unreliable.

Cover art by Melody Simmons

BOOKS BY JUDITH LYNNE

Lords and Undefeated Ladies

Not Like a Lady

The Countess Invention

What a Duchess Does

Crown of Hearts

He Stole the Lady (January 2022)

Cloaks and Countesses

The Caped Countess

The Clandestine Countess (July 2022)

PREFACE

My very dear readers,

In the spring of 1813, Britain is hard-pressed. Napoleon has control of most of the Continent, and forbids trade with Britain, which is after all a small collection of islands. The French Emperor suffered great losses in his attempt to invade Russia, but remains on his throne. The War of the Sixth Coalition has just begun, and the United Kingdom of Great Britain and Ireland has joined Austria, Prussia, Russia, Spain and Portugal, as well as Sweden and several of the German states, to try to defeat him.

Elsewhere, Britain has gained control of former French, Dutch, and Danish colonies, and banned slave trading (though not slavery itself). The young United States of America is harrying British ships in the Pacific, and so the war with them drags on. The African Company of Merchants, run by men from London, Liverpool, and Bristol, makes immense profit in western Africa.

And after twenty years of its current method of operation, during which it has effectively assumed control of India, the East India Company is due to be reauthorized by Parliament.

Let us have a care for the duke of our tale, who has tried to do his best for his country and whose private life has been far less interesting than London society speculated in *The Countess Invention*. It is about to take a turn, for he has met an extraordinary woman, though almost no one knows that yet.

But he does. And you do.

Your obedient servant,

Judith Lynne

AN UNEXPECTED ENGAGEMENT

*F*or Selene, running meant rushing into the unknown. But to save her mother, she ran.

She heard the parlor door hit the wall as she burst through. "Dr. Burke! Is Dr. Burke in here?"

"I'm here, Selene, what is it?"

"My mother, she's collapsed!"

She felt him *whoosh* past her, then his boots pounded up the stairs.

Selene couldn't follow as fast, but she did her best, hanging on to the polished handrail the whole way. She couldn't hear anything but the sound of her heart pounding so hard and the awful silence that had fallen in her mother's room.

Dr. Burke was slapping her mother's hands. She *hoped* that was her mother's hands. In the small quiet room that held her mother's bed, the horrible sound echoed. "Mary! Can you hear me, Mary?"

Selene tried to shrink behind the chair, forcing herself to stay still and be small until something, anything, woke her mother. She could stay there forever, if only her mother would wake.

She'd been knitting to the friendly creaking of the rocking chair, and her mother had just… stopped talking. In the middle of a sentence. Selene couldn't remember what they'd been talking about. She desperately wished she could remember.

"I shook her as hard as I could. Even her face felt cold. Is she...?"

"She is insensible, not dead. Mary! Will you wake up, Mary?"

Her mother didn't answer, and didn't answer, and didn't answer...

The physician slapped her hands again. "Mary, wake up. I need you to wake up now. Can you hear me?"

"...'m awake. What is it? What's happened?"

The relief hit Selene hard, and she slumped; only her grip on the back of the chair kept her upright. Her mother's voice was faint, but *there*.

Cass was at the door. "What can I do?"

Dr Burke answered. "Sit with Lady Redbeck for a few moments, will you, dear? I'd like her to stay awake. Just talk to her. Selene, let us fetch your mother some cool water."

"I'll be back immediately, Mama, will you be all right?"

Her mother seemed to find that rather funny. She'd been bedridden nearly a year, after all. "It's not as though I'm going to walk away, dear."

As they left, Selene heard Cass start talking about levers and fulcrums.

That would put her mother to sleep.

"Walk down with me, Selene."

Breathing deeply—she must remember to breathe—Selene followed the doctor at a sedate pace. She knew about doctors. They only wanted to say things one didn't want to hear, and they preferred to do it where the patient couldn't hear.

When they reached the floor below the servants' quarters, Dr. Burke said quietly, "Are you quite all right?"

"What happened? What was that? Will she—?"

"As I've explained, your mother's heart is not as strong as it should be. I believe her heart just could not push enough blood to her brain, and she fainted. It's not painful, Selene."

"How can we make her better?" She'd keep asking until he gave her a new answer. He didn't *have* a new answer. But she needed one, so she kept asking.

Dr. Burke's voice was gentle and understanding. "There's not much I can do for her. I'm sorry."

"Is there anything *anyone* could do?"

His hesitation made her hopes swoop high, then crash as he finally spoke. "I believe that the heart works like any other muscle. Perhaps hers could be trained to be stronger, unless it is badly damaged. It may be. I cannot tell. If it is badly damaged, moving more could kill her. I'm sorry, Selene."

For Selene, standing tall was both nature and habit. They kept her upright now. "Please don't say that. I *need* to hear what else we can do for her. What *anyone* might do for her. I cannot lose her, Dr. Burke, I simply cannot."

And with that, her last nerve snapped, and Selene burst into tears.

And that was when she heard the Duke of Talbourne's voice just behind her.

"What's going on?"

The abrupt question shouldn't have been calming, but it was. She knew His Grace.

He was as stiff and formal as a stone pillar, and at the moment nothing seemed as welcome as a stone pillar. The sturdy kind that held things up.

He'd seemed so since the day she'd accidentally met him while dusting in the library. His silver honey voice had startled her. He'd asked gravely, suddenly, "Miss, would it be better for both of us if I moved to another chair?" So close by that she realized he was there at the same time that she realized she was about to trip over his feet.

She'd gasped, and laughed, and apologized for not knowing he was there, and for a moment she had been Lady Selene again, the earl's pretty daughter, the one pretty enough to marry well even if she was blind.

Unforgivable in a housemaid, and even now the thought of it made her face burn. But no one had seen her, so what did it matter? Her cousin's household was very informal.

And she hadn't been flirting. Not really.

No one would ever accuse His Grace of flirting. Or of being particularly happy, or sad, or any other thing that feeling people did. He was just inescapably *there*, excruciatingly proper even while they talked together, unchaperoned... and alone.

He never made her skin crawl, though so many other men had, from viscounts to fishmongers. She had always trusted her own instincts, and that one especially. And he had always spoken to her just as he was speaking now. There was something *bracing* about that.

Fighting for calm with her fists against her mouth, Selene heard Dr. Burke explaining quietly to His Grace. Her mother had fainted and frightened Selene, but was awake now.

Her sobs slowed. She ought to say something. Her mother *had* woken. She was alive tonight, and that was reason enough to save the rest of her worrying for tomorrow.

Someone gave her a handkerchief. A crisp linen square that smelled of lemons and rosemary.

Selene was the maid here. *She* ironed Dr. Burke's handkerchiefs, and everyone else's in the house. With lavender water.

This handkerchief must be His Grace's.

It was amazing how bracing lemons and rosemary could be.

"I am well, I promise."

"And your mother?" Brusque could seem rude. To Selene right now, it felt intimate. And welcome.

She opened her mouth to tell him, but her voice still would not work. She couldn't force the words out. She needed a little more time to figure out how to be this frightened.

"Dr. Burke, can you tell me more about Lady Redbeck's health?"

"Selene?" Dr. Burke was leaning in. "May I?"

She just waved the handkerchief. She had no secrets worth keeping from His Grace.

After all, after months of referring to her, quite properly for a housemaid, as Selene, the Duke of Talbourne had started calling her Miss de Gauer.

He'd found out who she was.

Which had given her the pleasure of no longer worrying about it. As far as she knew, the Duke had guarded her shame as gravely and steadily as he did everything else. It freed her to devote her time to plotting how to make him laugh someday.

He'd sat in the House of Lords with her father. He knew the key facts. Her father was dead, and they were destitute.

He may have suspected some details: little rooms, then one room, then a room so damp and cold that her mother came down with a fever that had left her this weak.

Those didn't make pleasant conversation, so neither of them sought to discuss it.

She *had* told him pleasanter things: about oranges, and games, and awarding herself points for dusting to keep track of her place. He knew she had been blind since childhood, with nearly no memories of light and color.

He even knew that what Selene had most regretted about losing her debut London season, was dancing. Not that she regretted losing the season anywhere near as much as she regretted losing her father.

Selene didn't recall how that subject had come up or why she had told him such a personal thing, but he knew.

She *didn't* tell him terribly personal things. How she missed her father's voice reading her history books. And how she missed the constant swirl of Redbeck Hall's fascinating visitors: the Dahomean king who had once ventured into the great African desert; the tiny, ancient Italian *comtesse* who had told her *very* inappropriate stories; the Frenchman dressed all in satin, who had sounded like dry grass walking.

No gentleman was amused by a lady's stories of *taxes*, so Selene had kept those entirely to herself. She missed talking to traders who'd been through the dissolving Holy Roman Empire, and through Russia, to Chinese Tartary and beyond.

The Duke brought news of Britain's politics, and those Selene drank down like water, ignoring her hunger for the tales one got from American diplomats of uncountable trees and extraordinary animals. A lady let a gentleman choose the topic of conversation.

A housemaid even more so.

Her parents had always told her she would be a countess, perhaps a marchioness. Her whole world was different now. She was *grateful* to be a housemaid.

A tiny world in which she had become someone who only spoke to the members of her cousin's odd little household, and, very occasionally, the Duke. She had learned to give up being charming for being quiet.

A tiny world that revolved around her mother.

"Lady Selene." The Duke's voice was very close; her mind had drifted. Had Dr. Burke gone?

"Don't call me that, please." She *had* once been Lady Selene. Now? She really was not.

She had also learned humility. The kind of humility it took to convince her mother, finally, to write to Cass, a distant and unfamiliar cousin. To ask for advice. Cass had sent back that they must come live with her.

Selene had argued like a lion for Cass to let her work; she couldn't do nothing day in and day out just because she was blind. She'd learned work she once would have shied from, work with linens, and dusting, and laundry pails.

And she'd hoped every day that the one thing she wouldn't lose was her mother.

Her shoulders hunched, and the sobs shook her again. Into the Duke's scented handkerchief.

If she lost that hope, crouching on a staircase, bawling her eyes out in front of a duke, she lost everything.

"Miss de Gauer," the Duke tried again. "May I speak with your mother?"

Deference. From a duke. Absurd. His Grace was never absurd. Oddly, the absurdity steadied her a little. "Surely it is just Selene. Now more than ever." And she mopped at her face, which must look revolting.

His Grace didn't seem to be revolted. Not that he would have given it away if he did. "I should never have addressed you so informally, Miss de Gauer, but I enjoyed our conversations."

Speaking informally to her had been entirely proper, because she was the *maid*. Their conversations had been thrilling for the flavor of the old days they brought back. And she'd so wanted that.

Perhaps His Grace had liked it too, because he added, almost as if he were admitting something, "It's hardly as though you called me Nicholas."

"Your name is Nicholas?" She was surprised enough that her unrelenting tears stopped falling, just for a moment. She felt him take the handkerchief away, and he dried a few spots that she had missed, then gave it back to her.

"It is."

That was reassuring to know, somehow.

"May I visit your mother, Miss de Gauer, if Dr. Burke allows it?"

"Yes, of course, but you needn't—"

"Please, miss, just a quick visit. I will return down here directly."

She sat up a little straighter. *Were* they alone? "Dr. Burke?"

"Oh yes. Lady Redbeck is quite well enough to speak, though she may fall asleep."

The Duke's footsteps as he went up the stairs were so slow and measured compared to Dr. Burke's just a few minutes before. His cool calm at this moment seemed as indomitable as the ocean. Attractive? It was practically seductive.

For nearly a year, that calm had fueled what was left of her daydreams.

But daydreams were daydreams. Selene told herself not to get silly, though silly was preferable to despairing. Or lonely.

Cass' little household included many who spoke the manual language for the deaf, and for Selene, that was just silence.

Not to mention that Cass and the other maid Peg both were married, and Selene... was very grateful to have her mother for company.

Dusting, she suddenly recalled. The topic they'd been discussing, when her mother's voice had just faded away. *Dusting.* Her mother would talk about *dusting*, if it was for her daughter.

This household wouldn't be family without her mother in it. If her father had been her world, her mother had become even more than that since they had come so far together without him. There was no way Selene could lose her now.

* * *

Selene lost track of time, sitting on the stairs with a straight spine and crushing the Duke's handkerchief in her hands. His footsteps coming back down seemed almost to wake her.

"Miss de Gauer," said His Grace's measured voice, "Your mother and I have agreed that she should be removed to Talbourne House as soon as Dr. Burke agrees that it is safe to do so. You will of course come with her."

"What? I don't—" Selene ought to stand. She stood. She had to remind herself to keep hold of the sadly squashed and tear-soaked handkerchief. She'd lost control a bit. "I mean, thank you, sir, for the offer, and my sincere apologies for the overflowing emotion—"

"Please do not apologize. I have enough footmen to carry her comfortably, if Dr. Burke approves the plan. Would this evening be too soon?"

Would this evening be too *soon*? Selene didn't even know what he was *talking* about.

"Lady Redbeck should be fine to travel a short way," said Dr. Burke, who didn't sound entirely certain. Was he confused too?

A firm hand just cupped Selene's elbow. It must have been the Duke's. Some of his habitual calm seemed to seep into her at the touch, and without thinking about it, she let him lead her down the hall.

And he kept talking. Asking the most amazing things.

May they pack her belongings? Her mother's too? Did she own anything delicate they should take care in placing in the carriage?

"Your Grace—what do you actually mean?"

"Miss de Gauer, your mother needs more care than can easily happen here. I shall remove you and her to Talbourne House, in about twenty minutes if you agree."

If she *agreed?* He was offering her something more precious than diamonds. It was like the moment at the end of a fairy tale, when everything came right after all.

She'd never before been handed a rescue along with a handkerchief.

Her memories of softer, younger days receded even farther, overcome by the allure of sturdy stone pillars. An allure she might follow into just about anything.

Surely he was just being kind. She ought not to take his offer too seriously, though his voice was as serious as he always was.

As serious as he almost always was.

The offer was too generous; she should give him a graceful way to withdraw it. "Sir, I ought to see my mother." In half an hour he would come to his senses, if she only left him to it.

"*She* has agreed. I think she assumed that if it was best for her health, you would accompany her? Talbourne House has far more staff. And of course I can engage nurses. But if you prefer to stay here...?"

"*Prefer?* No, but..."

"Very good. Mr. Adams, please do give Gerald those valises. Miss de Gauer, is there anything you ought to take that isn't in your rooms?"

"I should talk to her before..."

"You can speak in the carriage, of course. Dr. Burke, perhaps you would accompany Miss de Gauer to the carriage? Or perhaps your wife would be so kind? I shall stay with my men, they are bringing Lady Redbeck down in a chair."

"A *chair?*"

Dr. Burke took her hand. "Selene. It's quite safe." He led her toward the parlor. "Come say goodbye to Cass."

In moments, Selene was enfolded in her cousin's long arms, and Cass' familiar voice made the world a little more normal.

"This is so lucky for your mother. Oliver tells me that what your mother really needs is a little gentle excitement, and care. Talbourne House would do it. A change of scenery! I would hate for her to be trapped in the four walls of that room, if—But what about you? I have known His Grace for years, but to put you entirely in his care—"

"I can risk anything, for my mother. But he isn't even family! I do not understand his effort on our behalf."

"He knows *you*, Selene."

Did he? Well, yes. He knew Selene the housemaid. She was a housemaid now. They'd learned at least a little about each other.

The thought was so tempting. That the Duke of Talbourne was helping because he *knew* her.

To be kind, not romantic. She had better remember that.

"He is a duke, he knows *many* people! Dr. Burke, tell me the truth. Will this help my mother? I was so frightened, I just—I *cannot* lose her, I cannot."

Dr. Burke took both Selene's hands in his, and Cass' arm around her shoulder held her close. "Selene, her heart may never be strong. And His Grace can provide... well, anything. If it does not completely heal her, it certainly will not hurt. New surroundings may be quite helpful."

Cass wasn't as sure. "He seemed to have a plan in mind? And he said that he and your mother had agreed? If you won't be alarmed to go to a new place... I cannot think it anything unsavory. Though you needn't! I feel... well, responsible, as your older cousin. This is new, Lady Redbeck's episode. We can find a physician more knowledgeable about her condition."

"Cass," and Selene put her lips close to her cousin's cheek, both to kiss it and to keep the words between themselves. "You gave us a home when we would otherwise have slept in the street. You never need to apologize, not to me."

Cass' arm squeezed again. "You are always a part of this home, you know. Our great-grandfather's house, and me. That will not change."

Then one of the Duke's footmen announced that it was already time to depart. They were leaving.

The world was about to become larger again.

* * *

IT WAS a long way from the carriage's door to the seat. Selene traced its side with her hand, searching for the seat for what seemed like ages. The thing was the size of a small cottage.

And seconds later, her mother was lifted, by several strong young men, into the space with her.

Selene helped her shift from the chair to the carriage's broad, upholstered cushions. "Are you quite well, madame?"

The pat she got back was soft, but it was there. "I feel surprisingly well for such a fast trip down those stairs. Truly dear, I was only unconscious for a moment. I am not sure why all this fuss."

"His Grace said that you had agreed that we be removed to Talbourne House?"

"Oh yes. I did."

Her mother sounded far from alert, but clearly some sort of conversation had occurred, and that was as good as Selene was going to get.

Especially as His Grace suddenly filled the vast space of the carriage with just his quiet voice. "Ladies," he said without preamble, apparently arranging himself in the seat opposite.

She wondered if he was looking at her. But surely not? Or, rather, naturally he was looking at her; he was sitting opposite. She was nervous, this was fantastical, he was being kind.

"This is an extraordinarily kind gesture, Your Grace," Selene said softly.

His response was only a noncommittal noise.

Was he *her* duke? Now outside the parlor, in this vast carriage, he seemed distant and strange. And she so wished him to feel familiar.

Perhaps now, with her mother there, Selene would have confirmation that she could make him smile.

"It's odd," said Selene, "I never really thought of you as kind before."

He seemed to smother a snort, and her mother made a distressed noise, as if she had stepped on a mouse.

Selene took heart from that smothered snort. Surely a snort was just around the corner from a smile. "I will be sufficiently repaid if you always speak so frankly to me. Miss de Gauer."

She'd ask her mother later if the smile had been there. Not in front of the Duke.

"Lady Redbeck, will you play Three Kingdoms with me? Just to while away the drive."

"Without His Grace?"

"No thank you, madame," the Duke declined the implied invitation.

"His Grace doesn't play games, madame." He didn't mind hearing about them, so far as Selene knew, but he didn't play.

So Selene and her mother chattered softly about animal, vegetable, and mineral things, the daughter with her arms wrapped around her mother, trying to protect her from any jouncing. Outside the vast, plush carriage there were sounds of people drinking and shouting, and children playing in the street. Those faded away as the carriage rocked out of the more densely built city into more open lanes, the sounds of people replaced by the sounds of trees rustling in the night breeze.

Inside, Selene held tight the last member of her immediate family and hoped with all her might that moving her mother to the residence of the silent duke sitting opposite was the right thing to do.

* * *

"The man's barely taller than I am, and yet he seems to take up all the air in the house. In fact, all the air in the street." Dr. Burke watched the carriage doors close from the townhouse door.

"It's all those servants." Cass waved as all the footmen scurried around the enormous vehicle, which was blocking their small street as it so often did. The spectacle usually drew peering neighbors. They were probably peering now, out their darkened windows.

"It's not all the servants. He matches the woodwork, ought to blend into it, and yet one feels compelled to keep one's eyes on him."

"He is a *duke*. I think the grey in his hair matches his eyes and looks distinguished. Or... do you not trust him?" Cass looked at Oliver with surprise. His Grace had visited them many times, and Oliver had never said any such thing.

"Of course I do. Who am I not to give a fellow the benefit of the doubt? And it seems they've spoken, I don't mean Lady Redbeck and the Duke, but the Duke and your cousin? It's just... There goes your cousin and her mother in his yawning abyss of a carriage. I wish I could have done more for Lady Redbeck. It's guilt, I suppose." Oliver watched as the massive carriage began to roll away. "Just a bit of guilt. They will be fine."

* * *

SELENE WAS RIGHT, of course. Nicholas wasn't kind. But it wouldn't do to admit that in front of the young lady's mother.

Especially not when that mother had provided such a spectacularly convenient reason to carry Selene away into the night.

If he had wanted to display his feelings, the only correct way would be to rub his fingertips together with glee and cackle like a pantomime villain. But Nicholas had spent a lifetime cultivating an impassive face that did not display his feelings.

Nor was this light fun. It was deadly serious, to him.

He had her. She was *his*.

He was thankful he'd been able to move fast. But it was no accident. One happened upon crossroads every day. Being able to take an advantageous turn depended upon preparing for it.

And Nicholas didn't believe in luck, even when he was looking straight at it.

Because it had been a bit of luck that he had rudely visited the Burkes' house—Lord and Lady Howiston—right after Lady Redbeck's collapse.

It had been luck, and craving.

Now he was carrying Selene de Gauer off to *his* home. The temptation was right there, to think of her as *his* as well.

But it would be foolish to think so. She would only be where he could constantly improve his chances. Nicholas didn't know if he might reach his ultimate goal in a week, a month, or a year, but a step in the right direction was a step in the right direction.

It wouldn't be so odd for her and her mother to join Talbourne House's revolving collection of nearly-permanent guests. She would get to know him. The rest of his plan would naturally follow.

Had he been a different man, he'd have cannon firing salutes.

But he was himself, so his elation showed itself only through one finger tapping on the head of his walking stick.

Yes, it would have to be slow. Selene was so innocent. His short conversation with her mother had confirmed it. But she was far from stupid. Nicholas stayed where he was, on his side of the carriage, determined not to do anything to give himself away. If he wasn't careful, she might figure out that he was bundling her away to Talbourne House for purposes that were not based on kindness.

But he did let himself look at her. He never tired of looking, waiting for her next smile.

There were a thousand things about her, as he had slowly discovered, that drove him nearly mad with distraction. The way her good humor and determination showed in her face was his absolute favorite.

If I play my cards right... No, this wasn't that kind of game. Cards were for people who thought that good luck and bad luck came in equal measure. Nicholas didn't believe that, and he didn't play cards.

But he did like this move. Selene would be in Talbourne House. He'd be able to at least see her whenever he liked.

And then one day...

He rapped on the front window and told the answering footman, "I would like to see Mr. Lyall immediately upon our return."

If his luck held, no one would see them arrive but his own servants.

* * *

JONAS CAMERON, Baron Callendar, was as surprised as anyone that he was still at Talbourne House after three days. The trip to London proper was over an hour, so he put it off; and the staff, by some miracle he didn't understand, kept producing clean clothing.

It seemed to be the custom here to come and never leave. The dining and gaming tables featured plenty of people who, at some point, had done the same thing.

In three days, he hadn't yet seen the Duke of Talbourne. The Duke did not attend his own musicales or gaming tables. Jonas had heard that he usually dined with the household, but what *usually* was, hadn't happened either.

Jonas didn't care. If he weren't a guest here, he'd just be a guest somewhere else. And he didn't intend to leave till he learned if the rumors were true.

Word in political circles was that His Grace had come to life like a statue enchanted, and was actually planning to propose a new measure for vote.

London's politics were like sugar for Jonas: sweet, addictive, and probably unhealthy. Everyone in London knew how much he loved them, so everyone tossed him the same poisonous candy. Such a surfeit of candy, that now Jonas' tastes were becoming more refined.

He wanted truly rare confections.

If the stony Duke of Talbourne was planning to actually do something, Jonas wanted to be the first to know.

He'd play cards with everyone and keep his eyes open.

* * *

"MISS DE GAUER. May I take your hand?"

Talbourne House must be huge. She could hear servants everywhere: meeting the carriage, opening the door, greeting His Grace as he alighted.

Then he turned back to *her*.

"Oh yes, thank you for asking. I never mind it if I must walk somewhere."

He did take her hand and placed it on his arm to lead her. It was a shockingly familiar way to touch a lady, and an unheard-of way to touch a housemaid.

And it gave her the most peculiar urge to ask him to go right back into the carriage.

Being with him in there, rather than out here, seemed far more appealing at the moment.

New places were disorienting, and while Lady Selene had adored new people, housemaid Selene often found them less than charming. And she *was* a housemaid now. If he introduced her to anyone, what would she *say?*

His arm was hard and warm beneath the fine wool of his sleeve, making her think of warm beds and stone pillars at the same time, which was also a little disorienting.

The troop of men carrying Lady Redbeck in a chair scuffled along just ahead. Trying not to worry about them dropping her mother, Selene focused on gathering any clues she could about Talbourne House.

To her left there was singing, with several stringed instruments; rich earthy smells wafting across what was clearly a vast foyer betrayed someone's delicious late dinner. Girlish laughter tumbled like little bells somewhere off to her right.

Along with the irregular tapping of many pairs of high-heeled slippers across the inlaid floor. Tapping that stopped as their short procession drew near. Then a flurry of light feminine voices whose words she couldn't quite hear. Some group of girls, watching them progress across the elegant open hall of Talbourne House.

But none of them spoke to her, of course. They did whisper as she passed.

The yearning that flooded Selene in that moment, to make a friend she could talk to, surprised her.

Selene straightened her spine.

The girls didn't speak to them directly but a young man did. To the Duke, quite close. "Your Grace. A generous host even to late guests."

"Lord Callendar. Lady Redbeck has been quite ill. You'll forgive me if I see to her comfort."

"Of course. Will I see you later at the tables?"

"I don't usually join."

Nicholas' tone rebuffed his guest more than his words. His tone was musical, but the way silver was musical: cool and unyielding. Didn't he know this Lord Callendar? Who was here in his house?

Lord Callendar sounded as if he did. "Then we'll miss your sparkling wit."

Selene's first instinct was to answer Lord Callendar's pleasantry herself, but instead she drew back a little, as if to hide behind His Grace. She felt… compromised.

It was one thing for the Duke to touch her so, it was another thing for others to see it.

The stranger's cut-glass accent and careless air also reminded Selene of the state of her clothes, her hair. What she must look like. What she *was*.

It was the scent of Talbourne House, she realized, that reminded her she was out of place. That scent jerked her into the past. It was familiar.

Now that she smelled this particular smell again, she could pick out its components, the mixed scents of hot crushed flowers, warm silk and velvet, polished silver and wax candles.

It was the smell of being rich.

Of having possibilities.

The Duke clearly did not wish to talk more with his guest. "I believe I see Lady Hadleigh waiting to escort you to the tables, Lord Callendar. And Lord Burden is talking to Lady Fawcett over there— he considers himself quite the card-player. Excuse me."

All those silk-and-beeswax people, were they looking at her? It must be obvious that she was out of place. A servant.

Or even, she realized with a flash of insight, a lady of ill repute.

The very idea made her want to cover her face again. No one had even *insinuated* that she might... do any of that, when she was the Earl of Redbeck's only daughter. And when she was poor, the things people shouted at her in the streets made her wonder why anyone would *want* to.

Touching Nicholas was something entirely different.

She ought to stop touching him. She didn't want to stop touching him. She *wasn't* compromised, she was *poor*. Gentry could be poor.

Selene's possibilities were long gone. She was in no danger of a marriage made of contracts. She didn't have a dowry and she didn't have to live for anyone but herself and her mother. There was a freedom in that.

Selene the housemaid was free to touch the Duke and dream of his arms holding her up.

Though it was a long leap from touching to holding, a gap her imagination wasn't quite able to fill.

The Duke didn't say anything else to the young man, and Selene heard the man's boots walking away. He did say, "Mr. Lyall. I'd like to settle Lady Redbeck on the east side of the family wing. I believe those rooms are ready for guests?"

"Sir."

The Duke transferred Selene's hand to the elbow of a servant. "Talbourne House welcomes you, Lady Selene. Rest well."

* * *

PETER LYALL WAS a bald man built like a stone country wall and just as worn, with eyes that looked even older. He ran Talbourne House, but was rather more valuable to His Grace for his ability to find things out, from the depths of the bays of Scotland, to the gunpowder supplies in the West Indies, to the drinking habits in the royal palace.

He was the one who had given His Grace everything the world knew about Selene de Gauer and her mother.

He'd worked for the Duke long enough to know that when the man spoke of one thing, he often meant another. He'd called Lady Redbeck his guest; but he'd led in the girl himself.

And it was the girl he was watching leave.

"She's very pretty."

His Grace didn't acknowledge the remark, so Mr. Lyall pressed further. "But I have seen you turn down..." Every woman that had crossed his path for all the time Lyall had known him. "May I know the reason for your interest in this particular young woman, Your Grace?"

"Mr. Lyall, I doubt you would grasp it."

Lyall shrugged. Hadn't hurt to ask. He thought he knew the Duke of Talbourne better than anyone else in Britain, and he still wouldn't dare to try to guess what he would do next.

His Grace paid him to ask and answer questions.

So he hinted that His Grace might do well to answer this one. "I do grasp a great many things, sir."

"My apologies, no insult intended. It is... difficult to describe."

It must be, Peter Lyall thought to himself.

Because at thirty-eight, widowed two years and in the prime of health, the Duke had no women at all.

Lyall had never seen his head turned, not by country milkmaids or London virgins. That girl was important. "May I ask why you wanted me to observe the young lady's arrival?"

Talbourne did not look away from where Selene was disappearing up the wide, sweeping staircase. "She's here, Mr. Lyall. We must... see that she stays. Happy and well. I trust you will see to it."

"Of course, sir," and Lyall withdrew, knowing from long experience that His Grace had nothing further to say about the young lady or her mother.

* * *

NICHOLAS SELDOM DRANK.

There was therefore no reason to have liquor in his apartments. For the first time, he wished for some.

That was a new wish too.

He let his valet help him off with his boots and then waved the fellow away as he sank into a chair by the huge glass window that looked out over his gardens.

It wasn't that he *never* drank. Never drinking was noticeable. He drank when it was customary, so that neither drink nor the lack of it would be noticed.

At this time of night, the window opposite showed him his own face, reflected in its black surface, cut into a dozen copies of itself by the mullioned panes. Not a view he relished.

He knew he had no scruples, because it had crossed his mind in the carriage that if Lady Redbeck had only been unconscious for the trip, he might have gotten away with touching Selene a good deal more.

And he *liked* Lady Redbeck.

Damn it all, he wished that bevy of silly girls that Lady Villeneuve took with her everywhere hadn't seen them come in. It wouldn't just be all over the house, it would be all over London. He should have had Lyall clear the place before bringing her through. And who was that Callendar boy?

He'd just been following his gut urge to *get her in the house*. But he ought to have learned as a child that his gut was a terrible guide.

It was madness, thinking that this would work out. Things *didn't* work out, and this wasn't going to work out either.

But no. He wouldn't let his thoughts swirl in that same endless circle. Wait long enough for something to go well, and before he knew it, his life would be over, wasted. It had taken him years to realize that, and he didn't have more time to waste.

He was his father's son. He never expected to be good. He wanted to be *fair*. If he could carve out one role to play, it was that of a voice of reason in the House of Lords.

Quickly.

He'd inherited his seat so young. And his father had done nothing with that seat. No one blamed Nicholas for not doing more with it but Nicholas himself. Now he had a goal, to use his habit, his talent for remaining calm, cool, and collected to make sure that the United

Kingdom peers heard hard truths, when it was what they needed to hear.

Nicholas had no faith in his ability to make decisions of a moral nature for himself or for anyone else. He did have faith in his ability to see things clearly.

But the way he felt this constant pull toward that young lady shook that faith. Five years ago, ten, it would never have even occurred to him to want to touch her hand. Now he pictured it as many times a day as there were panes in this glass. With his eyes closed, he could still feel the warmth of her fingers on his sleeve. He could imagine far, far more.

He hadn't brought Miss de Gauer to the house because it was the moral thing to do. He had done it because he wanted to do it.

He thought he'd trained himself out of wanting. He was wrong.

He wanted to be fair, and this didn't feel fair.

He was going to do it anyway.

* * *

ALISTAIR FILLWER, Earl of Burden, had just lost spectacularly at cards. The instant after he realized it, he told himself that it didn't matter.

He nodded to Callendar over the cards and crystal, calm as a summer breeze. Even a loss like that one—and he felt it—couldn't do him any real damage. The voices of his childhood reminded him of that and took the sting away. When he had even the ghost of the idea that *this could really hurt him*, it faded into nothing, chased away by the bright sunshiny voices of older people telling him "Oh surely not, Alistair."

That didn't mean that he couldn't give Callendar a good glare.

Callendar looked pleased with himself, and that was tasteless. Alistair tried to say so with his eyes.

"Off to bed, Lord Burden?" Callendar asked as he rose. There was a rustle and more murmuring, and the crowd drew back, now that the last exciting head-to-head round was played.

"I'm off home," and he raised a hand to summon a footman. "I'll have a carriage."

"Sir."

Callendar looked a little surprised. "It's late, sir, you had better stay here."

"I would rather my own bed."

"Good night, then."

Alistair would teach them all a thing or two about how a gentleman took a loss, nodding appropriately as he went.

The butler approached him as soon as he reached the hallway. "We beg your pardon, Lord Burden, but there is some confusion. There is no carriage of yours on the grounds."

That's right, he'd come out of town with Lord Halworth when he'd seen him passing the druggist's shop.

"I can help you out of your confusion. I was of course asking for one of the Duke's carriages to be readied to take me home."

"To the city, sir?"

"To the Mayfair area, of course."

The butler's mouth seemed to be confused too, about what shape to take. "At this time of night we'd have to wake footmen as well as a driver to accompany you, sir, plus the groomsmen."

"Of course." Alistair couldn't do the man's job for him any farther; surely he saw now what was needed.

"I see, sir. If you will wait here just a few moments, I'll see to it, sir."

"I'll wait in the blue parlor." His loss was fine, it was fine, but he wouldn't stand out here in the open space for anyone to gawk at as they passed by.

"Very good, sir."

Hopefully they'd be quick, thought Alistair as he strolled past Talbourne's collection of far Eastern vases.

The evening had still been well spent. He'd accomplished something in just seeing that pretty girl in servant wool who'd walked like a queen, straight into Talbourne House on its owner's arm. He'd know a great deal more about her by the time he came back tomorrow and talked to Talbourne about his proposals regarding imports.

It occurred to him that his proposals had better make good, or his coffers would soon run short. The business he'd inherited from his father earned him far more than the lands, but his income still didn't quite match his household costs.

Alistair didn't ask himself what his father might have done differently. He'd lived for so long in a chorus of voices telling him that he was magnificent, all was well, and everything would be fine, that he never heard anything else.

RECONNAISSANCE

*S*elene woke up drooling on something silk. How had she landed on this bed? She'd dreamed about washing laundry, and... washing His Grace's *hair*. That was odd. She didn't even know what his hair was like.

Then she'd dreamed she'd dusted all the inside of a carriage the size of a house.

Wait, that carriage was real.

"Mama?" She put out her hand and tried to sound awake.

"Yes, dear," came her mother's voice, tired but calm, her dry small hand patting Selene's, and all Selene's insides settled.

Her mother's voice. *Her mother.* Alive, and for the moment, well.

They *were* in a room in the Duke's residence, and from the sound of their voices—everyone's voices—this room was *huge.*

She squeezed her mother's hand. "Are you quite well? Did you sleep?"

"Beautifully, dear. Even with Fran constantly waking me. What a comfortable mattress-maker His Grace has discovered. The people you hear are flocks of maids bringing linens now, and feather pillows, clothes brushes, playing cards, and flowers, now that you are awake." Lady Redbeck sounded both delighted and awed.

It must be the aforementioned Fran who interrupted, just a little amused. "I woke your mother every two hours, miss, just as her doctor told His Grace to see to. She answered my questions clearly, so I let her go back to sleep. There was no need to disturb you. I've done a bit of nursing before."

Selene pushed herself upright. "How may I help?"

"Not at all. The rest of us are just arranging things now, and it'll be completely sorted in half a minute. I'll like keeping your mother company. It won't be so bad, will it, Lady Redbeck?"

"I am sure you are lovely company, dear, but I plan to continue to sleep." Her mother's voice still sounded tired.

It was a feature of her illness, Dr. Burke had said; she was often tired. Selene wanted her to sleep. But Selene was awake, her dream fading, and the worry—and unanswered questions—of last night coming back to her. "Mama," she whispered. "What did you tell His Grace?"

"He will tell you, dear," was all her mother said. Then she fell silent again. She must have drifted back to sleep.

Surely it was sleep and not the deadly cold silence of lost consciousness. Selene tucked the coverlet more closely around her mother.

Well, Selene would figure out what to do next.

She felt, well, sticky. She'd slept in her clothes. Clothes soaked with tears, no less. Selene never cried like that. Yesterday evening had been *years* ago.

How long had her mother talked with Nich—with His Grace?

"Fran, might there be a place where I can wash before I speak to our host?"

"Of course, miss."

* * *

FRAN WHISKED her through a door before Selene could make note of where it was and seated her at a dressing table.

"And Fran, Dr. Burke suggested that my mother would benefit

from gently moving her limbs, rubbing her feet to encourage her circulation. Do you think you can arrange that?"

She reached to find the brush on the table before her but Fran was already untangling the great mass of Selene's hair with her fingers.

"Of course, miss. Dr. Burke had several instructions for your mother's care. He also said that if you yourself were comfortable, that might make your mother more comfortable. So let's get you into the tub as well. I have some water in the fireplace."

Selene heard water splashing, and in moments she was ushered into a deep, pleasantly hot tub.

Relaxing despite herself, Selene decided that learning where she was in the room could wait.

She had missed luxuries like this. She had missed the sense of enveloping, relaxing warmth, and the fresh summery smell of roses that rose from the thick bar of soap even though it was barely spring.

She had *not* missed the sensation of feeling lost.

In fact, it was all too familiar. Selene rubbed the soap between her hands, making sure to clean under the fingernails of her laundry-roughened hands, and wondered how many life-changing shocks lay still ahead of her at the ripe old age of twenty-four.

Hearing the door close again—Fran leaving, surely—Selene let her head loll back against the tub.

Her mother was safe. They were safe, and it was because of the Duke of Talbourne. Nicholas.

The man with the strong, warm arms.

Holding was really too much to think about. Dancing, that must have been the word she'd wanted, last night in all the rush.

Dancing would be just the right amount of appropriate, it would have nothing to do with... those things she'd thought when he'd touched her in public. Dancing happened in specific times and places even if dreaming about dancing—with Nicholas—spilled everywhere in her head.

For right at this moment, he did seem to be everything. Even the silky warm water was a little like his voice. Not that his voice was exactly warm. But it did surround a person.

Would he dance that way, she wondered? Surrounding her?

She imagined his steady arms leading her through a polonaise—no, for his arms to surround her she would want a waltz. He would be so sure in his steps, so predictable. She would be able to rely on his direction in every move, even as he drew her close…

The fairy tales had been vague about what happened if dancers got too close, but dancing all night was a real and possible thing.

It would smell like this, Selene decided, like the lush opulence of a rose garden, fresh sweetness edged with silver frankincense.

Oh, she did like the idea of that.

It would be heavenly, but apparently, the Duke didn't enjoy himself. If he didn't take any part in his own games, just downstairs, it seemed unlikely that he danced.

No games, and likely no dancing either. It was sad. It made Selene think of him drowning in silk and beeswax, all alone.

If Selene were a part of the party, she'd make sure he had at least a little fun. If she couldn't make him laugh that was one thing. If he never laughed, that was quite another.

But she was not actually part of the party, was she?

She splashed her fingers in the rose-scented water.

* * *

NICHOLAS HAD KEPT his feelings to himself since he was eleven years old and he wasn't going to stop now.

Staff always watched. Particularly his staff. He could never be sure how loyal any particular person was, no matter how well paid or well treated. So he would not give away to the staff that he was particularly interested in Selene.

Given the way he had whisked her into the house, late in the evening and along with her mother, there would already be more gossip than he wanted.

Thus he was awkwardly cracking his breakfast egg, and trying to decide how to ask his own servants what he really wanted to know.

He paused before biting into his toast, as if it had just occurred to him, and told the footman, "Oh, make sure something is sent up to Lady Redbeck; and see if her daughter is coming down."

"Sir," said the young chap and leaped to it.

The table would soon be swarming with guests just as it was every other morning. He wanted to see *her*. If she came down soon, he might get to see her alone. If she didn't, he would have to make sure to leave *before* she arrived; he didn't want anyone to see them together. It wasn't just habit, it was good discretion not to give any interest away. What if his plan failed? He'd already compromised her reputation.

Though he could make that work in his favor.

The soft, salty sweetness of butter on his tongue only made him wonder what it would be like to kiss her.

Surely this incessant preoccupation would stop now that she was here. Though he wasn't proud of the thought, here, he might see her when his craving struck. So the craving would fade.

More defensibly, here she would be safe.

Mr. Lyall's skill at uncovering facts was practically uncanny. Nicholas knew, as surely as he knew his own name, that what Mr. Lyall had uncovered (that Selene had never mentioned) must have worn on her the most. Nicolas could guess a great many things about the series of little rooms where they'd lived before they had found their way to Lady Howiston's house: the little food, the endless grinding hours of sickness, the worry about tomorrow. Selene had been through too many of the levels of hell, he was sure of that, and he could make it so she'd never worry about tomorrow again.

Gossip was inevitable, but it would help his plan if he could keep it to a minimum.

* * *

"Fran?" Selene stepped gingerly out of the tub, wrapped in drying linens and hoping this was the right place to drip.

"She's returned to your mother, miss." Some new maid, one with an interesting French accent, slipped a soft chemise over Selene's arms, then her head, without introducing herself. Then a gown. The gown didn't feel familiar.

"Thank you. I am Selene de Gauer; will you please tell me your name?"

This maid wasn't nearly so talkative. She paused. "My name is Selene, miss."

"Never tell me so! How confusing that will be, both of us having the same name."

"Céline, miss. The accent on the first syllable, not the second."

Everything about the young lady's tone indicated that her name was the right one, and Selene's was *not*.

Selene decided that inappropriately named women should dress their own hair. "I can finish my hair, Céline, if you will point out my comb and the hairpins."

But the maid continued to toss and twist hanks of her hair.

Selene liked her hair, and it rankled a little that the maid seemed to be treating it primarily as a problem to solve.

"I've been asked to see to your hair and dress, miss."

Well. *Lady* Selene might have been quite curt at this treatment.

But then, Lady Selene's servants were all gone, and come to think of it, her friends had disappeared too.

Now Selene knew what it was to *be* a servant, and she wouldn't snap.

So she kept her hands folded tight and her lips folded tighter as Céline braided her hair snugly and pinned the braids close to her head. It pulled a bit, here and there.

Well, I must look like a tidy workman's lunch bundle now, Selene thought a little acidly.

"Will miss be breakfasting downstairs, or have something here?"

She wanted food, but she *needed* to know what His Grace intended to do with her and her mother. How long might they stay? Might her mother have a physician who knew more about her illness?

She shouldn't have made a joke of his kindness. Their lives hung on that kindness now.

"Please, I do not want to sound rude but I really must speak with His Grace."

There was a long silence. Apparently this request was in the category of wanting to dress her own hair. "I will deliver your message, miss."

Selene wondered to whom she would deliver it. It sounded like she planned to deliver it to the bottom of a well.

"If you believe he is engaged, perhaps you would show me Talbourne House a little, so that I may orient myself."

"I will deliver that message as well, miss," said the maid, and then the door closed.

Well. Apparently that meant *no.* Selene was left alone.

To count the hairpins in her hair.

Her mother usually showed her new spaces. But surely her mother was asleep.

Selene wasn't going to sit here counting hairpins.

Her fingernail tapped on a particularly unpleasant hairpin. "What are we doing here, mother?" she wondered out loud.

Good heavens, perhaps he wanted her to be a maid here!

No. These rooms were grand, and even a surly lady's maid was a genuine lady's maid. Housemaids didn't rate them.

Well, guests ought to be free to explore.

* * *

FEELING along the wall looking for the door to the corridor, Selene instead heard a man's voice coming from another room—was that her mother's?—and came upon its door. She tapped on it and pushed it ajar. "Lady Redbeck?"

"Your daughter, I'd wager," said the man.

"Oh yes," Lady Redbeck tiredly confirmed as Selene moved to her side.

"There's a chair here by your mother's bed. I am Dr. Billingsley, and I must do something about my reputation for it seems to have done me a disservice. Either that or His Grace enjoys sending messengers to pound on my door in the wee hours of the morning."

That didn't sound like *her* duke. But then, she barely knew him. "I am so sorry for the disturbance, sir."

"Not at all, not at all. I have written a few things on illnesses of the heart; His Grace flatters me. Pleasure to meet you. I've just been speaking with Lady Redbeck, and I'm delighted that she's so strong, as much of the work will fall on her."

Her mother was *not* strong. Selene's hopes began slipping. "Doctor Billingsley, I hope my mother has not failed to explain her illness completely."

"Selene, really." Her mother still sounded tired. And perhaps a little cranky. "I have given him a full account of the details, I assure you."

"Strength of will is what's needed to recover from these things, miss, and I think your mother has it." He sat on the bed. "Life gives us a great deal to bear and we must decide to bear it, and that is half of any battle with illness. You and Lady Redbeck have been through a great deal, and deciding to go on without your father, your husband… you two made that decision, have you not?"

Selene found her mother's hand and squeezed it. They had. They both had.

"Then you will do what I prescribe, won't you? And I can rest too, knowing you are taking my valuable advice. When I see you again, I am sure you will not disappoint me, Lady Redbeck."

"I certainly will not," her mother said, still faintly, "but I am going to fall asleep again now if you will permit me."

"May I take your hand, miss?" asked the doctor and, when she nodded, helped her up and towards her own door.

They had already slipped through it before Selene realized what they were doing and started back. "I should sit with her." They might play Three Kingdoms or Cross Questions; any talk to wipe away the memory of that dreadful silence.

"Fran will sit with her. I think she loves it. Your mother is a lovable patient, after all. And if I may, you must rest too. You have also had trials, I can tell, even if you think you escaped undamaged. Give yourself a little time to adjust. You have no life-shattering decisions that must be made today."

If only that were true. "I have no skill for staying still. My mother doesn't either, despite what you see today. There *are* things I must do." She *had* to speak to His Grace. If only to thank him for engaging this man.

Selene's earlier relief had given way to a cold worry that there was some misunderstanding, that she and her mother would be sent packing at any minute. His Grace could afford to play games with charity that Selene and her mother couldn't afford to play.

"Do rest. I have less luck persuading younger women to take my advice—must be something wrong with my face," Dr. Billingsley mused. "Though you would be immune. Still, if you are wise, you will take it. And you strike me as wise."

* * *

FROM HIS CORNER, Jonas could move in any direction if the need arose; he chose to stay there, pretending to look at a porcelain vase and staying far away from Burden.

Who was being himself in the middle of the room, where anyone could see.

Lord Burden was a man whose appearance unfortunately matched his personality. Both his lips and his fingers seemed to be constantly pinching something, and his narrow, balding forehead gave the impression that it had been pinched at some point as well.

"The damned duke must be keeping you waiting for a reason, Callendar."

"Tch, Burden. That's how you refer to one of England's august peers? His Royal Highness would not like to hear you so abusing one of his dukes." Jonas worried that if he stepped any closer, someone might think he was a friend of Burden's.

Burden wasn't a man who had things like friends. Buttons and self-importance, yes. Friends, no.

It wasn't hard to guess that they both wanted the same thing: to know more about the lovely young lady in shabby clothes Talbourne had escorted in last night.

But Burden clearly couldn't help being obvious. Callendar would stay right here and pretend to examine hand-painted birds on the blue wallpaper while Burden did it.

And maybe needle the man a little. "I thought you wanted Talbourne's vote on your proposal to block American imports."

Lord Burden shrugged a shoulder that managed to be both bored and disdainful. "Talbourne is always a champion of doing nothing. Import bans are established and America is still an enemy, Why should Talbourne squawk?" He waggled his finger at the wallpaper. "Abominably bad renderings of birds."

One graceful loss at cards didn't make Burden appealing, and that wasn't going to help him if he planned to suddenly take his seat in the House of Lords seriously.

Jonas had no vote in the Lords. He said so all the time. He was still terribly popular, because lots of people wanted something from Parliament, and because all of them knew that his grandfather, the esteemed Lord Langdale, voted however Jonas told him to vote.

And his grandfather followed Jonas' advice because Jonas was too smart to say "Talbourne" and "squawk" in the same sentence.

And here was the Duke of Talbourne himself.

No woman, though.

"Lord Burden. Lord Callendar." Talbourne gave each of them a short bow of the head but properly addressed the senior man first. He was always correct, Jonas mused to himself. Not warm. Just correct.

Which was when Jonas realized that he and Burden were both wasting their time. Talbourne never gave his true feelings away. He wouldn't even let his true feelings be seized by force.

* * *

SELENE STOPPED SHORT when someone asked, "Do you need help, miss?"

"Oh yes, please." She kept her fingertips against the wall. "That hallway crosses this one, I can tell. Does it not lead toward the front entrance of Talbourne House?"

There was a pause before the young man spoke again. "Yes, miss. Visitors of state reside along that corridor when His Grace the Duke of Talbourne entertains them. This goes toward the foyer."

"I did think so! Do you know where I might find His Grace?"

"The Duke is seeking funding for a canal to speed shipping to London. I believe the proposed route will cross others' lands, so he has several people to persuade." His tone made it clear that the Duke was far too busy and important for Selene to hope to be able to bother.

Selene was thankful just to have found such a well-informed footman. "I hate to disturb him, but my questions are quite urgent. Do you know where I might find him?"

Her worry about what was happening was starting to eat at her, making her stomach twist. Even things that seemed pleasant in fairy tales often weren't. That girl who had been enchanted so that every word made flowers and jewels fall from her lips. How unpleasant must that have been?

The young man seemed somewhat taken aback. "I am... somewhat familiar with his schedule. I can show you to his study, he frequently spends his mornings there."

"Oh, would you please? Would you mind terribly if I took your elbow to follow your lead?"

* * *

NICHOLAS REGARDED his visitors with all the excitement of a man who didn't want them.

"Your Grace. So kind of you to receive us." Burden spoke as though he and Callendar had arrived together, even as he stepped forward to bow on his own. "We know you must be busy."

Burden was stupid and stupid was boring, but Callendar should be watched till his plan was accomplished.

The doctor had visited, he knew, and Lady Redbeck was likely sleeping. So where was Selene?

Nicholas couldn't concentrate on the usual endless parade of conversations about things he probably could not help. Shipping of supplies to their soldiers abroad, controlling the price of mutton in London, cutting down disease by forbidding farmers' open carts. There were always a hundred issues for his attention, even aside from his own goals. And he could not focus.

He was half-wondering what she was doing right now, and that wouldn't do. He couldn't afford to appear distracted.

Especially when he was.

"I am happy to make time to see you two, sir." It was obvious enough that he did not mean it.

"Really?" Burden lifted an eyebrow in a way he probably thought was witty. It wasn't. "I understand you have made a recent addition to your household, one I would assume would be taking up more of your time." Burden added a smile to the eyebrow. It wasn't witty either. "Especially in the morning."

Ho ho ho. A graceless jab. A jab that implied that, at long last, the icy Duke had a mistress. In his own house no less. Ho ho.

Nicholas just looked at the man. He knew exactly why this was a topic that would fascinate Lord Burden, and Nicholas was not going to feed that fascination.

Alistair Fillwer, Earl of Burden, was trying to play a game that was so far beyond his capabilities that it was embarrassing to watch him try to play.

Jonas kept his mouth shut. Apparently willing to let Burden sink.

And Burden was sinking.

Very well, Nicholas would push him down a little farther.

"Ah. You've heard about Lady Redbeck falling ill. Yes, I have been remiss in my debt to her late husband in not calling on her more often. I found her yesterday so unwell that I felt my only prudent course was to remove her and install her more comfortably here."

"Her husband?" Burden's confusion was obvious. They *all* knew Lady Redbeck wasn't the woman Burden was talking about.

"Of course. Such long service together in the House, you understand. You *do* understand, don't you. We have served together a few years ourselves, haven't we, since your father passed away… is it four years ago now?"

"Three, sir." Burden looked flattered.

* * *

IN HIS CORNER, Jonas wondered if he could actually damage himself by rolling his eyes.

"Of course. So important, the continuity we provide, isn't it? Especially with so many new members entering the Commons this year. In fact your eye is exactly the one I'd like on the addition I'm proposing to the window tax."

"Is it?" Now Burden showed his startlement. Jonas could have kicked him.

"Yes. Exactly so." Nicholas raised a hand, and a footman leaped forward from where he had managed to blend in oddly well with the bird-spattered wallpaper. "Take Lord Burden to the green room and show him the draft on the desk there, I'd like his opinion."

"Sir."

Burden bowed. "Of course, Your Grace, immediately." And the man actually looked pleased that he was being led away to be shut up in a room for upwards of an hour to read a long law. A law about which the Duke did not care one bit, Jonas deeply suspected.

The door closed behind them.

Jonas, his fingers still running over the delicate vase, said, "I expected that to be blunter. Not cruel, of course, but not so kind."

* * *

THIS WAS the second time in the space of a day that someone had called Nicholas kind. He must be slipping.

Something about the way the man's hands touched the porcelain made Nicholas faintly uneasy. As if the younger man might push over the rare vase at any moment, just to hear the crash.

Maybe it was the way he grinned, as if they were friends.

If Nicholas had had friends, which he did not, they wouldn't include Callendar.

"If Lord Burden has come all this way to discuss taxes, I can certainly give him a few minutes on the questions at hand."

"Taxes, surely, you don't care about them. But not last night's mysterious woman."

There it was. Callendar was a treasure-seeker. And Nicholas only had one new treasure.

His father's training had assured that Nicholas knew how dangerous it was to give away that something mattered to him. As at breakfast, even a question might give it away.

But sometimes one had to risk it. "Are you here about some mysterious woman as well?"

What he wanted was for Jonas to immediately, and believably, insist that he had no interest in Selene at all.

Instead, what Jonas said was, "Beautifully phrased. I like the way you don't admit there *is* any mysterious woman. Though I saw her arrive with you last night, as I'm sure you recall."

"Are *you* chasing a vote? On the window tax, perhaps?" Nicholas wouldn't confirm anything.

Jonas finally let the vase alone and came towards his host. "In another moment you'll be threatening to bundle *me* off to read tax amendments. Mightn't I just be checking on a friend? You seemed in a fraught situation when I saw you last, with two women on your hands."

Nicholas memorized every detail of Jonas, from tousled gold-brown curls to polished boots, as was his habit when faced with someone dangerous.

"To find myself with such a new friend all of a sudden rocks me back a bit."

Jonas waved a hand as if magnanimously overlooking the fact that no one had ever seen the Duke of Talbourne rocked. "I heard a rumor you were planning something new. I hoped to learn more about it."

"You wish to hitch your wagon to my horse."

That made Jonas laugh. "Your Grace, you *have* no horse. No ears, either, of other men in the Houses, so no one's votes. You've been in the Lords long enough to know that. I know," he put up his hand to ward off contradiction, though none was coming. "The Duke of Gravenshire is willing to support you, if you support him. And *his* concerns for an overgrown London are compelling. No one knows what your concerns are, so they can't support them. That is simply fact."

Possibly, but Nicholas wasn't about to reverse the habits of a life-time and spill his hopes all over the floor. Let the *other* man talk. "Your grandfather wants an end to the American war and to resume their trade, does he not?"

"I would love to know what *you* want."

Nicholas managed the world's tiniest shrug. "I understand your grandfather's position. Britain is starving for wood and much else, and the Continent is closed to us."

"True. So deftly put. And without betraying a bit of your own interest. I imagine you could summarize the opposite side of the position just as generously."

"As who could not? The Americans want us to recognize their sovereignty. It does nothing for them, they think, to be drawn into quarrels between European nations. Attempting to force them to give up their neutrality is not going very well," Nicholas reminded him.

Jonas shrugged. "Sweden may not have the coffers to help us win the war against Napoleon and build manufactories at the same time."

Nicholas wondered why they were discussing this. They both knew Britain was squeezed for resources between American colonies who wanted no part of their problems, and a Sweden that had prob-lems of its own. Sweden and the other countries of the Coalition.

They must win the Continental war. Nicholas was thinking about afterwards.

Both Sweden and the colonies were caught up in the new passion for government driven by the will of the people rather than a king's words. Their newly appointed Prince Regent didn't care for the plan.

Despots were like that.

Deep down inside, where memories of his father lived, Nicholas had a near-demonic hatred of despots.

It was painfully uncomfortable to skate so close to being something he hated.

But he would keep on telling himself that he wasn't keeping Selene prisoner. He was helping her, helping her mother. He didn't have to tell her how hopelessly determined he was that she stay.

Nor would he admit to Callendar that he was willing to talk about anything to keep the topic away from her.

"Friends share each other's perspective," Callendar said, "Perhaps you can tell me more about yours?"

He could; he received letters from Sweden and America often. But those thoughts kept scattering. They fled like mad sheep escaping their pen, and whenever he gathered them back together, it just happened again.

Was this how most men got through their days, desperately distracted by feminine charms? It explained a great deal about government if it were the case.

"I have had some correspondence that might interest you. Perhaps we can walk through the puzzle garden and discuss it." Keeping an eye on Callendar easily meant keeping him close.

"I would be happy to do so, Your Grace."

"This particular garden was created in the reign of Queen Anne and is very fine."

* * *

THIS FOOTMAN SEEMED willing to take her all over the impossibly huge house, and Selene counted herself lucky to have found him. "You are so kind to take the time to escort me. Am I keeping you from your duties?"

"None that matter."

He must be being kind. Surely he was supposed to be doing something somewhere.

"His Grace has been such a kind host, I hesitate to make any further demand upon him at all, but I truly must."

"I do not know if he will grant you an audience, miss."

A lowering thought because it was true. A guest might have a right to interrupt His Grace in the middle of the day, but what was she?

Selene would not be able to settle herself to anything else until she understood something of his mind about why she was here. It must not come as a shock if her mother's coddling only lasted a matter of hours. "Of course."

"Since we did not find His Grace in his study, the west state room or the yellow drawing room, we ought to check the receiving rooms. In fact—I shall return forthwith, madame."

Startled by his suddenly dropping her hand from his arm and stepping away, Selene put out her hands and found a wooden rail. With columns; the balustrade. It was the grand staircase she had climbed just last night. "Oh... of course."

Abandoned in the vast space, Selene felt very alone.

TALBOURNE HOUSE WAS TOO grand to be a house, but too polite to the Crown to style itself a palace.

The wide stairs were framed by balustrades forming two graceful arcs sweeping up, and the staff kept the wood shining.

Lord Callendar's awe as they came into view of it did seem real. "I have observed that the greater the power, the grander the staircase."

Nicholas shot Jonas a look. Was he talking about Nicholas? "When I inherited it—"

A flutter of blue caught the corner of his eye. He looked up.

Far up.

Selene. Selene was near the top but bent over the balustrade, bent backwards—her whole body teetered on the wooden edge and her toes struggled to find the carpet. Had she tripped? Fallen? She clung to the wood rail, fighting to regain her balance twenty feet in the air, and her hands looked small, so small.

She looked about to lose her grip and topple backwards into space.

His life stopped.

In the space of one beat of his heart Nicholas could calculate the spot on the bare floor where she would land, how little protection would be afforded by her fluttering gown, and how likely she was to shatter with the impact.

He had just learned how to dream, and his dreams would die.

He was too far to reach her by running up the stairs. Instead he found himself standing just below her, staring up at her fingers grasping for purchase on the slippery wood.

His hands reached up but he was too far away.

All he could do if she fell, would be to break her fall with his own body.

Callendar, two yards closer to the staircase, had leaped forward and was taking the stairs three at a time. Nicholas saw him seize Selene around the waist. Saw him pull her back over the balustrade, and set her on her feet.

It took Nicholas a moment to grasp that she was fine, *Selene was fine.*

In fact he didn't grasp it until she stood before him, at the bottom of the staircase, laughing, both hands clinging to Callendar's arm as Callendar tried to join in with his own choked near-laugh.

She was on her feet. Safe and in Talbourne House.

Nicholas breathed again.

And she was laughing! Actually laughing. But then, she could not see how far she might have fallen.

"There must be better ways to meet than through my clumsiness, sir," Selene was telling Lord Callendar as Nicholas drew near.

The words escaped him before he could stop them. "You are not clumsy." At least Nicholas still sounded calm. He could always sound calm.

"Your Grace!" Selene curtseyed. Was she wobbling a little? Yes, Callendar was steadying her arm. She'd been shaken after all.

"Why was no one helping you down the stairs, miss?"

"A footman was with me just moments before, sir. I had no intention to come down the stairs; I was standing at the top."

Nicholas felt something pounding in his head at the idea that a servant of his had left her there to possibly fall to her death. But that would not show.

"So? What footman?"

"I did not ask his name. Your Grace! He'd only left me a moment before. No need to be angry with him."

Nicholas Hayden, Duke of Talbourne, knew with every fiber of his being that he sounded calm and cool. No other person in Britain would have thought him angry.

Without denying it—nothing drew attention to a betrayed emotion like denying it—Nicholas said, "And you decided to come down alone? I cannot recommend it, miss. This staircase is broad, and the stairs high." And she was unfamiliar with it, and she was blind, and those shoes were new and probably why she tripped, and, and, and... Nicholas had to work harder than he had in years to keep himself in check.

"It was not my intention, I assure you! Someone must have been hurrying—someone bumped into me, from behind, moving so fast, and I tripped trying to place my foot; I ended up hanging on to the rail instead!"

His eyes travelled up the staircase.

He did not second-guess himself. He had no doubt that someone had tried to push Selene.

Someone who did not expect her to catch herself, or to be so strong. Someone who did not know her well.

That was everyone currently in Talbourne House.

And as he met Callendar's eyes he saw the younger man reach the same conclusion.

There was no time to pull him aside, but Callendar seemed to be of Nicholas' own mind regarding not alarming the young lady. "How fortunate that I came along at just the right moment to give you a hand."

"More than fortunate! I can tell this room is very large, and I might have had quite a fall!" Selene withdrew her arm from his grasp only to squeeze his hand. "I owe you a great deal, sir."

Tossed in among the roiling jumble of unwanted feelings of every possible sort was the certain knowledge that Nicholas also owed Callendar a great deal.

That felt unpleasant.

That was what was causing that sensation of having a cold stone in his stomach, Nicholas thought to himself, watching the man smile at Selene, and watching her pat his hand.

He had miscalculated. It was too dangerous for him to convince her slowly. Dangerous in too many ways.

He needed to accomplish his plan before she even realized she was caught in it, or his hopes would be gone.

His only other course would be to let loose his inner despot and lock her in a tower to keep her safe, and close.

That he would not do.

"I believe I have kept you waiting, miss," he said. "Lord Callendar, my apologies. We will have to discuss it another time."

"Of course, sir. And you, my lady, I hope we meet again under better circumstances. Though we have not yet actually met! Your Grace, would you be so kind?"

Nicholas' gut said that Callendar had not had a hand in the accident, but he didn't know that for sure. It would attract attention to refuse to introduce her. Damn, now the man would have her name. "Miss de Gauer, this is the right honorable Baron Callendar."

"A pleasure to make your acquaintance, Miss de Gauer, though the circumstances are most regrettable."

"Thank you, my lord. I am delighted to meet you, with all my gratitude, truly." She squeezed his hand again. Nicholas wished she would stop doing that.

"Let me escort you, Miss de Gauer," and Nicholas made her stop touching the younger man by simply taking her hand and placing it on his own arm. His study. He'd take her there. "We have so much to discuss."

FORMALITIES EXCHANGED

*B*y the time they reached his study, Nicholas was worried that he'd been too hasty and too importunate. "My apologies for taking your hand so abruptly, miss."

"Quite forgiven."

"I hope your chambers are comfortable. And that your mother is settled." Nicholas stayed just on the edge of his chair. Because he intended to wrap this affair up quickly.

And because from here it was possible to lean close. To Selene.

He could just faintly smell roses.

"Your Grace, you have been exceedingly kind, but you should know that my mother is not expected to get well."

"I do understand that, Miss de Gauer."

"But then... you cannot expect us to simply live here on your charity. For perhaps years."

Go gently, Nicholas thought, forcing himself not to force this. Let her suggest the solution... but quickly.

Out loud he said, "Did you wish to leave your mother here? I had thought you would not want to leave her alone."

"Alone? Of course not!"

"Though I quite understand the position in which it places you."

"Sir, I am thinking of the position in which it places *you*."

He could work with that. "I am sure my reputation can withstand a few knocks, miss."

"But I was thinking of… of the penalty, sir, for your charity. You don't… Do you think people will *talk*? Because of us?"

"A trifle." How thickly should he lay this on? "I doubt it will harm my support on the votes that really matter to me, such as the Talbourne canal, or the import tax."

He'd gladly trade his canal for some progress on getting his peers in the Lords to listen.

Those peers didn't care how many women he kept in his house.

But Selene didn't know that.

He liked the way she leaned a little on the arm of the settee, with the blue silk of her gown hiding her gentle curves and falling to her feet. She looked as if she were a queen posing for a portrait. Though there was something wrong with her hair.

Selene squeezed her thumb against her fingers.

He'd always seen her before with some sort of work in her hands. This gesture, though, seemed to indicate thinking.

He waited, knowing that whatever she was thinking probably supported his cause more than him trying to push her.

It did. "Your Grace, I must insist. My mother and I cannot be the downfall of any of your work. We ought to return home right away, and—"

"Is your mother comfortable? Does she need more nurses, do you think?"

"Oh, ah—Fran is wonderful, and there seem to be quite a few young women helping her. A physician has already attended her. I am so grateful for your help."

He saw her lips part to take a breath, but before she could add anything Nicholas murmured, "A good deed I should have done sooner."

"But why, sir? You owe us nothing. Your charity is overwhelming."

"Charity? Not at all. A loan repaid, at least a loan of kindness."

Here Nicholas had to be very, very careful. He made it a point never to lie if the lie could be found out. But Selene had only a few loved ones that he could use, and it was too dangerous to make something of his connection to Lord or Lady Howiston when she knew all about their connection already.

No, it needed to be her father.

Nicholas moved to the opposite end of her settee. Restrained, but informal.

She'd be most likely to be comfortable like this. Restrained but informal.

"Your father supported a cause of mine when I was very young, and new to the title," he said softly. Selene jumped a little at the closeness of his voice. "I owed him. I did not pay heed to what became of his family. Until your cousin told me who you were, I had no idea my chance to repay him had been waiting there in front of me for so long. And then I could not decide how to raise the idea. I have been remiss."

"What cause did he help, sir?"

Dammit, she wasn't supposed to ask for details. She was supposed to accept the excuse.

Her father had been dead for five years—more?—and Nicholas had ascended to the title young, at twenty-eight. Something far back. Early, when she was too young to have noticed.

"I inadvertently offended one of the new Irish members at the time, and your father smoothed things over for me."

Selene's fingers stilled. "After the union."

"Just so."

"I'm glad he did, but you still cannot keep his widow at Talbourne House for no reason."

She wasn't getting it. He would have to nudge.

Nicholas sat back, and it was easy to sound doubtful. "Should I marry Lady Redbeck, do you think? For appearances' sake?"

Some sort of sound half-choked her.

"Are you well, Lady Selene? Perhaps I should have some tea brought for you?"

Selene pressed a hand to her throat. "I am fine," she croaked. "My mother has fifty years and more, sir."

"Truly? She does not look it. But then, I am a plain man and an old one myself, and I do not expect any fresh young ladies to fall at my feet only to be my second duchess." The rueful chuckle was genuine too. "Or I should say, I doubt I would make a comfortable marriage with the young ladies who might do that."

"There are no young ladies you like well enough to marry?"

He had her. "What young lady would be willing to throw away her youth on an old curmudgeon like me?"

Oh, she was thinking. Nicholas was smiling inside; indeed, there might be some part of him, hidden far away, clapping like a child. He could *see* her thinking it over. Her face often had a gentle half-smile in repose, but he could see her thumb rubbing her fingers.

She would never be so bold as to propose to him. Not even his Selene would do that.

But after a long pause, she did say, "You are not old, Your Grace."

Yes, he definitely had her. "Nearly forty, miss. Well, only two years shy. With a grown son. It's unnerving watching the parade of young ladies of the *ton* dragged before me by their mothers. They're Edward's age. None of them are dying for my company, I can tell you that."

There *were* parades of young ladies, but Nicholas was well capable of ignoring them. Still, it ought to help him to sound a little sad. He could manage that.

"I find that hard to believe, Your Grace. I always enjoy your company."

Hook. Set. Reel her in. "But I daren't hope a sweet young lady like yourself would be willing to marry *me*."

Nicholas had no problem making the last word drip with disdain. No young woman with a heart should be saddled with him, especially not Selene, who brought out feelings in him he didn't even understand.

But she *would* wind up marrying him, if she said her part.

And she did. "A young lady like me would be honored beyond belief to be asked to marry you."

Her voice was so quiet that he could barely hear her say *you*.

But she'd said it. And that was enough.

"Miss de Gauer." He hadn't put the tremble in his voice; he didn't know where that had come from. "Your mother and I ... when we discussed you coming here, I didn't dare hope that you would... that I could hope."

"You've thought of it. Marrying me." She sounded utterly disbelieving.

He'd thought of nothing else for months. He had to rein it in. Sound calm. Sweet, even.

He *couldn't* sound sweet.

But he could sound calm. That was second nature. "I have, Selene. Are you saying you would be willing to marry me? To protect my reputation?"

"You're teasing."

"You always tease me. I thought it appropriate."

In fact, that was what he noticed first about her. She wasn't rude, but she wasn't shy, and she hadn't hesitated to tease him—first, about being willing to let a woman keep him waiting.

Nicholas didn't even remember what he'd said in return. He only remembered the way her eyes crinkled in the corners, and the way she laughed.

And the way that had made him feel.

But Selene looked shaken. "Don't—don't tease me about—"

Instantly he realized his mistake. "No no, Selene, I was not teasing that way! I would be honored if you would have me for your husband."

"You cannot be serious."

"I think you've told me I'm always serious. In any case, I am serious about this."

"A duchess. Your duchess."

The words made something inside him sing like a plucked string. "Yes, of course."

She was young, but she was of age. And she was descended from one of the oldest families in England. That alone made her perfect for his purposes.

She had not been formally presented at court, nor had she been formally chaperoned every day of her life since then. That alone made her disastrous.

But in fact it didn't matter. She was the only woman in all the world that he had ever actually wanted.

And he *would* have her.

Selene finally moved. Just slightly, in her seat. "You need a duchess so badly that you are asking me."

* * *

SELENE'S PULSE had already been racing, from her accident on the stairs. Now there were new alarms, one after the other, and her heart was not slowing *down*.

She had assumed he was not serious. Now he sounded as if he was. Thinking back, she remembered how little he did tease, and that more than anything else alarmed her about this conversation.

"I would be less shocked to find us discussing a betrothal if you had ever once mentioned the topic of marriage." Selene was proud of the way her voice did not waver.

"Miss de Gauer, I had assumed her ladyship your mother had informed you that I... had inquired about you." He added more quietly, "Is it such an awful prospect, becoming Duchess of Talbourne?"

"It is not that it is an awful prospect, Your Grace, as much as it is a very startling surprise."

Marriage?

His marriage?

To *her*?

Was it actually possible that in all these months, Nicholas Hayden, Duke of Talbourne, had been visiting *her*?

She had never suspected it. He had never been the least bit forward, even behind a parlor door! She'd have sworn that she'd heard him rise whenever she entered the room. Rise. For the housemaid.

The teasing way she had just spoken to Lord Callendar was the way Lady Selene would have spoken in her father's house. To anyone. It was not the best of manners, but it was her, and her father had always laughed at it.

She thought she had a bit of charm but the Duke of Talbourne was... *a duke.* Solemnly playful in his own way, but always a duke, always formal and polite.

Formal, polite, and a bit sad.

Sad enough for her to try to make him smile, letting the work she ought to be doing wait in the kitchen or the laundry.

But this?

Surely her mother would have mentioned something about marriage discussions if she had actually had an offer of marriage from a duke. *Her* duke. Her sad, polite duke.

Her duke who now apparently owed some debt to her father that he wanted to repay. No, that story didn't ring quite true.

Yet, here she was.

"Sir... I am honored, but..." Selene paused. "I have never received a proposal before, so please excuse me if I seem ungrateful or rude. But this plan seems likely to harm your position, not help it. Does it not?"

Things were spinning out of control. She had no idea what she was wearing, or how to find her way back to where her mother was. She had fallen into the puzzle that was Talbourne House and this could not possibly be the right way out.

It was a bit too close to fairy tales for comfort.

"Miss de Gauer, we should talk more of how... easy, really, I would wish it to be for you to become Duchess of Talbourne. Perhaps we may dine together this evening?"

Selene tapped one fingernail on the wood of the chair's arm. "Do you truly not mind if I speak as freely as we have spoken in the past?"

* * *

HER SPEAKING FREELY WAS his favorite thing about her.

No, perhaps truly that was the crinkles at the corners of her eyes.

Her eyes themselves were a warm brown that he knew others would probably admire. But for him, it was the crinkles.

It wouldn't do to let her try to talk him out of the idea. He needed to put her off a bit, let his plan sink in a little. "Speaking while we dine would be wonderful. You can give me your answer then."

* * *

No, it wouldn't, and no, I won't, thought Selene with rising concern. Waiting another day to go home would not make this easier on her mother; it would make it worse. To have all this comfort within her grasp, and then to snatch it away?

But if she remembered only one thing from all her mother's attempts to drill her in the proper behavior for a young lady whose last name was de Gauer, it was never, ever to contradict anyone with precedence before her father's.

A short list, but it certainly included all dukes.

"As you wish, sir. I apologize for the interruption."

When she had arisen, the Duke took her hand and placed it on his arm. "If you will permit me," he murmured as he led her to the door.

* * *

SURELY HE COULD GET AWAY with escorting a young lady down the hall if she was blind. Not entirely appropriate. But that damn young Callendar had just had his hands on her repeatedly. And after all, Nicholas intended to marry her.

He *was* going to marry her. Marry her and let her do exactly as she pleased, and it needn't give him away.

No one watching would know how her scent haunted him, that combination of roses, old books, and warm skin that he associated only with her.

No one knew that all the soap at Talbourne House smelled of roses because they reminded him of her. Brought him back to that parlor, with Selene dusting and arranging flowers, even when he could not invent any plausible excuse to be there.

And now she was here.

"Are you sure?" she said back just as quietly, matching him.

If she was asking about his proposal, he was not going to explain himself now. Nicholas chose to pretend she was asking about his suggestion of dinner.

"Miss de Gauer, nothing would give me more pleasure than to dine with you this evening so we can at least have more time to speak, if not more privacy."

She nodded even as he moved her hand from his arm to the footman's.

The plan called for it, but he was reluctant to let her go.

* * *

THE FOOTMAN DELIVERED her to her mother's door, said a crisp "Miss", and disappeared, apparently not grasping that a blind person might need further assistance.

This house had a serious problem with disappearing footmen.

She tapped. "Lady Redbeck?"

"I'm awake, dear, and there's nothing between you and my bed. Be careful of the carpet. I sent Fran for some fresh air. She *is* sweet."

"You sound better!"

As Selene sat on the edge of the bed, her mother practically bounced. "I feel better!"

"I worried the sudden move would tire you."

"What could tire me about moving to a *duke's palace*? Because Talbourne House is a palace, dear, do not let the name mislead you. This is everything I always wanted for you ever since you were born. It is such a *relief*, my darling!"

Selene wished she were relieved. The idea of disappointing her mother weighed in her like a cold rock. "Just being in this house doesn't change our situation, madame. What are you—*why* did you give His Grace the impression that I would marry him?"

"Did I?" Her mother sounded vague for a moment, and Selene had a moment's panic, wondering whether she wanted her mother to deny the whole idea, or confirm it. Her mother did neither. "If he wants to marry you, why on earth *wouldn't* you want to accept?"

"Madame." Selene bit her words back.

They ought not to have been penniless when her father died. His heir—in her head Selene always silently snarled *that man* at the thought of him—had left them penniless, with nothing of the widow's share her mother ought to have received. She'd pushed her mother to seek legal redress; Lady Redbeck refused.

Selene respected her mother's decision.

But she didn't understand it. Certainly didn't understand how her mother failed to realize that with that same decision, she'd made marriage proposals for Selene impossible.

Had made *this* marriage proposal impossible.

"Madame, you know I would never complain of your decisions. But you insisted years ago, not to press that man for your legal share of my father's estate. We have been destitute. Our lives have hung from threads." You nearly died, Selene wanted to add, but didn't. "Perhaps you recall living in a garret room? That wasn't the first clue, that was the last. Young ladies do not recover from such a social fall. That does not happen."

And she did not *want* to be a duchess. Not any more.

She wanted little things, for herself. She'd like to know what the Duke's laugh would sound like if she could rest her ear against him and truly listen.

That is, if she could make him laugh.

But what else had she had to wonder about, the dishpans? He was practically the only man to whom she'd spoken in ages. Who *wouldn't* daydream about that voice?

Like the Frenchman in satin, who'd turned out to be an expert swordsman, or the shocking little Italian *comtesse*, the Duke of Talbourne was one of those people who kept getting more interesting with the passage of time.

How could she *not* wonder what his hands could do?

No, voice, she'd been thinking about his voice.

Her mother's shrug was in her answer. "You are a de Gauer, and that is more than enough for anyone in the realm, including His Grace."

Her mother was back among the contracts. Selene had moved on to wondering entirely different things about marriage.

The Italian *comtesse* had explained something of what men and women did together, but it did not sound plausible, let alone pleasant. Neither had it fit with the way marriage was described in the fairy tales her governesses had read to her. Selene had not asked those governesses to explain the gaps.

The fairy tales contained a good bit of obeying, and that hadn't interested Selene much.

"What are you thinking so hard about, Selene?" her mother asked, but Selene just patted her hand.

Among the bits and pieces she could recall, like the girl who spoke jewels and flowers, she remembered most of a tale in which a princess had demanded to see the ambassador who'd brought a marriage offer from a prince (seeing was always terribly dangerous in those stories). Then she'd demanded to have the ambassador. Run away with him as his lover.

They'd wound up shipwrecked on a desert island of squirrels. Selene definitely remembered the squirrels. And when her lover had got too hungry, he tried to kill the princess to eat her.

That was how those fairy tales went. No practical information. Why would the man try to kill the woman he supposedly loved on an island full of squirrels? Why not eat the squirrels?

That princess had gone on to marry the prince, as she ought to have done in the beginning, and then the story ended. The story had praised the prince for marrying the runaway princess. As if it were her fault that the ambassador arrived first. The princess had been hasty, certainly. Of course, she hadn't *known* she would end up in that squirrel situation.

Selene wasn't stupid. None of that had *anything* to do with being an actual duchess. Or being married to an actual man.

Talbourne House must have a library. Perhaps it would have a history of Eleanor of Aquitaine.

"Madame." Selene used the tone that her mother had always recommended when firmness was necessary. "Please say that you know this idea is claptrap. Say it. This isn't going to happen."

"Please do not say 'isn't', dear, contractions are so common."

Selene wasn't *prepared* for this.

And the worst thing she could imagine was that her mother had somehow talked the lonely duke into this.

"*Mother.*" Selene took her mother's hands. They were small and cold. "This is dangerous for his reputation. He needs a duchess, not a housemaid. I am a housemaid now. Did you forget?" Because her mother could conveniently forget. She'd certainly forgotten the cold lodging rooms that smelled of mold.

"Lady Howiston is a relative, dear. For all anyone knows, you moved in with your second cousin when our financial circumstances required it."

"Don't call her Lady Howiston; she hates it. Cass gave me a position as a housemaid."

"Because you would not take her charity. And really, what good was all that pride?"

What good was *pride*? Her mother had raised her on nothing but pride! If a de Gauer never wavered in his defense of his lands, if a de Gauer stood for his principles, if a de Gauer ruled over his domain with fairness and firmness, how could a de Gauer take money from a woman working hard to keep her own house?

Selene had never realized before that her definition of pride was very different from her mother's.

"You must have simply misled His Grace somehow. He needs a duchess, someone whose social position will be influential and unimpeachable. I am not duchess material."

"The de Gauers have been peers of this realm for hundreds of years longer than most of His Majesty's court. Your bloodline is impeccable."

This, this was why she'd been grateful to be out of it. *Influence* and *children* were two entirely different things. "What can that *matter*? He has two children already, both boys!"

"Rest her soul, the man's wife has been dead for two years. He needs a duchess like you."

Like her? *"Mama. His Grace may need a duchess, but he does not need *me*. Did you claim that I had some special ability to help him? Is that what prompted this?

"You always underestimate yourself, Selene. You have extraordinary skills. You have simply been in an unfortunate position and unable to use them."

If extraordinary skills included re-soaking tea leaves four times and spreading peas on her toast instead of butter, then fine, she had extraordinary skills. Selene couldn't imagine them being of much use to a duke.

"I know you are ill and you have been tired, but I cannot imagine why you did not mention this last night, or even this morning."

"He wanted to talk to you first. Has he not?"

If the conversation she had just had with His Grace counted as explaining his sudden and bizarre urge to marry a housemaid, Selene was a plucked chicken. "He said he wished to marry me. In fact, he didn't even say that. The idea just sort of... bubbled up in conversation."

"What did you expect from a duke to a second wife? Sonnets? Just imagine how he is hounded by young ladies fresh to the social scene. Or the widows, they are even worse. They all have terribly sad eyes."

Said her mother the widow. "How much personal discussion did you have with His Grace about all this?"

"Quite a bit."

"*When?*"

Her mother patted her hands. "Darling, this was always where you really belonged. Oh, not Talbourne House precisely, but something like it. And he *likes* you, Selene, he likes you! How lucky is that!"

The way her mother described it, His Grace wanted a duchess much the way one wanted a coal bucket, or a bootscrape: to solve a small but immediate irritation. That didn't sound lucky at all.

Whether he was lonely or needed a coal bucket, it wasn't about dancing. Nor did it appeal.

But wait. If Nicholas wanted a duchess, he had his pick of women in the realm, even to be a titled coal bucket. He *had* picked her. Hadn't he?

"One question. Did you bring up the topic of his marrying me, or did he bring it up?"

"Who can remember?"

Selene was very familiar with the airy way her mother dismissed questions she did not want to answer. "Was it you? Who?"

"Honestly, Selene, I don't remember and badgering me won't make me remember." Apparently common contractions were good enough for her mother when the lady was irritated.

"Madame, he wishes me to say tonight if I will marry him. The moment to remember is now."

"I know you will make the right decision. Do let me alone, Selene, I need to rest."

That chilled her. Her mother *could* die.

Of course her mother wanted Selene's future to be secured.

But Selene kept thinking over and over that somehow there had been a mistake. And if this was not somehow a misunderstanding— What was it? What was he asking of her?

And could she do it?

She hadn't really thought about marriage in years. Faced with it now, she knew it wouldn't be about dances. She'd have to find a way to help the Duke, if she were to be his duchess.

And then what about Nicholas the man?

They barely knew each other.

But then, didn't they? Didn't the little moments tell you more about a person than almost anything else?

"Mother," Selene said softly, "I want you to rest. But please, please, tell me honestly you did not talk him into this. Tell me you did not play upon his sympathy. *Please.*"

She heard her mother rustling down into the thick pillows and soft sheets. "Do you know, Selene, it's the funniest thing. I really do think it was his idea. But as I think back on it now that you ask, I do believe I did almost all the talking."

Stifling a sigh, Selene patted her mother's hands before tucking her securely into bed. "Rest well, madame."

* * *

"MR. LYALL," said the Duke of Talbourne without looking away from his balcony's view, "someone attempted to push Miss de Gauer down the front staircase today."

Peter Lyall's blood froze, and it was nothing to do with the cool spring breeze on this balcony. Talbourne wasn't given to long explanations; he'd failed, as *keeping her here* would certainly imply keeping her *alive*.

He wasn't exactly afraid of the Duke. Not exactly.

"An attempt to kill her?" was all he said.

"I'm going to assume so," and now the Duke looked at him. There was something burning deep in his eyes, something Lyall had never seen before. "You're going to assume so too."

"Consider it handled. Did you want the culprit turned out, or…?"

"In this case, that won't be enough."

Lyall understood that too. That was all his employer would be saying about that.

And indeed the Duke moved on. "On that other matter. You engaged that solicitor to investigate the matter of Lady Redbeck's inheritance, did you not?"

"Yes, sir. He would like a private moment to speak with Lady Redbeck."

"No."

That topic, also, was over.

Not that Peter Lyall wasn't perfectly accustomed to carrying on business for His Grace on very little information.

"Perhaps it would be best if Miss de Gauer kept to the east wing, the lower two floors, just to take some more care about who sees her."

"No, Mr. Lyall. Never pen her up."

"Only until we track down this odd threat—"

Talbourne just looked at him. The look made it unnecessary for him to say *never* again.

"Sir," said Mr. Lyall, and left.

* * *

IF THE MAID Céline had been cool before, her manner while dressing Selene to have dinner with the Duke was positively icy.

Selene had to take a deep breath. Several times.

It was triply uncomfortable when they were in such intimate proximity. Selene had never been shy; she had grown up glad to be helped with laces and buttons that she not only couldn't reach, she couldn't see.

But, already unnerved by the pending conversation with His Grace, in this silence Selene found it awkward to have Céline slip the chemise over her skin, then settle her stays into place and lace them.

When Selene's hair began to be tugged the way the stays' laces had been tugged, she thought it might be time to draw a line. She couldn't get through tonight with a lunch bundle for a head.

"I have been used to dressing my hair for some time, Céline. If you will show me the hairpins and the brush, I will do it."

"Not at all, miss," was all the maid said, using the comb to unbraid her hair and making it feel like she was in a fair way to pull much of it out.

"Céline. I can do it. Please."

"I have dressed the hair of two marchionesses, miss. I assure you that it will be most correct."

Selene didn't want it correct. She wanted it becoming. It was hard enough trying to figure out what to say to the Duke when he seemed serious about this proposal, and her dancing daydreams figured nowhere in that proposal.

Feeling like a shaved field mouse did not bolster her confidence.

So she changed the subject. "Is there a gown I should wear? What is it like?"

The comb pulled at a new section of braid, then another, before Céline said, "Does it matter, miss?"

That pulled Selene's spine straight. Was the maid implying that she didn't care what she wore because she was blind, or because she had to accept whatever was offered? The first was untrue, the latter was unkind.

"It matters to me, yes, Céline," was all she said.

"It is a purple Empire gown by Madame Dudin."

Gracious. "Where did that come from?"

"Your cousin sent it, miss? That and the silk you wore this morning."

Cass had sent it? "My cousin is easily several inches taller than I am. We brought these in our luggage last night? Did you alter it?" Had Céline stayed up late altering the thing? That would explain her crankiness.

"Of course not, miss. We have two seamstresses here, and one of them altered the blue silk last night, the other altered this one this morning."

Of course not. Selene had forgotten how jealously servants could guard their work. Her cousin's house had run like an extended family, with most of them doing whatever they could do when they could do it; the cook had even doubled as a housekeeper. Here, every person had a speciality and no one would thank her for implying that they overstepped each other.

At least that explained the fit of the gown. Cass was tall and slender. Selene's bust barely fit inside the bodice. Shortened, though, the gowns were wearable.

"Please do thank the seamstresses for me," said Selene.

But the maid didn't answer.

Which was impertinence on anyone's score.

Selene couldn't bear to resolve this now, when her stomach was all tied up in knots and she still didn't know what she was going to tell His Grace.

So she said cheerfully, and *very clearly,* "And my thanks to you as well! I shall finish my hair. I will not need you till this evening." Surely that was enough?

Apparently it was. Almost no one ever really moved silently. That fabric rustling was Céline, probably curtseying, and then withdrawing.

Alone at last, Selene picked up the brush.

She wished His Grace's odd proposal could be dismissed as easily. Her father's dreams, her mother's, her own, all of them were colliding with something a little too real. She did not relish the responsibilities of a duchess, yet if she took them on to save her mother's life, she could not then ignore them.

This was not, in fact, a romance. The Duke of Talbourne had never spoken of love. He needed someone in the role of duchess, and out of extreme charity or need or both, he was offering it to her.

And there was something he wasn't telling her.

But he seemed to have some idea that she could do this.

Selene twisted a lock of hair around her finger. Just six years ago— very nearly exactly—she was very busy imagining how her first London season would be a great success. Her main worry had been about her gowns. She'd spent Christmas planning a wedding in a grand hall full of music and sweet beeswax candles. She'd learned by then that jewels were mainly just hard stones, so she pictured herself dripping with flowers, rather than jewels and flowers like the girl in the fairy tale.

Just a few short weeks after that, she had lost her father, the only home she'd ever known, and those particular wedding dreams. Later, the gowns, sold, one by one.

She never missed the gowns. She missed her father every day.

Those daydreams of being held in Nicholas' arms (and washing his hair, good heavens!) were in the same category, she realized. Selene could give them up in a second for even a little more time with her mother.

The hairbrush picked up speed. She split off a section of hair to twist.

Time, and a home. Both the histories and the fairy tales were pretty clear about that. If she traveled from the land of laundry pails and dishpans to his palace to marry him, then the palace became hers too. It was more daunting than reassuring—Talbourne House was so huge—but it would be their home. Her mother would be comfortable, and Selene would learn how to do whatever duchessing was needed. If Nicholas didn't need a wife with a dowry or a particular family tree, she'd have to find out what he *did* need.

She could do it. She could go back to her girlhood dreams and make something of them now. She'd have to do it with others watching her every moment of every day and every night. Because that was what it meant to be a duchess.

The happy, silly, pampered girl she'd been…

The hairbrush almost fell from her hand.

She couldn't go back.

But she might be able to go forward. Make those dreams over yet again. She'd made Lady Selene into a housemaid; perhaps she could make the housemaid into a duchess. Perhaps.

Even in her mind she could only commit to *perhaps*. She wasn't brimming with confidence today.

She could barely get the maid to leave her hair alone.

It was entertaining for Jonas to watch Lady Fawcett and Lady Hadleigh both attempting to herd the guests into different conversations. Lady Fawcett was a delicate little golden thing, Lady Hadleigh far plumper, earthier, and louder. In a wrestling match, he would have easily put his money on Lady Hadleigh.

In this verbal competition, however, fragile little Lady Fawcett was holding her own. There was steel in her eye when Lady Hadleigh suggested a game of questions.

Perhaps he should start some betting on the two of them.

Then a footman brought in Miss de Gauer, and Jonas decided that the betting had changed.

The young lady looked forlorn for a moment, till another gentleman engaged her; then her face lit up with a smile.

The kind of smile that even drew the eye up from where that gown was a little too snug around the bust. Jonas wanted to thank someone for that fit, and the color; the gown set off the golden tint to her skin —did she have some Welsh ancestor?—and the bright shine of her hair, which had decided to stop short of ginger in a very well-bred way.

Jonas' steps toward the lady were blocked by Burden, who approached and nodded as if he were doing Jonas a great favor by greeting him.

Jonas wished the man would go away. "I didn't know His Grace had invited you to dine." He didn't want the Duke associating the two of them together.

But here was Burden and all his buttons, still mixing himself into the perpetual swarm of guests that Talbourne House seemed to support.

The man who'd greeted Miss de Gauer—was Sir Malcolm his name? Stout Scottish fellow—was introducing her to Lady Fawcett.

Jonas' interest in her had nothing to do with her figure in his arms, though thanks to the incident on the stairs, he had a clear memory of that. Of course he was curious about her mysterious appearance in Talbourne House, and now here was the lady, if he wished to talk to her directly.

Yes, that was it. He just wanted to talk to her.

"Well of course Talbourne invited me to dine," Burden was congratulating himself. "He wanted my thoughts on that tax bill, you recall."

It would be a cold day in hell before the Duke brought up that tax bill to Lord Burden again. The fact that Burden didn't know that was almost sad.

"I would have thought after the drubbing I gave you at cards last night, you might stay in the city and avoid the gaming here."

Burden just gave him a cool glance down the bridge of his nose.

"Don't flatter yourself, Callendar. One can amuse oneself at Talbourne House without gaming with you."

True and still uncharming, Jonas thought to himself, wondering how he might move in the lady's direction yet still keep Lord Burden from bothering her.

The lady's smile was sweet and naughty at the same time. She didn't deserve to have Burden inflicted on her.

But then, no one did.

Miss de Gauer also had slight shadows under her eyes—she had not entirely shaken off the strain of her near-accident.

She was too far away, with too many people between them. Perhaps he'd be able to speak to her after the meal.

If not, he would be back tomorrow.

* * *

AFTER HER HOURS of agonizing over what to say, it was a cold shock to find that she and the Duke of Talbourne were not dining alone.

Nor was her dinner companion even that charming Lord Callendar from the embarrassing incident on the stairs.

No, her dinner companion was a baronet by the name of Sir Malcolm, a Scotsman with quite sixty years behind him, Selene thought, and two glasses of wine in front of him. He told her so.

He had a great deal to say about the wine. "I won't lie, I wish it were whisky. As it isn't, we'd better drink it anyway."

Selene just nodded and sipped. She had no intention of trying to keep up with Sir Malcolm in drinking.

A Lady Hadleigh also sat near her and provided endless commentary on the dinner companions just out of reach. "Just look at Lady Fawcett, leaning so close to Lord Halworth you'd think she might be attached to him with pine tar. What that woman won't do for his company. Like a horse with four sore feet since His Grace showed her the door. Metaphorically, I mean, for here she still is."

"My goodness." Here she still was? How *here* was she? "Lady Fawcett had hopes regarding His Grace?"

"There's not a woman in here who doesn't," Sir Malcolm snorted.

"Shush up, you old Scot," Lady Hadleigh said with some good nature. "I don't."

"There's half a dozen who do," Sir Malcolm nonetheless persisted.

"Go back to drinking." Lady Hadleigh wasn't having it.

"My goodness." Selene couldn't help it coming out a little more faintly this time.

Why on earth had His Grace invited her to dine with him as though they would be settling this marriage question tonight? Of course, he would not be dining alone with her if they were *not* to be married.

It was inconceivable that he would choose her from all this.

Selene needed to know more. "Surely there is more entertainment than just drinking."

"There was some splendid music last night," Lady Hadleigh agreed.

"And that Callendar fellow gave Burden a mighty wallop at the card table. That was capital."

"Oh! What did His Grace say about it?" Sir Malcolm made it sound as though Nicholas and Lord Callendar might really be friends, despite the way Nicholas had spoken to the younger man last night and had been so chilly to him after the episode on the stairs.

"Eh, His Grace wasn't there."

"He's never there," added Lady Hadleigh.

"Really? What amusements does he favor, usually?" Selene was trying to sound uninterested.

"Talbourne?" Sir Malcolm sounded surprised.

"Amusements?" Lady Hadleigh was also clearly thrown by the idea of *Talbourne* and *amusements* in the same sentence.

If he didn't care for company, why was the dining hall of her sad lonely duke full of people?

"Oh, I see," Selene lied, and wondered if she ought to have more wine after all.

She could hear Nicholas' voice. He was only a few yards away. She couldn't quite hear what he was discussing; it might have been a proposal for Parliament, or a proposal of marriage for all she could tell.

Perhaps this was his idea of a test. Selene thought about bristling when that idea occurred to her. Then she tossed it away. She simply wasn't a person to be irritated by social maneuvers, and she liked the Duke. At least, she had before he proposed. Behind a parlor door, he'd been attentive, gracious. *Funny.*

She'd never quite made him laugh yet, but he made her laugh all the time.

Her father had always said that people had reasons for the things they did that made no sense. He'd said that if you found out people's why, you found out who they were.

Silently Selene applauded the idea, but doubted she would have time to unwind the mysteries of all His Grace's *whys* before she and her sick mother were shown the door.

But then again, they might stay… in whatever manner most of these people were here. Perhaps His Grace had lost control of his dinner table. Especially if Lady Fawcett was unwanted but still dining here. *Was* she only dining here? Or did she live here too?

Did she find the Duke's voice as appealing as Selene did?

Her stomach sank. Perhaps he was simply known as easy prey. It didn't match what she knew of him, but why else did he host all these dinners and entertainments when he didn't care for any of it himself?

It was always possible that the Duke was nothing like what she supposed him to be. That he was madly debauched, keeping all these women at hand for… convenient debauching.

Perhaps he was a despoiler of virgins!

No, that didn't seem right. It didn't seem to suit him, and that sort of pastime would require a constant supply of virgins. He had widows everywhere, most of them older than he was.

Wasn't it more likely he'd simply asked her here from an excess of charity? And that the same excess was responsible for the surfeit of guests?

She ignored the chill that chased down her spine as some part of her pointed out that if he was a despoiler of virgins, she was the only one here.

She let Sir Malcolm gossip on while she wondered if she were annoyed with His Grace, why he didn't rein in all these people exploiting his good will, and what she should say to him when she was exploiting his good will too.

The usual small challenges of eating in public while blind were negated by the fact that she barely ate at all.

* * *

NICHOLAS RATIONED his glances at Selene, making a point of looking all around the table when he did and trying not to let his eyes linger.

He knew he wasn't giving longing glances; he hadn't lost that much control. But it rubbed him the wrong way to look at her out here, where anyone might see.

She didn't eat. Didn't she like the food? It looked as though she was at least prodding each dish—the slab of meat, the baked apple, the soup—but they didn't suit her.

When the dessert came, he was sneaking a glance her way—was it sneaking? To himself he decided to be honest and call it sneaking—and saw her lean over to Sir Malcolm to say something before picking up her spoon and feeling around the dish with it. Delicately, she used the fork in her other hand to push a bit of the lemon ice into the silver spoon.

She didn't close her eyes, but she made a little sound when the sweet, tart ice touched her tongue.

It hadn't been loud. But it carried to him, and it called to him as if it were the only sound in the room.

He could hear it more clearly than he had ever heard anything in his life.

* * *

IT AMUSED JONAS, the way Talbourne so nonchalantly cast his eyes around the room now and then, pretending that he wasn't watching Selene.

Of course he was watching Selene. *Everyone* was watching Selene. Most did not know who she was, she was packed into a dress the color of a summer plum, and her hair shone like rays from a sunset. Her blindness was the least of the reasons that her appearance here would cause a wave of gossip.

Talbourne *was* watching her, Jonas was nearly sure, and watching Talbourne try to hide it was worth sitting through this dinner and listening to Lady Fawcett's tennis tips.

Everyone in London knew that the Duke had no lady loves. While there must have been a stalwart few who believed that he was touchingly faithful to his wife, many people in the *ton* assumed he preferred the love of men, and disparaged him accordingly.

Having spent a little time with him, Jonas found himself believing that the man was simply too stiff to climb into a bed.

But his second guess would have been that men were the Duke's preference; his third, no one at all, which was more common than unobservant people thought.

Curiosity only made Jonas watch the man more closely. And that was how he caught it.

Not a motion; a lack of motion.

Miss de Gauer licked a spoonful of lemon ice, and the Duke nearly lost his mind.

Had she made a sound? She must have. His Grace had quickly turned his eyes away so he wouldn't have to see, but he must have heard.

The man froze, just for an instant, and the planes of his face hardened with a hunger that, had an artist captured it with paint on a canvas, would have looked feral.

Jonas would have given gold weighed in pounds to know what sound Selene had made, that made him look like that.

He looked around the table. No one else appeared to have noticed, but then these people were friends of His Grace, not Jonas.

Still, Jonas would have heard if the Duke of Talbourne was in the habit of inviting young ladies to dine at Talbourne House and then spending dinners looking as if he wanted to eat them.

The tennis tips weren't so bad. Jonas was very interested in this evening, and was learning a great deal. Some of it might even improve his game.

* * *

SHE'D HAD ENOUGH.

As soon as the party had risen from the table, she thanked her dinner companion and asked a footman to return her to her room.

In fact, the whole day had been too much.

The Duke of Talbourne clearly did not want to speak with her, as he hadn't, not once. She had just been one of the women dining at his table.

Self-consciously she touched her hair. Perhaps it wasn't right.

She was exhausted. She hadn't lunched, and spent too much of the day learning this house, a task she now saw was pointless if she would not be staying. Not to mention all the effort of rearranging everything inside her head, and her heart, to accommodate her new reality. And what she'd thought was his proposal.

While Nicholas had been talking earlier, it had seemed obvious that she would stay; now she realized she must have misunderstood. He was not truly lonely; there were plenty of ladies at his table.

And if his reputation was in no danger from them, it was in no danger from Lady Redbeck.

Selene was still in the same sticky position: her mother needed care, Nicholas seemed willing to provide it, and Selene couldn't bear to be without her mother. And Selene was unmarried, though not out, and rumors about her would soon travel. By strict rules, she had even been unchaperoned at dinner.

Given the penchant for gossip around His Grace's dinner table, Selene had no illusions that her presence had gone unnoticed.

Surely rumors about an unmarried woman might even damage his work in Parliament, if she let this get out of hand.

All at once she realized that the footman escorting her had not turned down the corridor to the wing where she and her mother were housed.

"This is not the way to my chamber."

"Your pardon, miss. His Grace asks for just a moment of your time."

Had he? That seemed a bit direct for Talbourne House.

One way or the other, she was ushered into yet another new room, and deposited inside its door awaiting goodness knew what.

Was Selene imagining it, or could she smell the lemon and rosemary of the Duke of Talbourne's cologne along with the soft burr of old cigar smoke and wine? Smelling even better than that lemon ice had tasted?

He *was* here.

Why now? Why alone? Why here?

Something snapped into place inside her. Learning to be a housemaid hadn't made her less than Lady Selene; she was more.

If His Grace wanted to play games, she could entertain him; but she wasn't playing, not with her mother's life and not with her own.

Now she knew what she would do.

All she offered was a curtsey and a short, "If you please, Your Grace," assuming that he was here.

* * *

SHE LOOKED TIRED, Nicholas thought as he rose and handed her to one of the heavy carved and upholstered chairs. "Was Sir Malcolm an unpleasant dinner partner, Miss de Gauer?"

The barest ghost of a smile came and went. "Not at all, he was charming."

Making her smile felt marvelous. He could enjoy getting good at it. "He isn't charming so much as gossipy, and occasionally drunk. Was he drunk this evening?"

"He was only very slightly drunk."

70

"You are too kind."

The silence stretched a little between them.

They at least used to be able to talk. What was he doing wrong?

But Nicholas couldn't think of anything to say that might not damage his chances of this going well.

He was glad that Selene solved the silence for both of them by saying, "There are too many ladies here."

"Really? For what?"

"You have any number of women to choose from if you wish to marry, sir. You need not marry me."

Perhaps his dinner plans had not been the best. Nicholas felt his pulse quicken. "You don't believe that I am lonely?"

"Your Grace, are you playing a game with me because you are bored, or because you thought I would not notice?"

The hair on his arms stood on end.

When in doubt, play for time. "I think of you as intelligent, Miss de Gauer."

She nodded. "So do I. But I'm also really quite tired. And I do not think you so desperate in your options that you would seriously consider marrying my mother—*or* me."

"You think I'm awash in options?" Surely he could manage to pretend to be amused, if it covered his near-panic that his whole plan was about to burst into flames.

"I counted four women here tonight who would be happy to marry you."

"Four?"

"I'm not leaving out Lady Villeneuve." Selene folded her hands in her lap.

"Not at all, I thought she made six."

This, this was how they did this. Light, playful volleys that made it fun to say little of import. This was how it had been in that little parlor.

"Six? Was there actually more than one Raffington? I thought I had misheard."

"Two Raffington sisters, and Lady Withers ought to be counted, don't you think?"

That ghost of a smile came and went again as Selene slowly shook her head. "Lady Withers wouldn't have you; she wouldn't have anyone. She talks constantly of the failures of her past two husbands. Especially about their failing to live. Truthfully, sir, I doubt you should trust her."

"I believe I can trust you." He *knew* he could trust her. "And there are no others who would put up with me. I am not an easy man to live with."

Her head tilted as she seemed to consider this. "Earlier you said that your failing was that you weren't warm."

"Only one of my many failings."

He *wasn't* warm. He'd always been an icy stone of a man, sexless and emotionless.

His departed wife Alicia had preferred him that way. They'd been required to marry, at eighteen and twenty, and produce an heir as quickly as possible. Unpleasant for them both.

Alicia hadn't welcomed "interference", as she called it, for years after that, which was just fine because Nicholas didn't offer it. Talbourne House was vast and only one of his holdings; Nicholas seldom even saw her.

Eventually, they'd rescued an amiable relationship from the painful awkwardness of their early years. A second child had been her belated idea, and Nicholas was amazed that it was so much easier. Rather than forcing his body to do things it just didn't, he knew her, he liked her, and the whole business went so much more smoothly.

Still, it was pretty clear to Nicholas what was vitally necessary to other men wasn't for him.

Until.

Nicholas said, "I am hoping you know me well enough to get along with me and that we will ignore my failings together. Is that not appealing? I have never made flowery speeches to any woman. At my age I don't expect to begin."

He had to draw the line somewhere. He hadn't expected to feel desire either, and look where that got him.

Before he knew it, Selene had gone from a diverting acquaintance to an obsession. Selene, with many reasons to be bitter but who always laughed. All the details about her burrowing under his skin. And then, one day, setting him aflame.

With a ravening hunger that was very, very different from his friendship with his lost wife.

She would be more relaxed if he sounded casual. "Marriage for a duke is usually a chilly affair, laced with assurances and alliances. At least ours would be friendly, and then the matter would be behind me."

For the first time in his life, just imagining his fingers stroking a woman's cheek made him *yearn*, it made his *blood* boil.

He couldn't help it, couldn't stop it. Secretly, his famous control was gone. It hadn't been control, it had been absence where now there was presence. *Her* presence.

He didn't even care what she thought of him as much as he cared that she *stayed*.

* * *

SELENE COULD DO with some assurances and alliances, she thought. Those at least were a sound basis for joining together, if it wasn't for love.

She could press him on what he wanted his duchess to *do*. Her father would, if he were here. But that wasn't the concern that rose to the top of her mind.

She wanted to ask what he meant by *friendly*.

The idea of wedded intimacy frankly alarmed her, and describing it as *friendly* rather than *loving* made it worse.

* * *

SHE WAS WONDERING what *friendly* meant, Nicholas was sure. As long as she didn't ask, he wouldn't have to decide what to say about how little he knew of the answer himself.

He had no idea how to appeal to women, either from his marriage, or from his father, who had always insisted that Nicholas not want women even as he himself was chasing barmaids. Those poor barmaids.

Nicholas was fairly sure he'd never even appealed to his mother.

He could figure this out; he just needed time. She'd grow used to him. If she was safe, and his, the rest would follow.

He settled on a more tepid version of the truth. "Other women might be willing to marry me, but I am asking you. You are perfectly eligible, and I wish you to live here."

"I'm *eligible.*" Had she just made a ladylike snort? "You're not warm, you're hard to live with, you'd like to get this over with, and I'm eligible. I shudder to think where this list will go. Would you marry a peacock if she were the daughter of an earl and you met her dusting books in a library?"

"If the peacock seemed not to dislike me, I might try it."

If he knew one thing about his Selene, it was that she was loyal to a fault. She'd stood by her mother's decision to fall into poverty rather than take her father's heir to court. Selene might have *died* from that loyalty. He needed that loyalty committed to *him* before she found another way to help her mother. She could. And then he would lose his only chance at being necessary to her.

"I admit, I do not blame ladies for their willingness to marry me for my money or my title, but you can't blame me for wanting someone who cares for Talbourne, at least, as well." That was as blunt as he could bring himself to be. She could interpret *Talbourne* however she liked.

"Now I'm desirable for my interest in the public welfare of your lands. An interest we've never discussed at all."

Well, that was how she'd interpreted it. "As you say." She was making this too hard. "If it is for life, I would like a wife who at least likes me well enough to speak to me every once in a while."

"Sir, that is gambling far too much on stakes that seem very small."

"You would be surprised how few women do speak to me."

"I *would* be surprised. You are not that unpleasant."

He pounced. "Am I pleasant, then? Sufficiently pleasant to marry? It is only getting married, after all."

That made her silent for what seemed a long time.

"What a breathtaking way of looking at it."

He had her. He could feel it. The next move ought to be hers. He *had* to wait.

And when she spoke, he'd won.

"Your Grace, no lady in my position would turn you down. You knew that when you asked. For my mother's sake alone, I will not turn you down either. Nevertheless, an offer can be irresistible and still be a huge mistake."

Selene leaned toward him. "Your first marriage was arranged for you, if I recall, as a state affair. You ought to be able to remarry for love."

She had cut through his maneuvers with a few words and a hard realism that was eye-opening. Yet she talked about love as though he must be looking for it.

She was only right to the extent that he'd certainly never seen it.

If she was here and he was here, he'd find some way to charm her some day, even though he wasn't charming. Wanting her the way he did must be worth something.

Innocents, he suspected, did not place their faith in desire.

But she didn't even have to know.

Not yet.

"Miss de Gauer, I never had the impression that you were one of these young ladies who spent their afternoons sighing over imagined love affairs."

"I've never made a plan to sit down and sigh, true, but I am not entirely cold-blooded about the idea of marriage either."

The Duke snorted outright. "Very well; let us assume that I *am*. Why should I not offer you the vacant position of Duchess of Talbourne if it seems to me the best way to help you?"

The very idea made her want to shift nervously in her seat. She didn't. "Because it is not a *job*, Your Grace."

"It is very much a job, miss."

"It is not only the position; it is the job of being your *wife*."

"It need not tax you greatly."

Selene had rolled her hand into a fist; she began tapping her thumb against the other fingers, a habit when she was thinking, a habit her mother had tried to break.

Something about the *way* he offered her marriage didn't lighten the heavy worry in the pit of her stomach. In fact, it made it worse.

His Grace had the ability to take away Selene's grinding worries about her mother's health. But surely it was only a trade of that constant threat for this one? This tight feeling of dread about where this would all end, perhaps with him putting her aside as if she were a cup of tea?

She would need to become necessary.

"I do not lie fainting on couches dreaming of romance, but I have never before heard marriage described solely as work, either. If we suppose you need a duchess, we must assume there are thousands of women who could do the job better. Why marry *me*?"

* * *

SHE WAS VERY good at continuing to ask questions. That didn't worry Nicholas; he was very good at continuing not to answer them.

"I have grown tired of being invited to so many functions where boring girls are paraded in front of me like cattle. Men I must persuade, in my work in the House of Lords, make sly remarks about my widowhood and constantly ask about my mistresses, as if any duke must have many."

"And do you have mistresses?"

This was the Selene he knew, come out to play. Well, not amused, but not shying away from the shocking question, either. He had many reasons that he wasn't ready to share, including that he was out of excuses to make the hour-long trip to Lady Howiston's parlor.

"I do not."

"Surprising. Your duchess will apparently be able to enjoy your fidelity."

Was she pleased? He hoped she was pleased. She didn't look it. He wished she were.

But then she went on. "You *must* be lonely."

When he said nothing, she pressed him. "You *are* lonely, aren't you?"

The question threatened to crack something open inside of him which must remain closed.

"I have never used that word, Miss de Gauer. I am not proposing to inflict much of my company upon you, if that is what you are asking. I am an old man, and a plain and boring one. You need not fear that I expect you to wait in attendance upon me."

* * *

"ON THE CONTRARY." Now Selene sat back, and she managed to smile. "If I am to do the job of a duchess, I would expect at the very least a little of my duke's company." She did not consider him old, doubted he was plain, and knew that he was far from boring.

He didn't seem to suspect the way he featured in her daydreams. And he did have a duke's disdain for romantic feelings.

Well, perhaps she would recover Lady Selene's disdain for romance too.

If she were to be married to the man for the rest of her life, it would at least be easier if he continued to like her. And she him.

She *needed* them to spend some time together.

* * *

"MY COMPANY IS no bargain for you, miss." Nicholas tried a glower, but of course she did not see it. He felt a flush of concern. His glower was an important weapon for keeping people at bay; he realized for the first time that of course he would never be able to use it on her.

She was undaunted. "No, I like the idea. Are you willing to play a game, sir?"

Nicholas stifled the urge to both laugh and groan. "This is not a parlor and you are not entertaining me while I wait."

"But you know I like games! And we ought to have one, for it will lighten what you describe as a heavy work, this marriage business. I propose…" Her thumb rubbed against her folded fingers, so he knew she was thinking. "I propose that we must spend at least a quarter of an hour together every evening, or the person who fails must pay a forfeit."

He could not stop his smile. Thank God no one on his staff was here to see it. His reputation as the iciest duke in Britain would be shattered. "And what sort of forfeit? I suppose you would play for a divorce? Annulment? You won't get out of the arrangement so easily, I promise you."

SELENE HOPED she managed to hide her reaction to the cutting chill that went through her when he mentioned such things so easily. That answered at least a few of her questions. Divorce and annulment were things that ruined lives, and would ruin hers, but he mentioned them as if they were nothing but game pieces on a playing board. If she did not please him, he would put her aside the way a pawn was eliminated from the board.

She did not shiver. If she accepted him, she would already have played away her future in exchange for her mother's life. It would be worth it. In Talbourne House her mother would have company every hour of the day and night, footmen to carry her wherever she might want to go, beef broth and sweetmeats whenever she liked.

Selene could risk going on as they were, but it risked her mother's life, and she was only trading away what the rest of the world no longer valued anyway.

Before she grew too despondent thinking about *that*, Selene remembered that she had been in the middle of a proposition.

"A forfeit of the other person's choice, of course. What do you say, Your Grace? Are you willing to play?"

She still did not know what he wanted from his duchess. He wasn't warm, he was hard to live with, and she was *eligible*?

Lady Selene would not have settled for such a lukewarm courtship; even as a housemaid, she wouldn't have settled for it. And she wouldn't say so, but she wasn't going to settle for it now.

This entanglement would have to grow into something stronger. What that was yet, she wasn't exactly sure. But she would have to be a real duchess. She would have to figure out what to make of *that*.

This was going to be a very long game.

And even if he didn't love her... oh, she could teach him a thing or two about playing games.

It was a small thing to have fifteen minutes a night in her arsenal, but a great deal could be learned in almost any game well played.

"If you like," he said as if he didn't much care one way or the other. "If that suits you, we can arrange the ceremony for tomorrow."

The carelessness with which he tossed out the idea of holding the marriage ceremony almost made her dizzy. "Tomorrow?"

"Why spend more time waiting when the result will be the same?"

"Aaahhh. I forgot, you wish to put it behind you." His offer just got better and better.

Selene's hand spread out along the arm of the settee, feeling its carvings.

Sometimes one could discern the shape of an object from the hole it made in sand, or snow. There was something here that Nicholas was hiding. She *would* find it out. And she could only hope that whatever it was, she could keep some memory alive of the young, daydreaming core of herself.

She tried match his careless tone. "Fine. But if you find that my company chafes, you will kindly remember that it was you who set the date. You must have a bishop in your pocket to so quickly acquire a license; but I tell you, sir, I do not undertake marriage expecting it to be annulled." It was only a fair warning.

Then she thought of something else her father might have said, and Selene felt her face getting hot. "It would not be fair if I—if I bear you children." After all, if he didn't have mistresses, he must expect her to...

She *didn't* want to discuss it. But the prospect hung about the room. He wasn't offering waltzes or word games. This was a marriage proposal of financial support and occasional conversation. Against that backdrop, the possibility of... getting children seemed more alarming than anything else.

Not that anyone would make love to a coal bucket.

* * *

THIS WAS a topic on which Nicholas knew he had to be reassuring. The pressure on Alicia to get with child right away had been as unbearable for her as his father's insistence had been on him. They'd never really talked about why intimacies had not gone well till much later, or why such things had never drawn the two of them together.

Why talk about it when she'd adored Edward? And Thomas had been her idea. Her best.

Whether or not Selene wanted children, she mustn't feel pressured. At all.

In his brief conversation with Selene's mother, Lady Redbeck had made it a point to tell him that her daughter was a complete innocent. One that Nicholas had no illusions was mad with passion for *him*.

He had to tread lightly. He didn't want her nervous, thinking he would pounce on her at first chance.

Which he wasn't. He reminded himself that he wasn't going to do that.

"I have two children and both are male. I do not require that you provide me more. I know that... ladies do not... welcome men's advances unless they are utterly necessary."

Selene wasn't smiling now. "They don't?"

Did she sound... shocked? Sad? Appalled?

Surprised?

He shouldn't have pretended to know what ladies thought.

But Nicholas doubted she had ever even held a man's hand in an intimate way. Surely this was an assurance she wanted?

He needed to conclude these negotiations before he ruined them entirely.

"Selene, I *am* old, and plain, and boring, but I am quite aware that you are not. I have made no secret of the fact that I enjoy your company. I enjoy it so much that I would like to have you here, where you will be secure, and nearby, and your mother well cared for."

That was the plain and simple truth; it ought, therefore, to have the virtue of being persuasive.

Selene chewed on her lip. "What a convenient coal bucket I must be," she muttered to herself, and Nicholas stifled his own laugh.

He'd *been* a sexless icy stone of a man.

He'd waited this long to want *anything*. If Selene were his duchess, he could wait centuries more for her to want him back.

He didn't know how to make that happen, but he hoped with his entire being for the chance.

"Selene," he said her name again softly, "I am asking you to be my duchess. And we are well-disposed toward one another. Is that not what young ladies seek in a marriage?"

"I *hope* not." She had both hands clenched tight now. "But as we've said, I am not a fainting novel-reader who believes in romance. Surely it is better to know where we stand before we marry than after? You understand that without my father to speak for me, I must be as forward and careful as I can. We cannot—My father was gone... so fast. And then when my mother fell ill I... I am only reluctant to take any step that might put us in any new danger."

"You will be safe in Talbourne House. Both of you will be safe." He *would* ensure that. "I am so glad you are sensible enough to accept my offer."

* * *

WELL. She *was* a sensible coal bucket after all.

A safe one. If that didn't sound wonderful, it didn't sound bad.

Nicholas' reassurances weren't romantic, but they were working. On him, too. There was something in his voice, something satisfied and purring. And, she noticed, he was talking as if she had already accepted.

In fact, he continued to do so. "Very sensible. It's only getting married, after all."

"Yes," she murmured. "You said that." She had no idea what was about to happen. But then, did any woman when she was about to marry?

At least she wouldn't get eaten on a squirrel island.

So before she lost her nerve she quickly added, "Fifteen minutes a night, Your Grace. Or else a forfeit. If I know we will have our little conversation at the end of the day, I will know you haven't regretted your... well, your choice. Do we have a bargain?" With fifteen minutes a day she ought to be able to find out what he needed, what he wanted... how to make the two of them into a pair.

She could build on that. She *wanted* to be home.

"This is your answer to my proposal of marriage?"

She smiled. "You say yes first."

* * *

THAT ALMOST SHOCKED him into a laugh. But he suppressed it. "Very well. Yes, I accept your proposal, Selene."

* * *

HAD HE ALMOST LAUGHED? There'd been a hitch in his voice as if he'd held something back. She'd win that laugh yet. "Then I also accept your proposal. Nicholas."

"Excellent!" He stood so fast she barely had time to register it before he added, "We shall be married in the morning. Let me dispatch a message to the bishop."

"In the morning?" Selene flushed hot all over, then cold. "Do I not have time to talk to a clergyman, or... or anything?"

"Yes. The bishop. In the morning. To say that you will."

She would. Good heavens. She would.

"And my cousin? She will be there?"

Nicholas answered instantly, "I thought it would be best not to bring any further... attention to your cousin, given her difficult situation."

Selene could not argue. Cass had been through hell the past winter, and had only recently arrived at a carefully balanced—and limited—position in society. It would not be to anyone's benefit, least of all Selene's, for Cass to draw attention to her ongoing business relationship with His Grace.

Or her familial relationship with Selene.

Still, it didn't feel right. To Selene, it made the affair seem not only cold, but cutting.

Then it struck her. "Your Grace! Your mother! And your children! I have not met your children!"

Nicholas made a sort of *pheh* noise that seemed to dismiss both ideas. "I doubt my mother will interest you; she is in London to launch the season, of course you will meet. And children are children. Besides, Edward is full grown. He will barely notice a new stepmother."

Selene had little experience of children but she was fairly sure that they would notice a new stepmother.

"Isn't your younger son quite young still?"

"Thomas has a tutor and a nurse, and will hardly bother you."

"I had not thought that they would bother me, sir, but rather that I might bother them."

"Selene." This time when he captured her hand, he drew her up to stand with him. "This is *our* marriage. We have come through much to get here. We can do as we see fit. Edward will understand that my choice of a calm and helpful duchess will do more for his position than almost anything else. Eventually Thomas too will need to choose a wife. You will be an excellent example for them no matter what."

An example. A calm, helpful, eligible coal bucket.

Even when she'd thought she would marry a man with a title, these were not the topics she had expected to come up.

But then, just like that, Selene's insides settled. She'd have to trust that he knew best when it came to his own family. And, she realized, she liked that he had spoken of all this with *her*. Her father was gone and her mother disinclined, but she had asked the pertinent questions, trying to safeguard herself, and he'd answered.

That sturdy, respectful reliability had certainly appealed to *her*; perhaps he liked that she seemed to be made of the same stuff. He thought she could be what he wanted. Selene felt there were things that he *needed*. They were an odd pair, but perhaps the right one. She could do this.

"A calm and helpful duchess. I hope I can be that. And I'm serious about you learning to enjoy yourself, Your Grace. You need not always be so sad."

At that, his hand tightened spasmodically around hers. Something raw in him seemed to claw its way out. "How did you...?"

But then he apparently gathered himself, and in his more usual voice he only said, "I will see you to your chambers. Tomorrow you will be moved to the duchess' chambers; never fear, your mother's rooms will still be close by."

He placed her hand on his arm and led her through hallways she was beginning to recognize. The sound of their footsteps, the texture of the floor or carpet, everything seemed quiet and muffled as they went, till she was again at a door she assumed was her own.

Only until tomorrow. When she would be the duchess.

"Good night. Nicholas."

"Good night, Selene."

And she comforted herself with the thought that his beautiful voice would be the voice of her husband from tomorrow on, for the rest of her life. A voice that, yes, *would be* lovely when he laughed.

And refused to worry that he had not even sealed their betrothal with a kiss.

* * *

"LORD CALLENDAR, SIR."

Jonas opened one eye, then the other, trying to make out the head silhouetted by a sun that was bright and in the wrong place.

"What?" he asked intelligently.

"I would never wake you, sir," apologized his valet in the middle of waking him, "but an invitation has arrived for the Duke of Talbourne's wedding. *Today.*"

The urgency of the *today* still didn't stir him, until a thought shot across his brain as if from a cannon. "Wedding to *whom?*"

* * *

"I SAW Lady Gadbury walking around the square and you'll never guess what she told me!" Lady Burden burbled as she circled the breakfast table four or five times. "The Duke of *Tal*-bourne is being *marr*-ied to-*day!*"

"Peculiar," said Alistair, cracking an egg.

"I cannot believe it, I simply cannot believe it! You must have met the young lady, haven't you? Lady Gadbury said it was Lord Redbeck's daughter. I remember him, naughty man, he drank your father under the table once."

"Surely not, madame." That was not a picture of his father he cared to contemplate.

"You don't suppose we will be invited as well?" She sounded a little hopeful, eyes wide and hopeful too as she finally alighted on her chair.

"Surely not, madame," Alistair said again, "it is late for a breakfast, weddings are usually quite early."

"Oh. I had thought we might."

"I mean, of course, that I am sure we are invited, but it is too late to accept."

"Oh, I see what you mean, I do see what you mean."

Instead of eating anything, Lady Burden bobbed out to the front of the house to ask the butler again if there had been any messages.

Unconcerned, Alistair ate his egg.

A TENTATIVE ALLIANCE

*N*icholas had made this sound so easy.

"Céline, I have said very clearly that I prefer to dress my hair."

"Miss, I have been assigned to do it, and I will do it." There was a nasty edge to the maid's tone as she added, "It cannot have any mistakes today."

Selene's jaw dropped open before she regained control of it and closed it. What had been wrong with her hair yesterday? For that matter, Céline hadn't even seen the final *coiffure*.

She definitely didn't want to argue about her hair while wrapped in damp linen, sitting on a dressing bench, and preparing to be married in less than an hour.

"I did ask you to leave the combs and hairbrushes here." The dressing table's surface was empty and smooth; Selene ran her fingertips over every inch of it. "I can dress it perfectly well if you will only leave me to do so." Didn't she have enough to worry about, preparing to marry a duke who thought she was calm and helpful?

"The style must be fashionable today, miss. This much hair cannot be styled fashionably. You will look like a battleship under sail if we do not cut some of it away."

"*Cut* it? But I don't want—"

Selene heard the metallic *chink* of a pair of scissors opening.

Throwing herself off the dressing bench, one hand keeping her bathing sheets wrapped around her as the last thin veil of protection she had, Selene backed herself to the wall.

Her last nerve snapped. She *was* going to do this, and she was not going to have her hair chopped off before she did it. "*You will not cut my hair.*"

The maid seemed to waver. "It is not—"

"I will style it. *I* will style it. It is no longer a matter for debate."

Selene heard the scissors rattle on to the dressing table. She let out a breath she had been holding.

The maid was spitting mad. "Pah. Go ahead then, build yourself a platform for ships like Madame Capet, Madame Déficit. Or country braids for a milkmaid."

"Pardon me?"

She heard Céline flouncing towards the door. Yes, she heard it; that was definitely flouncing.

The maid tossed back over her shoulder. "If he wanted to marry a servant girl, I know a dozen younger and prettier than *you*."

And with that last cut, the young woman was out the door.

Panic cut off her breath. She'd known. She'd known that Selene was just a housemaid.

That the Duke of Talbourne was joining together in marriage with a housemaid.

She breathed, in and out. She had nothing to be ashamed of. She must remember that. She'd saved herself from starving and from going mad from boredom. Saved herself and her mother.

Selene gripped the top of the bath sheet until she had sliced it with her fingernails.

She'd never expected such treatment from that quarter. Even knowing that Talbourne House might not embrace her without a few ripples, *that* had never occurred to her. What had she done to cause *that*?

Later.

Not now.

She did not have time to search the room by touch. She needed help. Real help.

Trailing her fingers along the wall to find her mother's adjoining door, she threw it open, heedless of who might be there.

She heard a bevy of young women fussing over her mother, and among all their light, laughing voices, her mother giggling. Giggling.

Selene smiled. That was what all this was for. Just that.

Still, she had to get married.

"*Ladies.* I am in dire need of assistance."

EVER AFTER SHE could not remember what exactly happened to her in between appearing in her mother's door wrapped in damp toweling, and the moment sometime later when she stepped through that door again for a final inspection.

Selene's gown was white jacquard, she knew, with an overdress of silver lace, edged with fashionable small tassels, and accompanied by white gloves. She couldn't imagine what Nicholas had done to get it.

"My beautiful daughter! A dress fit for a queen. Is it a bit tight in the bust? Well, it is a wedding," her mother said, which made no sense to Selene at all. "Your beautiful hair! Very becoming, dear."

"Is it too old-fashioned?" Selene refrained from asking if it looked like a platform for battleships. She'd arranged her hair in smooth twists low on the back of her head, leaving a few curls to drape around her face. It ought to be flattering, but she wanted someone to confirm it.

"Only slightly, but very tastefully so. His Grace is not known for fashion and you need not be if it doesn't suit you. Your hair is lovely, and there is so much of it. A touch warmer than I'd like, but very nice."

Lady Redbeck was not given to unrestrained complements. Selene had heard for years that her hair had developed a slightly copper tinge that her mother didn't care for, but apparently made up for it through sheer tawny quantity.

"And we have orange blossoms for you! Come, let me pin them in your hair myself. It will be my little part in your toilette."

Selene sat on the edge of the bed. "You are not over-taxing yourself? The footmen will carry you down?"

"Oh yes, dear, and the Duke's son no longer uses that lovely comfortable rolling chair that Miss Cullen—that Lady Howiston designed, you remember the one. He no longer needs it at all and I am to have sole use of it."

"Please do tell them if you tire at all."

"I will tell them to bring me straight back here the moment I am fatigued. And Fran will be with me." Her mother sounded very certain. More like her old self.

Selene relaxed.

Her mother finished pinning the orange blossoms in her hair. As they warmed, they began to release their scent, the essence of clean spring air.

"Such a lovely bride." Lady Redbeck's small hands slid around her shoulders and pulled her close. "I am so glad that I lived to see this day," she murmured into Selene's ear, and Selene knew those were tears captured between her cheek and her mother's.

"I as well, Mama, so very happy."

She *was* happy. Selene almost thought she could be happy forever, just sitting here with her arms around her mother's neck.

But she did have to go get married.

"Miss de Gauer," came a voice she thought she'd heard before, a low one like a shovel full of gravel.

The man introduced himself as "Peter Lyall, the steward, miss. I will accompany you to His Grace, and there are four more footmen here to take care of Lady Redbeck."

Selene stole one more hug from her mother. "When I see you again, I shall be an old married lady!" It wasn't possible to decide if she was crying or laughing.

"Don't spoil your face! You will not be old for a long, long time."

Her mother must have gestured for Mr. Lyall, as the man was suddenly beside her. "Are you ready, miss? May I?" And, at her murmur of agreement, using just one finger, placed her hand on his arm.

Forever afterward, Selene didn't recall if the gravelly-voiced man said anything else during the walk down.

She remembered moving slowly down the grand staircase, Mr. Lyall on one side, her other hand on the polished balustrade. She remembered Mr. Lyall leading her to a small room behind the stairs, so small as to practically be a closet, and she remembered smelling His Grace's cologne, the crisp lemon and rosemary scent of his handkerchief, as she entered the room.

And she would always remember the noise Nicholas made as she came in, though it was a noise she couldn't decipher. Something in between a grunt of surprise and a very satisfied murmur, like a dog cuddling a coveted bone.

Then Nicholas said quite clearly, "I ought to have given you some diamonds," and he tucked her hand into the crook of his elbow most securely. "In combs for your hair, perhaps, as a tiara risks offending the crown."

She leaned close as well. "Shall I tell you, when I was a little girl I wanted to be married dripping in jewels and flowers. Isn't that silly? My father read it from a story, I didn't even know what jewels were. Then when I got older, I found they were just hard stones. I much prefer the flowers." She touched one of the blossoms in her hair. "However were they found so early in the spring?"

"Somewhere in London, nearly anything can be had for a price."

Selene could not stop smiling. "Spoiled already," she confided as she patted his arm.

Nicholas did not answer.

"I can see that the young lady is marrying of her own free will," said another voice, and Selene realized that she had been so caught up in Nicholas' presence, she had not even noticed the presence of the bishop.

"Your lordship. I do, sir." She curtsied to him, even as Nicholas kept tight hold of her hand. Perhaps he didn't want her to fall over.

"Well. Let's give them a few moments to settle your mother—I understand that she has been ill? I hope she will feel better soon?"

Selene pushed away the thought that the bishop's concern came a little late. "She stays roughly the same, sir, but she has become so much better just since her arrival here—His Grace has ensured excellent care for her."

"I believe I met Lady Redbeck when she was younger. It is my failing that I have not seen her since your father passed away. I will visit her."

"Your lordship."

The Duke of Talbourne, who had been restlessly shuffling himself back and forth in the small space, seemed to run out of patience. "Surely they are ready."

He didn't wait for anyone to confirm whether they were or not. When he led her from the small anteroom, she heard several footmen in front of her as well as several behind.

"Why such a processional?" Selene murmured, leaning toward him again.

"The doors to the ballroom are large. They will leave us to march along the aisle by ourselves."

And the doors did open.

Selene very distinctly heard the sounds of many people rustling, breathing, and awaiting a wedding.

Many, many people.

"Nicholas!" she hissed under her breath, tightening her hold so that he wouldn't move. "How many people are in there?"

"Not so many. Two or three hundred."

"Two or three... *hundred*? You are joking!"

"I don't think so," her soon-to-be-husband said matter-of-factly. "Almack's often has more than five hundred. For the wedding of a duke in London, it is practically small."

He didn't add that people were curious. He didn't need to. These people must have received invitations in the middle of the night. Yet still, they came.

To stare at her.

"Nicholas! I can't do this!" She just barely restrained herself from clawing at his sleeve, suddenly terrified he would drag her down the aisle and everyone would see her battleship-platform hair.

"Selene. Not only can you do this, you can do this beautifully."

Her feet were glued to the floor. She couldn't walk with her feet glued to the floor.

Then he leaned closer, and she could hear the smile in his voice. "It's only getting married, Selene."

Her laugh was gasping, barely drawing in a breath. But it steadied her.

It's only getting married, after all.

* * *

WHEN SHE SAID "I WILL", the words seemed to ring. The crowd rustled and murmured.

Nicholas pressed her hand into his arm as he led her back down the aisle, as if he would never let go.

Back in the tiny office under the stairs, the bishop fumbled a bit wondering how she should sign her name.

"Let me make my mark, your lordship, as all unlettered people do, and Mr. Lyall will witness it."

In contrast to his earlier restlessness, now Nicholas was in no rush at all. He stood quietly as the bishop fussed with pen and paper, scribbling everything that needed to be scribbled.

But finally they were done with the formalities and he sounded almost jolly as he asked her, "To the breakfast, Your Grace?"

Well. It was beyond odd to be addressed as a duchess. A starving one. "Yes! I am famished."

And he led her to the reception hall, which was filled with delicious smells and the sound of many dozens of people circulating and talking.

Nicholas seemed to summon two footmen with a wave, for he leaned close and said, "They will take care of you," before he disappeared, leaving her to be greeted by three or four ladies all at once.

And that was the last of her husband's company Selene enjoyed at her wedding breakfast.

* * *

LORD HALWORTH LET his horse walk, the sound of the gelding's hooves muffled by the softer spring ground toward the edge of the lane.

When Talbourne Hall was as full of people coming and going as it was right now, he preferred the quiet out of doors. The way the air smelled wet and green refreshed something inside him. Along the road's edge, new grass defied the churned chaos of mud to stab upwards to the sky, the tiny blades coming together to form a soft new carpet.

Life was amazing.

The rattle of tack and wheels made him look up. Wasn't that the Duke's older son Edward, driving the Talbourne gig?

When the little two-seater drew abreast of him he saw that Edward was indeed driving it, and that sour Lord Burden was with him.

He walked his horse over a bit to make more room on the lane for the gig. Edward stopped.

"Lord Fettanby." Halworth tipped his hat. He tried to be as formal as the Duke preferred, though it was sometimes hard with Edward, whose flyaway clothes and distracted look gave him something of the air of the nursery he had left behind not long ago.

"Lord Halworth," the young man said just as formally. "Are the festivities spoiling your peace?"

"Oh, no, a little merriment can't hurt me." He nodded. "Lord Burden."

"We are intending to be fashionably late to the breakfast," Burden said in that way he had where he thought he was funny.

Halworth couldn't think of a kind way to point out that, unlike Talbourne House's everyday affairs, the wedding breakfast was by invitation only. Well, maybe Burden had one. He didn't think the man was to the Duke's taste, though.

And Edward was against it. "I say there's no need to go at all."

Halworth looked at the young man again. Yes, he was spitting angry about something. "You needn't," Halworth assured him mildly. "There are plenty of guests to eat your share and keep each other amused."

"Surely not." Burden didn't look amused now. "His Grace has been speaking with me constantly on a vote for which he wishes my support. I am sure he wants my attendance."

Halworth nodded but said, "I'm sure, but there are many in London who have not received invitations." To assuage the man's feelings he added, "I believe he considered it a family affair."

"I wonder what family," Edward muttered.

Burden wasn't flustered. "Now then, Lord Fettanby, no harm done. If we find that there has been some oversight and I am not a guest, we'll simply drive back home."

The idea that Edward would be perfectly willing to miss more of his father's wedding to drive someone who was *not* a guest all the way back to London struck Halworth as, to put it mildly, odd. But Edward seemed to take it in stride.

"Good day, then," and Halworth tipped his hat again as Edward shook the reins and the gig moved on.

He hoped the boy would root out whatever was eating at him. It was too nice a day to be bitter, and it was spring.

* * *

"What sort of event will you hold when you come to Bath?"

"Have you heard any news of the East India Company's reauthorization in Parliament?"

"It is appalling to see shopkeepers' daughters masquerading as our equals—do you not agree?"

"I say, if we taxed the jam at an event like this we might pay the Regent's bills, what? Har har."

"The lamb is delicious, isn't it?"

"Do you drink wine in the daytime?"

"What do you think of the new ministers joining the government?"

And all of it with an endless chorus of *Your Grace, Your Grace, Your Grace* that all seemed to be referring to Selene.

This role wouldn't require that she be silent.

Well, she'd figure out how to be a *Your Grace* if it was the last thing she did.

After a quarter of an hour she wondered if she should send one of the footmen shadowing her every move to find the Duke.

After half an hour she wondered if she had done something wrong already.

After an hour she wondered if she had been jilted at the altar. But that could not be right, because the ceremony *had* been performed. The bishop had concluded it and everything. She had been there.

After two hours she considered asking someone to bring her a knife and she would go find her husband herself.

The bewildering array of people never stopped. They introduced themselves, but they also talked over one another and she could not always keep track of who was speaking. They all talked as if they already knew her, and the worst part was that some probably did; they might have attended her father as earl during his lifetime. She did recognize a few.

Her mother had only spent a few minutes in the crush and then had mercifully been removed to her chambers again.

The food was clearly for show. She had her place at the table, but eating in public was one thing that did not always go easily for a blind person, and especially not in front of all the people who were watching her. She dared not spill soup or meat on the precious gown, so she ate nothing.

Except a smidgen of cake.

Her wine glass was kept full by attentive servants, but as a rare drinker, the wine made her light-headed more than anything else.

Again, Selene could hear Nicholas' voice at the table, only a yard or two away, but he was addressing people around him and he did not speak to her.

And when the interminable meal was over, the crush of guests returned.

"What draper created that lovely gown?"

"Is there a chance that the Continental war might soon be over?"

"Have you decided which parties you will be attending?" was a thorny one, since to the best of her knowledge no one in London even knew she existed until the last hour, so she doubted she had any invitations awaiting her.

And the one that struck real fear into her heart, "Will His Royal Highness be here, Your Grace?"

The last thing, the very last thing she wanted was to meet the Prince Regent right now.

She'd prefer to put off explaining why she had not been presented at Court. And she'd prefer much more warning. The Prince had a well-known taste for amusing married ladies, and it was unnerving to think that her marriage might have made her an eligible target. She'd never worried before about the kind of man who made love to married women.

When Selene heard a familiar voice at her elbow, she nearly whirled and clutched at the man out of pure relief.

"You make a beautiful bride, Your Grace, but then you were beautiful before as well."

"Lord Callendar! What a pleasure to see you again. Perhaps you can help me find my mother."

She knew perfectly well her mother was not in the room and probably so did he, but it gave her an excuse to nod to the people accosting her on all sides and move at least a few steps away.

And graciously, he played along, leading her aside.

"I am surprised you put it that way, Your Grace, since strictly speaking, you have never seen me at all."

Selene laughed. His informality was as refreshing as cool water on a summer afternoon. "I cannot speak for all blind people, my lord, but I believe most of us find it easiest to use English as the general population uses it. You would not expect me to say that it is a pleasure to hear you again, would you? Or perceive you? It might quickly be awkward."

"You could never be awkward. It is a pleasure to see you, and I say it most accurately. There is something so melancholy about attending the wedding of a beautiful woman, and here I am doing it of my own free will."

That made Selene laugh again. He was so effortlessly entertaining. "Not only attending the actual wedding but celebrating it afterwards!"

"I am quite smug that I received an invitation not only to the ceremony, but to this celebration as well."

"And how did you arrange that?"

"I am hoping it is because I referred to His Grace as a friend." Jonas sounded as if he rather surprised himself. "In fact, I am also to attend the ball this evening."

"This evening! Never say so. I am already exhausted. And I have met a hundred people I could not possibly recognize if my life depended on it."

"Ready to escape already?" Jonas asked lightly.

Which drew her up short. No, she wasn't. If this was the wedding day Talbourne required, so be it. She suspected that Nicholas would not have done all this if it were not necessary.

She had told Nicholas that she would be his duchess, and she would. She was.

"Not escape. I did not sleep well, that is all, and I wish this beautiful silver lace did not poke me so terribly."

"The suffering of the rich and noble. Let me serve as an assisting pair of eyes for you, may I? Many of the revelers seem to have retired. There is a clear path to the door, and if we reach there safely, I can send you up to your chambers to rest for a while, perhaps with your mother? Would you like that? And then you will have plenty of time to dress before you come down and dine and dance with us mere mortals here below."

"You are a genius." Selene did not want to ask, but she *did* want to know. "Do you see my husband anywhere about?"

Husband fit awkwardly in her mouth, especially saying it to Lord Callendar, a near stranger.

But Jonas took it quite in stride. "I believe he left perhaps half an hour ago? No doubt to attend to some pressing matter so that he can enjoy the rest of the festivities with you later. His Grace is famous for his attention to duty."

Was he? Perhaps she knew nothing, really, about the man whose life she had just joined to hers. Selene felt foolish, and small.

But wasn't she a duchess now? She would not show it.

Giving him her widest smile, Selene put out her hand, allowing Jonas to place his own arm beneath it. "We will carry out your plan of attack, my lord," she said as if she had not a care in the world.

"Brilliant."

And as he had promised, Jonas delivered her to the door where he summoned a footman.

"Do not stop to talk to anyone on the stairs," he admonished as he let her go.

"Never fear, I have run out of small talk on every conceivable topic," Selene assured him.

Still, he said the same thing to the footman. "Don't stop on the stairs. Off you go."

How kind he had been to help her escape, thought Selene.

Where the *devil* was her husband?

*   *   *

IT HAD ALL GONE PERFECTLY.

The most difficult part of his plan was complete. She had married him. She wouldn't leave now.

He was a bit hazy on what to do next. But Nicholas wasn't worried. The critical part was done.

Half of London had seen the ceremony for themselves. There was no doubt that Selene was his duchess; no one could question that.

At the same time, especially after the incident on the stairs, he wanted no one in London to know how much she meant to him. It was too dangerous.

Still, it was done, and as long as he didn't show it, Nicholas could be as happy as he liked. In, in fact, a good mood.

He could even spare an ear for these two, debating the approaching Parliamentary task that *actually* mattered to him. It was possible to concentrate, knowing that soon he would see Selene again, because she was his wife.

Practically humming with good cheer, Nicholas listened to both men say the same things he'd heard them say before. In his mind, he'd dubbed them Mr. Willy and Mr. Johnson, as he found both of them absurd.

Both men were certain that they knew what to do about the reauthorization of the East India Company, based on nothing but their interest in being rich or being contrary. He was there to give them someone to talk to, since they refused to talk to each other.

Not that his mind was on their argument rehearsals. His mind was on the signed and sealed wedding documents. A written agreement was a solid basis on which to build. No one could separate them now without the approval of the Prince Regent himself, and that would not happen; Nicholas would not ask for it and neither would she.

They were both smart enough to stay out of the orbit of the self-indulgent Prince.

He liked the idea that she could enjoy herself here. No more red knuckles from scrubbing laundry at all hours. And her mother was here. She could amuse herself however she liked and as she grew accustomed to him, she might find him a comfortable enough companion.

Perhaps even comfortable enough to allow to come quite close.

Nicholas didn't like that he thought of it that way. He knew Selene was not a wild animal, or a figurine under glass. Still, he thought it safest to approach her slowly and cautiously. Because he *was* going to approach her sooner or later. He wasn't proud of himself for thinking it, but he was honest, if only to himself.

Selene had looked exactly like a duchess, the silver gown making her glitter and glow among the swirl of all those far less interesting people. Her hair had shone as if the rays of sunlight had crept inside only to find her.

She had looked like *his* duchess.

He had hated leaving her alone, but it was important. Every single person there needed to believe that his attachment to her was only slight.

It wasn't only his father's training. She had already survived one attack. Not that he wanted anyone to know that, including her. Surely that would *not* make her comfortable.

Another man would have frowned at the thought of his wife nearly being murdered. But Nicholas Hayden, Duke of Talbourne, did not make facial expressions involuntarily.

It was better that he'd left. People made up their own explanations for anything he said or did. And she wouldn't want him hovering over her, surely, when they barely knew each other.

Mr. Lyall would get to the bottom of the threat. Nicholas had to turn his attention to the blowhards repeating themselves for the eighth time.

"The Company has had sole control for too long already."

"If you damage the Company's prospects you damage the prospects of every peer in Britain."

"The African Company stands to surpass the income of the East India Company."

"You think that recommends them? Since the trade in slaves has been abolished? How are they earning so much? They are on a course for a review of their practices that will rival the Hastings impeachment."

Which gave Nicholas a wonderful opening to make exactly his point. "Speaking of Mr. Hastings. Gentlemen, the time when we may affect Parliament's decision is growing short. Mr. Hastings ought to be able to address us."

As expected, the one gentleman scowled at that. "The embarrassment of the House precludes it."

And the other used the opening to attack. "Had you not spent seven fruitless years investigating the man, embarrassment would be no obstacle. We are not *all* embarrassed."

Nicholas cut off the recriminations by cutting in. "Warren Hastings consolidated the Company's various holdings in India. He repelled France's attempt to wrest India from our grasp. We need to know his thoughts about allowing other merchants to trade in India."

The embarrassed gentleman continued scowling. "He spent his time collecting zoo animals and languages. And bribes."

The other gentleman did not let that pass either. "Seven years of investigation that nearly bankrupted him proved nothing of the sort."

Nicholas had to get them closer to deciding. "We are not re-investigating Mr. Hastings. We are asking him for his knowledge based on ten years governing in India."

"Knowledge? Just consider the source."

Nicholas fixed the man with a look. "That is exactly what I am asking you to do."

This had gone on long enough. Nicholas had done what he could for now. Now, he would do what he wanted. "Gentlemen, let us speak again soon. Please enjoy the hospitality of Talbourne House."

As he expected, they immediately took their leave of each other, leaving him through separate doors.

Now he could be with Selene.

The guests had dispersed from the dining room; his duchess—his duchess!—must have retired.

He would no more have betrayed his eagerness by taking the steps two at a time than he would have taken off all his clothes.

But it only took him short moments before he was at Selene's door with the footman announcing him.

* * *

IF HE HAD NOT SPENT a lifetime training himself to betray no emotion at all, he would have frozen in place upon seeing her.

Selene was sitting at the bench at the dressing table, crushed white orange blossoms scattered on its surface and a tidy pile of hair pins in front of her.

She stopped in the act of brushing the thick cascade of her hair forward over her shoulder, and turned her face toward him.

The subtle shapes of her, every single aspect of her, just struck Nicholas as *right*.

It had confused and roiled him, but it hadn't crushed him, discovering at his age that he was subject to such feelings. Somehow, because it was Selene, it was all right.

The urge to touch her seemed to press on him everywhere.

It was awkward at best, not only because it was a new sensation, but because Nicholas had learned from painful experience never to betray that anything or anyone was dear to him.

It had never been so difficult before.

He closed the door behind him. "Your Grace?"

Selene wore a very slight frown. "Am I? You disappeared so long ago, I assumed you needed the time to track down the church registry and tear out the page where we signed our names."

Perhaps the marriage wasn't going as well as he'd thought.

He stepped inside. "There was an opportunity to create some crucial discussion on a voting matter I am... trying to steer toward a particular conclusion. I thought it best to seize the moment."

"A voting matter. Well. That certainly puts our marriage into perspective, doesn't it?"

Perhaps he should have spoken to her more before he left. "My apologies, madame..."

"No need. An eligible coal bucket only rates so much attention."

Nicholas took note of the way her knuckles were whitening around the handle of the hairbrush. He kept one eye on that just in case she threw it. "I take it you are feeling quarrelsome?"

"I seldom have before, Your Grace, but I do believe I am now."

"I thought I had handled any difficulty that might arise today, madame. I regret anything I overlooked."

"I cannot imagine how you could have anticipated anything which has weighed on me today. Six years ago I went from being the daughter of the oldest earldom in Britain to being a pauper. Yesterday I was asked to go from being a pauper to being the Duchess of Talbourne. Why shouldn't I feel light as a feather? Aside from worrying about my mother's health and my magically disappearing husband of twenty minutes, I've been introduced to half the United Kingdom, none of whose names I will ever remember; I've had no food and too much drink; I've been moved again to this new chamber, when I had not even learned the old one; and I've been threatened with a pair of scissors. It could have been tougher."

"Who threatened you with a pair of scissors?"

Selene waved it away. It made her let go of the hairbrush.

Nicholas was no longer worried about thrown hairbrushes. "Selene, *who* threatened you with a pair of scissors?"

"It was nothing, Your Grace." She sighed, and he could almost see all the energy drain out of her. "A disgruntled maid. I've no idea where she has gone; this house is practically a city."

"What maid?"

Turning toward him again, Selene put out her hand, leaving it there in midair until he took it. "You're frightened," she said half under her breath.

Her distressing habit of being able to discern his emotions would have to be dealt with later. She'd offered her hand and he could take it. No one could stand in his way.

Dropping to one knee upon the plush woolen carpet, Nicholas lowered his voice and kept hold of her hand in both of his. "Tell me what she said."

"Nicholas. I'm sorry to worry you. I'm tired, that is all. She was the young woman who has been waiting on me since we arrived. I doubt you know her name but it was Céline, if you can believe it. She seemed to feel that my name was my fault."

"What did she *say?*"

"She threatened to cut my hair—which made me more nervous than I already was. I heard the scissors in her hand, you know that little noise they make? I had to insist that she would *not*, and she told me to go ahead and make my hair into a platform for battleships, like... what was it? Madame Déficit? Which made no sense. My French is not good, Your Grace. Yes, Madame Déficit, Madame Capet, that was what she said. And she called me a servant."

Nicholas should have remembered. It was never safe to want things, and things he wanted were never safe.

All abruptly, he leaned in and gathered her up in his arms, holding her completely even as she sat there on the dressing bench.

He had her softness and her hard-edged wit, her curves and bones and spirit and smile, all held tightly against him, belonging to him, belonging here, and he had never before been so happy and so terrified.

He felt her rigid astonishment relax, just a little, and found himself amazed at the way she fit against him when she did.

"Selene," he murmured against her hair, "those are references to the French queen who was beheaded at the guillotine."

In his arms, her spine snapped straight.

"You cannot think that she—but—"

"I can think it. There are many who are angered by what the privileged class does with its privileges. Seeing the same things they see, it is hard to disagree. But they should not be working in your chambers." Brandishing scissors at my *wife*.

"I am—should I be sorry? I—"

"How can you be sorry? I am sorry that I did not do a better job of ensuring that you had only trustworthy help, you and your mother from the moment you arrived here. *I* am sorry, and I will regret it for the rest of my life."

Selene was silent for a moment, her mouth fallen open in astonishment.

Finally she said, "I was not hoping for such a sweeping apology, Your Grace. I only had hoped to spend a little more time with you on our wedding day. Dance with you."

He ought to let her know that dancing with her risked ruining the illusion that both of them needed to maintain. It wasn't just his father's training, which had hardened into his own habit. She had only been in danger since she had come *here*. Someone hated that she mattered to Nicholas; he must appear as though she didn't. He hadn't danced in years and ought not to change that now, for this, for her.

But he couldn't bring himself to say it.

"She knew I was a servant," Selene said again.

"That is of no import. Forget it. Forget her." He settled her back in her seat. He had to let go of her. "Your Grace," he said, soothing and quiet, one of his thumbs lightly stroking the back of her hand, "you have had a trying day, with all this marrying business, and you should get some rest. We will have guests for the ball this evening. Tell me what you need."

"I thought I just did."

The thudding of his heart in his chest would give him away if she heard it. He had to control it.

He could not control it if he stayed this close to her.

He said quietly, "Madame, I do feel that we should begin as we mean to go on, so you must trust that I did not mean to make you feel abandoned. A duke and duchess married today; what will get you through the rest of it?"

That little speech seemed to soothe her. He'd at least done that right. "Thank you, sir," she responded just as softly. "I do need a lady's maid, to help me dress for this evening. And—more than rest, I wish to visit my mother. I meant to, but the footman brought me here and left so quickly."

"There is no trouble there." Drawing her up to stand, Nicholas tucked her hand in his elbow. "It will be easier for you to follow me this way than with your hand upon my forearm, will it not?"

She nodded.

"It appears to be five long strides to your door? No, that would be for me. Let us follow the wall from the dressing table." When they came upon what seemed to be a small accent table crowned with a brass *cloisonné* urn—they both heard its rattle when she bumped the table slightly—Nicholas added, "And I will have that removed before the end of the ball this evening. Perhaps you will count the steps from here?"

Selene's fingertips, used to learning about the surrounding space, bumped over the tiny join in the wallpaper. "Perhaps I will count panels of wallpaper, Your Grace."

"Very clever."

When they reached the door, Nicholas placed her hand on the fluted brass of the door's knob, let her open it, then followed her through, always close enough for her hand to stay on his elbow. If she needed to learn the way, he would let her find it.

"This hallway is the family wing," he told her, and they paused. "My chambers are on the right; that is where the wing ends. I have a lovely view of the lake and its closest garden, about which you won't care at all."

That made her chuckle.

Just a little chuckle, but it lifted some of the weight in his gut.

He went on. "To your left is the rest of the wing, crossed by a hallway that continues toward the front of the house. Where lies the main staircase, you doubtless recall. We can follow the wall on the left until that hallway cuts our path; it is quite broad, I'm afraid, to allow for ladies' skirts and men carrying buckets and such, but let us count the steps."

He let her set the pace as they left the guiding wall behind, counting for her, till the left wall again was in reach.

"Only four steps? I think your stride was longer that time." He sounded almost as if he were teasing.

"I will become used to the distance and judge it without thinking eventually," Selene assured him.

Nicholas let her trail her fingers again along the wall. "That room is empty now, then here is the room you were in earlier, and then here is your mother's." He paused, reluctant as always to let go her hand. "I do reserve this area closely for friends of the family. Sir Malcolm is the only guest here, and his door is just before the last, four more doors down. My mother has an apartment on the lower floor, on this side; she prefers the garden view and hates stairs. But she is currently in a townhouse I own in the city."

"And the children?"

* * *

SELENE FELT HIM SHIFT; waving a hand, no doubt. "Where children are. Upstairs. There is an entire suite of rooms designated a nursery. Edward has left the nursery but remains along that corridor."

"Thank you, Your Grace."

Nicholas leaned a little closer. "You are welcome, Your Grace. And while you can of course ring for assistance at any moment, let me also tell you there are two footmen awaiting your or your mother's pleasure along this hallway right now, and you can also simply open your door and ask. May I ask, why did you not eat?"

"It's no great matter."

"Madame, you must eat."

"Cutting can be difficult, and I daren't drop anything on this dress."

"Hang the dress. Shall I take you back to your chambers?"

Taken aback by what had almost sounded like vehemence, Selene shook her head. "I will go see my mother first, and find my own way back." She wanted to thank him again, but if she just kept thanking him over and over he would know how tangled up and tired she was right now. "I know I will see you at the ball later, but... afterwards? Our fifteen minute wager should begin tonight."

"I thought this would count as our fifteen minutes. Does it not?"

His genuine surprise threatened to start her laughing, hysterical laughing that might end up as sobbing. How could he be so thoughtless and so thoughtful at the same time?

Somehow she managed to keep her voice even as she said, "I can make an allowance for our wedding day, sir, but keep in mind I mean our fifteen minutes to close our days in future."

"You never specified that."

She had. "Then I am unpredictable. Who knows how the rules may change?"

"I am not unpredictable. Count on me, madame. I will see you this evening."

She listened to his footfalls moving farther away till the carpets muffled even that remnant of his presence.

Great heavens above. He thought he was predictable.

She had misjudged *that* from parlor conversation.

"Selene! How sweet of you to visit me! How goes the party? Is it lovely?"

Selene heard at least two other people moving around in the room, perhaps more. "How goes the party in here?" She put on a smile for her mother.

Her mother's happy voice was all she really needed to hear. She'd been right to do this. Even if her mother's health didn't improve, she would at least be very comfortable. And not lonely.

Not being lonely seemed important just now.

Her mother sounded quite jolly indeed. "Fran has decided I need my feet rubbed, as walking to that rolling chair turned out to be surprisingly painful. Deidre has decided to wash and dress my hair for the ball, as I am to make an appearance. Your father would be so proud! And then Ann is taking in a dress for me, another of Lady Howiston's gifts. I am afraid it will be too youthful, but Ann assures me not."

"A gray watered silk, becoming on either of you, Lady Redbeck," Ann assured them both, most likely from a position bent over her needle, "and how lucky you are that your figure is so like your daughter's. The draper will be sending more things for Her Grace soon; I am sure your daughter does not mind sharing this one with you, madame."

"Not at all, but... I hate to inconvenience you all, but might I have a few words with my mother alone?"

There was a chorus of feminine outbursts of "Of course!" and "Right away, Your Grace!" and the room cleared surprisingly quickly for a group of young women all engaged in so many tasks at once.

"What is it... Your Grace?"

Selene took care not to tear the silver lace on her gown as she sat on the edge of her mother's bed. She wanted to crawl up and rest her head on her mother's shoulder as she had when she was little.

The feeling was in sharp contrast to the title her mother had just used for her.

Gently, carefully, she leaned down farther and laid her head on her mother's arm.

"Oh, Mama. I'm not sure of what I've done," Selene whispered.

"Oh no my child! You have done brilliantly."

"So you and Papa would say. Very well, I have accepted the Duke's proposal. But now I must... now I must be his duchess, and it may be harder than I ever thought for all kinds of reasons I never suspected."

"Has he not been kind to you, darling? Husbands, especially dukes, aren't always affectionate, but they must be kind."

Selene's eyes began to prickle with tears. Tears would take ages to fix. She was not an expert about ladies' toilettes but she did know that. "I think he is kind, in a way."

"Well then! That truly is what marriage requires most of all, dear. And he will continue to be. I ought to have reassured you yesterday. I did your father's duty and told him that you have been completely gently bred, innocent of men's baser nature, and that you would expect him to continue to be a complete gentleman once you were under his protection."

"Meaning what, Mama?"

"Meaning just what I said! It is barbaric for men to feel they must establish their ownership claims by dragging a girl's innocence away on their wedding night. This is not a feudal fiefdom and you are a lady. He must respect your disinclination to submit to his baser nature, at least until you know each other better. If at all."

This was news to Selene. She and her mother had not had conversations about men's baser nature before. Only to bar the door against them when they had been in those moldy-smelling thin-walled rooms at the top of rickety stairs.

The few times Selene had considered men's baser nature, it seemed likely to her that there must be such a thing as women's baser nature too. That princess hadn't broken out of her tower for nothing.

But she hadn't had time to worry about either one when her primary problem was whether her mother's health would improve on a diet of peas and parsnips.

At Cass' house, Selene had barely *talked* to any men.

Except Nicholas.

And she had not shared her daydreams about Nicholas with her mother.

It at least explained some of his reassurance that he could happily leave her bed alone. Nicholas was under the impression that she was... well, frightened of him. Nervous of him.

And she might be, a little, but not because of his baser nature.

It was because he really was so very... startling. When she'd imagined leaning on him, she'd imagined it very differently.

And he'd implied that her life as a servant could affect his reputation, when he was discussing the idea of marriage. She knew he had. Yet now, apparently, he didn't care.

Like the knowledge that he had a bishop available to him day or night, it was unsettling. He was *not* steady, or predictable; and she was beginning to wonder how they could establish a steady orbit around one another when his motions were so erratic.

"Can one skip one's own wedding ball?" Selene rubbed her cheek against the sleeve of her mother's dressing gown.

"Just rest, dear," Lady Redbeck murmured, rubbing the spot between Selene's shoulderblades that had always soothed her. "I'll wake you in a very short while."

She could not possibly fall asleep. Selene did not even hope for that, so she did not try.

* * *

WHEN SHE WOKE, her mother was saying softly to a footman, "Just there, please."

"What is it?"

"Your new husband has sent you some food, darling. I don't know when he learned what you like, but there is some smoked trout, a dainty boiled egg, some very fine buttered bread and a cup of coffee. I hope there is enough for you to give me a taste of that coffee."

"Dr. Burke forbade you coffee," Selene remarked as she went and found the little table. That new husband had heard her, it seemed. The Duchess of Talbourne would have to be less quiet about what she needed.

She was still wearing the dress, but here she could use a napkin to protect her front.

And everything was cut into very manageable pieces. Accompanied by a spoon as well as a fork.

This wasn't just the kitchens. The Duke of Talbourne had put thought into something she needed.

What about what she wanted? Perhaps he would remember her request about a dance, too.

It was a bit mortifying to remember that she'd said that out loud... but it was true.

"I hope you are feeling better, Lady Redbeck."

"So much, darling. And how has the nap left you?"

Selene swallowed the bite of bread she was chewing. Sleep and food cured so many things, along with the memory of the way he'd hugged her. It had been like a blazing fire all in an instant, one that was then just as suddenly put out. "I think I will be all right."

* * *

"YOU'VE DONE LADIES' hair before, Martha?"

"Oh yes ma'am. Ever so nicely. I know the styles these days and just what will look pretty on Your Grace."

Martha had been sent up to be Selene's new lady's maid five minutes ago, no doubt an answer to Selene's request of His Grace.

Selene had forty minutes before she was expected at her own wedding celebration.

She had little choice.

"Martha, you must choose a dress and any accessories for me. Obviously I cannot choose them for myself. Can you find something becoming in which I can dance?"

"Oh yes ma'am!" Martha sounded very confident.

There was nothing for it but to take the plunge. Selene needed to appear downstairs very shortly.

"Martha, let us aim for glory."

* * *

Peter Lyall again came to lead her down.

When they reached the bottom of the grand staircase, Selene heard music drifting over them, a lovely set of string musicians, and voices. There were guests in the foyer, and no doubt drifting through the closer rooms, waiting to dine.

So many voices.

"Mr. Lyall—"

But before she could finish the thought, there was—

"Her Grace the Duchess of Talbourne!"

And all voices dipped in volume as Selene could practically feel all eyes turning to her.

There was a murmur that ran through the air. Selene had a feel for the murmurs of crowds. This one was surprised, and perhaps a little disapproving? Was that a giggle from someone farther away?

"Your Grace." Nicholas arrived to escort her.

"Your Grace." She let him place her hand more formally on his forearm as he had done when they walked in towards a bishop to say their vows.

"What is the problem?" Selene managed to whisper nearly soundlessly.

"No problem, madame. I suspect a few souls are surprised to see how young you are, that is all."

"Why, how young do I look?"

"In a simple rose-colored gown without overlay or ribbons? With your hair swept back into the crown of curls that every young lady in her first season is wearing? And no jewels, and only a lace choker? You look about seventeen, madame."

Selene suppressed a groan.

"Never fear." He had mastered the art of pitching his voice not to carry. She'd wager he barely moved his lips, too. "I believe it will be only to my benefit. To have chosen a fresh young girl. I will be perceived as cheap, perhaps, in that you do not wear an obvious wedding gift of jewels."

"I do not suppose it will matter to anyone that I don't particularly care for jewels."

"Not at all. Truly, do not let it distress you, madame. As long as whatever people imagine does no harm, it is not worth noticing."

But it would do harm. Even a calm coal bucket full of peacocks ought to elevate the dukedom, and here she was making it seem shabby.

Indistinct words in many voices moved through the space like a shocked fall of rain. The murmuring pitter-pattered in one spot, then another.

Selene simply kept her head up and nodded to anyone who greeted her. She had no idea what any of their names were. Just nodded her head repeatedly, like a broken toy.

IT SURPRISED Jonas to find he had meant what he'd said. It was melancholy to attend a beautiful woman's wedding. Even more surprising, he didn't regret telling her so.

She looked quite calm and took her place at the table with a grace that spoke of years of practice. Seated opposite the Duke, at the far end of the table, throughout the first course she spoke to the person on her right, and then with the next course to the person on her left.

Selene had not become this type of duchess overnight. She knew what she was doing.

He ought not to be staring at her. Well, it was looking. But he did keep doing it. It was a wedding, surely it was allowable to look at the bride?

Without much finery it was even more clear that Selene glowed in the candlelight, and it was her air of paying attention to people as much as her hair or her smile that worked that magic. Her eyes looked off into nothing, yet she was the most present person at the dinner. The way she tilted her head toward whomever was speaking—she *listened* with all her being. And that was entrancing, somehow.

It also was the sign of someone for whom these sorts of dinners weren't new.

There was no mystery as to why Lady Selene had not had a season. Her father had died. All of London knew it. There might be some who wondered where she had been since then, but not many. People were expected to keep their problems private, reappearing in society if they solved them, politely dying quietly somewhere if they did not.

Reappearing and instantly marrying a duke would cause some comment. But not much surprise. Disappointment, especially among the ladies—Talbourne was young for a duke, and average-looking enough, Jonas supposed, in an utterly unremarkable way—but no great shock. And a marriage to a daughter from an old earldom would only be expected.

The *ton* tended to behave as if touching something beneath them changed a person. Here was a de Gauer, descendant of hundreds of years of British nobility, and if she'd somehow been or done something inappropriate while she had been out of the public eye, they would expect it to show.

Since she was entertaining her guests just as she ought—though she herself ate very little—no one would think anything ill of her disappearance and reappearance in society.

Not unless gossip framed them otherwise.

So when Burden attempted a snide insult, remarking to the lady on his left that it was a shame that "the duchess looked like the little ash girl before the fairy godmother arrived," something in Jonas snapped.

Jonas got along with everyone. Everyone got along with him. He enjoyed doing favors, and he enjoyed collecting them. And he enjoyed being a prize in London society.

Yet he forgot all that in the momentary desire to shut that man up.

"Lady Fawcett, I am looking forward to a dance with you this evening." He stepped away from his dinner companion to catch up with Burden. "Burden, a word."

The man seemed surprised to be addressed so informally at a public affair. "Only a moment, of course, *Lord* Callendar."

Jonas looked at the man's pinching face and upturned nose and found nothing to counter the wave of dislike that had come over him. "Burden, don't let me catch you disparaging the Duchess of Talbourne again in my hearing."

"I beg your pardon." All those buttons practically quivered with indignation.

"You'll beg hers if I hear of it again, and I will see to it personally. If you can't leave your disagreeable qualities in Parliament, at least keep them out of people's homes."

"Ah, I see. The Duchess has a defender."

"Never attack her again and you needn't find out," Jonas assured him in a low voice before leaving him standing there.

* * *

NICHOLAS WAS HOLDING Selene's hand. Out where everyone could see.

More properly, the Duke of Talbourne was holding the hand of the Duchess, preparing to start the first dance.

How good it felt wouldn't show.

Nicholas had never intended to actually dance with her. They were here, as expected, and now he should leave her side again. Let the people there wonder if he had married her for money, or alliance, or some other gain. He had *her* and that was all that mattered.

But it wasn't all that mattered. She wanted things too.

Nicholas had a visceral hatred of anyone being forced to do anything they did not want to do. But above and beyond that, there was a type of pain, too, in asking for something over and over, and not being heard. He couldn't even remember any more if he had ever asked for anything. But he must have. For he could too easily imagine that type of pain.

He couldn't do that to Selene. Not again, not today. Not unless he had to do it.

Thank goodness she was not a romantic girl who would be disappointed in the wedding dance of a duke of the United Kingdom of Great Britain and Ireland.

* * *

HE RAISED her hand in his. "A polonaise, Your Grace?"

Selene's heart jumped. She *wanted* to be swept away in his arms. In something shocking and sensual, like a waltz. Or... or not even in a dance, if they were alone. She wanted to feel *him*. She wanted to be back in that hug that had happened so fast that she almost missed it, yet still felt imprinted all over her.

But she knew somehow that hug had been for them, Nicholas and Selene. This was the performance of the Duke and Duchess for the audience.

Apparently, she could not have both at the same time.

At least he would dance with her. She nodded.

It took a few moments for the shape of the polonaise to come back to her. Nicholas moved smoothly, guiding her through the steps as though he had been dancing with a blind wife all his life.

What had her dance teacher said? To be an extension of his hand. To float at the end of his fingertips.

But it wasn't that way. They made one shape out of the two of them. They both seemed to move together, at the same time, keeping the same rhythm.

There were other dancers, of course, but without discussing it between them, the Duke and Duchess did not change partners. They must have broken a set. Perhaps other dancers were scrambling to fill the gaps they'd left behind by staying together. Terrible behavior.

If so, her excruciatingly correct duke never wavered.

It was more delicate than a waltz, and far more surprising.

As the music drew to its close he drew closer, making of the two of them a small but definitive promenade, walking to the music side by side.

And then his hand let her go.

The loss left her hollow.

Had she completely lost her bearings, or had that dance begun with the Duke and Duchess and ended with Nicholas and Selene?

When his hand came back to hers, placing hers on his arm, something had gone from the connection.

What did she expect? Duchess was a title, not a relationship. And one couldn't feel a title.

Since these dances were meant to show off her finery, and apparently she wasn't wearing any, Selene just held her head high as her mother had always insisted, and wondered if she would understand how that dance had felt later.

There'd been no empty rooms full of music and he hadn't held her close.

But she felt married now.

That feeling of being married trickled away as people's voices came back into focus. The crush of people was speaking to her, to both of them. Around them there were more people having their own conversations, and around them more, seemingly endlessly more. All thinking many things of her, and of Nicholas, that had nothing to do with that dance.

All clamoring for her attention. For his.

As they would be for the rest of their lives, presumably. The last feeling of that dance trickled out her toes and was gone. The plaintive sounds of the stringed instruments said everything she could not say. They were longing, and she was grateful for their voice.

The music *was* lovely.

"I am dismayed that I did not arrange to have you dripping with flowers and jewels," Nicholas said quietly to her during a lull in other's voices.

He was kind. He *was* kind. He wasn't the least bit in love with her, but he was kind, and she was already failing to fulfill the tasks required of a duchess. She didn't look the part at all, and it had little to do with his failure to drape her in jewels as well as flowers. He was doing his part to be the duke, and she didn't feel yet that she was a duchess, not to London's unforgiving eyes.

When the music paused again, she heard Sir Malcolm's voice close by as he said, "I hope to dance with the bride, Your Grace."

He was one of the few people she had actually met at Talbourne House. Yet Sir Malcolm seemed to be addressing Nicholas, not her. And Nicholas responded by saying, "And here is the Duke of Gravenshire, clearly hoping for the same. Your Grace, may I present the most honorable the Duke of Gravenshire."

"Your Grace," said her new acquaintance, and led Selene away.

She understood perfectly. The order in which she should dance with the guests would be determined by their precedence.

* * *

"AND THIS IS LORD FETTANBY, Edward, His Grace's son. You must have met."

The earl Selene had just danced with—she had already forgotten his name—sounded offhand, whereas Selene was seized with the moment. He was introducing her to her stepson! Edward, Lord Fettanby. This was Nicholas' older child.

"I apologize we are meeting this way, Lord Fettanby. I have looked forward to our meeting."

"No need to apologize, Your Grace. I understand that in matters of love my father can be impetuous, carried away by his depth of feeling."

The world seemed to tip; Selene grabbed the arm of the earl to keep from falling over. That gentleman was surprised at her grip. "Are you well, madame?"

"Yes, yes thank you," Selene managed to say.

Because Edward's voice was the voice of the footman who had shown her some of Talbourne House just yesterday morning.

The footman who had left her at the top of the stairs.

The stairs where she had nearly fallen.

"And my apologies again, my lord. I believe we *have* met," Selene managed to add.

That made him pause, but Edward only added, "A whirlwind courtship like my father's takes everyone's breath away, madame, not just yours. How impetuously mad love has made him." Though most of his words were calm, there was a bottomless pit of bitterness expressed when he said *love.*

The earl cleared his throat. No one had the impression that the Duke of Talbourne was impetuously mad with love. Pointing that out at a wedding, *his* wedding, *Selene's* wedding, seemed in poor taste.

But Selene was not going to be further rattled by further expressions of dismay at her wedding. "I hope we have time to get to know each other far better, Lord Fettanby. You are residing here, are you not?"

"For the moment. I expect to remove to the duchy as soon as the season is finished, and remain there. My grandmother will be there." *And you and my father are not,* Edward managed to convey with his tone.

"I look forward to it, sir," Selene inclined her head, wondering how she had angered Nicholas' son already, and if he had been angry yesterday when she mistook him for a footman. Or when he had left her at the top of those stairs.

JONAS MADE a point of checking on Burden every so often to make good on his promise.

He still wasn't sure why. The new Duchess barely knew him.

Saving her life seemed like a decent foundation on which to build, though.

When Jonas saw her slip out the French doors, he waited a moment or two in case anyone was watching before he followed.

NICHOLAS HAD MADE a point of leaving the ball early. No one expected him to enjoy dancing. Though he *had*. He'd liked dancing with his wife. It had been unexpectedly engrossing.

He wouldn't do much of that in public.

She was so adaptable. She would become accustomed to serving as the sole hostess of gatherings at Talbourne House. It would be a relief to get away from his own guests without Lady Hadleigh and Lady Fawcett squabbling with each other about which of them should act as hostess in his stead.

She would be the face of Talbourne.

And no one need guess how much she mattered to him.

It was his practice to retire to his rooms when social affairs were happening in Talbourne House; no one even batted an eye as he left his own wedding ball and used the servants' staircase to slip upstairs.

Whereupon he loosened his cravat, and immediately walked out to his balcony to see anything that was happening on the grounds.

And saw that Selene was wandering as far away as possible already.

He turned back towards the room, looking for some distraction from the sinking sensation he got from watching her walk away. His eye fell on a chess board standing to one side, the pieces frozen in opening position. If one never played, every piece was safe.

He couldn't not look.

Turning to face the dark, Nicholas watched as she crossed the lawns: a lady who looked too young to be married, with a bare head and no shawl, gliding slowly on a footman's arm all the way out to the gazebo next to the lake where there were Talbourne swans.

The dew had fallen. Her feet must be cold.

Nonetheless half a dozen footmen were there, and he could see her from here. No one could hurt her, and as long as no one could hurt her, she ought to do what she liked.

He watched the gleam of a white shirt as some gentleman crossed the lawns after her.

Was that Callendar?

Damn the man. He had better not touch her.

Not that he would with all those footmen around.

Still.

He'd invited the man because he still didn't know what Callendar wanted, and he could prove useful, though not because of his empty words about friendship. Maybe a little because he'd saved Selene's life.

He hadn't expected the fellow to openly follow Selene around like a moonstruck calf. Hating Callendar was beginning to seem like a very attractive idea.

But then again, Nicholas did not believe in strong emotions.

* * *

"Your Grace! What madmen have let you come out so far on the grounds without a cloak, and this early in the spring?"

"Lord Callendar. I'm afraid I insisted."

Selene was not sorry to be discovered shivering in the gazebo.

The ballroom had grown warm and close, and one of the French doors had stood open. The breeze had beckoned like the door out of a prison. She'd asked the nearest footman to take her as far out in the grounds as she could go.

Selene had imagined a few minutes' respite, safely hidden in some nearby garden hedge. Instead it seemed to be miles before she was in the gazebo. The ground was damp and her slippers ruined.

Her feet were cold, and she wanted an excuse to turn back, yet she couldn't yet bring herself to just go.

Jonas did not wait for her agreement. "You two, follow us back. You, run ahead and fetch Her Grace a cloak."

"I'm not ready to go back."

Jonas sat beside her. "Ah. So you *are* ready to escape so quickly."

"Not escape, but..." Selene didn't have the words for the swirl of emotions this day had been and all the many ways to fail she had never imagined.

When she realized that once again her husband would not be returning to her side after their one and only dance, Selene's heart had sunk to the floor.

And she could not imagine what might lift it again.

"Your Grace..." Jonas pitched his voice quietly, not to carry, though undoubtedly the remaining footmen were still near enough to hear. "You have done what many women dream of. To marry a duke! It is the stuff of girlish dreams, and you have done it. If... Whatever your reasons for marriage, they are surely reasons any woman would understand."

"What reasons do you mean, sir?" she asked sharply.

"I assume you play chess? If you'll forgive the comparison, you have managed to promote a pawn to queen. You have an unassailable position here that no one can gainsay save the Prince Regent himself. You... and your mother, perhaps? Will never have another hungry day. Physicians will dance around your mother like flower girls round a May pole. And if His Grace is not the sort to give you a wedding gift now, when the Dowager Duchess passes away you will be positively dripping in jewels."

He knew way too much, and yet so little. Selene was neither a pawn *nor* a queen. She was not on a gameboard; she *played* the games. "I had not thought you foolish till now, sir. Sharp rocks are not an interest of mine."

"I see. Still, I would prefer to see you celebrating. To marry a duke. This must be what you wanted."

Selene's irritation washed away. No, it wasn't. What she'd wanted was to help her mother. And she had wanted to help him, her sad and lonely duke.

Well, she had. And she still could.

He had needed a duchess, he said. He had never professed love. Or even interest. Indeed, he seemed to have accepted her mother's suggestion that he stay away from Selene's bed without the slightest fuss.

Despite being reared to marry exactly this way, and despite being all too aware of the probability of poor outcomes for princesses in fairy tales, some part of Selene had managed to become romantic about marriage. Thank heavens it was a tiny part.

The reality was that dukes, the descendants of former kings, helped or hindered the Crown, funded wars, and shaped Britain. Their wives needed to provide heirs, consolidate fortunes, and build bridges to valuable allies.

He had asked none of that from her. He had offered her everything she needed and asked nothing in return.

She had practically had to arm-wrestle him to get him to agree to fifteen minutes a day with her.

Selene didn't know much about her husband, but she knew with certainty that he needed a great deal more than that.

His older son was quite angry, but she would stay out of that. Someone had bumped her at the top of those stairs, but she didn't think it was Edward; he hadn't been an *angry* footman. She couldn't just arrive here and start casting aspersions on Nicholas' heir, even if she wanted to. And she didn't. Wars were lost by engaging in too many small battles.

Nicholas never enjoyed himself. *That* was something she wished to change.

And though he hadn't said so, she suspected he had Parliamentary plans with which she could help with as well. There were so many highly-placed people here. It couldn't be for no reason.

She could do this. She could help him, more than he could imagine.

But she was definitely going to need some help herself.

"Lord Callendar, you are so kind to venture out here; perhaps you would also be so kind as to return me to the ball."

"Ah, good. Ready to go back now? To the ball, or just to retire? Many of the guests *have* left."

Not a very jolly ball, then. Or perhaps they simply needed to retire early, in order to begin describing her gown to the gossip rags.

Wonderful.

Selene brushed it aside. "To the ball, until the last guest leaves. And if you would, please send someone for Mr. Lyall. I have a message which must go out tonight."

She was a duchess now.

THE WATCHTOWER LIGHTS GO OUT
AT DAWN

Selene woke drooling on a cool, smooth pillowcase under her cheek.

She was *married*.

She was married *to Nicholas*.

Her hand shot out to feel around in the bed.

Of course he wasn't *there*. He wasn't that type of husband. This wasn't that type of marriage.

Still. She was going to start duchessing today.

Poor Martha had stayed up so late for her. Selene hadn't breathed a word of the dress disaster. No reason to upset the poor young woman. She was sure Martha had done her best.

It was cold for exploring; still, Selene slipped out of bed and poked around the room in her nightdress, reminding herself where everything was. The warmth of the fireplace told her there were coals, but she couldn't find any wood. She wondered how the servants would react if she asked them to leave a stock of wood here for her to replenish the grate herself.

And over a chair she found her simple gown and chemise from last night, presumably waiting for Martha to collect them. And under them, the cape that Lord Callendar had had the servants bring to the gazebo.

It wasn't hard to wiggle into the chemise, then the gown. She couldn't button the buttons in the back, but it was on. And she tossed the cape over it. She ought to ring for Martha.

But Talbourne House was her home now, wasn't it?

She'd just dash down the hall to see her mother. What time was it? She was so sleepy, but the day seemed late. It would take a while to adjust from a housemaid's hours to a duchess'.

Yes, her mother, she thought, resolutely telling herself she had no interest in turning the other way and investigating the chambers of His Grace.

Telling herself that all the way up till the moment her fingers were on the latch of the door that she supposed led straight to... her husband.

A *husband*. What an odd thing to have. How did a signed paper and a title make two people fit together? It seemed like such a slight connection.

If the footmen were about, they didn't announce themselves, and if they were going to ignore Selene, she was going to ignore them.

Her fingers ran over the latch again.

What if she knocked?

What if she just *went in*?

She didn't remember any fairy tales about princesses breaking *in* to towers.

She knocked.

Then she panicked.

But before she had taken two steps back, the door opened.

"...Madame."

Her husband. Her husband. Her...

"Nicholas," she whispered.

"Are you all right? What has happened?" She heard him instantly step closer, his hands clasping her upper arms as he moved her behind him. "Jonathan, is anything wrong? Where is Henry?"

She heard the footman's voice coming faintly, from all the way down near her mother's room. "Nothing, sir. He's just gone to fetch her ladyship's breakfast, sir. Shall I do the same?"

"Stay where you are till he returns, and let Mr. Lyall know when you see him there should never be less than two of you here."

"Sir."

The door swung to. Had it latched? She didn't think so. Did that make it less inappropriate to be in a man's room? Though it couldn't be, could it, if they were married?

"Nicholas, I only came to say good morning. We're married, you know."

As soon as she said it, Selene wanted to stomp on her own foot. She was neither a girl nor a saucy maid. She needed to learn to be more formal. Even with him. Maybe *especially* with him.

But he didn't seem to mind. Was that an actual chortle? Maybe just a snuffle. "I do recall it, madame. Good morning."

After an awkward second or two, Selene let out half a sigh. "Say a little more than good morning. It's awkward to make conversation on the morning after one's just been married."

"Good morning, and thank you for marrying me."

Now he'd gone and made her insides all warm and that wasn't what was called for either. She was sure it wasn't. "I had only—I thought I would learn your room."

More silence and Selene realized how peculiar that sounded since she'd never been in it before and hadn't been invited now and... Should she have stayed away? Why weren't there etiquette lectures on this?

Foreign royalty had been easier.

And why did his voice sound like that? "I would be happy to acquaint you with the rooms, Selene."

"Oh, ah... we needn't now, of course. You must be busy. Are you busy? What time of the day is it?"

"Quite early; I have yet to dress. I had planned to keep my usual schedule."

Of course he had. "And you don't… need anything?"

"What do you imagine I need?"

Well, *that* was what she got for being polite to the man she'd just married. What an odd combination of insinuating, and surprised, and amused, and suggestive he sounded.

And it was unbalancing, when he usually sounded just calm.

"If I ought not be saucy, you need not be either," she said with all the dignity it was possible to muster in an unbuttoned gown and cape at her husband's chamber door first thing in the morning.

"I never said you shouldn't be saucy."

Which was an irritating response inasmuch as it was true. "Help me a little, Nicholas. I must learn to be a duchess. Your duchess."

"Mmm." The half-purring, half-growling little sound was so brief she wondered if she imagined it. When he spoke his voice was, as always, perfectly calm. "You already are my duchess, so you needn't do anything further."

"But what do you expect me to *do* all day?"

"Whatever you like. That's what duchesses do."

He really wasn't going to help her at all? "You don't need anything?"

"I won't ask you again what you think I need, since you just scolded me about that. I have a valet. His name is Philip. He's been dressing me for years. I could describe the work of the cook, the butler, and the housemaids too, but I think you know enough about them?"

That was a low blow. "You said this was a job, Your Grace, I only want to know what to *do*."

"You are the lady of Talbourne House. What do you *want* to do?"

That was a question… that she couldn't answer. It had been so long since she'd done anything merely because she wanted to do it. Except, she'd come here this morning. Solely because she wanted to do it.

"I suppose if I am lady of the house I should get to know it. And I started with your room."

"Of course," and she still had the idea that he was amused, though he sounded solemn enough. "Let me take you around the edge as we did with yours." He immediately took her hand and laid it on his arm.

Very well, she would pretend that it was exactly what she'd intended.

And one of the first things she found was a doorjamb, closer than she would have expected, so close that it startled her into saying, "That ought to connect to my rooms."

"And so it does. I haven't yet unlocked it." Had he actually paused for a second as if thinking about what to say next? "The key is on your side," he added.

"Oh."

The key is on your side. So casually intimate. Her formal Duke was familiar, but a casual husband was something else. Something unsettling. "We needn't do... a full tour just at this moment, sir. You must, as I said, be busy."

And Nicholas seemed just as ready to drop the tour as continue it. "Of course."

But that felt wrong too. "Are you... *laughing* at me?"

"Never. You think I haven't felt as you feel now?"

That thought stopped her. It made sense that in his past there had been a moment when he had felt as unsure about all these intimacies as she felt now. It was graceful, and touching, of him to admit it to reassure her. "Then why is your amusement rubbing me the wrong way?"

He moved even closer than they already were. Her hand slid from its usual resting spot and wound up cupped over the muscle of his forearm. "Should I apologize now for being amused? I'm sorry. You are welcome to be just as amused at me. I have no idea what we should say to each other this morning either."

"Why *is* this so awkward?"

* * *

Nicholas fought down the urge to pull her into his arms and bury his face in her hair.

It was awkward because they were standing this close, because she had come to him, walking toward something that he suspected she wasn't ready to find and that was consuming him whole.

"Perhaps you didn't think we were so close." He didn't know if he meant their rooms, or the inches between them now. "People can be this close and still be worlds apart."

Her hand moved a little on his arm, and warmed his skin through the cool linen of his shirt.

"You are quite safe to explore." He could pretend he meant Talbourne House.

"I like to know where I am, and I usually make someone guide me till I do."

Christ.

"In this case—" He stopped to clear his throat before he could go on. "In this case, you can rely on yourself."

Her head bowed a little, as if she was thinking, and her other hand joined the first one. He could stand there forever and support her hands if she wished.

Then, amazingly, one hand floated upward and laid softly against his chest.

"Your heart is beating so hard. *You* aren't nervous, are you?"

Yes, he was. "Not nervous, no." How could he say this right? "I will never tell you that there is anywhere you cannot go. Only that there are some places you should be sure you want to discover before you cross the threshold."

Selene didn't move, and Nicholas used every knack he had ever learned for staying still. He followed his breath into his body, letting it calm his pounding heart, let everything wild in him freeze, then melt and run away, letting himself just be here with her, letting himself enjoy the soft warmth of her skin through his shirt because no one would know, not even her, and because it was bliss.

"Selene?"

"I am... only looking around to see what I find."

Yes. She didn't want *him,* not yet. And he didn't want her to come to him out of duty.

Duty wouldn't be enough.

He laid his hand over her hand on his chest, just briefly, before turning so that both their hands would fall away. He walked her back to the door to let her leave just as she'd come in. "You should go, and do, whatever you wish," he said quietly as he swung the door open.

"Thank you."

She looked like she was going to say something else, but when he waited, she didn't. She walked out his door, an experience oddly pleasurable and painful at the same time. She was still there. She would never be so far away again that he would have to worry.

As she trailed around the corner, he waved his hand at Jonathan the footman that he should follow her.

She *should* go anywhere and do anything that she liked. But she mustn't ever be in danger.

The last inch of her cape disappeared, and Nicholas wanted to run and catch it.

But that wouldn't do.

It would be like Sir Malcolm's habit of drinking till the intoxicant overcame him.

It couldn't be healthy, it might be dangerous, and he ought to try to live without it.

* * *

"WHO IS WITH ME, PLEASE?"

Selene had reached the second room before she asked. She could hear someone following her. Didn't he realize that?

"Jonathan, Your Grace."

Of course it was. Footmen always, everywhere, in this house.

She felt prickly, irritated by more than the trailing, silent footman.

There had been something there, something between her and Nicholas, and it had seemed huge and terrifying, and she had walked away from it.

Walking away from terrifying things wasn't her habit.

But she'd had reason to suspect that cliffs and murder and other dangerous things might be right around the corner, and blundering into such things was not a good strategy.

Her fingertips explored the carvings on the armoire. This room was huge, she could tell; she'd just explore by the doors a little. By the cool smell of the air, these rooms weren't much used.

Perhaps she would change that. She would surely have guests today, if her message had gone out.

When in danger, consolidate forces.

But that hadn't been a game. Why had it felt so risky when Nicholas had been, truly, kind and friendly?

He could afford to be so, Selene decided. He hadn't laid the trap; he *was* the trap. She *liked* being close to him; what if the trap closed on her when she wasn't ready? Heavens, she'd walked straight in there. What else would she have expected him to... offer?

He might have said the same to any woman who walked right through his door.

Even if he didn't despoil virgins, or widows, as a general rule.

Before she made any more sorties into foreign territory, Selene needed far more time to understand their risks—and not get too caught up in wondering about their immediate rewards. She had a long-term objective.

And she needed more allies in the event of catastrophe.

Yes, her messages should have been delivered. She should ring for Martha, *not* tell her about the reception to her look last night, and truly dress for her first day as duchess.

* * *

As SELENE CAME DOWN the sweeping grand staircase, the indistinct voices of two ladies resolved clearly into words.

"Lord and Lady Ayles ought to be woken to break their fast." The porcelain chirping of Lady Fawcett.

"Nonsense. His lordship's past fifty if he's a day and he must have seen the sun come up, he went to bed so late."

"They have not been visitors before, and they did not bring servants with them to attend to their things." Lady Fawcett sounded as if whatever *things* were, they ought to be attended properly.

"They came all the way out here from the depths of London for a wedding, and ended up enjoying themselves. I imagine that's exactly what they thought would happen when they made the trip. We are not so close to the city that people just dash back and forth, you know."

"All the more reason to—Your Grace. Good morning."

Selene realized she meant *her*.

"Good morning, Lady Fawcett. Please, do not let me interrupt."

The two ladies seemed to need a few moments to decide among them how to continue. As Selene might have guessed, it was the more forthright Lady Hadleigh who made the difficulty plain.

"We have been used to—well, to splitting the duties of a hostess between us. But now... do you know what His Grace would prefer we all do?"

Heavens. Hadn't Nicholas told them anything either?

And why did they want to know what *Nicholas* would say?

When in doubt, say something pleasant. "I am so very, very grateful His Grace has had such friends as you to count on."

"I hope so," she was surprised to hear tiny Lady Fawcett say first. "He seldom enjoys our company, but it is here if he wishes it."

Surely that formal, fragile little woman couldn't mean anything inappropriate by it. She seemed as regretful as Selene was that the Duke didn't enjoy himself more. "I hope I will be able to count on you just as he does. Please, give me your advice on what we should do with Lord and Lady Ayles."

"We ought to wake them."

"What does anyone need to wake up for before they wake themselves, when they're recovering from a late night of fun?"

Their squabbling hadn't changed at all.

Well. They were her husband's friends. Selene also half-suspected that one, or both, still cherished a hope or two regarding her husband.

Until she might learn better, she'd keep a little distance. Those weren't the kind of things, after all, one shared upon slight acquaintance, and certainly not with the woman who had actually married His Grace.

It would help her find her footing if she had a few friends of her own.

Hopefully they would be here soon.

GATHERING THE TROOPS

*L*etty Grantley was following the butler so closely that when he stopped to announce them, she nearly smashed her head into his armpit.

"The Lady Howiston. Lady Grantley. Mr. Anthony Hastings." The butler's voice sounded able to carry to France.

Letty peered past his shoulder.

Her Grace the Duchess of Talbourne, an appealing figure draped in flowered green and crowned with a great quantity of copper-tinged tawny hair, was standing, with a footman, next to an overturned table.

She had a pocketknife clasped between her fingers.

As Letty watched, the knife flew; then there was the thunk of a knife point successfully burying itself near the middle of a circle drawn on the wood.

Earlier that morning, far too early, Letty's friend Cass had arrived at Letty's townhouse with a hired carriage. "Just come with me," she'd urged. "This is the first I've heard from Selene in two days, she wants company, and apparently somewhere in there she got married. I need to make sure she is well."

Now, Her Grace laughed a delighted laugh, and clapped her hands.

She *looked* fine.

"Did we settle on what I was going to win? Or did we quite forget to set a wager? You didn't think I was going to be able to do it, did you?"

Letty liked the laugh lines in the corners of the lady's soft brown eyes.

The footman looked abashed. "Of course not, Your Grace. I mean, of course I expected you to be able to do it. I mean, I was just showing you the game, Your Grace."

Anthony, Letty's brother, took pity on the man. "Perhaps the Duchess would like to continue the game later."

"Of course, sir. Ma'am." The young fellow gathered up the pocketknife and the table, tucking the latter under his arm, and scurried for the door.

"Oh, the woodwork on that table," Cass murmured as he left. She sounded as though the footman had been torturing kittens.

Selene reached out a hand. "There should have been a peal of thunder as your name was announced, Cass. I have so been wanting to speak with you."

Her tall, willowy cousin ignored the hand, wrapped her cousin in her arms. "I am glad to hear it! I have been so worried that I did the right thing in letting you go. You see how restrained I am by not demanding to know everything that has happened." Cass let her go just a little. "But... what has happened?"

And the lady answered as if the question had been about her mother's health, and not about her sudden marriage. "His Grace has engaged an excellent physician, and my mother is practically chipper. But I hope your husband will call as well. As a friend, if he likes."

"Friends we will still be." Cass played along. "And here I have brought you, oh, friends more than guests, I think. Do you remember Lady Grantley? And her brother Mr. Hastings?" Cass waved her hands about, apparently slightly at a loss whether to ask if the others remembered Selene. They *had* met her, Letty recalled. When she was a housemaid.

But Selene only had a gracious smile. "Under other circumstances. Welcome."

Letty put in, "I can vouch for Anthony's usefulness in any situation."

Selene paused for only a moment, her thumb rubbing over the fingers of one hand before she said, "Lady Grantley, Mr. Hastings, I sent for my cousin for advice. I need allies, and she is my only place to begin. But I don't wish to burden new acquaintances."

"Fuff." Letty settled her skirts in an upholstered chair close to the settee. The little woman's toes barely touched the floor. "We should all sit, somewhere close enough for Cass to hear us, and you give us some idea of what you are facing. I am sure there is a way we can help."

"You are extremely kind, my lady. Do call me Selene. I'm finding that I will soon miss the sound of my own name in someone else's mouth."

"Mmm…" Anthony shook his head a little. "That we ought not to do, madame. In a residence such as this, one is never truly alone."

Selene was wry. "We will see if that is true."

Cass took her cousin's hand to lead her to the settee. "How can you be lonely if the footmen are teaching you mumble-the-peg?"

"Things are not… going quite as smoothly as they may seem." Selene sat as gracefully as a queen upon a throne, her hands in her lap. "My mother has all the attention she needs, never fear. But I will not even begin to tell you the horrors of my lady's maid situation." She stopped short before, apparently, even more situations came to light. "I will not rampage around the house throwing tantrums. But I must find a way to take some things in hand."

Letty watched her brother move a chair closer for Cass. "I believe I know exactly what you mean. While relatively well behaved in London, my husband tends to bellow up and down our Roseford home, and I have never noticed anyone listening to him. In fact I think it has the opposite effect."

Selene's fingers were rubbing together. "A de Gauer ought to be able to make himself heard. I have two good examples in my parents;

but to support His Grace's name and position, I must be perceived to be a duchess."

"We are quite ready to be your privy counsellors, madame," Anthony said as he settled himself next to her, "tell us what you need to do."

* * *

AFTER A LONG, long conversation, Letty finally yawned. "We ought to just hire some sign painters. *Don't come in unless you can be pleasant.* Or *I am the duchess now.* Whatever you like."

Cass gasped. "Letty!"

Anthony chuckled. His sister had already shared that she was with child, and *he* had already shared that the condition had made Letty even more direct than she had been before. Which was quite a bit.

Selene knew Letty meant well. "I think being direct with London society, or even this household, will get me no results at all. And that is far too direct. Especially for a duchess."

"But your plans will take so long! I feel I must stay with my husband right now, and the person I can send in my stead may not be helpful at all."

"I also need to stay with my husband—not because I am in an interesting condition, but because things do tend to happen to him when I am not watching." Cass' voice was rueful. "I'm so sorry not to be able to stay here. The chance to look at the woodwork!"

"I will return," Anthony reassured the lady, "and the substitute you will send will be most useful."

Selene turned toward him. "Oh, Mr. Hastings, I cannot thank you enough for your insights. It is as though you already knew the ins and outs of Talbourne House."

"Fancy that. Well, we know each other well enough now that when we see each other again, you must call me Anthony."

"Oh, now we are exchanging given names? In Talbourne House, I must assume someone is listening," she teased him.

Letty was still not sure. "My replacement, as it were, will definitely be entertaining. Is entertaining good enough?"

"Well, she'll also be quick—tomorrow, I imagine—whereas mine will take a few days to arrive." Cass sounded tired as well.

Selene regretted forcing her to sit here and listen hard to voices that were probably difficult for her to hear.

Her guests needed refreshment. "If we stay in here much longer, we might solve the Continental wars, or we might die of hunger. Letty, ring the bell, won't you? You must dine here tonight, Cass. We will find you rooms to rest a little before we dine."

"Oh no! You don't want me dining at a duke's table, not in my black sketching gown with a penknife in my pocket." Cass sounded horrified.

"Is that what you are wearing?" Selene put a hand to her head in mock horror. "In the residence of a duke? Well, you made that bed, my dear, you must lie in it."

"I won't," Cass said with the sort of new decisiveness she had adopted with her sketching gowns. "I'm tired of trying to read everyone's lips, and my plans are made. I know you will forgive me."

"Anything," Selene said, squeezing her hand and meaning it.

"Oh but I want to dine at a duke's palace!" Letty burst out. "I'm sure I ought to—oh, it takes hours to make my hair lie flat, but if one can dine with a duke despite frizzy curls, I'm dying to try it."

"If Her Grace will have us, I will be happy to accompany you," Anthony reassured his sister.

"And then—" But Selene was interrupted.

"His Grace, the Duke of Talbourne!"

* * *

THE BUTLER'S voice sent a shock around the room much like that of an earthquake. All of them shot to their feet.

The Duke seemed so average, Letty thought. Average height, slightly waving hair of an average brown turning gray at the temples;

his eyes were a cool color between brown and gray, and his features were even but unremarkable. A forgettable face, thought Letty; he ought to blend in to his surroundings, except that his surroundings were so incredibly grand.

The way he silently studied each of them did not put his guests at ease, either.

Selene simply said, "Your Grace. I have just invited my cousin and our guests to stay for dinner."

"Indeed."

Cass approached him and curtseyed. Letty expected the man to soften at seeing his old friend, but he did not.

Cass said, "I hope we do not impose."

"You have been a kind hostess to me many times, Lady Howiston. I am happy to provide some small hospitality in return."

Letty looked around at the classical medallions hand-painted on the walls, the silk embroideries upholstering the furniture, the porcelain vases of fresh flowers among silver enameled figurines and the ormolu clock. "Your hospitality is quite large, Your Grace."

Cass waved toward her guests. "Lady Grantley, may I introduce His Grace the Duke of Talbourne. Your Grace, Lady Grantley is a dear friend of mine, and this is her brother, Mr. Anthony Hastings."

Nicholas' look measured Letty and Anthony right down to the length of their shoes.

He said, "It is kind of you to grace my home with dear friends of yours. Lady Grantley. Mr. Hastings."

It was a perfectly polite speech, and His Grace's voice was velvety, with something of the smooth expressive purr of a fine piano. But it contained no emotion at all. He sounded as though he were reading it from a piece of paper someone slipped to him. Letty had no idea if she were really welcome or not.

The Duke went on, to his new Duchess. "I wished to know if your mother is well enough to dine with us, madame."

"I think not."

"I see." He had nodded, a reflex, but then added the words as an afterthought, apparently remembering that Selene could not see him. Letty decided that he might not be made entirely of stone. Perhaps.

"And I will see you after dinner as well, will I not, Your Grace?" put in Selene.

The look the Duke gave his wife was even longer, and gave even less away.

Finally he said, "Of course. For now I will leave you to your guests." And with a curt, small bow, he left.

Everyone left in the room took a collective free breath.

"How awkward," Letty muttered to herself.

"Truly, I've never seen anything like it," mused Anthony. "Here I thought I had a face that gives nothing away. And you *are* married, Your Grace?"

Selene's thumb was rubbing over her fingers. One of them wore a gold band. She laughed. "We most assuredly are married, sir."

"I apologize," Anthony added instantly. "That was thoughtless of me."

"Selene, you know," Cass said softly, her hands covering her cousin's "if you want, you can always come home to me."

"Thank you, my dear. But nothing dire has occurred." As if she were speaking to herself she added under her breath, "It's only getting married, after all."

* * *

THE SILENCE that settled over the room reminded Selene that she oughtn't say such things aloud. Perhaps it sounded awful. They obviously didn't realize it was far better than being murdered and eaten on a squirrel-infested desert island.

Perhaps she shouldn't mention that was the measure she was using.

"That sounded dire when it isn't. *He* isn't. It's—you know, complicated, as these things can be so complicated."

"Why is it complicated?" asked Letty.

That just reminded Selene of her very complicated morning.

He hadn't made fun of her; but he *had* challenged her.

It was complicated because those fairy tales ended at the wedding, and she was past that now. Because in her daydreams, he was the hero in a fairy tale, but he might not be one.

She'd use her fifteen minutes a night to see who he really was. Safely in her territory, not his, she thought, conveniently forgetting that she was the one who had laid her hand on his chest.

If Nicholas would give her the slightest hint what he needed... other than whatever that was, everyone would forget the housemaid and the girl in the plain pink dress. She knew she could do it.

Selene's head went up. "Let us get you rooms to refresh yourselves before we dine, as I said. And Cass, you might wish to see my mother?"

No one pointed out that she hadn't answered Letty's question, and Selene had forgotten all about it.

"Absolutely," Cass said, with the kind of genuine warmth anyone would have expected of a family member, which threw into relief that His Grace the Duke of Talbourne had shown his brand-new bride none at all.

* * *

THE SUN cast shadows behind the pillars at the door of Talbourne House by the time Jonas arrived with a full purse, ready for anything. Because he couldn't discern any pattern to Talbourne's invitations, it was tempting to think that there was none.

But he'd seen up close the cool eyes that chose carefully whom to follow, and those exhaustively. Talbourne was anything but aimless.

Perhaps having Jonas come and go, helped disguise how often more important men were coming and going as well.

Which was odd, because Burden had been right about one thing: Talbourne's reputation was that of a man who was supremely uninvolved. Not a lazy man, but a motionless one. People said he read everything and did nothing.

So Jonas was interested. And absolutely would dine at Talbourne House.

And it had nothing to do with its Duchess at all.

* * *

HER GRACE WAS the first person he saw when shown into the yellow drawing room, but she was already speaking to someone else.

So Jonas settled for the Duke.

"Your Grace. So kind of you to invite me. An honor given to few." And it was. The crowd was small tonight. Lady Hadleigh, Sir Malcolm, Lady Fawcett, a few others whose names didn't immediately come to mind, which proved how removed they were from the action of the House of Lords.

They also weren't family, or financial connections. Frankly, it was odd.

Jonas hoped that, given the opening, Talbourne might explain it.

He didn't explain it. He stood there, looking at Jonas with those silent eyes.

Jonas knew he was over-inclined to talk. This might be a place to experiment with silence.

It was hard, but he let the silence around the two of them puddle and grow into a bubble that contained only them.

Just as Jonas knew he was going to lose this game, his host decided to talk. "I am grateful for your quick action in saving my wife."

That *was* surprising. "Anyone would have done the same, sir."

"I doubt it, but that's not the point. You did."

When Talbourne was done talking, he was done talking; Jonas waited for some long moments to see if his host would add anything more.

When he didn't speak, Jonas thought *he'd* try saying something. It cost him nothing, after all. "I'm happy to be of any service. We never got a chance to discuss your new proposal for the Lords."

"Government begins in the Commons," Nicholas recited as though he thought it was expected. "You needn't look for influence here."

"You take your seat seriously. And I have an interest in those who do."

"I'm not sure it behooves you to so openly curry favor with men with votes when you have none."

"Whew!" Jonas pretended to wipe off his forehead and check his hand for blood. "Must you always strike like a mace? You don't have many friends, do you?"

Nicholas said nothing.

Jonas just grinned. "I am still ready to walk around that garden. Look. You can do nothing for the rest of your life just as most of your predecessors in the House of Lords have done. You've got a good start. Ten years of warming up. Or, if you want to make something happen, you're going to need an *ally*."

"So what are you offering?" Nicholas' eyes had that measuring look. "Guidance, I suppose?"

"Sir, I barely know you. Or anything about you. You seem to have good taste in wives," and Jonas nodded to where Selene stood with a small woman with frightfully flyaway hair and a dark man with his back to the wall. "I assume those are friends of your wife, since I have not met them before."

"Indeed."

"Some men ask their wives to give up their friends upon marriage."

In a deliberate, measured way that in no way matched the vitriol of the words themselves, Nicholas said, "There are many men in London who are vicious, controlling fools."

Jonas rocked back on his heels. "And now I know more about you than I did before. That wasn't so hard, was it?" He even considered clapping Talbourne on the shoulder, just to celebrate the accomplishment of getting a personal thought out of him.

Something in Talbourne's expression told him not to.

So instead he said, "Had we better dine? I see your butler waiting to catch your eye in the doorway."

Nicholas didn't look at the butler, he kept his eyes on Jonas. "You've been kind enough to take a care for Her Grace's well-being twice."

"Twice?" Only the stair incident was coming to mind.

"You offended Lord Burden by requiring him to keep his bad-natured gossip to himself. I owe you for that as much as the other." For the first time Jonas thought he caught sight of something other than cool watchfulness in those eyes. What it was, he couldn't tell. But Nicholas actually tilted his head forward a little—was that a bow?—and said, "Any defense of her is a service to me."

"Very well then." Jonas just nodded, keeping his tone light in deliberate contrast to Nicholas' somberness. "The basis for a sound friendship, perhaps."

That got him no answer at all, but Jonas hadn't expected one.

* * *

LETTY WAS A DEEPLY entertaining dinner guest, with much to say about the crystal, the gilt on the chairs, and the tiny temples chased with vines, made of unglazed porcelain instead of sugar, that decorated the Talbourne table. Selene hadn't asked, but Letty was seated to her right, as her guest of honor, with Mr. Hastings beside her.

Letty clearly was *not* used to dining in surroundings like these, but was very quick. Her brother only had to stop her twice to prevent her describing others at the table. Selene would quite have liked to hear, but Anthony was of course correct.

Selene was sure his corrections had been too subtle for others to see. He had a care for how his manners here reflected on her.

And Selene's plates were prepared now for her. Someone had gotten instructions that stuck.

But not from her.

Dessert featured a pineapple that had appeared during all of yesterday's swirl, and been counted a wedding gift. Selene learned this as everyone else did, the explanation along with *ooh*s and *aah*s traveling around the table as people realized the prized fruit had actually been cut up to eat and not just kept for display.

Her wedding gift as well as Nicholas', though no one had thought to ask her opinion about its final disposition.

Selene decided to consider that kind, as she wouldn't have enjoyed it as decoration and it *was* delicious.

The taste of possibility, Selene thought as its tart sweetness burst on her tongue.

She was in danger of being more of a decoration than a duchess. That was what happened to those fairytale princesses, always looking beautiful in one castle or another, if they avoided being cut up and eaten themselves.

Riches would help her mother, but beyond that they wouldn't get Selene what she wanted. She could spend endless amounts of the Duke's money and still not be counted a duchess.

Possibilities now depended more on friends than pineapple. Lady Grantley was a darling, and Selene very much liked her brother. He had a quiet steadiness to him that Selene sincerely hoped would prove more reliable than her stone pillar of a duke had turned out to be.

She must thank Letty, and Anthony too, for never questioning her need to make plans.

* * *

JONAS CAUGHT Selene just as she was leaving the table. "Will you be gaming tonight, Your Grace?"

Selene turned to face Jonas with a smile. "Yes, but not with you."

"Ouch! Have you been learning to fence from the Duke? Both of you are far too ready with the conversational knife. Have some claret."

"No thank you, not at the moment. What did you say to offend him?"

"Well! I like that! Am I an offensive man, madame?"

"I will leave your character for others to judge who know you better, sir. Are you well supplied with drink yourself?"

"Well enough. I think I need to keep my wits about me."

Just as Jonas was wondering what else clever he might say to keep her talking, Sir Malcolm stopped by their side. "Cards, Callendar?"

A man could grow tired of games, Jonas realized. "Ah—" To Selene he said, "Will your friends be staying?"

"Their carriage is on its way to the door, and it is taking my cousin away too, so I must bid them farewell. Enjoy yourself tonight, sir, you are quite welcome to anything Talbourne House can provide."

Well, he knew she didn't mean *that*, Jonas thought with some genuine sadness as he watched her go.

Sir Malcolm gestured toward a different door, both eyebrows raised in question. "Willing to settle for us mere mortals, then?"

She was gone. "Cards will have to do, I suppose."

* * *

NICHOLAS DID RETIRE to his chambers, as was his habit, as his guests moved on from dinner to drinks and games and the fine musicians someone had engaged for the night.

But he immediately emerged again to walk the four steps to Selene's door.

He almost shoved his way into Selene's chamber before the footman was done announcing him. He didn't want to alarm the lady. But he felt impatient.

It was new to him, being impatient.

All these feelings were so new, and new was dangerous. He ought not to have been so free with her this morning.

If he made a misstep before he understood the rules, everything he wanted could be yanked away. He had plenty of experience with that. Callendar had made conversation and friendship and things sound so easy, when Nicholas knew they were traps.

He was still at least as suspicious of Callendar as he was grateful.

But he'd sidestepped all the traps when it came to Selene. He breathed in, slowly. She was *his*, and her loyalty was set in stone, and everything would be fine.

She stood in her chamber, hair clashing gloriously with the reddish lilac of her gown, and Nicholas felt his own face smile against his will before he even closed the door.

"Please," he said, "sit."

"I need to stand each time you enter a room, do I not, Your Grace?"

"Of…" Nicholas caught himself before he said "of course". Nicholas observed every ritual of his title, primarily because someone would notice if he did not. But Selene must be comfortable; she must *stay*. "If people can see," was how he decided to answer.

"Ah."

She sat back down, waving at a small table set between two comfortable chairs. "Please do sit," she said right back to him.

Nicholas paused, then settled into the chair, peering at the table as he did so. "Are those… rocks?"

He put down between them the small wooden case he was carrying, and picked up one of the objects. It was indeed a rock. A pebble. She had a pile of them.

People didn't surprise him. Not even Callendar, with his easy open ambition, surprised him. But somehow Selene surprised him.

She had *prepared* something? For *him*?

She had. "I can only assume I will have fifteen minutes, sir, and I wanted to use all of them. Have you played the game of nim before?"

"You needn't teach me games."

"But I am going to. It's a simple game of drawing stones out of a pile. You don't want to be forced to take the last one."

"No one wants to be forced to do anything. But speaking of stones… I did promise you a wedding gift. The case before you."

Selene ran her fingers over it, smiling before she even opened it. "Thank you, sir."

His "Mm" was the audible equivalent of a shrug, but he watched as she took out three combs, then a necklace, and finally a bracelet. The stones in them caught the candlelight and threw flashes of fire. "Some more rocks. I know you will enjoy them little, but indulge me."

"What are they?"

"Rubies set in gold with diamonds on either side. All three pieces, though the combs are ebony."

"Will they make me look like a duchess?" Selene held the necklace up to her bare throat.

They made her look like a queen. "Very appropriate, madame," was all he said.

She'd always looked like a queen. Likely that was why he had overlooked buying her jewels. From their first meeting, she'd intrigued him with her slow graceful movements and her thoughtful expression, an expression that changed in an instant when she laughed.

Her genuine smile—he could see it in the corners of her eyes. As she returned the jewels to their case, Nicholas wished that he'd given her something she would enjoy more. He could do better. He would think of something better.

He could watch her all he liked. She wouldn't catch him gazing longingly at her. Still, by force of habit Nicholas tore his eyes away from her, never willing to be caught showing any true interest.

He was too old for such things anyway.

There was another new box on her dressing table, one with many little cunning drawers that would let her find things with ease—her cousin must have brought it. Plus a mirror from someone who'd clearly panicked about giving a gift, a pair of cameo-carved crystal goblets, an ivory fan he thought he recognized as once Lady Hadleigh's, and a bottle of liquor that only Sir Malcolm would have given.

His eye lit on two curiously long poles leaning against the wall by her dressing table. "Have you been injured? You need a walking stick?"

"Oh, my gifts. There have been a few." Selene didn't seem overly interested, yet they were sitting by her dressing table.

Nicholas leaned over and picked up the one that had first caught his eye. "Rosewood inlaid with silver. Heavy."

"So heavy that it would tire me quickly, unless I need it to beat someone senseless. Lord Burden sent it."

He picked up the other. "And a long light clouded cane with only a silver tip."

"Lord Callendar's. Actually I think that one would be useful. It may help me find my way around on my own. One can use it to locate the stairs, and the like."

"Take a footman." Hopefully she would assume the sharpness he couldn't hide was because he was jealous—which he was—and not because he feared for her safety. "Have a servant accompany you. Always."

Selene nodded as she sat back, her thoughtful expression returning.

He wanted to know what she was thinking. "What?"

"What do you mean, what?" Selene countered immediately.

"I wondered what had occurred to you. I can see you thinking."

"Your Grace," Selene said evenly, "if I can hear you thinking and you can see me thinking, we are going to trip over many little occasions where the other person does not want to share their thoughts, aren't we?"

Nicholas' eyes narrowed. "I won't admit to that, madame."

"Neither of us has to." Selene leaned back. "Shall we play?"

"There is a small pouch in the bottom of the chest you have yet to take out."

Surprised, Selene explored the velvet lining with her fingers, and discovered a pouch she'd missed, made of the same material. She drew it out.

"One moment." Nicholas poured the pebbles from the small porcelain dish before him, and placed it empty before her.

Selene carefully emptied the little velvet bag into it.

"What are they? So round! But they don't feel like glass?"

"Pearls, madame. I thought you might find them less pointy and more comfortable than rubies."

Selene put one in her palm, rolled it around there with her fingertip. "They grow warm to the touch."

Nicholas felt a pool of something melting, growing, roaring inside him.

Her lips flushed and parted as her fingertips rolled the silvery orb on her skin.

He wanted to be that pearl.

He had two urges at the same time: to have her portrait painted just this way so that he could relive this moment over and over again, and to lock the door to keep the rest of the world from seeing her this way. To keep this perfection for himself.

Of course, he would never lock her door.

He might have her portrait painted.

"If you like them, I will look for more." He'd have ships scour the seven seas for them. "These have not been drilled, and I understand they can only be drilled when they are fresh from the ocean, so you cannot wear them around your neck; but they are sufficiently large that I thought you might enjoy them made into hairpins one of these days."

"You seem to like bejeweling my hair," she teased.

"You have beautiful hair."

She froze, and he stopped breathing. Was a compliment too much? Was it wrong? It was surely a sign of weakness. He would pay for it somehow, now.

But all Selene said, softly, was "Thank you," and Nicholas let out his breath.

She hesitated and Nicholas wondered if there was something else he should say next, something good. But before he thought of anything, she went on. "A gaming duke should play with pearls. Let me explain the rules. We will be drawing from this little pile; it will only take a few moments to play. Tomorrow I will expect you to play me with the stones and I expect you to try to win."

"I will try to win now. I can hardly do anything else."

"Me too, Your Grace," Selene said as she placed the pearl-filled dish between them.

* * *

IT DIDN'T TAKE LONG for Selene to explain the rules, and by the time they had played a trial game or two, the slight awkwardness between them had fled.

"Your friends returned home," Nicholas observed.

"You can't expect everyone who comes to Talbourne House to stay forever!"

"Only a select few."

Was that another compliment? Selene didn't know how to take them. They didn't seem to suit His Grace's—Nicholas' personality. He'd never said anything like that before.

But she liked them.

"And how do you choose them? I'm surprised you don't entertain gentlemen from the Commons more. They might help you if they knew you better."

Nicholas didn't speak of his interminable houseguests, but he did say, "I am not a great voice among them, I assure you. In fact, I am making my first effort, as it were, trying to steer the Lords, and it is not going all that well."

Selene almost held her breath, willing him to say more, and when he didn't she said, "You must allow yourself a few tries to find the footing that you want."

"Perhaps that's the problem. I should have tried before something important arose."

"Something very rare?"

"If it turns into something that may interest you, I will entertain you with it then." Was that regret in his voice?

She wanted to pound her fist on the table. "You can entertain me with it at any time you like, you know. These evenings are for both of us. We could indulge in some nice hot tea and I will listen very thoroughly, I promise you."

"Did you want tea? Why don't you have tea, then?"

"I didn't want to join the late supper downstairs. I preferred we stay here."

She wished he'd say that he preferred it too, but instead he just said, "For heavens' sake, Selene, if you want tea, have it. You don't have to attend the entertainments for that—or to do anything else."

"I had never thought of asking for tea anywhere in the house."

Nicholas was quiet for a moment, then said, "Talbourne House can seem... austere. Don't let it. You should have anything you wish, to be comfortable, to be happy."

Selene's voice softened. "That's the first time you have ever mentioned anyone being happy."

"If anyone should be happy, especially here, it's you."

That pleased her far more than she'd have thought a few words could. He cared if she was happy. It must mean he cared about her. Not just as a... woman in his bed, and perhaps not yet as a duchess. But as someone in his home, albeit one of many.

That care, she realized. She wanted to trust that *that* was the Nicholas she would find if she went to his bed.

"I do take back my saucy remark in the carriage, sir. You are indeed kind."

That made Nicholas shift around uncomfortably. "You are the one who has gone to this effort to entertain me, madame."

"Was it worth missing the entertainment and evening fare downstairs?"

"Definitely."

But then before she grew too excited by yet another compliment, Nicholas added, "But then I never do attend the evening entertainments downstairs."

* * *

When Nicholas couldn't think of another reason to drag the time out, and bid his wife good night, it didn't improve his mood to find Lyall waiting for him in the hallway outside.

"Your Grace."

"No news on that maid?"

"No, sir."

"Keep looking."

"Of course, sir."

He could be patient about waiting for Selene to want him, he truly could. And he could be patient waiting for party men to see reason. And even for Mr. Lyall to find out who the woman was who had threatened his wife.

He didn't see why he had to be patient about all three.

* * *

MARTHA BUSTLED in as soon as the Duke departed.

Selene was pleased. He'd stayed nearly half an hour, by her guess, before bidding her good night.

That was a good start.

He was still so—he didn't talk freely. He still didn't trust her enough to tell her about his work. She wanted that; somehow, she *needed* it.

And there had been none of... whatever that was between them this morning. She'd pushed too far by going to his room, that was all. Or maybe he'd remembered no one talked that way to an eligible coal bucket.

Still, at one point she'd dropped a pearl, and he'd fetched it for her, made a dry remark about her already so accustomed to being a duchess that she could drop jewels wherever she went, and he'd laughed when she teased him about losing even the teaching game.

Well, he'd snorted a little.

It was all very promising. Those precious snorts felt valuable. She knew she would lie awake in bed, if she insisted on going now, replaying them in her head and wondering about all the things they might mean.

She intended to build something of that snort. Something that would support a lifetime.

With all the pity in the world for a lady's maid wanting to keep reasonable hours, Selene was too wound up to sleep.

"Put me in something I can get out of myself, and go ahead and retire, Martha. I may go check on my mother."

Then she remembered a question. "Oh, and Martha. Who assigns the maid's work?"

"The housekeeper, madame."

"I assumed, but what is her name?"

"Mrs. Wilkes, madame."

"And where would I find her?"

"Oh but you—you wouldn't go down there!"

"Down where?" Martha made it sound as though she planned to go down to the gates of hell.

"Mrs. Wilkes lives in the silver cupboard."

"You don't mean she actually lives there?"

"No, no! I mean—you will find her in the silver cupboard. On any given day."

Peculiar, thought Selene, but she ignored it in favor of changing and letting Martha go.

There was still so much new territory to discover.

First, she'd look in on her mother.

Lord Callendar's gift would come in handy. It was smooth and light in her hand. She certainly did *not* want to tumble down the stairs.

It was easy to retrace the steps Nicholas had shown her last night to her mother's room.

But once she was standing outside the door, Selene stopped. Someone was *laughing* inside.

Someone—probably Fran—was playing cards with her mother, and her mother was laughing.

Her *mother* was laughing. She had the *breath* to laugh.

Selene had already won that.

She wouldn't interrupt their little party. Her mother might feel she had to put the cards away, since those were games Selene couldn't play.

"Is there a footman here?" she said softly, remembering Nicholas' explanation that someone would always been waiting in the hall to help her if necessary.

She half-braced for her stepson Edward's voice, now that she knew it. Half hoped for it.

But it was Jonathan, the footman who had been teaching her to drop knives into a circle. "Yes, madame."

"Say that it's you when you greet me, won't you, Jonathan?"

He remained silent.

So. Nicholas could ask for her plates to be prepared and they were, everywhere.

But a request from her? Went nowhere.

Well, one thing at a time.

Including, eventually, the silver cupboard.

But first to go beyond this wing. Nicholas had called this the family wing. She took the turn.

She used her new thin stick to feel ahead of her several steps, and her hand to guide her along the wall. When the hallway ended, she walked slowly forward till she felt, with the tip of the walking stick, the floor fall away. The grand front stairway. The rooms she'd explored this morning, the unused ones, were to her left.

She turned right, and followed the wall all the way to the end of the hall, where she discovered a much smaller staircase.

Up one floor, Jonathan trailing a few steps behind her, Selene only paused on the landing for a moment.

Just one floor further up, she heard a loud voice making a vehement case for *something*.

She decided to investigate.

* * *

"I AM Lord Thomas Hayden and I flatly refuse to go to bed!"

Selene would have much preferred to listen at the door for a while, but apparently duchesses didn't do that. "Her Grace the Duchess of Talbourne," Jonathan intoned at the door before she could stop him.

"Thank you *so* much," she muttered as she passed him. "My lord, I am so very glad to meet you at last. Will you shake my hand? As we are related now, and I cannot see my way to anything as formal as a bow." She put out her hand.

For a moment she wondered if the little boy—he was about eight, if she remembered correctly—would give her the cut direct, but he finally grasped her hand. He had a sweaty, little-boy hand. Selene didn't think she had ever held one like it, yet somehow she recognized it instantly.

Thomas said, "You ought to be formal. I am Lord Thomas Hayden and I refuse to go to bed."

"Lord Thomas!"

"No need to be shocked, Nurse, I quite understand Lord Thomas' point of view. We ought to be as formal and correct as His Grace himself, oughtn't we?"

Selene wondered if Thomas was watching her as closely as she was listening to him. Interestingly, he had not let go of her hand.

He said, "His Grace is formal. But he says that I am young and lucky not to go in public, so I may say what I like."

Selena repressed a smile. "And he is certainly correct, sir. But I do not think that he means that you may contradict your nurse."

Thomas seemed to consider this for a moment. Then he said, "But he never said that I couldn't. And he never said that I had to listen to you, either."

"Lord Thomas!" This time the nurse had real despair in her voice.

Selene had to work to keep from laughing out loud. "It is a sad truth that we all must live with, Lord Thomas, that we are supposed to behave appropriately from general rules, rather than do whatever we like unless it is forbidden."

This seemed to make the little boy think very hard. Like his father, she could practically hear him thinking, even when he said nothing. And like his father, there was something about his voice she found indescribably appealing when he finally spoke and said, "I don't recall my father saying that I had to obey general rules."

"And you won't take my word for it?"

"For sure not! We have just met, and my brother tells me that you will not be here for very long."

Selene burst out laughing. His words stung but his reasoning was flawless.

"Loooord Tho-mas! That is more than enough, young sir. Enough of you."

"Never mind, Nurse—what is your name, please?"

"Nurse Carter, Your Grace, thank you kindly."

"Nurse Carter, I am going to borrow your charge for just a few minutes. He sounds wide awake, and I think that he should make the acquaintance of my mother Lady Redbeck."

"Oh no, ma'am! He's not dressed, and—"

"Lord Thomas, do you think that your current costume is sufficiently formal for a brief visit?"

The boy seemed to consider this seriously, as he did everything. "Not for sure, but perhaps good enough. Will she mind the sticky spot of jam on my pocket?"

"I've no idea. Let's see."

As she led him out into the hall, he said, "But you won't see anything."

"Yes and no." Holding his hand in one of hers, and the cane in the other, she had to awkwardly feel across her body for where the hallway turned into the staircase. But the walking stick was long enough; it worked surprisingly well. "I will perceive, and we will use the word see for that."

"You'll see with your stick." The little boy seemed oddly pleased by that.

"Just so." Downstairs, along the front hall, and left. Then left again, and she faintly heard the laughter still coming from her mother's room. But this time she knocked lightly, and opened the door.

"Clear away your winnings, Lady Redbeck, Lord Thomas has come to visit you!"

There was a chorus of cooing sounds as the maids scrambled to move the cards. Perhaps Lord Thomas was a more adorable-looking little boy than he sounded.

"How good you are! And how kind of you, Lord Thomas, to visit an old lady. Will you sit?"

When the boy started forward to take the chair that Fran had probably vacated, Thomas kept hold of Selene's hand, dragging her closer with him.

And that was all it took.

She was in love.

Lady Redbeck was tickled too. "Ought I to be enjoying your company at this hour? Surely you are to be asleep by now."

"In fact," Selene informed her mother, "we were just discussing that very topic."

"I am Lord Thomas Hayden and I do not wish to go to bed," the little boy said, really relishing saying it again.

"Ah, I see. That puts me in a difficult position, Lord Thomas. Because I would like to discuss with you very important questions about apples and sailing boats, but I cannot take advantage of your complete abandonment of your nurse's schedule."

"Also questions of pocket knives," Selene put in helpfully. As she had recently found the topic fascinating herself.

Thomas let go of Selene's hand, apparently from sheer excitement about this topic. But Lady Redbook sounded mildly horrified.

"Pocket knives! Certainly not pocket knives. Whatever gave you such an idea? Pocket knives are not an appropriate topic of conversation for gentlemen at this age."

Lord Thomas begged to differ. "Pocket knives are interesting," he assured his new acquaintance.

"Well I agree they may be *interesting*, but they are certainly not appropriate."

"You know, madame, perhaps," Selene said as if it were just occurring to her, "if Lord Thomas agrees to go to sleep tonight, you would have time for such fascinating discussion tomorrow."

"What do you think, Lord Thomas? Might you have time to discuss these things with me tomorrow?" Lady Redbeck sounded utterly sincere.

"We could do it tonight!"

"These really are the rewards of doing as one ought. I ought to be asleep myself, as I have been ill, so perhaps we should set a good example for each other, and you will allow me to beg your leave to retire." Lady Redbeck sounded so entirely reasonable that Selene herself felt silly for being up so late, and nearly stifled a yawn.

Lord Thomas displayed more graciousness and forbearance than many a peer when he magnanimously agreed, "Of course. I hope you feel better."

And the good lady sounded most sincere as she said, "If you visit me again, Lord Thomas, I am sure that I will."

"Good! Then I will do that. And thank you for not seeing the jam spot on my pocket." When the little boy climbed down from the chair, he grabbed Selene's hand again.

But it was quite unnecessary, she was already head over heels in love. "Let us return to Nurse Carter and let her get you ready, shall we?"

Thomas was silent as Selene led him back to his room, but before they left the staircase, he pulled on her hand a little and whispered, "Your Grace."

"Yes, my lord?" Selene bent down and whispered back.

"I hope you won't go away *too* soon."

Unable to stop herself, Selene found herself kneeling in the hall hugging the little boy tight. He was so small, and it was so easy to sweep him up in her arms and hug him so close that his feet left the floor.

"I hope that wasn't too much of an imposition," Selene said as she returned him to his feet.

"That was a very good hug," Thomas responded with his characteristic thoughtful judgment, that reminded her so much of his father. And he added, "My father gives hugs just like that."

"Does he? I am so glad to hear that." She was glad to hear he hugged his little boy. The hug she'd had was excellent too. It warmed her heart to think they agreed on this.

Thomas added, "I miss my mother's hugs."

And just like that, Selene had to hug the boy again or cry into his hair. She hugged him. "Of course you do."

"No one likes it when I say that. But I do."

"I think it is only reasonable, and I don't mind you saying it one bit."

"Don't you? Edward made it sound as though you would be here instead of her and that I wouldn't like it at all. But it's not so bad."

"I'm not here instead of her, sir. She had to leave you, and I am here now, that's all."

She put her hand on his head to stroke his hair and felt him nod.

Selene whispered again. "I'm tired too. Let's get you in bed."

* * *

HER HEAD WAS TOO full of everything that had to be contemplated, but she had to put it down and try to go to sleep.

What an odd sensation, knowing that Thomas had so easily, so quickly captured her heart.

She didn't think she'd ever felt anything quite like that before. And yet she knew it, knew it absolutely for sure.

And it wasn't because he was charming, or sweet, or even nice. There was just something in him that fit together with something in her. Just as he was, he was perfect.

And she would do anything for him.

She wished she had met Edward differently. Perhaps he would have struck her the same way.

Was there only ever one chance to fall in love?

Marriage was awkward when one wasn't in love with one's husband. Ought it to have happened in the first moments, if it were going to happen at all? Or when he had first taken her hand? Well, it hadn't.

He wasn't like that. Perhaps she wasn't either.

But she was still determined to find a way for them to fit together. Like Duke and Duchess ought to do.

Or man and wife.

As she finally laid down, Selene clutched the thought to her like a lifeline.

He hugged his son. *He hugged his son.* And he had hugged her too, when she had most needed it.

There was something there, she didn't yet know what, but if she kept looking she would find it.

* * *

UPON ARRIVING at Talbourne House in the middle of a clammy gray morning, Lord Burden was shown directly to the study of the Duke himself.

Ought he introduce the topic of the window tax directly? Yes, thought Alistair, best get it out of the way so he might move on to the more pressing topic of the import ban. He had a business connection who was growing impatient and Alistair had promised action.

"Ah, Lord Burden," said Talbourne, not rising from the table at which he had several letters in front of him in various stages of completion.

"Your Grace."

Burden's bow was interrupted by the Duke. "No need to be too formal, Mr. Collins will see you out in a moment."

"But I've only just arrived."

"Yes, I know." Talbourne scattered a little sand on the document he'd just signed. "My apologies, sir," he said in that way he had, which conveyed no sorrow at all, "but I will not be able to help you with the vote you are seeking."

"But we haven't even discussed it yet!"

"Yes, I know," his host said again. "You will forgive me if I state plainly that I cannot spare the time to give it the full consideration it deserves just now."

This surely wasn't the last word. "Sir, I have made several trips to Talbourne House to discuss this with you."

Talbourne just looked at him instead of saying *yes, I know* a third time. "What a burden."

"Are you being witty?"

"No."

Alistair was too confused to bristle. He put on a dogged expression, and ground his teeth a little. "I really think it is in both of our best interests if you listen to my proposal."

"I know you understand how the pressures upon us shift unexpectedly from time to time. I'll have Mr. Collins show you out with my regrets."

Alistair found himself shaking his head back and forth in a tiny wave of "no". This wasn't how this was supposed to go.

He sputtered, "Perhaps I should have said that it would be in *your* best interest to listen."

"Is that your attempt at a threat, Burden?"

All the Duke did was rise from his seat, and the few vertebrae that had managed to hold up Alistair's defiance broke apart and scattered to the winds. His Grace's dark coat was not so broad in the shoulder, his height not so menacing, as to give anyone pause; yet his look had a solid immobility that sliced through Alistair and left him stepping back.

"An unworthy thought."

Talbourne bowed his head, just an inch. "My apologies again," sounding no more sorry than before. "These misunderstandings happen with everyone from time to time. I am sure we are both willing to overlook them for the sake of everyone. For instance, imagine how awkward it would be for me to apologize that my staff admitted you to my wedding breakfast even though you were not invited. Too delicate a matter to speak of, I'm sure you agree."

"I suppose so." Alistair was in a daze, trying to gather what was left of his thoughts. Why was this going so poorly? Alistair was a man of importance, with important ideas that Talbourne ought to be willing to back.

The man never *did* anything; why not use the power he wasn't using anyway to help out Alistair?

Alistair had a few other methods of persuasion in his pocket, plans that he and his associate had made, to use only if necessary. Alistair had never thought they would actually be necessary.

He made one more valiant attempt. Mustering all his guts, he managed to look Talbourne straight in the eye. Well, for a moment.

"You really ought to listen to me, sir," Alistair said to the curtains. "You'll simply have to, one way or another."

"No," Talbourne said again, "I won't."

The Duke stepped to the door and opened it, waving the butler back in. The butler who had waited. No doubt told to wait.

"Mr. Collins, let me know when the Duke of Gravenshire arrives, and please show Lord Burden out. And don't worry, there won't be any more confusion. When he is invited to return, the invitation will be written."

Knowing that meant that he wouldn't be invited to return, Alistair bowed, and followed the butler out.

* * *

JONATHAN DID NOT SEEM excited to greet the new day by visiting the silver closet.

Well, that was his problem, thought Selene, as she herself was dying to visit the silver closet.

It was a narrow door, into a small space that smelled of silver polish, and once inside it, she heard the stiff rustle of quite a few starched petticoats. "Your Grace."

"I assume that you are Mrs. Wilkes?"

"Yes, madame. Mr. Lyall ought to have introduced us before this."

"I am told that I can quite reliably find you here when it is necessary."

Mrs. Wilkes said nothing about *that*.

Selene was starting to see a pattern in the occupants of Talbourne House. Perhaps she'd fallen into it herself.

"Martha has done sterling work as my lady's maid, but I would like someone more familiar with the task of dressing a lady for the station."

"A maid can't take the place of a lady choosing things for herself, ma'am."

Selene contemplated that for a moment. That was either a dig at the maids, or a dig at Selene for being unable to choose her own fashions by herself.

Selene decided to ignore it, like she had the dig at Mr. Lyall just seconds before. In one minute she had already grasped Mrs. Wilkes' methods. She blamed others, and otherwise kept her mouth shut.

"Are you worried about someone stealing the silver?"

"Ma'am?"

"I said, do you have reason to think someone will steal the silver? For you to spend your whole day in here, I mean."

Selene amused herself by counting to see how long it would take Mrs. Wilkes to decide what to say to a veiled barb at herself.

Six, seven, eight…

"Talbourne House servants do not steal, Your Grace."

"Of course not! I am glad to hear it. You must be relieved not to be chained to this room. Do send another lady's maid to assist Martha as soon as you can, please." Cass and Letty's friends might arrive at any hour, and Selene was nearly desperate for allies of her very own. "And when my guests arrive, please place them along the front hallway, on the same floor as my chambers."

"Those rooms are reserved for royalty and other guests of state, ma'am."

"Are they? Then they must be very nice."

* * *

SIR MALCOLM PUT down the decanter of liquor at the clatter of what seemed like a herd of elephants stumbling down the front stair.

When he reached the foyer, Lady Redbeck was just being settled onto the inlaid floor in Edward's old rolling chair.

"Good God, lads, you're not pitching hay."

"I'm quite well, Sir Malcolm," Lady Redbeck said as her nurse Fran tut-tutted to herself and tucked a lap rug around her ladyship's lap. The footmen stood in a group, abashed.

"I'd better roll you wherever you want to go. Where were you headed?"

"I heard the long gallery gets quite good sun this time of day, and one can see the lawns."

"One can see the lawns when one's on the lawns. Beautiful out, we must try it."

"Well…" Lady Redbeck's twists of silver and gold hair glinted even in the absence of sunbeams. The foyer had no windows to let in the sun, or to let her see out. "The long gallery first, then we'll take a look. If Fran agrees we might make a small outing."

"Anywhere you like," said Sir Malcolm as they set off for the long gallery with Fran and the gaggle of footmen coming along behind. This was far more entertaining than drinking alone.

* * *

"I THINK you are being bad at this on purpose." Thomas' voice carried far more open disappointment than his father would ever show.

Selene gently dropped to her knees and collapsed on the fine grass, laughing so hard she feared she might hurt herself.

Thomas' accusations didn't let up. "I think you know where the stone is."

They had been playing hopscotch for quite some time, and for some reason Thomas was convinced Selene knew where the stone was and yet still deliberately, repeatedly, failed to find it.

Even being allowed to use her walking stick to keep her balance, Selene was fantastically bad at the game. She kept bumping the sticks used to mark the squares, and the marker stone made almost no sound in the grass when it landed; truly, she had no idea where it was.

She played because Thomas was enjoying it.

And for some reason she found his despair over her badness side-splittingly funny.

He also seemed to think lecturing her would help. Selene hoped he hadn't picked *that* up from his father. "Losing isn't funny."

"On the contrary, Lord Thomas, losing can be *hilarious*."

"This isn't the way you lose."

"It can be." Rolling to her knees—this was undoubtedly not proper behavior for a duchess, and she hoped the dress wasn't ruined—Selene reached out to find him and ruffle his hair. "There's no shame in losing a game. And I fully expected to lose this one."

"If you thought you were going to lose, why play?"

Selene felt the sun falling warmly on the top of her head and Thomas'. She thought of arguments for fresh air and exercise, but those wouldn't have persuaded her and she bet they wouldn't persuade Thomas either.

So she told him something she really thought. "If you don't play, you won't have had the fun of playing. And if one is going to play anything, one needs to know how to lose gracefully. It's as good a place as any to start mastering a game's strategy. So thank you for the practice."

"Practice at losing? That's silly."

"I assure you I meant it sincerely. I hope your father has had practice at losing, as if he doesn't I suspect he will get it tonight."

Thomas jumped away, startled by something. "There's Edward! Edward, will you play hopscotch with me?"

"Her Grace is doing that now." The older lad's—the young man's voice was a good deal more sullen.

Fortunately Thomas did not take much notice of it. "She is *awful* at this. And apparently, I need to practice losing."

Clever boy.

Feeling for and finding her walking stick, Selene rose to her feet and brushed at her skirt a little, probably not affecting what she assumed was most of the damage. "I would love to leave you two to the pursuit of excellence in hopscotch, Lord Fettanby, if you are willing to take my place."

"I don't have your talent for taking other people's places, but I'm willing to play."

Selene elected to ignore that. She barely knew him, so it wasn't her he was angry with.

She wanted to bathe before she dressed for dinner... and the lesson she had in store for the older gentleman of the house.

NICHOLAS STARED at the table in disbelief.

Selene was in an excellent mood, humming to herself and smiling. She'd poked into many nooks and crannies of Talbourne House, as she'd reported to him in entertaining detail; she'd taken Thomas to visit her mother again and then out onto the grounds, and now, she'd won three games of nim in a row.

And she'd made Nicholas speechless.

All that good mood became sugary condolences that he strongly suspected she did not mean. "My goodness, Your Grace, bad luck. Would you like to try for five out of seven?"

Nicholas narrowed his eyes at his duchess. "Madame, you have swept the last three games. I am not so foolish to think that I would win one in the future when I have not won one yet. What is the nim equivalent of someone who sharps at cards?"

"I did not cheat." His duchess fluttered her eyelashes. Nicholas half-grunted, half-laughed at the exaggerated gesture. Selene added as sweetly as she could, "You had a day to learn the rules of the game, sir; how much more of a handicap should I have given you?"

"I like how you say that you did not cheat, not that you would never cheat."

"It's flattering of you to notice, sir," and she batted her eyelashes again. She could be so deliciously absurd. For a card sharp.

He chuckled.

Which made Selene look smugly pleased.

"So this was just to teach me a lesson? Or get my attention?"

"Why not both?"

A saucy Selene was practically his favorite. He liked wanting to laugh. It could be his new favorite thing. Feeling like this, and looking at her. "What lesson? And why did you want my attention?"

"I have demands."

"Demands?" His voice lowered. "Is this a negotiation?"

That made *her* laugh. "I have guests coming to stay for a while."

"Fine. I will always welcome guests of yours."

Selene seemed surprised at how easy that had been. And yet pressed on. "I want your support with Mrs. Wilkes. I would like to see some changes made in the household."

"Such as?"

"The fish."

"What fish?"

"The fish we ate at luncheon today. I hated it, and I imagine you did too."

"Don't touch the fish."

"Honestly? The fish is where you stand firm? You *must* have hated that fish. It was mushy, it smelled of saltwater, it—"

"I buy that fish from a duchy that has access to the sea. My lands have no access to the sea. I want His Grace to remember the goodwill of my people when it comes time to vote on the canal I am attempting to have built to connect my lands to London via the Thames. And I want him to rest assured that even when I have access to the water, I will buy fish from him."

Selene thought.

She surprised him by asking, "Is it necessary for you yourself to eat the fish?"

"Yes. And for the guests at my table to eat the fish and see that I eat the fish."

She was rubbing her thumb over her fingers. "What if we find a less disgusting way to serve the fish?"

"Fine. But we will continue to buy the fish and eat the fish."

"I can do that."

She would do that. Nicholas felt something well up inside him. Had anyone ever offered to do something for him, just for him? Much less eat disgusting fish? "Why must we be serious over fish? *You* don't even have to eat the fish."

"When it would help you if I did? How would it look if your duchess refused to honor your bargains? Truly, Nicholas, you should be able to expect more of me. Do you—" Now Selene had stopped smiling and sounded more subdued. "Is that why you did not introduce me to your children?"

He hadn't had *time*. "I did not wish to burden you."

"Thomas is no burden. And Edward—"

"He doesn't speak for anyone else at Talbourne House." Nicholas' mind filled with a jumble of images from Edward's babyhood, his illness, his recovery. "I have not seen much of him these last few months."

"Not because of *me*."

"No. Parliament began sitting in January, and you know the Lords meet all evening most nights."

"How does he spend his time?"

"However young men spend their time." Nicholas made a point of not having Edward watched all that closely, which he wasn't going to say, as it might draw Selene's attention to her different situation.

She was quick, and she would notice if she hadn't already, but he wanted her to feel safe in Talbourne House.

Nicholas added as if as an afterthought, "That age, you know. He will find his footing again."

"Well. Perhaps he and I will have that in common."

"He enjoys how people come and go here. Perhaps we should hold an entertainment. You should meet a sponsor or two from Almack's."

"Everyone who wants something from you comes here. Why don't I plan an entertainment for them—or people whose help *you* seek?"

Nicholas would rather she be comfortable sleeping in the room next to his than that she feel she must be de Gauer's daughter working for Talbourne's benefit. "You needn't."

"But if it is what I *want?*"

It *would* be the more likely thing for her to want.

A little hollowly, Nicholas just said, "You should do as you wish, madame."

His lack of an answer seemed to ruffle her feelings for some reason. "Perhaps I will concentrate more on people in London, and less in Talbourne House."

"If it pleases you." His mouth felt a bit dry. "Would it?"

"Your Grace," and Selene leaned forward over the table, resting her cheek in her hand and apparently coincidentally showing her *décolletage*, "if you don't answer questions, why should I?"

What was he supposed to make of *that?* Did she *know* how he could see her skin practically glowing where it threatened to overspill that dress?

Long game. Long game. Best to quit the field while he was ahead. Or at least, considering the nim games, only behind on the less important things. "Our fifteen minutes is long gone, as well."

"Then thank you for the games. Sir." Selene sat back and she did smile a little, her fingertips playing with the stones in their dish. "Next time there will be a wager, of course."

"Should I bring some coin?"

She shrugged one shoulder. "I haven't yet decided what we will wager. I'm only giving you fair warning."

* * *

I'M ONLY GIVING *you fair warning.*

Nicholas could hear her voice all through the next morning—unfortunate, as at one point it distracted him from the Duke of Gravenshire, whose vote he needed on his canal.

"Everything all right, Talbourne?"

Nicholas shot a look at the older man. "I am quite well, sir." *Just unfortunately fascinated by my wife.* He found himself wanting to win whatever she wagered. "I don't suppose you've ever played a game called nim."

"What?" The question took Gravenshire by surprise. "I am not a gamester. My daughter plays cards quite well. Ask her at our ball on Thursday."

Nicholas never had any intention of explaining himself in any situation; he was not going to explain all the ways in which that would be too late. "Thank you."

"Lady Tella is quite interested in meeting your duchess, you know."

Meaning his daughter, Lady Donnatella, hoped to be the first to feature the new duchess at her *soireé*. And she would be, because her father was one of the few dukes who actually sat in his seat in the Lords, and Nicholas wanted to continue their good relationship.

Well, working relationship.

"What do you do for entertainment, then, Gravenshire?"

The broad-chested, silver-haired duke just stared at Nicholas, jaw agape.

"What?" Nicholas felt somehow exposed, being gaped at like that.

"You've never asked me anything of the sort before. Are you sure you're quite well?"

"It was a friendly question, nothing more."

"That's my point. You're not friendly. You astonish me, sir. Marriage must agree with you." The other duke took a puff of his cigar, still looking askance at Nicholas as if he might bark, or fly.

"I suppose it does. I will speak to Her Grace but I expect we will enjoy your hospitality."

"Good, good."

"But seriously, Gravenshire, do you know anyone who plays nim?"

SKIRMISHES IN THE DAYTIME

Selene hummed under her breath as she wove the stems of the daisies together with her fingers. "Am I doing this right?"

"Oh yes," said Virginia, who'd finally arrived as Letty had promised. The *yes* was all Selene really heard before her mind wandered.

He'd said he liked her hair. Perhaps she'd wear these in her hair.

What if he didn't like it? On the other hand, how would she know unless she tried it?

Selene couldn't have explained why it seemed like such a difficult problem, how indecisive she felt about whether she wanted to... well, *seduce*, seduce her... well, her husband.

Then she realized that in fact she could explain it perfectly well. Nicholas had *reassured* her that they needn't make love. While he was *proposing* to her.

They'd had that odd moment in his room, yet he didn't trust her to entertain his alliances?

Perhaps she was not the one confused on how they should proceed in this marriage.

She ought just to tell him to ignore her mother's warnings about startling Selene with that innocence-dragging-away-business. That those weren't the final word on the subject. But Selene suspected that the business *would* be startling, and still wasn't sure how, or whether, to go about it.

It was the unknown, she realized. People wrote those fairy tales and read them because the land of lovers was an unknown land, and for all anyone knew, it might well be full of squirrels and murder.

It would be so much worse if she didn't already know something of Nicholas. She did. He would never try to eat her no matter how hungry he was. It was just that not being eaten was a low target at which to aim.

And his morning challenge appeared to be rescinded. She'd been as obvious as she could last night, and… nothing. Perhaps she didn't know how to be obvious.

Maybe she couldn't be obviously willing and obviously unsure at the same time.

This would all be so much easier if he would only tell her what votes he was trying to win. She could woo him with votes.

She heard the footman approach before he cleared his throat. "Lady Viola Evelyn has arrived, Your Grace. Lady Viola, may I present Her Grace the Duchess of Talbourne, and Miss Virginia Díaz de la Peña."

* * *

VIOLA STARED at the heaps of English daisies of all colors scattered around the gazebo, and the two young women sitting among them, one of whom, the bright-haired blind one, was the brand-new Duchess of Talbourne.

A duchess who clapped her hands like a girl and said, "Oh splendid. I am *so* glad you are here, Lady Viola. Join us, Miss Díaz is just showing me how to make a flower crown."

"Though you should carry a flowered branch rather than wear them in your hair, as you are the duchess." The arresting young lady sitting at Selene's feet brushed leaves from her skirt as she stood and came to greet Viola.

A young lady even more startling than the Duchess.

"You are not appropriate," Viola blurted out before she could stop herself.

And then immediately blushed so red that she could actually feel her face heating up.

But fortunately the other young lady, taken aback, laughed uproariously. "Well, neither are you, if you go around saying such things to people!"

"I don't, I truly don't. Please forgive me. I have heard of you, Miss Díaz, that is all."

"Well, I have heard nothing about you, Lady Viola."

"That is as it should be, I suppose," mumbled Viola, though she didn't sound particularly happy to be so un-notorious.

The two young women regarded each other, both dark-haired and dark-eyed, but those were their only resemblances. Viola was slender, a bit pale, with haunted eyes, while Virginia was round and glowing, her dark skin polished golden in the sunlight and her figure set off by a yellow gown with a saucy short striped spencer. Viola, in her mauve gauze, imagined that if she stood next to Virginia, she would fade into the woodwork. Had there been woodwork.

"You have arrived at the perfect moment, Lady Viola, as Miss Díaz and I were just discussing how I should make a splash in London society."

"Don't," said Viola in the same subdued tone, taking a seat on a low bench nearby.

"Ah, I must. There are people in the *ton* who remember me as a child, and they haven't seen me in years. They will want to know how I have fared. I don't wish to say. I must give them something else to talk about." Selene grimaced. "And I have not made a good start."

"Thus, me," said Virginia with a grin as she sat again at Selene's feet, resuming her braid of English daisies.

"Oh no, Miss Díaz, I am grateful Lady Grantley convinced you to come in your own right."

"But..." Viola could think of no polite way to say what she was thinking, which was that Miss Díaz, though her existence was known, had never appeared in society, and could not distract at events she could not attend.

But Virginia seemed perfectly happy to do Viola's share of the talking as well. "I am received, you know, for all that I am the offspring of Lord Gourgaud's shocking marriage and my mother's shocking marriage too. I am not wholly Spanish, I am not wholly British. I own property; I am exempt from the ridiculous marriage market in which you British women must gamble. And I *like* parties."

Viola refrained from adding something about the very dark color of Virginia's skin. Virginia had summed it up quite well, after all.

"Lady Viola," Selene gently interrupted her thoughts, "your sister-in-law, my cousin Cass, thought that you might be willing to help me. But you need not do anything you don't wish to do. I am happy to have you as a guest in any event. We are distant relations of a sort and I will enjoy your company."

That would be new; no one had ever enjoyed Viola's company before. "Your Grace, I would be happy to do anything I can for the sake of our mutual relatives. But I don't—I am not... I am not fascinating and beautiful like Miss Díaz, and I'm afraid my experience of society has been filtered through my mother, who is... also not in demand at social events."

"Ah, fascinating and beautiful, thank you!" Virginia was delighted. "I much prefer that to merely odd."

Selene did not waver. "Your mother has given you exactly what I need, Lady Viola. I understand that you know who everyone is in London society, that you have a thorough knowledge of Debrett's guide to the peerage, and further that your mother absolutely delights in sharing gossip with you even when you don't want to hear it."

"That is all true." Viola picked up a beheaded English daisy. Stemless, it was useless, but she would keep it. It was a lovely color.

"It will be a perfect mix for me with Miss Díaz, who has been widely talked about, but not seen."

Virginia saluted with the pink pouf of petals in her hand, though Selene couldn't see it. "I will be the distraction."

"Just so. If people are talking about Miss Díaz, they cannot be talking about me. And while they are not talking about me, I can learn a great deal more about *them*, through you."

"You had better call me Virginia, if I am to be your designated distraction," Virginia said, tucking one of the blooms into her hair, where it looked stunning.

Viola didn't think it fair that someone so beautiful was also so easy to like.

Selene clearly wasn't bothered by Miss Díaz' beauty, but why would she be? She couldn't see it. And she was quite pretty enough herself.

The Duchess said, "I would be honored, Virginia, and delighted for you to call me Selene. If I am to chaperone you two to London's finest parties, I am sure you shouldn't call me that; but I wish you would. And Lady Viola, I hope you, too, will be a friend." The Duchess' hands paused among the flowers. "I need friends more than anything."

A little uncomfortable with actual emotion, Viola looked around. "I assume you *want* us to be meeting in a gazebo, with no servants around, and any that approach can easily be seen?" She squinted. "Except for that footman who doesn't look much like a footman and who is staying ten paces away even though that is a foolish place for him to stand and do nothing."

Selene's eyes crinkled at the corners. "As astute as I was told, Lady Viola. Ours is an outlying territory, but it is secure. This had better be where we hold war councils, at least unless it rains."

"You might as well call me Viola too, if only out here. If it will not be too confusing to have two confidantes whose names begin and end the same."

Selene laughed. "I suppose I would have chosen differently, if that were a great concern."

Viola was not used to friends or confidantes. She had spent the better part of the year staying with a married friend in the far north, and that had been its own special kind of torture, only pleasant in comparison with life under the same roof as her mother. Being on first-name terms with a duchess was novel, and being on first-name terms with a renowned mystery lady was even more so.

Virginia shaded her eyes with her hand and looked out across the lawns. "Out past the footman, there is quite a procession coming—a lady wheeled in a chair by two footmen, and a small boy with his nurse."

* * *

SELENE HADN'T REALIZED that her day could get better, till it did.

It was a curious sensation, being so vehemently in love with the little boy. Just knowing he was on his way made her so glad that she couldn't avoid showing it.

It had given her a great deal that was new to think about, on the topic of love.

Plus she had to brace herself for more jam stains.

"Just what the day requires to make it perfect. Ladies, I do not want to rush you, so let us enjoy this mild weather with Lady Redbeck and Lord Thomas. But after luncheon, we must apply ourselves. I am in dire need of a serious lady's maid."

* * *

THE SOUND OF NICHOLAS' voice in the dining room made Selene stop short in the corridor outside.

She distinctly heard the Duke say, "My lord, this is unbecoming to both of us."

"I cannot even pretend interest in your new idea of what is *becoming* to this family." It was Edward, and he was practically *hissing* with anger, and Selene's stomach sank. Apparently they were having this discussion in the luncheon room, in full view of guests.

His Grace was silent; Edward went on. "I suppose it is becoming for you to show all of Britain your new-found ability to think with your—"

"*Sir.*"

Selene's skin crawled at being described this way, among people she barely knew. What *ailed* Edward? But she was a de Gauer—and more, she was the Duchess of this house. She wouldn't be kept out of the dining room. Time for a definitive entrance.

"Good morning, all. I trust everyone is in good health today?" She put out her walking stick for the nearest footman to take, which he did as he handed her to her chair.

"Good morning, Your Grace," Nicholas said most properly as she was seated. "I believe everyone is quite well, except for my son, who was just leaving."

"I wasn't—"

"Oh, I think you were," Nicholas said almost off-handedly.

"If you think I will be silent while you replace my mother with this... Why you couldn't keep your by-blows somewhere else like every other peer does is beyond me. I suppose you will have the King annul your first marriage in favor of whatever comes out of this—"

"Lord Fettanby, it is past time for you to retire."

"I will retire to the dowager residence. I'll be out of your hair."

"I would prefer that you do not."

Both father and son seemed uncomfortable at that—Nicholas sounding as if that simple statement was dragged out of him and Edward apparently frozen to the spot by it.

Then Edward, perhaps unwilling to be stared at any longer—for undoubtedly every guest was now sitting at the table with their mouths wide open—left without another word.

How this would be handled by the guests' gossip, Selene knew, depended on what was said next.

Quite blandly, she said, "His lordship is not happy."

And just as blandly, Nicholas answered from the other end of the table, "Apparently not."

"How is the seed cake this morning?"

"Good enough." She took his silence for very dedicated chewing, as if to investigate her question thoroughly. "The quince jelly is quite good."

As appalling as the situation was, it felt good to support her sad and lonely duke. To be on his side.

And it felt good that he seemed to be on hers.

Perhaps they could figure out how to be on Edward's side together.

"I'll have the quince jelly on my seed cake too. And a boiled egg." As the footman moved to gather Selene's plate, she vehemently hoped that that would be the end of that.

* * *

IT WAS NOT the end of that.

"I am not accustomed to Englishmen showing any passion. I was taken aback."

Virginia paused just to turn to Mrs. Wilkes' latest candidate. She asked the girl, "Have you ever burned hair while curling it?"

The young girl wrinkled her nose in thought. "Hasn't everyone, miss?"

"It can be difficult, can't it? Thank you," Virginia said immediately but kindly. "Tell Mrs. Wilkes to send up someone with a little more experience with hairdressing, would you please?"

The girl curtsied and left.

"That one seemed a little annoyed. I cannot blame her." But then Virginia returned again to her primary topic. "His face was so red! I thought he was going to attempt to strike his father right there at the table!" She sounded half-admiring.

"Oh no." Selene's dismay was obvious. "I had no idea he felt so violently. I... knew he wasn't happy about the marriage, but..."

"Being unhappy about his father's remarriage is one thing. Announcing it over luncheon is quite another." Viola's distaste for the scene seemed to equal Virginia's fascination.

"He might as well have taken out an advertisement in the London papers," Virginia agreed. "His father seems so... perhaps quiet is the word? So much the opposite of his son."

"Ladies, we have too many targets and a limited number of arrows.

For now, I need someone who can dress me to appear old enough to be a duchess. I must look like I can hold my own with others in the Duke of Talbourne's circle."

"It is *never* the goal to look old." Virginia was firm on that one. "You must be pretty, charming, but also faithful, yes?"

"Don't *ask* it. Yes, of course faithful!"

"Don't snap! We have only recently met, after all. Many women who are safely married cannot wait to get the bit in their teeth and run, as we say in the stables."

"Don't say it *outside* the stables. I am not a runner."

"No, of course not," and Virginia's voice was soft.

Wonderful. "I am sure you are not *pitying* me, Virginia. I pitied myself quite enough, dressed as I was at my wedding ball. We must fix the impression I left on London, ladies, and immediately."

Another lady's maid was announced.

Virginia didn't even let the maid finish her curtsey before she asked, "Have you seen the latest number of *La Belle Assemblée*?"

That made Viola finally pipe up. "Let us not be absurd; what maid purchases Bell's magazine?"

"Which is why I only asked if she had seen it."

Selene interjected. "It's quite all right, it's just a few questions. Might you have followed the hairstyles or the fashions for ladies this season?"

The maid answered promptly. "Why would I, Your Grace?"

Selene just nodded. "And quite right. Thank you for all you do here. Would you ask Mrs. Wilkes to send up another option?"

"Of course, madame."

"None of them have any idea what you need." Virginia found that far more disconcerting than Edward's luncheon fit.

"I expected that. Mrs. Wilkes, however, doesn't seem to realize that I can do this until she runs out of unsuitable options and long after. I *will* have a good lady's maid. And I will definitely need your advice on dressing, both of you."

"We will be happy to help!"

Selene had to smile at Virginia's excitement, possibly at the idea of unlimited choices in fashion.

Viola was far less gleeful. "I have been away from London for the year. I am not sure I would trust Miss Díaz's choices without… perhaps comparing them to what ladies are wearing at a few events early in the season."

"Pardon me!" Virginia huffed.

Viola marched on, undeterred. "And we should take *La Belle Assemblée* ourselves and as many of the other similar papers as we can get. But your appearance, Your Grace, should reflect how you want to be remembered. What is the impression London should have of you?"

"Lady Viola, just as I said, you have already justified Cass' faith in you, and now mine. That is the question, indeed." London had a passion for appearances. Now that she had help, she had the tools to devise the right appearance—but not yet the answer of what *was* the right appearance. Who was the Duchess of Talbourne?

"Not a *runner*." Virginia was now lounging in her chair.

"No." That idea did *not* suit her.

"No, not a runner," Viola agreed. "And are you… excuse me, are you… in an interesting condition?"

What an oddly painful question. So many people seemed to be assuming that she was; it was peculiarly unpleasant to have all those people *talking* about her that way, assuming all sorts of things when Selene wasn't sure of any of them. While she didn't want to die a virgin, she had no credible information about the alternative. Difficult all around.

Virginia and Viola were wonderful company but Selene doubted either had any more information than she did. And her mother was steadfastly unforthcoming on the most important topics.

It didn't matter. Selene would figure it out herself.

"I am not in an interesting condition," she assured Viola quietly.

"And you are, I think someone said you are twenty-four years of age? Certainly not young. Miss Díaz is right, it would be disastrous to appear old."

"I am fourteen years younger than His Grace!"

Viola sounded bored by that. "Not such a great difference in a marriage in the *ton*, especially not a second marriage. No, you mustn't be girlish but you mustn't seem experienced either. What do you like to do?"

The first thought that popped into Selene's mind was *talk to Nicholas*. But she wouldn't say that. "Play games. Books of history. Meet new people, always."

"Really? I find new people a torture," Viola said matter-of-factly. "Can you do anything else? I assume not archery or sports of that sort. But needlework? Sing? Play any sort of instrument?"

"I can sing, yes, and I don't do fancy needlework but I can knit."

"Knit? Surely that won't do!" Now Virginia sounded appalled. "Knitting is for grandmothers and you just said she mustn't seem old!"

"Knitting is something many women do at home. Knitting will do well. We are about to start a fashion for knitting, Your Grace." Viola sounded serenely certain.

The footman announced another maid.

This time Virginia barely let her get in the door. "We just wanted to ask: have you ever had responsibility for jewels before?"

"Why no, miss!"

"Quite all right. Would you let Mrs. Wilkes know we have need of another maid?"

Clearly quite confused, the maid gamely responded only, "Yes, of course, ma'am."

Selene just nodded as the door closed behind her. "We can do this all day."

SKIRMISHES AT NIGHT

*I*t was a peculiar sensation for Nicholas when he won the second game of nim, and an unpleasant one.

Because he was certain Selene had let him.

He was not a man who needed to chase in order to catch, nor was he the sort to be threatened when someone else excelled. He was quite aware of his shortcomings, which was why he could honestly say when someone else had gone around them to give him an undeserved win.

"Madame," and his voice dropped low, "I trust you do not put me in the category of men so weak they cannot lose a fair game to a woman."

"My apologies, sir. Stricken from the record. Shall we begin again?"

"I doubt it will help."

Selene was gathering up the stones, one by one, and dropping them back in their dish. "If you prefer," she said slowly, "you might entertain me with stories of your progress concerning your Parliament plans."

He almost sighed. There was a gambit he'd been expecting. And he didn't want to stay silent. Why should he? This was his wife; more important, it was *Selene*. Talking with her had been a keen pleasure long before they'd married, and he needn't give it up.

But he wasn't sure what to say. "In truth, madame, the men I must convince bore me, and I am running out of time."

She nodded.

Then, just as suddenly, he did *not* want to talk about it. Aside from his old ally Gravenshire, few were interested in the simple proposition of letting a man give them expertise they desperately needed. He was sure Lord Callendar might be willing to lend a hand... but he didn't trust Lord Callendar, who spent far too much time entertaining his wife with a thoughtful look in his eye.

"In fact, I'd rather play nim."

"Are you getting a feel for the game, do you think?"

He wasn't. "You take the first turn."

His entire court had no one in it who was able to strategize at nim, a fact Nicholas displayed quite clearly by losing two more games.

"There is a trick to it."

"No sir," Selene said instantly, "there are rules. There is strategy."

"Where does one learn it? Because I confess it can't be learned in Talbourne House."

Her mouth opened with astonishment. "You *did* try to improve your game!"

"To no avail, obviously."

But Nicholas couldn't feel bad. It had shifted something inside him, having something to think about during the day other than whatever was going wrong in his plans for Parliament. They were unwilling to allow Hastings to testify, and he would *not* give up.

It had been a pleasure to be able to rest and spend some moments thinking, not just of Selene, but of their game.

He'd had a tiny thought, somewhere deep inside him, that she would stop captivating him once she was well and truly his. It had been wrong. "You obviously know something I do not."

"Many things," she said with that crinkle to her eyes that made him smile too. "For instance, I know what we wagered."

Please, let it be something that involved him touching her. "By all means. What must I give you?"

"It is what you must take. Come," she said a little more loudly, and a footman came in.

With a dog.

With an enormous, brown-and-white, blunt-headed dog.

Nicholas froze as if confronted with a weapon.

"Come now," Selene said when he continued to be silent, "you lost fair and square, and you must take her."

"Take her?"

"Are you quite well, sir?" Selene half-rose. He sounded so hoarse, and not at all like himself—except that one other time he had sounded as though his voice had escaped from deep inside him.

"…Yes."

Nicholas couldn't think of what else to say. The dog sat staring up at him with its sappy grin, tongue lolling about, its tail sweeping a slow arc across the floor. It was a huge, friendly… dog.

A dog.

"I cannot take a dog, madame."

"Of course you can."

"I do not have time to care for a dog."

Selene was not yielding. "All the care she needs will be your attention and a little of your company."

"Literally anyone else in this house can spend their time with that dog as I am unlikely to do it."

Selene had bent forward a little to rub the dog behind its ear. The dog approved. Nicholas could tell from its doggy expression.

She also seemed to agree. "Of course, Your Grace! Jonathan, for instance, would do very well. He told me he loves dogs."

"Not Jonathan. He has other duties."

"So Jonathan is following me around for a reason, then?"

Nicholas fell silent. It was a more serious flanking maneuver than any game, getting him to admit that. "You did that on purpose."

"It does seem likely, Your Grace."

Nicholas thought it was time to put his foot down. "I will not be taking this dog."

"I would like to make two points, sir," purred Selene, leaning toward him and resting a hand on the dog's head again. "One is that though I have been lenient, wagers are wagers, and you would not wish to be known as a man who does not honor his wagers."

"Blackmail," said Nicholas.

"If you like. The other point is that apparently I must have Jonathan follow me around whatever I do. If I must accept a short leash held by a footman, you must accept the dog."

* * *

THIS GAMBLE NEEDED to pay well, thought Selene, concentrating on staying calm. She had already made the effort of asking Mr. Lyall to locate a suitable dog, and it had been an effort; she found Mr. Lyall, with his gravelly voice, somehow more intimidating than Nicholas.

She was making an enormous guess, based on memories of her father's friends, and on what little she knew of Thomas. She was gambling that what might appeal to the littler gentleman, might appeal to the bigger one too. She could spend a lifetime deciphering how father and son were the same, or different. But something told her that Thomas might adore the friendly company of an agreeable dog, and that his father might be the same.

Dogs didn't talk. That ought to suit Nicholas.

Something about Nicholas' reaction bothered her. It was far more vehement than she'd expected, especially given that Nicholas simply wasn't vehement. She ought to have guessed that he had it in him, given what she knew of Thomas. But no matter why the dog affected him so, she hoped Nicholas would accept it. The dog would be an important ally, she was sure, in introducing a little more fun in Nicholas' life.

Plus the dog would be someone who didn't beat Nicholas at games.

* * *

DISCOVERING desire had been hard on Nicholas. His life had always been tightly bounded, and fitting in new feelings had caused him no small discomfort. By bringing Selene here, he had hoped to fence in those feelings, at the very least keep them from intruding in his day.

Now when he looked at Selene, he felt not just desire but a host of other complicated things that threatened to spill out, not just into his day but into his life. What was she doing to him?

She'd made an enticing weapon out of a dog.

And gotten information out of him doing it.

Well, if he didn't win fair and square, he'd best be good at losing.

"Has it eaten?" Nicholas mumbled ungraciously.

"As it so happens, Jonathan truly does admire dogs, and he has made some effort with this one; I believe she has just come in from dining with him. I did not want to bother Mr. Lyall about it."

"Or Mrs. Wilkes?" He'd heard some rumor that something was going on between the new duchess and the housekeeper but was ignoring it. Lyall would tell him whatever he needed to know.

She was quite calm about that. "Mrs. Wilkes has been very busy finding me a new lady's maid."

Nicholas would bet heavy money that if he asked Mrs. Wilkes what she'd been doing, she would describe it differently.

Selene shrugged a shoulder. "I am sure she will find me someone to help before the Duke of Gravenshire's evening."

"I'm sure she will."

Nicholas just kept staring at the dog. It—she?—had expressive eyes that were watching his every move—appropriate, he thought, for a Talbourne dog.

Selene asked, "What will you name it?"

"Doesn't it have a name? From whoever whelped it?"

"It's your dog now. You have to find its name."

There was an absurd thought. He was a duke of the realm. He would simply give it a name.

But looking into the dog's eyes, Nicholas thought—no, he felt—that he would wait and find out what name would suit the dog.

"Very well, madame."

"Aren't you going to say thank you?"

"For a dog I didn't want?"

Selene looked very pleased with herself as she gathered up the nim playing stones. She'd noticed that Nicholas had used the past tense.

Nicholas picked up one of the stones closer to him, took her hand and turned it over to give her the nim stone. His finger slowly traced a circle around the stone in her palm.

He wanted so badly to kiss her there.

To kiss her everywhere, he realized.

Selene just sat with her lips slightly parted, surprised, apparently, by his touch.

"Tomorrow we're playing chess," he grumbled.

SLEEP PROVED DIFFICULT TO ACHIEVE, as the prickling burn of his touch stayed in Selene's palm well into the night hours.

She closed her hand around the feeling; she didn't want to push it away, she wanted to keep it.

Two Talbourne men had taken her hand in the last two days, and both gave her much to think about.

It was so uncomplicated, adoring that little boy.

And so complicated, feeling so many different things for his father.

Nicholas' touch was so tempting. Intriguing. *Thrilling.* She wanted more. Wouldn't it just be the same but more, if they made love? Wouldn't it just be like that, but all over?

Would it be that thrilling even if they weren't in love?

It wasn't the sort of thing Selene could know before she tried. And if she did, and then Nicholas put her aside, would she really have lost something?

Her life had stopped, she realized now, when her father had died.

She hadn't just become poor; she'd become nearly hopeless. Nicholas had given her so much, including, well, all kinds of possibilities.

To be the duchess of Talbourne, to be part of his family—both the glad and the sad parts of that, she wouldn't give them up. To be his wife—

She wished he would explain what *he* thought of that. But she was afraid that if he did, she would find out how much less she was to him than she wanted to be.

Her father, she realized, had never said out loud what it meant to him to have Lady Redbeck as his wife. They had simply *been*, two halves of the same whole, and she now realized that there must have been mountains more to that relationship that she had never known. Being inside a couple was very different from observing one.

Her mother wasn't going to start being forthcoming now.

She ought to ask her cousin Cass, but Cass was a very different person. She had always taken risks with her reputation that Selene would never have taken when she'd had anything to lose. Cass was still paying for that. Selene wasn't sure how that translated to what happened in the bedroom, but she still didn't think Cass' advice was what she wanted.

Or maybe she just didn't want to have to ask.

Maybe she still thought she could figure this out on her own.

Maybe she would continue to avoid it in favor of swaying London's opinion, which seemed easier.

HER KEY WEAPON in the plan to reach more of London arrived the next morning.

"Mr. Hastings, Your Grace."

Selene turned toward the door. "Mr. Hastings! I had expected you sooner. Miss Díaz de la Peña, Lady Viola Evelyn, you must know Mr. Anthony Hastings."

Viola looked the newcomer up and down before resuming her

drawing. "I believe my brother Oliver has mentioned you, Mr. Hastings." She managed to convey that the mention hadn't been flattering.

Virginia, however, stood to greet him. "I believe we have met, Mr. Hastings, have we not? And you have cut your hair."

* * *

ANTHONY'S EYES held hers for a moment, as the last time he had seen her, he had not been introduced as a member of society. "You are kind. And yes I have, Miss Díaz. My sister insisted I look more fashionable."

"It becomes you very well." She gestured toward the settee where Selene sat.

"Forgive me, but… Your Grace? If I may have a private word with you?"

Virginia was stopped in mid-gesture. As she and Viola left, they could hear Viola saying, "I assure you. My brother says he is always like that."

Anthony paid it no mind whatsoever. "Madame, I came to extend my apologies. I will not be able to help you."

"I have need of someone to help me learn more about the men in Parliament my husband is attempting to sway. And the people who visit here."

"I would love to be able to help you, but… I must not return to Talbourne House."

Selene stopped.

After several long moments she slowly asked, "When you came here today, is that what you intended to tell me?"

"Your Grace is quite astute enough without my help."

"Not at all. If all you can say is that you cannot help me, you might have sent a note."

"Not privately, as madame would not be able to read it."

"It doubt it would be private if I could. Mr. Hastings. I really need you to tell me what has transpired."

That he would not. "Only that I will not be able to return to Talbourne House. I am so sorry."

Selene clenched her teeth and did not let the question go. "So then whatever happened, has happened inside Talbourne House since you arrived."

"Truly, madame, it is like speaking to the Delphic oracle. I beg you not to press further." After a moment's pause he added, "I believe I may be able to send someone to help you, but I cannot guarantee even that."

"So you cannot enter Talbourne House but someone else can, even if they know you."

"Madame," said Anthony, taking her hand and brushing her knuckles with his lips as he stood, "you are an inspiration. Truly, I've only met one other woman who equals your wisdom."

"Really. I would like to meet her."

"Both easy and difficult to arrange. She is my sister's housekeeper."

JUST MINUTES after Anthony had left, Virginia and Viola both returned. "Is he gone already?"

"So abrupt, that's what Oliver said," Viola confirmed.

"Ladies," Selene said slowly as she rubbed a thumb over her fingers, "I believe I've lost a chess piece that I very much needed."

AND IT HAD to be to Nicholas.

She had not agreed to this game.

This, thought the new Duchess of Talbourne, did not make her trust the Duke of Talbourne more.

"ARE YOU HAUNTED BY GHOSTS, Lord Callendar? Or bill collectors? Or perhaps spurned ladies." Lady Hadleigh was a bit peeved at the way Jonas kept peering around her at the door.

Other people's crystal and silver rang softly all around them as the cold late supper was served, but Lady Hadleigh would not abandon their *vingt-et-un* game.

"Wondering if our host would join us." He hoped she wouldn't pry further.

She pried. "He never used to join before he married and he certainly has not since. You cannot imagine that a man newly married cares for card games."

Jonas tapped his cards; she dealt him another. "The marriage does not seem to be a love match."

She scoffed. "It doesn't have to be a love match."

"Disappointed, Lady Hadleigh?"

She waved the venison pastry she was munching in between hands of cards. She had spilled claret on her jacquard skirt and there was a slice of fruit cake awaiting her attention. "Do I look disappointed, sir?"

"A woman old enough to have known disappointment before might be able to cover it up quite well with a bit of claret and cards."

"What an odd combination of compliment and insult." She nodded toward his cards. "You have nineteen, you know."

"Do I?"

She turned over another card for herself. "And I have twenty-one."

"Dreadful. Did we have a wager?"

"You can answer a question for me and save your money."

"Done," and he tossed his poor cards her way. "Will you be spreading my answer through the gossip mills?"

"Possibly. After a fashion. I don't let sharp points get back to anyone they might hurt."

"What is it you wished to ask, Lady Hadleigh?"

"Is it all the game of politics for you? Are you chasing the Duke's support? Or... is there a lady you are chasing?" She slid the cards back into the pile one-handed. "The lady Duchess?"

"I met the Duchess right here. I attended her wedding."

She winked at him and kindly ignored that he hadn't answered her question. "Oh, then it's me you are pining for."

She was older than Talbourne by a few years, at least fifteen years older than Jonas himself. Nonetheless, it occurred to him that he could do much worse. "I am not that wise, alas."

"Alas for *me*, you mean."

Jonas contemplated her smooth, rose-flushed cheek as she finally set the pastry down on its porcelain plate and wiped her fingers. The few strands of silver in her elegantly arranged braids did not detract from her still-attractive face; neither did her tendency to wave her pastry about detract from her slightly generous figure. "You look like a woman who knows how to enjoy herself, madame. Why are you here instead of finding a second husband of your own? Are *you* pining for someone? The Duke, perhaps?"

She did not look up. "You do not get to ask a question, sir. You did not win the game."

There was something about the set of her mouth that emphasized how closed it was. He let her be.

Everyone in Talbourne House kept themselves to themselves and no one was quite getting what they wanted, it seemed.

Jonas had to admit to himself that he wasn't getting what he wanted, either.

He almost regretted that Burden hadn't been back in a while. Jonas would have enjoyed tossing him out. He liked new pleasures, not to revisit pleasures he'd already sampled.

Truly Jonas ought to be spending his evenings in some new place, enjoying being flattered on account of his uncle's importance and endearing himself to hostesses and hosts alike.

It wasn't surprising that the Duke and Duchess of Talbourne were not attending the card games.

The question was why Jonas was.

His mouth thinned as he pressed it shut. He would not admit how much he hoped he would see... her again. Miss de Gauer. The now Duchess. Selene.

No, he would not admit that.

Not even to himself.

* * *

THE DUCHESS' skirts fluttered as she moved through the colonnade that lined the east courtyard of Talbourne House.

Edward's impulse was carried out before he'd even recognized it. "Do you need help, Your Grace?"

Selene turned and paused, the line of her shoulder gleaming in the candlelight that escaped through the windows. "Lord Fettanby. You asked me that before. Is it habitual, asking wanderers if they need your assistance?"

Edward didn't answer. His father got by on never answering questions; Edward would just follow suit.

Selene just sighed. "Not answering a blind person renders you invisible, sir. Are you trying to frighten me? If you are, I should warn you that I seem to have a bodyguard; he can't have gone far. If you are not, please speak."

That made Edward ashamed, and rather than feel ashamed he retreated into another wave of the cold rage that had gripped him since a footman—*a footman*—had informed him that his presence was requested at his father's wedding the next day.

"Not trying to frighten you, madame." He had no practice at being the sort of cold stick that his father was. Perhaps he should start.

"I was grateful for your assistance. I wish you had introduced yourself."

"Why?" Edward knew he sounded sulky but he couldn't help it because he *was*.

"Perhaps so that I might meet you for your own sake, though I would also have gladly met you just to know the Duke's son."

"Your marriage was only a day away, madame, you must have had a great deal more on your mind than meeting me."

She started to say something, then stopped. "As it happens I did," she said, apparently instead of whatever she'd decided not to say.

"Never fear, I don't expect more of you. You must be busy being his new…"

Selene just waited for him to finish his thought, and he couldn't do it. Not to her face.

She seemed awfully cool about obviously having been his paramour before arriving at Talbourne House. No one married a woman they'd met the day before, and men did not know ladies that were not out in society unless it was in illicit circumstances.

It burned Edward's gut that his father had apparently had a mistress for some time and just never saw fit to mention it. Not that one necessarily discussed such things with sons, but still. Edward was full grown even if he was not yet of age, and he had thought that his father at least liked him a little.

It was hard to tell, with his father, but he'd been pretty sure.

He desperately hoped that the affair had started after his mother's death.

"Lord Fettanby," Selene finally said as the silence stretched between them, "I think it pains your father that his marriage has made you so unhappy."

And even though he knew it was churlish, Edward's resentment slipped out of his control. "I doubt the two of you spend much of your newlywed time discussing me."

"I do intend to see His Grace this evening and you are right, I hadn't planned to discuss you." Her shoulders straightened. "If you would like to apologize to him, I think you should, but that is between the two of you."

"If he can find the time, what with him spending so much time being *married*."

Something seemed to amuse her. Why did she seem so much older than he was? There was not such a great difference in their ages, and that rankled too. The feeling she gave him that she knew so much more than he did rubbed Edward the wrong way.

"As it happens, tonight he's going to spend time playing chess. And I am not feeling merciful. So we will see how it goes. Good night, Lord Fettanby."

* * *

IT DID NOT GO WELL.

"I offer you a draw, sir."

Nicholas took a long moment to study the board. It had belonged to his grandfather. It was old, and worn, the pieces a little smudged from long use. He'd learned to play chess on it thirty years ago.

At least, he'd thought he had.

"Are you offering the draw because the conclusion is so inescapable, or simply because you are bored?"

"Are the two things terribly different?"

She wasn't smiling now. This was not his playful Selene. Her mouth turned down at its corners, her fingers drummed on the table; she was flaying him alive, yet not enjoying it.

She might be right. The game did not look so hopeless to him, but it was already clear she was a far better player. Even with him moving the pieces for her and her need to keep the board in her mind, she had played him to a rook ending that he knew would not go well, and they'd already agreed to a draw for that game. This one was supposed to go better.

It was late, they were tired, and the offer of a draw was nearly an insult.

His goal had never been to win. He wanted to spend time with her. "Is there nothing that would make it more appealing to play the game through?"

"Such as? Are you thinking of pearls, or rubies? Because I am thinking of a friend who had offered to help me, and today he ran away as if you had set fire to his coat."

"Ah. The Hastings fellow." He'd be damned if he elaborated.

She didn't need him to. "He would have been able to carry messages for me, and much more."

"Any footman would—"

"Nicholas, I accepted your help for my mother's sake. I didn't ask for help for myself. I can conduct my own affairs, unless you are now going to block me at every turn."

"You can ask for anything for yourself that you like! Why don't you have tea?"

She wouldn't be dissuaded by tea. With a ramrod straight back and her set mouth she looked even more than usual like a queen from days of old. One of the cranky ones. "If you won't help me, don't hinder me."

"I did nothing! If the man abandoned you, he abandoned you."

"I get the feeling Mr. Hastings has never abandoned a promise before in his life."

Then he was a weak reed, Nicholas thought to himself. A few questions about his family, his background, and the man had darted for the door. Nicholas would have to look into it a bit more; no one leaped away like that unless he'd hit a tender spot. Not that he had time to worry about that now. He was the wrong sort of Hastings, apparently not related to the Indian governor-general Hastings, and of no use right now to Nicholas.

His wife put a hand out to hover over the board. "Are you accepting the draw?"

"I may have other moves to make!"

"I doubt it."

It was her certainty that flicked him on the raw. He was positive they were no longer talking about chess.

"Are you so desperate to have your hand in the politics of Parliament, madame?"

"Are you so desperate to keep me out of your life? As you did your son, who blames me because he thinks I was your secret paramour? The poor boy probably wonders if it was while his mother was still alive."

"Damn." What had Edward been saying to her? "I apologize for my son's behavior, madame."

"I'm not really speaking of his behavior. I'm speaking of yours." She leaned forward, fast. "Surely you knew enough about me to realize what interests me and what doesn't. Behind that parlor door we talked about everything, dissecting the latest moves on the Continent, the Regent's benefits and drawbacks, even the price of sugar."

In truth, what he remembered was her voice and her laugh, and that burned, both that she clearly had not been as concerned with him as with the conversation, and that she undoubtedly knew more than he about what he was trying to do. "If I don't want to discuss politics with my wife, that can't be a reason to *blame* me."

Selene leaned back. "If you don't trust your wife with the closest parts of your life..."

Why did she never stop pressing? He didn't want to share *trust*. He wanted...

"If you want a draw, madame," said Nicholas stiffly, "I will accept your kind offer."

* * *

It was unfortunate in many ways that Nicholas took his losses at chess far less well than anyone expected, including, apparently, Nicholas.

He took it so badly that even the next day, luncheon was grim. Usually the gentlemen, including His Grace, ate something with the ladies for luncheon at Talbourne House, but Edward had not returned to the formal dining room since storming out, and Talbourne's perpetual guests were talking.

Despite offers of truce with Lady Fawcett and Lady Hadleigh, Selene had made no headway in removing some of the other women who had stayed just to moon over Nicholas, apparently, even though he was now married. She hadn't even resolved the fish situation.

She was finding it hard to focus on fish and extra widows when she was still so angry at her new husband. Forget seducing him. Forget forging a lifetime with him. Right now she wanted nothing to do with him.

Sir Malcolm was already drunk, and Selene was worried for him but also oddly grateful, because it was drawing attention from the way Nicholas was slipping bites of something—probably the dastardly fish —under the tablecloth to his new dog. Perhaps he thought she wouldn't notice, but the dog's tail thumped excitedly each time he fed it and she could clearly hear it.

Selene was amazed that *anyone* could be that excited about that fish.

It was maddening that Nicholas both did not want to discuss it, and clearly was still affected by it. She half expected him to announce that he was Lord Nicholas Hayden and he had no intention of eating his luncheon.

At least she didn't think anyone else noticed his behavior.

And then the Duke calmly announced that he must leave, while his guests were just beginning to eat.

Well. This was a new form of sulking for grown men.

"Please do stay," Selene told the table at large as the conversation became a din of confused people preparing to leave as well, since a meal usually ended when His Grace had left the table. "I will return directly." Selene practically leaped out of her seat to follow her husband out.

Following the wall as quickly as possible, Selene nearly crashed herself into the doorjamb. Nicholas maneuvered her around it so that they were out in the hallway.

"Thank you," she said very quietly. "If you were going to be so disagreeable from losing at chess, you ought to have warned me before we played."

"You said you weren't very good at chess."

"And I am not! In a London tournament of players I doubt I would rank at all."

"So I am simply very bad at chess."

"Sir, that would appear to be the simplest answer."

Nicholas started down the hall; Selene started after him.

He stopped and took one of her hands and placed it on his arm. But it still felt like he was miles away.

When he started walking again, it was still with a long stride; Selene stretched her legs to keep up with him. The dog clicked along behind.

"Should I have let you win?"

He paused.

"No." He thought a little more. "I don't want a win as a gift. I did expect the contest to be not so hard-fought."

Selene felt it best to whisper. "You are *very bad* at chess."

"No one has ever brought my attention to that before."

"I *should* have been a more graceful winner. I was angry."

"Believe me, I could tell."

"I am being polite, Your Grace. You can also be an extremely bad loser."

"I'll get better. I'm getting quite a bit of practice."

Agghh. He *knew* she was angry about more than the chess game—so why did he not bend at all? He wouldn't tell her what he had done to Anthony. He hadn't warned his sons about his wedding. Or *her* for that matter. It was a habit that was going to get very old, very fast. "Are you going to tell me what you did to Mr. Hastings? I *needed* him."

"Talbourne House has dozens of people waiting to assist you, madame."

"Do not provoke me. I do not yet even have a lady's maid to dress me for the Duke's affair tonight."

"And yet you are dressed, madame."

"Do not think it is easy."

"Do not think I can help you. ...Though I suppose I could send up the dog."

"Your Grace." She pulled a little on his arm to make him stop. She *had* to rescue her position in London society, *especially* if she could not rescue her position with him. He must feel the same.

Very quietly she said, "You are just as interested as I that I make a good impression on society at my first public affair."

He looked down at her upturned face. "Madame, I am not."

* * *

HE WAS GOING to keep her, no matter what his damned son said, no matter what anyone in Britain said, so he didn't give a fig for the opinion of the *ton*. He was far more worried by Mr. Lyall's failure to find any information on who might have pushed her on the stairs, or where that counterfeit angry maid had gone—because Nicholas had no doubt that she had been counterfeit.

The Hastings man was no use, and the silly men Nicholas was trying to convince refused to be in the same room together. He had problems.

His son Edward worried him a little, but that would have to sort itself out. If Nicholas didn't have to control something, he tended to leave it to its own devices, and that category definitely included his heir. It nauseated him to think that he would ever control his son the way he himself had been controlled.

"Wear what you like. You will look lovely in anything."

* * *

SELENE WANTED to shake her head a little. Had that been a compliment? "...Thank you, sir."

"You liked the pearls, did you not?"

"I did, and I thank you for them again."

"...I've just realized, your mother likely has no jewels left from the dissolution of her estate, am I correct?"

"Very much correct. That man could not take them from her but we had to sell them, of course."

"Do you remember what she had?"

"Sir, it is a matter of no import, you—"

"Do you remember?"

Selene did not feel generous towards Nicholas' impulses right now, but he obviously wouldn't be swayed from the question. "I remember; she had a turquoise ring, a necklace and bracelet of links of smooth sapphires framed in enamel, a brooch with diamonds around the family coat of arms, and a gold locket with a miniature painted in it of my father."

Nicholas paused for a moment. "I'm sorry she had to sell that miniature."

"Thank you. She was sorry too."

"And why did she not take to the courts to get her just due from your father's heir instead of paupering herself?"

"She couldn't bear to have my father's name in court, she said."

* * *

NICHOLAS REFRAINED from expressing any opinion of the value of keeping up appearances when one was starving. "Did your father commit some crime?"

"Of course not!"

"Of course not. Madame, I have several things I must see to before this evening's entertainment. Your mother will be joining us?"

"Oh yes, I believe she will! The physicians have pronounced her much stronger."

Nicholas nodded and said out loud, "We can take a second carriage for her convenience, in case she wishes to return early. Let us take a few of her nurses as well."

"Sir, I—"

"I would love to help you but I really must be going."

Selene stomped her foot. "No you wouldn't! You wouldn't love to help me, you are enjoying watching me fail at everything I am trying to do in this house!"

Perhaps he was a worse man than he'd thought, because watching Selene stomp her foot with irritation *was* completely enjoyable.

Nicholas leaned close to her. "Madame, did you enjoy my losing so badly at chess?"

Selene bit her lip.

* * *

SHE COULD HEAR NICHOLAS' laughing all the way down the hallway. Well, she had wanted to hear it. She hoped there were servants to bear witness, otherwise no one would ever believe it.

* * *

"WILL IT DO?" Selene addressed the general room. "Do I look like a duchess?"

Being accepted as a duchess by London was looking like the only, and lonely, road for her life.

Virginia made a noise of pleased agreement. "Who needs ladies' maids?"

Her own lady's maid and Lady Viola's set up a chorus of *oh no's*. Virginia held up her hands. "I did not mean to offend, but none of us is versed in the height of fashion."

Martha traveled around the room picking up rejected things. "And I don't have an eye for it, I must admit. I see what people have done but I can't pick it apart and put it together new."

"Never you mind, Martha, you're run ragged just keeping me and my clothes in order. It is taking all of you to make me fit the part. We still need someone with inspiration as well as more hands." Selene quickly steered away from the topic. She suspected Martha had realized what a disaster her wedding ball dress had been, but hoped she hadn't.

"We will see the fashion forefront tonight," Viola said pragmatically, placing a last stitch in the edging that trimmed Selene's waist. "I hope this holds."

"You are so wise, of course, Viola, we will." That thought clearly delighted Selene.

Virginia snapped her fingers. "We ought to write down notes at this affair. Someone bring a pencil."

Selene couldn't tell if Virginia were serious or not. Before she could answer, there was a knock at the door, and Lady Redbeck was announced.

"Madame!" Selene rushed as quickly as she could toward the door, as she now knew its location well. "Will I do? Please tell me all our hard work has achieved something."

"Oh you look lovely, darling. Such a soft green suits you, and so nice for spring. Your rubies from His Grace practically glow."

"Your *modiste* at least does not need to be replaced," Virginia agreed.

"And what have you decided to wear, my dear lady mother?"

"The gray silk again, but it is the jewels! I must show them to you! Did you prompt him? For the Duke has sent me the most beautiful sapphires in a necklace and a bracelet—fine ones, they are. Quite the equal of the ones I—in fact these are more stunning. A blue that reminds me of your father's eyes."

"His eyes must have been quite something." Selene's voice was soft as she held her mother's hands.

She would not cry. She would not. It would ruin her face and they must go.

But Selene did feel, just a little, that she ought to have let Nicholas win a game of chess.

She could not understand him. He had questioned her about her mother's lost jewels in the middle of sulking like a little boy. She was *not* going to be able to know how he felt, about anything.

And she was beginning to worry she was not going to be able to decide how she felt about him either.

She was in this alone.

No, not alone. She had Virginia and Viola and her mother, who added, "And he sent these with a request that I give them to you. Which I thought was odd."

Selene opened the small box. Virginia's gasp told her everything she needed to know as she withdrew the rope of smooth cool pearls from their velvet bed.

"Add them to the rubies. You will look quite regal tonight," Viola told her.

Virginia's nose was so close to the pearls she was probably misting them with her breath. "Oh, they are *magical*. Only emperors have such pearls."

Emperors and one duchess, Selene thought, closing her hand around the tiny orbs.

"That reminds me. We must have someone check the library for a biography of Eleanor of Aquitaine."

AN ALL-OR-NOTHING ATTACK

Selene was not imagining the rustle of heads turning as they were announced. "His Grace the Duke of Talbourne. Her Grace the Duchess of Talbourne. Lady Viola Evelyn. Miss Virginia Díaz de la Peña."

Hopefully she *looked* the part of Talbourne's duchess tonight.

"You might help me a little by telling me whose good side you seek for your upcoming votes," she murmured to Nicholas as they walked. He could give her something, anything. One thing to work for. One thing to know about him.

"Do not concern yourself, madame, there is no need."

The man really had a thousand ways not to answer a question. It was too early in the evening to revisit her annoyance with him, especially when the smell of his cologne made her only want to walk closer to him. Not helpful.

She could hear people making way for them, the Duke and Duchess. Keeping her voice as quiet as his she said, "I am an eligible peacock of a coal bucket, but I would still like to justify your selection of me."

"It had nothing to do with your ability to help me with votes." Before she could ask more questions he wouldn't answer, Nicholas added, "The Duke of Gravenshire is just ahead, with his daughter Lady Donnatella Fairchild. She is our hostess, so if you intend to be gracious, you can start and end with her."

"I don't believe we've met. How old is she?"

"Only a year or two younger than you, madame, so I believe you had disappeared from society's sight by the time of her first season."

"And she has not married?"

"Her mother died some ten, twelve years ago. Left an uncle behind as well; he lives with them. I believe His Grace is happy to have his daughter as mistress of his house, and leave it at that. Not sure she's good at it."

Their hostess immediately confirmed part of his theory, sweeping up to them and fanning herself in something of a fluster.

"Your Grace, you honor our humble home. And Your Grace, I am so very delighted to make your acquaintance. You are all that London has talked of for a week; I am sure it will go on for the fortnight, so I hope it suits you. How lovely you look; you are quite a regal fairy queen for our theme of Spring. I hope it was mentioned in your invitation. My friend Lady Julia Harrell has actually arranged almost everything tonight, I was quite overset. Everyone is exhausted, how can one keep up excitement in a season that began in *November?* At least the Prince won't be here. I do prefer everyone to relax. Do you play cards? No I mean of course you don't, madame, but sir, do you play cards?"

The girl had yet to take a breath.

"No card games for me tonight," Nicholas reassured their hostess. "I am still recovering from a very bad loss at chess."

Selene did think of kicking him.

"Oh! Truly?" Lady Donnatella seemed quite confused. "My father has been so hoping you would attend. You never add your presence to these social occasions."

"Her Grace of course causes me to be a more social animal," Nicholas told her.

Had Selene snorted?

Lady Donnatella was looking at Nicholas with the shrewd eyes of a young woman who could add together His Grace's title and his money and come up with something quite interesting indeed. "Had you come to more social events, Your Grace, you might have married sooner."

"No," Nicholas just said, tucking Selene's hand into the crook of his arm, "I would not have. Good evening, Lady Donnatella."

"Do you like me or not?" Selene murmured as the crowd parted for them.

"Immaterial," said Nicholas, maddeningly.

Selene had never been prone to violence but already the evening seemed to call for it.

"I suppose you are going to leave me now."

Nicholas took a moment. "Likely."

"Well, get on with it then, I have things to do." She knew she sounded peevish and couldn't help it.

"As you wish, madame," and Nicholas nodded for the benefit of those watching as he released her hand and drifted away.

She missed his touch instantly and that was annoying too.

She was letting his mood affect her too much. There were plenty of other things to think about; this was her first ball as a duchess, after her own wedding.

Her first thought was that she should brazenly *ask* him to dance with her. See what happened to his reserve *then*.

Dismissing that thought, too, as foolish, Selene turned her mind to her task—and her companions. "Viola, are people flocking to Miss Díaz?"

* * *

"The men are." Viola tried not to sound disapproving, she truly did.

"Is the gold gown too much?"

Viola tried to catch a glimpse of it through the bodies of the men crowding around Virginia. "If the goal is to attract attention, I believe it is just enough."

"We must decide whom to meet; please do tell me everything you know about who is here. Do you know Lady Donnatella?"

"By reputation only, and you must have already divined what I know. A bit of a silly girl, freakishly tall, rotten good at cards; any one of the three might be reason enough not to be married at her age but I believe her father dotes on her too. And she just told you she did none of the work for her own party."

"She told me that she has a very good friend in Lady Julia Harrell. Let us see what else we can learn, Lady Viola."

* * *

GRAVENSHIRE USUALLY HAD his jaw outthrust in an expression of perpetual determination, beetling eyebrows drawn together.

Right now his whole face had relaxed and the effect was one of unwelcome pity.

"You may just not be cut out for this sort of thing, Talbourne," the man murmured around his glass as he drank. "You can't persuade people you look down on."

"What is there to admire? So wrapped up in their petty squabbles they wouldn't know a horse was nearby till it bit them on the arse."

The uncharacteristic show of feeling from Nicholas just made Gravenshire look graver. "Let's say I agree. You and I make only two votes. It is the nature of votes that one must have many of them on the same side to get one's proposal passed. And we don't. You can't only talk to the party leaders, you have to talk to some of the other men in the Lords. And convince them."

"It cannot possibly be of use to engage in more everlasting conversation."

"Not for you to judge, old man," and Gravenshire gave his crystal goblet to a passing servant. "Unless you are the Prince making everlasting demands, you're among us doing as must be done. And you want to do it. You'll have to wait twenty years for this chance to come around again."

* * *

"YOUR GRACE! WHAT A PLEASURE." For all his senses, Jonas thought. Selene looked like a banked fire with that hair and those rubies, she smelled like spring, and she sounded—well, not that happy to see him.

"Lord Callendar."

"What a fortuitous circumstance. I was just wishing you were here so I could ask you to dance." He was going to get her to agree, too, before that silent staring girl she had with her came back with punch.

"I'm—I will be happy to, if you will escort me to meet Lord Morgame afterwards."

Aha. So the Duchess was chasing votes.

Rather than offer her one outright—he would rather she be the first person to appreciate his company *aside* from what he could do in Parliament—he'd stick with her and see how he might be of service.

Not for nothing, of course.

"A perfect exchange. I believe there is a dance that will just suit us coming up."

* * *

NICHOLAS TRIED to watch those who spoke to him and not to let his eyes follow Selene around the room.

Her bright hair seemed to pulse in the corner of his eye, standing out among clouds of dark, dreary people everywhere.

The ache to touch her was all over him like a second skin.

That damn dog was the first… anything, that Nicholas had felt safe caring about in more than twenty years, and it was doing something to his insides. They weren't feeling much like stone any more.

But if they melted entirely, he would be gone.

He should have given Edward a dog. It wasn't Edward's fault that, because of things that happened long before his son was born, it would never have occurred to him to do it.

Was it too late? It felt too late.

Though he hadn't said it to anyone, in his head, the dog's name was Atlas. Atlas was fine with a silk bed and bones to gnaw. Watching the big animal amble through the palace wherever she pleased, Nicholas realized that he was giving the dog the run of the place much as he had Edward as a child.

It probably wasn't enough for children. But that was how duke's sons were raised. Confined to the nursery or free to roam, and Nicholas had chosen freedom for his son.

When Edward had fallen ill, roaming had stopped for a while. The rolling chair, all the devices Nicholas had acquired for him from Miss Cullen were so that his son could still do whatever he liked, so he would never feel trapped.

Though by Nicholas knew quite well that one couldn't always see a trap.

This party felt like a jail. Like a hall of ghosts. They all kept their distance from him and no one met his eyes.

Did he look down on them? Well, they made it so easy. The way they never looked below the surface of anything, much less other people.

He looked around at all their faces, the noises they made, the glances. He felt as though he were under a glass bell, seeing, but separate, while people swirled all around him. But was he such an odd man out? Were not most people spiky and unsatisfying?

He just needed more time to himself. He needed to absorb this newfound urge to… enjoy… things.

And to play with the damn dog.

Just because he wanted to do it.

Allowing himself to look casually around the crush for Selene, he found her bright head leaning close to another man—Lord Callendar.

Callendar, Callendar, Callendar. What Nicholas wouldn't give for the days when a duke could keep a decent dungeon.

He wasn't competing with Callendar. He was *married* to Selene. *She was his.*

Why did Callendar never seem to be trapped in a thick glass bell? How was he always saying, doing just the right things to set loose her smile?

Nicholas watched their heads lean close together again.

What if Nicholas Hayden, Duke of Talbourne, smashed the glass around him? What if he said something? Or, more suited to him, what if he *did* something?

Just because he wanted to do it?

A voice penetrated the silence around him. "Why, Your Grace, what ails you?"

"What?" Nicholas tore his eyes away from his wife.

Lady Donnatella was staring straight at him, nearly gape-jawed with surprise. Odd to have a woman looking down at him; the girl was truly very tall.

"Pardon me, Lady Donnatella?"

"Sir, you have backed yourself in between two large slabs of carved stone and you are shredding my flowers."

Nicholas looked at his hands. There was an enormous vessel of spring flowers on the stone to his right—he had indeed backed into a good defensible spot—and without noticing, he had apparently been ripping them violently apart for some minutes, judging by the pile of petals.

Nicholas swept the pile of petals into his pocket, as if that had been his intention all along.

"My apologies."

"You don't sound concerned."

He never did.

His eyes strayed over to where Selene was now dancing with that damned young Lord Callendar.

"I've heard a dozen rumors about your wife in the last week," the young lady of the house mused, "but I hadn't heard this one."

"What's that?"

"That you are in love with her."

"Lady Donnatella—"

"Never fear, I'm actually quite good at keeping secrets. Why, Lady Winpole owes me forty pounds from losses at cards and I've never told that to anyone. Except that I've just told you. Oh well."

"My lady—"

"I have heard that your wife has already been your mistress for years, and that you only waited so long to marry her because she is blind. There is a story that she is already carrying your child, and one that she is unable to carry a child, which is also why you hesitated. There is a story that your trifling with her in her youth caused her father to die of shame, and a story that your son is furious at your marriage because he is in love with her himself. I fully expected before this evening was out to hear that she is the natural child of Catherine the Great, and either she helped you convince the Russians to back out of their agreements with Napoleon, or hates you on behalf of her true father, Catherine's secret French lover."

"That last one is quite good. I thought Catherine hated the French. Also, she was nearly sixty when my wife was born, was she not?"

"What I did not expect to learn is that you love her."

"I'm afraid your instincts for drama have led you astray, Lady Donnatella."

"You are not the first man I've seen standing in a corner shredding flowers."

Nicholas looked pointedly over her shoulder. "Speaking of men. Is that someone from your uncle's former military brigade coming to toss me out for my violence to your flowers?"

Lady Donnatella looked over her shoulder at the massive young man making straight for her and scowled. "That walking tree trunk. I will leave you to your flower murder, sir, and advise you that you may yet have time to claim the next dance with your wife. If you don't dawdle."

When she disappeared into the swarms of young ladies, the young man followed her; but Nicholas ignored it.

He took her advice and didn't dawdle.

* * *

"THE NAVY CANNOT TAKE up the whole of Britain's purse. London is exploding and if we do not look to it, it will be chaos soon."

"On the contrary, sir. The wars abroad threaten the very existence of England herself. Or I should say, our united kingdom." Lord Morgame, whom Selene had danced with perhaps sixth or seventh at her wedding ball, was adamant.

Selene was holding her breath waiting for the Duke of Gravenshire's response. Finally, someone was speaking of issues that might touch upon Nicholas' goals. And neither gentleman was accompanied by a lady talking about ribbons. It was truly her heart's desire.

The Gravenshire response was forestalled by... Jonas. "Join me for punch?"

She restrained her sigh. Selene was here to understand the political theater of Britain. Jonas just seemed to want to chat.

"I don't—"

He leaned close. "Please."

"Oh, very well." She couldn't sound pleased when she wasn't.

"Your Grace. Lord Morgame." Jonas was bowing. "You will forgive me if I deprive you of the Duchess for a moment."

"A deprivation indeed." Lord Morgame sounded genuine.

Selene smiled back. "For me as well."

Two steps away, she wished she could secretly hit him with her fan. "I don't want punch."

"Talbourne has already promised Gravenshire his support on improvements for the city over the moneys for the Navy."

Selene was so astonished that she stopped moving.

"Don't stop, people will look. That's part of what you came to find out, isn't it?"

"Lord Callendar, I..." He was offering her something she wanted far more than jewels. And both of them knew it.

"You may yet find a use for me, my lady," Jonas said under his breath. "By the way, Morgame has never been to Talbourne House before he was invited to your wedding. I think Gravenshire and Talbourne both are recruiting him for whatever Talbourne is planning, which apparently all the party leaders hate."

"On what?" She held his arm tightly.

"That I have yet to learn. Ah, here are your spies, perhaps they can tell you."

"We are not spies." Viola sounded incensed.

Virginia was downright disdainful. "We are not *your* spies. If you will excuse us, sir."

"Of course. I promised Her Grace more punch."

It felt peculiar to be so sorry that he was gone.

"Why so mean to Lord Callendar, Virginia?"

Their heads were close and they kept their voices down, but Virginia said quite dryly, "Are we in favor of Lord Callendar or not?"

"It hasn't been an easy evening to judge. What news, ladies?"

Viola's voice was quiet but crisp. "Your husband is pushing for an end to the war in America to get the supplies he needs for his canal. Also, he is *for* the war, for the same purpose, as he intends to get his supplies cheaper from the Scandinavian lands that remain independent of the continent." It was clear that Viola disliked contradictions.

Virginia was much more entertained by them. "He intends to build manufactories in his lands; he also intends to forbid them. He has seafaring ventures that have gone badly, and he wants an end to the incursions in the Indies, east *and* west. But by far the more interesting stories are the ones about you. You must hear this one about Catherine the Great—"

Virginia's love of melodrama made her a less than ideal informant, Selene decided. "Let us try to stay on the topic at hand, Miss Díaz, surely."

"You are going to enjoy this story," Virginia assured her.

"No one is talking about the dog," Viola suddenly said.

"What?"

"What?"

"What is new for His Grace, besides his marriage? His dog. He takes it with him all day. No one has mentioned it. And many of these people love dogs. Stories about their own dogs come directly after their greetings. But no one has mentioned the Duke's."

"No one has seen it." Selene's head jerked a little with surprise. "Oh. None of these people have *seen* it. And the ones who have aren't talking."

"These aren't first-hand stories from within Talbourne House that they are repeating. Just rumors. No one really believes a word of it."

"Lady Viola, you *are* clever." Virginia's admiration sounded genuine. "You truly will enjoy this story about Catherine the Great, though—"

"Would Your Grace be willing to dance with me?" Nicholas' voice, velvet and low, appeared just behind Selene's shoulder.

His arrival was like a summer thunderstorm, bursting out of nowhere. Both Viola and Virginia mumbled apologies of different sorts as they faded away, seeming to agree between them without consulting Selene that this new situation took precedence over sharing information.

Selene stood with her chin up, facing the direction of his voice. It was an effort to keep her tone light and careless. "Why? What socially necessary reason has forced you to ask?"

When he was silent, and stayed silent, Selene prompted him, "Your Grace?"

Then his voice was closer. Almost right at her ear. She could feel the slight tickle of his breath. She suppressed a shiver. He said, "Would you be willing to *not* dance with me?"

"And do what?"

Instead of answering, he tucked her hand into his elbow in that way he had, and started to lead her off the floor. "You look warm, madame. Would you care to take a turn through the gardens with me?"

"I am not that warm. The garden is for lovers who wish to be caught, and for very long-married couples to be nostalgic together under the moonlight."

"We have been married for nearly a week. I am ready to be nostalgic."

That made Selene laugh a little. "If you will tell me what wars we wish to end or not end, and also whether or not you intend to build manufactories."

"Now where did you—never mind. Why do you not swill punch

and show off your jewels like all the other successfully married young ladies here? Is it only because you are blind, do you think?"

"Yes, I wish to help Talbourne and Britain and you solely because I am blind. All the blind people are very much for you, Your Grace."

"Don't you know what it would do to my reputation to actually laugh at one of these affairs?"

When Selene felt her skirts brush something, she put out a hand. It was a curtain. "Surely this is not the way to the garden?"

"This is an alcove on the way to the garden. Far more shocking." The drapery swished closed around them.

"Less nostalgic," Selene agreed. "More apt to cause talk. Your Grace, are you quite well?"

"I am no longer sure. But..."

Selene felt the gentle pattering of something small and soft falling on her hair, her cheeks, her hands.

And Nicholas' lips nearly brushed her cheek as he said very softly, "You are dripping with jewels and flowers and I know you want to dance but I..."

It surprised her when he moved closer, and took her hand from where it rested on his arm, perhaps to lead her somewhere else.

Instead, he turned her hand over in his, and pressed it to his cheek.

It was so oddly vulnerable and open.

And when he spoke, it was with that hoarse, raw voice. "Is it Britain, or Talbourne, or me?"

Before she could answer—before she really understood the question—he turned his face ever so slightly and kissed the palm of her hand.

Something had changed. Something was *different*. There had been times that Nicholas had touched her and still felt as though he were a hundred miles away. This was very different. This was like that hug. Like their wedding dance. At this moment he was *here*, putting not just a kiss into her hand, but all of himself.

And the raw honesty of his kiss, just the brush of his lips against the tender swell of her palm, crystallized something in her.

So she gave him honesty back. "It is you."

He kept her captured hand; but she still could use the other. And she wanted to touch him. Her hand slid up over his coat lapel. He always sounded so cool, yet he gave off so much *heat*.

When Nicholas let go of her hand to slide both of his down to her waist, she had both her hands to slide up the soft wool of his coat, and to touch the skin just underneath his jaw, a curiously intimate sensation. Selene's fingertips wandered on, till her arms were around his neck as his hands found the small of her back.

And their lips found each other just as slowly and far more sweetly.

He is kissing me, Selene thought to herself before all her thoughts fled and she lost herself in the taste and feel of Nicholas.

His hair curled at the nape of his neck. Her hands could tangle there for hours. As it happened, his hair was thick, and made waves under her fingers.

Her arms felt made to nestle around his neck.

With his hands practically burning through her clothes, she did have something like a coherent thought, something like *how large his hands feel on my waist*, and then something like *what if I lose track of where I stop and he starts?*

He broke their kiss to rub his rougher skin against the softness of her cheek. Their mouths opened in shock at the sensation. In the instant after that, they reached a silent agreement to press much closer, less two and closer to being one.

And both of them drew sharp inward breaths as they both realized at the same moment that her fingers were at his waistcoat buttons, and his were stroking up her back to toy with the closures of her gown.

As someone outside the curtain cleared his throat in a way that made clear that he expected them to hear him.

"Are you... quite well?" Nicholas breathed into her ear.

A shiver she could *not* suppress ran down Selene's spine.

But words came back to her with questions. "Why did you —what—"

But Nicholas Hayden, Duke of Talbourne, was no more inclined to explain himself than he ever was. One of his hands stayed in the small of her back, but he put a few more inches of space between them. She wished it wasn't so easy for him to do that. "Shall we learn who it is we must kill?"

That made Selene laugh.

* * *

NICHOLAS BRUSHED a few flower petals off his front. They would give him away.

And while his lady was laughing, Nicholas pushed the curtain back. Her laugh helped diffuse his anger at being so interrupted. What was he thinking, accosting her in an alcove like an eager rake? And how many people had seen them come here? What would he pay for the impulse, over which he already felt foolish?

But then his anger surged right back, because it was Lord Callendar standing just beyond the alcove and pretending not to be waiting for them to emerge.

And next to him was the current Lord Redbeck.

"Lord Callendar. Lord Redbeck." It was an effort not to let his emotions show in his voice.

Selene gasped.

"Excuse me," she said immediately, her hand splaying again against Nicholas' coat as if for balance, though she had not moved.

"I would be happy to show you to the dancing again, madame," Jonas said, capturing her hand and placing it on his arm. "Lord Redbeck wished to speak with you, sir."

* * *

"WHY ON EARTH would you do such a thing?" Selene made sure to keep smiling and keep her voice low, because nothing carried like hissing, there were people all around, and she did not want them to hear her hissing at Jonas.

And besides, she didn't want to hiss at him. She wanted him ejected from the room. Possibly from Britain.

"My apologies, madame, Lord Redbeck said that he had some business with the Duke of Talbourne and I brought him to the man. I had no idea you had strong feelings about your father's heir. Are those lilac petals in your hair?"

"Did you not?" Selene could not care less at the moment if were lilac petals in her hair. She wanted time to plot his slow demise.

Selene took her place in the quadrille and began the process of bowing to the partners at the corners. She was grateful the *chaine Anglaise* phase of the dance, in which one stood and bowed and did nothing else, took so long. She needed time to think.

Of course Jonas didn't know that she and her mother were at outs with Lord Redbeck. That had been her mother's decision. Lady Redbeck didn't want anyone to know that he had treated them so badly, and she had retreated from society rather than publicly feud with the man.

Such a retreat, that she'd sold all her belongings and nearly died rather than publicly feud with the man.

If Selene could have done it, she would have darted out of the dance and gone straight to her mother with her questions.

Jonas may have made an honest mistake. The question remained as to why Nicholas had business with the man.

When he'd kissed her—oh, she'd kissed him back—they'd breathed each other in like air, necessary and easy. She'd forgotten so quickly that not a quarter of an hour past, Jonas had told her more about Nicholas' goals than Nicholas had ever shared.

The man's kisses were no way to gauge his trustworthiness.

Especially not kisses like that.

* * *

"I BEG you to reconsider your suit."

"You have only to restore the lady's part in her inheritance, and I shall drop the matter." Nicholas didn't care if he sounded distracted.

Of all things to deal with right now, Nicholas rated this matter with Lord Redbeck close to last. And what he rated first was the woman who was dancing with that damned Callendar again.

Nicholas couldn't believe it. If there was one thing in this world he hated, it was how life could change in an instant.

If there were two things, the other was Lord Callendar.

Lord Redbeck had a tired, bitter sort of glare. "Your Grace. It ill becomes a peer of England to question another peer under the law."

Nicholas looked the man up and down. He was thin, with wheat-colored hair, and might have looked quite pale and weedy but for the way his jaw locked. Stubborn.

"It ill becomes a man, upon inheritance of his title, to leave a widow bereft of her portion of the estate."

"As I have told you through our solicitors, sir," Lord Redbeck muttered, drawing close so no one else would hear, "there was no estate to inherit."

"So you claim. Yet you hold all the lands and the title. It was on you to make Lady Redbeck whole. Her portion is yet due."

"The Redbeck lands are fallow, rents years overdue, the estate house in dire need of repair, the servants unpaid. What would *you* do in such a situation? Sell your own prior holdings to fund the widow's portion?"

"Yes." Nicholas didn't hesitate.

The younger man in front of him searched his eyes. "Yes, I believe you would. But I have no great attachment to the Redbeck lands or people. I must look out for my own survival. And you know as well as I that such an estate cannot survive being only what it once was."

Nicholas searched his eyes right back. "So. You would be happy for the Crown to take Redbeck off your hands. Give it to some favorite or absorb it."

"It seems the likeliest course of action. In His Majesty's hands, not mine."

"In the Prince Regent's hands, you mean. Lord Redbeck, you appear to have been poorly educated for your responsibilities. Let me inform you. Letting His Highness treat Britain's lands as toys is a poor way to serve the nation. We have just seen the dangers of the powers of a ruler who is not in his right mind, have we not? Perpetuating such capricious rule is dangerous to Britain."

"Nothing to do with me."

"No? Because you wish to be rid of your lands. Do you have a wife?"

"No."

"If you had, would you wish to keep her?"

Nicholas kept Redbeck's gaze. They both knew the Prince Regent had done exactly that—made a married lady his mistress, over her objections *and* her husband's.

Parliament and its laws had prevented His Highness from marrying for love, but they hadn't prevented that.

Nicholas went on. "Like it or not, part of your inheritance is the task of keeping the Crown in check."

The paler eyes of Lord Redbeck narrowed. "Seditious talk."

"Not since the Magna Carta, sir."

"You cannot sue for what does not exist. Lady Redbeck's portion was gone with the rest of Redbeck's money. Should I sell something to fund her? What? The land is entailed."

"Solve your own problems, sir. And please, limit our conversations to those carried out through our solicitors." Nicholas bowed, only an inch, and departed.

* * *

"Dare I hope for another dance so soon?" Jonas captured her hand again as soon as the quadrille was over.

He surely knew perfectly well she would not dance with him three times, married or not. Selene took her hand right back. "Lord Callendar, for what are you hoping?"

"I was *hoping* to waltz with you."

Waltz? While her body was still tingling from Nicholas' kiss? The very idea made Selene a little ill. "I meant with your introduction of Lord Redbeck."

"As I said, I had no idea you were not on good terms with your father's heir, madame. And I assumed if he had business with the Duke, you would already know it."

Selene stood, rubbing the fingers of her free hand with her thumb. When Jonas moved as if to perhaps pull her out into another dance, she pulled free.

"Lord Callendar, I had been thinking of you as a friend, but you give me reason to suspect I was wrong."

Jonas sounded as affronted as he could without calling someone out for a duel. "Never say so! I have been trying to be your friend since the day we met."

"If we are friends, you must not try to drive wedges between my husband and myself."

"I can think of one very good reason to do so."

"I won't agree."

"Talbourne is a cold fish. Madame, I have made no secret that I admire you. I have a vested interest in wedges."

"Don't. You don't know my husband." And you don't know me, Selene added in her head. Not that she knew *him*. It had not occurred to her that Jonas was actually trying to make love to her. Clearly, it should have.

That made twice that she hadn't realized that men might have secret agendas when she thought they were only talking. She thought of herself as a faster learner.

And it was dangerous, because Jonas offered her things she really wanted. Starting with a few votes and extending all the way, she suspected, to encompassing London.

But she was she ready to give up on becoming the duchess Nicholas needed?

That his *family* needed?

"Selene." Jonas bent his head close and the sound of her name from him was too personal and somehow indecent. "You married to save your mother. There she is, laughing and happy just a few yards away, enjoying her first society event in years. She deserves this. But must you sacrifice yourself so entirely? Cold and lonely locked up in Talbourne House for the rest of your life?"

"Lord Callendar, thoughts of you do not warm me."

His breath told her how closely he leaned, and unlike Nicholas just minutes before, Selene did not like it. He said, "You haven't given me a true chance yet."

"If you want to be a friend, Lord Callendar," and Selene took a large step back, slowly so as to be sure not to bump into anything, "reconsider what a friend could be."

"Better dance with me anyway." Jonas sounded cheerfully unconcerned at her rebuff. "Lord Burden is watching you from across the room with a look I would call baleful. You do not want to wind up dancing with *him*."

"Your Grace. You wanted me to let you know when cake was served." Virginia appeared at her elbow.

Selene tried not to look like she was clutching at a lifeline when she took Virginia's arm. "So I did!"

Virginia said under her breath as she led Selene away, "You looked like you needed to breathe."

"I do. Oh, I do. Is there anywhere to find a little peace and quiet?" The past hour had tumbled her in every possible direction, it seemed.

"There is always the ladies' private lounge for ladies about to faint."

"I won't faint. But I would love that lounge," Selene said grimly.

* * *

"WHY DID YOU DO THAT?"

Jonas knew that Nicholas meant bringing over Redbeck; the cutting ice in the man's eyes was too sharp to be explained only by his continuing to ask the Duchess to dance. He hoped.

"I didn't know she disliked him! She's never mentioned anything about it. Is that a habit that she's picking up from you?" Her rejection had stung enough to make Jonas realize that he really had wanted more from her, and that he was a cad for wanting it. He'd meant it when he'd offered Nicholas his friendship; his brain hadn't put together that he likely couldn't want both.

And what was worse, Nicholas seemed to know it.

"Did you do it to repay her for refusing to continue to dance with you? Is that the kind of man you are?"

"I am not! I've been nothing but helpful this evening!"

"Helpful? How? You—" Nicholas' eyes narrowed. "That Catherine the Great story. That was you, wasn't it."

Even dispirited, Jonas was rather pleased with that one. He prided himself on herding London's elite this way or that, and he knew that story was too good not to repeat. "No one is repeating Burden's vicious little stories about her working as a maid when there is so much more interesting information to repeat."

"I know."

"You *know*? What do you…" Jonas' eyes widened. "No. You haven't even said two words to anyone but Gravenshire since you arrived. When did you plant those other rumors?"

"Lord Callendar, one needn't be obvious to be effective. And if I am without friends, I am not without methods."

Jonas felt even more deflated now. He was sure he'd been the cornerstone of Selene's social defense. "Not much flair, though."

"No," Nicholas agreed without any emotion, "no flair at all."

* * *

"Her Grace would like some privacy, ladies—would you be willing to be so kind?"

All the ladies were perfectly willing to be kind to a duchess, apparently, and within moments the rustling of their skirts had died away.

Selene sank gratefully onto the empty settee Virginia showed her.

"Did Lord Callendar say something to upset you?"

Selene sighed as her rope of pearls slid over her hands where they were clutched in her lap. "Lord Callendar, the Duke of Talbourne, and most assuredly Lord Redbeck, whom I would rather have seen hanged than speak to at a party."

"Oh no! Lady Donnatella did not force such a meeting?"

"No, but Callendar did. I do not think we can trust him, Virginia."

"Men are not trustworthy," the young lady said, confident in her own wisdom on that point at least. "Ought I to fetch your mother?"

"Don't—do not interrupt her if she is enjoying herself. I am dying to speak with her, but—If she is, enjoying herself I mean, perhaps you should find Viola."

"Let me see what I can do. Will you be well on your own here?"

"Oh yes, quite well."

Alone, Selene felt free to let her head sink into her hands.

Marriage was difficult business, and... kisses were worse.

Why did Nicholas kiss her *now*? Here? Was he playing some sort of game?

And was Lord Callendar playing the same game? Because she needed him to stop.

The rustle of a skirt raised Selene's head again. "Virginia?"

The lady did not answer.

"I—"

Selene did not get a chance to finish the sentence. A heavy blow to her back sent her flying forward. She landed on the floor, bruising her hands and knees.

Then whoever it was landed practically on top of her. A knee pressed into the small of Selene's back, pressing her flat, and her hands were wrenched painfully behind her and her wrists crossed. Sharp spines from rough cord bit into her skin even through her gloves as her wrists were tied in place.

"What—"

Her attacker pressed hard between her shoulderblades, crushing her against the floor. Fingers pushed around the side of her face, pushing a wad of cloth into her mouth.

She had to think. She had to *think*. Surely if she could make something make a sound someone would hear—

In the next instant Selene heard the heavy *thud* of someone, or something, meeting flesh, and the weight of her attacker rolled off her back.

Instinctively Selene tried to wiggle *under* the settee next to her, hoping to keep the attacker from falling upon her again. She would not fit. Shoving upwards with her shoulder, she managed to overturn the heavy upholstered thing and scooted her back against its comfortingly solid bulk.

Why had the noise of it turning over not attracted someone?

She could hear grunts, and sounds of heavy breathing. Once, there was a sound of breath hissing outward, as if between clenched teeth.

She should kick the wood of the settee. That would bring someone. She should kick—

"Don't," she heard someone's voice, and then more scuffling. She kicked the wood again, hoping its hollow thump would bring someone.

A hand grabbed her ankle.

Selene drew a fast breath, prepared to scream into the fabric gagging her, when the gag was abruptly pulled out.

"Please don't scream, and don't kick any more either," she could clearly hear Lady Donnatella's voice now. "I don't want you to ruin this party."

* * *

LADY DONNATELLA BROUGHT the washbasin and rinsed the prickling wounds on Selene's wrists with cool water. "I would be so grateful if you kept this little problem to yourself."

"I am sorry I distracted you and the attacker escaped. It is as though she was never here. How am I to explain these to my husband?" Selene lifted her hands.

"Um. I suppose he will notice?"

Selene was feeling around her gown, which seemed undamaged; even Viola's last minute stitches had held. Her hair, however... "He is already worried that I was threatened by my maid. I had not taken it seriously, myself."

"Truly? Madame, you had better tell me about your problems,

quickly. I had thought this was one of mine, but I might have been mistaken."

* * *

"WHAT ON—" Virginia stopped abruptly just inside the door, probably startled by the overturned settee, then rushed in to find them sitting on the floor. "Are you quite well, Your Grace? I left only minutes ago!"

And Viola was right behind her. "You are—you look hurt!" Selene could practically hear Viola giving their hostess a good hard glare. Viola did not like mysteries.

But Selene still needed far more time to think. "My apologies, ladies, I will be myself directly; just a few more moments with Lady Donnatella, please?"

"Oh no!" "Never say so." "Terrible plan." "You ought to stay with us." "...If you truly must, we will be *right* outside." Viola and Virginia were for once united in disagreeing with Selene's request.

But both ladies left, even as they muttered between themselves, and Selene's heart felt a little healed by it. They were good friends, truly.

Selene faintly heard them talking to someone. Was that Jonathan, her footman? He sounded ready to rush in. Poor Jonathan. All his hard work, defeated by a dress.

"I cannot tell if this attack was meant for you or to cause problems for me," her hostess said quickly. "You had better tell the Duke everything, and I must hope that he can forgive me for allowing you to be so hurt in my home."

"The Duke has no reason to blame others right now," Selene said darkly. "But was it my old maid, do you think?"

Lady Donnatella hesitated, then said, "I think it was a larger woman than you describe, or even a man, but I could be wrong."

"Would others not have noticed a man entering this room?"

"When one makes an effort, madame, it is quite possible to appear as either. Trust me."

Selene frowned. "Who *are* you?"

Her hostess just took both of her hands gently and helped her up. "My friends call me Tella. Come. Let us repair your hair a bit, then I must let the servants know to tidy up this room. There must be other ladies, too, in dire need of a place to nearly faint."

* * *

IT WAS petty to keep looking towards the ladies' lounge, waiting for Selene to emerge. She was *his*. He needn't worry about the Callendar boy, he knew that.

Still, he wished she would return to him.

Her companions seemed to be discussing something urgently with Jonathan, but since the bodyguard was still there, Nicholas ignored them.

Mistake.

When Selene finally emerged on the arm of their hostess, Nicholas took one look and turned to the nearest footman. "I will need my carriage immediately."

He did not need to shove his way through the crowd; it parted for him.

When he took her hand and felt the faint trembling there, he said so quietly that only she could hear, "If you cannot walk, I can carry you."

"I am well," was all Selene said.

He didn't bother to argue. He already knew that she was not.

* * *

HE TOOK her hand and pulled it across him to hold it, placing his other arm around her waist. She felt him bearing her up, supporting her weight. She was grateful that she didn't have to stay upright all on her own; though she had thought herself steady, she felt herself getting wobblier by the second.

Sir Malcolm caught Nicholas' eye as they moved toward the door, his wife's companions following behind her. That gentleman intercepted them before they left the crowd. "Shall I bring Lady Redbeck?"

"Yes, she ought to return home with Her Grace."

Selene hated the idea of tearing her mother away. "If she is enjoying herself—"

Nicholas was not interested. "She ought to go home with you."

"*Go* with me? Pray where are *you* going, sir?"

* * *

Nicholas ignored the biting edge to her question. "I shall accompany you, then I must see to an errand."

An errand. *An errand.* A husband who ran hot and cold was one thing, but Selene was still shaking a little in reaction to being attacked and bound in the ladies' lounge.

Kisses changed nothing. Apparently he meant it when he said it was immaterial whether he liked her or not.

Then her mother was there, delivered in her chair through a burst of efficiency from Sir Malcolm. "Why Se—Your Grace, you look quite overset."

What must her hair look like? Virginia and Viola were staying silent.

It *would* be well to get out of view.

"I may be a little ill, Lady Redbeck, if you are willing to accompany me home."

"Of course! Should we not give our leave and thanks to our host and hostess?" Lady Redbeck sounded a little reluctant to cut short her first society evening in years, but the Talbourne carriage was already rolling up to them.

"I have given our thanks already," Selene assured her, just before Nicholas bent down to place her foot on the carriage step himself, then boosted her by the waist to put her, very firmly, in the carriage.

* * *

It was a long and silent drive, but for Virginia and her unexpected ally Sir Malcolm.

"More lace." Virginia said firmly, apropos of nothing.

"It is so fragile," Lady Redbeck objected to the nonexistent topic.

And Sir Malcolm, astonishingly, chimed in with "Practical doesn't make for pretty, you know."

Their chatter bounced around the interior of the carriage, keeping it from echoing, Selene thought, with the blank emptiness where her husband ought to be, even though he sat right there. He was a *million* miles away.

She could, however, at least recall the feeling of comfort.

Under cover of their chatter, Selene turned quietly to Nicholas. "May I have your handkerchief?"

"Of course, madame," he said, handing it over so instantly that Selene realized he would notice if she buried her face in it.

So she just clutched it to her chest, trying to find its fragrance as soothing as she once had.

* * *

Nicholas didn't even enter the house.

Selene heard him say something to Mr. Lyall, and the two of them left in the carriage without another word to her, her guests, or her mother.

Fortunately Sir Malcolm was apparently recovered from his excesses at midday, and ready to be gallant in place of her un-gallant husband. He tasked the footmen with removing Lady Redbeck to her room.

Lady Redbeck, who seemed to be covering a yawn. "Yes, thank you, Sir Malcolm, I *am* tired. It was the right time to make our departure after all. I don't suppose you young ladies would help settle me?"

Catching the nearest hand—Selene thought it was Virginia—Selene squeezed it a little and hoped it would be understood even as she said out loud, "I am so grateful we have friends to help us, my lady. I intend to wait for His Grace's return."

"Selene," Virginia said quietly, "we will stay with you. Your mother is fine."

"No, do go." Selene would stay up all night if that was what it took to speak to her husband. After his *errand*.

And until then, she intended to talk to Sir Malcolm.

And as soon as the ladies departed, that gentleman immediately said, "Madame, let us see what we can find for you to drink that's a bit stronger than wine."

"Do I look like I need something strong to drink?" She let him lead her to the vast parlor underneath Nicholas' chambers, and sat, listening to him lift crystal stoppers and sniff at the liquor. Her hair was half-tumbled around her but she was too angry still to care. She dropped the handkerchief clutched in her fist on the table.

"You look like you want, perhaps, a loaded musket and a saber at the same time. You don't usually look like that, my lady, I will tell you."

Selene wasn't even interested in whatever he'd handed her. It was a small glass; she tossed its entire contents down her throat.

If he expected her to cough, he'd be disappointed.

Whatever it was, it was bracing, and Selene steadied a bit. The liquor relaxed her muscles, she thought, but she wouldn't have another; she could not afford to relax her mind, not right now.

Sir Malcolm had had enough to be talkative, was her bet. "I am surprised that the Duke makes you such a free gift of his hospitality. And his spirits."

She had not expected her husband's arms to steady her so. Having finally felt them around her, during their kiss as well as during their hasty exit, she had not been prepared to lose them.

She wanted them *more*.

She needed to find her footing. Literally and figuratively. She'd thought she could help him while he helped her mother, and so here she was, with little help for herself.

She had to break out of this puzzle-tower or she'd be lost in here forever. If she had been wrong about Nicholas, she had to know that before there were any more soul-endangering kisses.

If Nicholas turned out to be the prince and the squirrel island murderer all in one, this duchess would have to find something around her from which to fashion some sort of armor. There would be no magical fish, or bird, or clover to save her.

And what she had to work with right now was a man who seemed to live off Nicholas' generosity just as she did.

A man with a liquor-loosened tongue.

"A-course, you wouldn't know why he lets me loaf about his table. He's far too good to me, and a good lad. I couldn't rebuild my estate when it burned down a few years hence—nor even a cottage. I wouldna squawked at any roof he gave me. But then he's always had a soft spot for me."

Selene wasn't sure she had ever heard Nicholas speak one word to Sir Malcolm. "A soft spot? Why?"

"Oh, because I took the lad's dog."

Her head seemed to spin and Selene did not know if it was from surprise or the drink. "His dog?"

"Sure, sure. But he won't thank me for repeating that old history." The man seemed to remind himself to stay silent.

That was the last thing Selene needed. "Sir Malcolm, I would *really* like to know why he is grateful to you for taking his dog."

Sir Malcolm was silent so long that Selene wondered if he had fallen asleep.

But finally, before she could decide to reach out and shake him, the older man said, "You never met the last Duke of Talbourne, did you?"

"No." Selene was practically holding her breath.

"Oh, he was a piece of work. Cold like iron and twice as hard. Any road, our estates bordered on one another, in Scotland you know, and one day Nicholas came to me at my house, came to me and begged me to take his dog."

"*Begged* you." This was impossible to imagine.

"Poor lad. He was just a lad, too, younger than Edward at the time but older than his little one. Perhaps ten? Yes, I think so, perhaps that old. Begged me with tears running down his face to take his dog. He was just as serious a little boy as he is now."

"But why? Didn't he like the dog?"

Again Sir Malcolm took his time in deciding to answer, but at last he said, "I think he loved that dog more than I have ever seen a boy love a dog, and that is going some."

"What on *earth*? But he must not have. He wanted you so desperately to take it, are you sure?"

"I took that dog and gave it a grand old life, chasing hares and eating about as well as I did—without the wine. Lived to fifteen years old, it did, oh, about fourteen of that with me. Talbourne lad never mentioned it again, never came to visit it. But after it died, he sent me a gold cup for no reason at all. I never knew how he knew. And when my estate burned, he sent me a note to come. More of a command than anything else. And here I am ever since. Waiting for him to tell me to leave, I suppose."

Selene drew a deep, trembling breath. "Sir Malcolm, thank you for telling me, though I don't know what to make of that at all."

"Me either, to tell you the truth."

"Would you mind ringing the bell? Did the footman Jonathan return with me?"

"No, madame, I noticed he went right off with His Grace and Mr. Lyall, in fact."

"I see."

She was so tired. She ought to go to bed. Deal with all this tomorrow.

But she was close, so close to something.

The footman's arrival startled her out of her reverie. "Please show me to my..." Was now really the time to give in to her tiredness? "Actually, no. Actually, I would like to speak with Lady Hadleigh, please."

"I'm sure she's asleep, ma'am," the startled young man said.

"Then tell her how much I regret that I need to speak with her. Now, unfortunately. And you may tell all the staff that when His Grace returns, I require his presence. Please tell him that I said so, and that it is *not* a request."

* * *

NICHOLAS HAD STRIPPED off his embroidered waistcoat and left it in the carriage.

Shrugging his dark coat back on, he still looked too rich. But he looked half-dressed, and more dangerous.

He said nothing as he grasped his walking stick and exited the carriage into a chilly night fog in a London alley with all the usual smells of piss and rain, Peter Lyall and Jonathan right behind him.

Nor did he knock at the door at which the carriage had stopped. He simply walked in.

Inside, a half-circle of men turned and, seeing him, rose in a rush, laying their hands on whatever weapon was shoved into their belts and forming a wall between him and the man at their center who stayed resolutely in his chair.

Nicholas did not stop for them either. He only moved purposefully, steadily, nudging one of the men aside with his walking stick and going straight up to the man they protected. He stopped a foot away.

Jonathan remained at his shoulder; Mr. Lyall stayed at the door.

"You know who I am and I know who you are. My man tells me you claim to have no knowledge of a spy in my house. Say so to my face."

The man finally rose to his feet, slowly, letting the papers in his hand roll themselves up as he let them go. His gaunt face did not change. His voice betrayed a French accent as he said, "I have no knowledge of a spy in your house."

Nicholas drew closer.

Though neither tall nor broad, Nicholas seemed to fill the very room even as his tarnished-silver eyes bored into the man. "I could have you back in France by morning. I could also kill you where we stand. I offer you this chance to survive only because I believe you want to free your country of its despot, not overthrow mine. That is all the patience I have. I will ask one more time. Did you place a spy in my house?"

"And who are you, that I should care to know what goes on in your house?" The man looked down the length of his nose at Nicholas.

Nicholas didn't move. He looked locked in place, fixed to the earth's core, and his eyes would soon bore through the man. As if the man's nose, which had clearly already been broken once, would likely be broken again before this interview was finished.

The ongoing and unnerving stare, and silence, finally pushed the man to speak again. "You are of no interest to me, sir."

Questions betrayed what mattered to the questioner. But right now Nicholas had no choice. "And my wife?"

At that, the man openly smirked. "What good would a woman be for our cause?"

His men standing around made a sound as if they were going to chuckle in agreement, but Nicholas' movement cut them off into silence. He raised his walking stick just slightly.

"If anything happens to the Duchess, I will find you. I can strike you here," and he pointed to the man's neck, noticing the knot there bobbing as the man swallowed, "and paralyze you, leaving you in the muck of the street knowing that you will never move again. Or I can strike you here," and he pointed to the man's skull, "and kill you instantly. You will have plenty of time to wonder which blow I will deliver between the moment something happens to my wife, and the moment I find you."

"Sir," and now the man's smirk was gone, "I cannot be responsible for a woman I have never met."

"Then I wonder what you will do to ensure her safety. And secure your life."

The gaunt man only nodded. He turned and spoke to one of his lieutenants, a younger man standing next to him and turning red with rage. The man burst out with some answer in French that Nicholas could not decipher; then in the next instant he pulled a knife from his belt and gestured toward Nicholas' bared white shirt.

The effect on the room was instant. The circle of men made some sort of noise, approving or not Nicholas never knew.

To them, Nicholas did not appear to move, but the head of his walking stick was suddenly pressed into the soft flesh up under the gaunt man's jaw.

Jonathan appeared between Nicholas and the red-faced man, with a dagger of his own.

And as a deadly silence fell again on the room, everyone heard the click of a pistol being cocked.

Everyone turned toward the door to see the bore of Peter Lyall's gun staring back at them.

Everyone turned, that is, but Jonathan, and Nicholas.

The gaunt-faced man was attempting to put his hand on the shoulder of his red-faced lieutenant and still not move. Nicholas eased up a fraction of an inch. The gaunt man patted his lieutenant's shoulder, apparently to keep him still, and said, "Do not kill me for what I am about to say."

Nicholas did not respond.

"I have heard of your wife, she is the Duchess who is blind, yes? There may be someone talking of taking her, just to make sure you are cooperative."

"Who? And where?"

"You think you are *le seul rosbif*, the only English bastard on my tail?"

Nicholas pressed harder. The man struggled to swallow. "Sir," said Nicholas, "I am your only worry right now."

BACK IN THE CARRIAGE, Nicholas rubbed his face with both hands. Something inside him wanted to go back and burn the place down, but it was just a reaction. Those men weren't the danger.

At least now he knew for certain who was.

He loosened his neckcloth. "By the way," he tossed in Jonathan's direction as he did so, "you are fired, of course."

To the man's credit, he didn't argue. He didn't ask whether it was because he had failed to protect Her Grace or because he had failed to tell Nicholas the instant he knew of the attack. There was nothing to argue about.

But Peter Lyall argued. "Her Grace will ask questions."

"You don't have to answer them."

"She knows Jonathan and she won't likely let his disappearance go easily."

"Are you cowed by my wife, sir?"

Peter Lyall always had an escape plan. He had twenty gold sovereigns stashed away where no one would find them and a pouch full of grains of shot on him now, as well as ten more bullets for his pistol. So he had a solid foundation on which to give His Grace a speech he would not want to hear.

"Sir, you have put another player on the board."

"What? That ragtag fellow back there? He was already—"

"Your Duchess, sir."

"Surely not!"

"I must ask you, sir, what is it that she wants?"

"To help her mother." With a quick glance toward Jonathan trying to disappear in the corner of the carriage, Nicholas went ahead and added, "To help me."

"And if she finds she cannot get what she wants, what will she do?"

Nicholas sank back into his seat. She could do any number of things. And if she couldn't help him, she might decide to start helping herself.

Dammit, Lyall was usually right. It was like overlooking the jewels. She had things she wanted, and she was serious about them. In a flash he saw the line of men she'd danced with at their wedding. Men of society. Men with *votes*.

What would happen to her loyalty if she stopped trusting him?

Which could well happen, if he did things like tear people out of her life without explanation.

And if she no longer felt loyal to him, what would she do?

There was no way in which she could not break him.

Maybe he'd known that all along. Maybe that was why he hadn't told her much of his goals.

He couldn't decide now if that had been wise or not.

His eyes flicked up and caught Jonathan watching him; the man looked away. "No, do look at me," Nicholas said, knowing it would only be reluctantly—and it was. Nicholas must look like the very devil right now. "You aren't getting another chance to prove you can protect my wife. You're getting one chance to prove you have a purpose other than digging post holes on Talbourne tenant farms."

"I understand, sir."

Nicholas sat back in the seat.

If Selene had become a problem, he ought to remove her from London.

It was the one thing he *could not* bear to do.

CLASH OF FORCES

*N*icholas had only just put down his walking stick when he heard his door open.

He grabbed the stick again and whirled.

Selene stood in the doorway, gleaming hair dangling in wrong places.

"Why aren't you asleep?" Nicholas dropped the walking stick again.

"I know the servants told you I needed to see you."

"I thought you were asleep."

"I *know* the servants told you I needed to see you."

He let out a quiet sigh. "You would be more comfortable in your chambers, would you not? I know you have not yet been through this room."

"If you will come with me, I would be happy for us to talk in that room as much as any room."

Damn. Where was the quiet housemaid Selene when he needed her?

He was too old for this. Too old for her. And far too tired.

She wasn't budging.

He tried one more time. "Shall I ring for Martha?"

"I'm afraid it is your help I need first."

She wasn't letting it go.

Fine, he'd rather see her to the room safely anyway.

But once inside her own chamber, she moved to the small table where they sat together, not her dressing table. "Nicholas, do come sit."

Her use of his familiar name did not match her tone.

"I am very weary and must bathe. I apologize that we did not have our evening together but I must beg off."

"If we add up the time through the evening, off and on, you've surely spent fifteen minutes." It was the first time he'd ever heard her sound genuinely bitter. "Sir. Please. Sit."

Nicholas took in a deep breath, tried to let it sigh silently out as he sank into the chair opposite her.

"Where is the chess board?"

His joke fell flat. "I know why Lady Hadleigh is here, Nicholas."

"No, you don't."

"I also know why Lady Fawcett is here, and Lord Halworth. I know a great deal I did not know a few hours ago."

"You ought to have gone to bed." He'd only left her for a little while —what had she been up to?

Selene was sitting in that way she had, her arm resting on the chair arm as if she ought to be holding a scepter. She still wore the rope of pearls, and the rubies he had given her. Her fingers were tapping on the table. *Irritated,* as with the chess game last night.

She had not changed or brushed her hair. What *had* she been doing?

"I have been talking to your friends," she said as though she could hear him think.

"I have no friends."

"They would be, I think, if you let them." Another woman would be pacing. Her fingertips took up a drumming rhythm. "And I suppose it ought to reassure me that you don't talk to your friends any more than you talk to your wife. But it doesn't."

"Madame, we have spoken every day."

"Nicholas," and here she flattened her hand on the table and her head turned toward him and there was no vestige on her face of a smile, "after tonight I realize we have never spoken at all."

"Be gracious and give me leave to retire." He was not going to go to battle with her, he was not.

"I know why Lady Hadleigh is here and those others, and I begin to form a pattern. But you will place the last piece in the puzzle or neither of us will ever sleep."

"Madame—"

"Lady Hadleigh's husband was discharged from service after six successful campaigns because one of his lieutenants accused him of firing on his own men. He wrote to her that he was firing on deserters, a letter he wrote before he hanged himself. You had her moved here after she collapsed and she has been here ever since."

"Selene." He sounded more warning now.

She pressed on. "Lady Fawcett's husband ought not to have accepted a further command on the Continent, he was older, he fought in Mysore nearly fifteen years ago. But he did. He died in battle on the same day as their only son."

"Selene. This is people's lives. Don't—"

"They talked to me quite freely, Nicholas, once I asked. The question is why you don't. Lord Halworth is dying, imbibing more laudanum every day for the tumor he says will kill him. He has an interesting story. He says that you met at school. He was two years older than you and saved you from a beating one day from a bully that had been plaguing you for months."

"Good night, Selene." The chair slid quietly against the thick carpet. He made for the door.

"All I know about Sir Malcolm is the dog."

Nicholas stopped. And turned to look at her.

He did not ask *what dog*.

He said, "Why would you tear me open—or anyone here—just to satisfy your idle curiosity?"

At that her fist came down.

She stood.

* * *

"WHY WOULD you leave me alone here when I—" She stopped herself from saying *when I needed you.*

He seemed to hear it anyway. "I'm sorry." His voice quieted. "I did not know you were frightened."

"Nicholas, *how* could you *not know I was frightened*? If it was not apparent, I assure you that you could have asked me or, and this is what I expected, *stayed* with me a moment or two longer!"

He had no good answer for that so he kept his silence.

But Selene was done with silence.

* * *

COMING AROUND THE TABLE, she walked to meet him in the center of the huge thick carpet. "You enjoy thwarting my attempts to help you? Fine. If that amuses you, you have the wherewithal to be amused. But I am done letting you slide away from questions even a housemaid ought to be able to get answered from someone she married."

The hand she put out thwacked him in the chest. He tried to take it. She twisted in his grip but he did not let her go.

And she said, "I'm done letting you be silent when I need you to talk. *I* need it. And you can start with explaining about Sir Malcolm and your dog."

* * *

"I CANNOT." He could, of course he could. It was such a small thing, a story sitting inside him; it was only that it would cut with a thousand razor blades if he pulled it out.

"Then tell me something true. Something I can believe."

"I think about you every minute of the day." It was out of his mouth before he could stop it.

Whatever Selene was expecting, it didn't seem to be that. Her mouth fell open. "*Why?*"

There weren't words.

He kissed her.

* * *

HIS KISS CAUGHT her by surprise and gathered force from there.

He had her, held her, supporting every inch of her against his body as he kissed her with a hunger that must have shocked her.

It seemed to shock him too. Murmuring tiny noises against her neck, he nosed down the length of her throat as her head fell back. She felt his teeth where her shoulder just began, and he gave her a tiny bite.

"Nic—" but he smothered his name in her mouth, moving a hand to sink into the tangle of hair at the back of her head, cradling it until she softened and opened to him. Then her hands slid up the outside of his arms to drape around his neck.

As he nuzzled her ear he whispered, "Are you frightened now?"

"I think not?"

"Your mother made it sound as though you might expire of fright if I held you like this."

"I don't think your holding me was her main concern. Nor will I expire. We might have discussed the question, but you have been quite difficult."

"I have been gallant and very easy to get along with."

"Sir, you have not."

She couldn't stop running her fingers through the edges of his hair where it curled against his neck. It was endlessly involving. "My strategy involved you losing many more games and becoming comfortable with my winning."

"If this is the game, and if you are winning it, I am comfortable now."

"Then tell me about your dog."

She felt him stiffen in her arms, from a warm solid presence to a slab of stone in the space of a moment.

But she didn't relent, though her voice was quiet. "Make a friend of me, or what shall we be? Enemies?"

"I have thought of you as a friend. For many months."

"Months. Never say so." She tried to stay serious, but she felt so exposed. She hid her face in his shirt. "Not really months."

"Months that lasted years. You cannot imagine I propose to a woman the moment the impulse strikes me."

"I'm not a woman, I'm an eligible bucket."

"I do not think of you so."

"You can tell me all your secret thoughts and I will be delighted to hear all of them." Selene's voice was unmuffled again as she leaned back, fingertips stroking his neckcloth. "You have retied this. What were you doing while you left me here?"

"Why are you so damned *smart?*"

"Why did you marry me if it does not please you? Please. Tell me *something.*"

* * *

Looking at her in the circle of his arms, Nicholas realized he was trapped. Much like a chess game, he had to sacrifice something important to keep playing.

Talking about why he married her was asking him to spill too much. It felt as dangerous as letting her know someone might kill her. It would drive her away.

His feelings for her were too new, too chaotic, and there was way too much to lose.

At least the story of the dog was only about what he had lost a long time ago.

"There is almost nothing to tell," Nicholas said in that voice that dragged itself out of him. "It was a dog. Beautiful mastiff. Short haired. She could outrun a hare. She—"

He stopped and swallowed so hard she could hear it.

* * *

SELENE LAID her head against his chest. "Does this make it easier? I have already heard many sad stories tonight. One more will not kill me."

His arms tightened around her.

"I gave her away."

"But why?" Selene's voice was very soft.

"Because... because my father found out that I loved her."

Selene stayed where she was, wondering if she was doing the right thing in asking him to let this out.

"I do not understand," she finally said.

"My father insisted I not want things. Not... care about things. Since I was very small. If I told him I liked my tin soldiers, he would toss them in the fire. I remember watching them melt."

"Oh but... *why?*"

* * *

NICHOLAS STARED into the air over Selene's head. He could see that puddle of paint and tin pooling in the fireplace as if it were there now.

"Who knows why such people do such things? I think at one point I tried to find an explanation for him. He was raised to keep Talbourne lands in Talbourne hands; large swaths of it have changed hands between my family and the crown four times. He failed miserably. He inherited the title young, declared he would keep his inheritance intact, and immediately the king claimed five thousand acres. The loss burned, and the humiliation never left him. But I doubt that really explains his fixation. I was never to want anything. Most urgently I was never to let anyone know if I did. Don't want new things, protect what you have, he would say as he threw away something I loved."

"A little boy?"

"You know how children are raised in these houses. I tried to stop him by never speaking, never letting him know what I was thinking. Which only meant my father was quicker to make a point of taking things away if he caught me caring about having them."

"Oh, Nicholas. Children cannot live that way. That's awful."

Selene's arms were clasped around him now. She was holding him tight. That did make it easier to talk. "He saw me rolling around on the grass with that dog and just gushing over her, I must have been appalling. I was afraid... I was afraid that he would kill her."

"Nicholas." Her forehead rocked against him. "I hope... I hope that was just your childish worry talking."

"I... did not dare to gamble on hoping so." Nicholas rested his cheek against her hair. It would be easier to keep going than to stop and come back to this at some future time, and she would want the whole story eventually. "A little while before I... gave away my dog he saw me laughing with one of the gardeners. The oldest gardener, in fact, well old enough to be my grandfather, the grandfather I never had. The man who showed me how to trim back the hedges, look for birds' nests, rescue baby rabbits... Old as a stone wall but he showed me how to climb a tree."

"You don't have to tell me this," Selene whispered.

"You might as well know. I don't remember what I said to old Will but I know I said something too much. My father heard it and then he was gone. Never saw him again. I was just a child, and I was convinced that he had died. But one cannot know for sure when no one will say." His head rocked against hers. "As I later found out, I was right, in a way. My father had sent him away. A far northern estate. He'd had no family to take with him. I looked for him when I inherited, looked for him as fast as I was able, but he had... died half a dozen years before."

* * *

SELENE DID NOT KNOW what to say. Her arms around him were not enough.

No wonder he had to be so stiff and unyielding. After all this time, what would he be if he bent?

"Did you never have anyone who was *not* cruel, to comfort you?"

She was wondering about his mother. But she would not push him more, not on this, not tonight.

"He wasn't cruel, just… cold. And I am cold. It runs in families, I suppose."

"Never tell me so!" She shoved at him hard—he did not move—but then she pulled him back against her just as hard. "He *was* cruel! And you are not cold! You would never treat your children so, nor me."

He thought of himself pressing the head of his walking stick into the throat of the French saboteur. "I have ice in me, madame."

"I am not interested in hearing you denigrate my husband. It is late, and we are both too tired."

"You had your fifteen minutes and more, my lady." Contradicting his words, his hands spread across her back, not letting her go.

"But we have not enjoyed ourselves," Selene admitted, sighing.

"Well, we competed. And you won."

This was not what she had wanted. She'd made him promise her time so they could play, laugh, get to know one another. Forge a marriage. This had felt like verging on warfare.

And it was not what she had wanted for herself, either. "I am more tired than I have ever been."

"Then you should sleep." Still not letting her go, Nicholas laid his cheek against the top of her head.

Her arms tightened around him again. "I have never been struck before tonight," she admitted, her face so pressed to his chest that he could barely hear her. "I still feel as if there are bees buzzing in my stomach. My hands won't stop shaking and I cannot sit still."

"Some soldiers tell me that the novelty of terror fades. It is easier to keep your head clear at such times with practice. But you never will, I promise you that." The way his fingers spread across her back as if to shield it was at odds with the casual way he spoke of getting practice.

His father had been *very* cruel, she was sure of that. "Is that why you are so kind to Lady Hadleigh and Lady Fawcett? Because their husbands knew what it was to be a soldier?"

"I know what it is to lose what you love. No one sees what they gave to stop Napoleon's empire. I only gave them a little help."

It wasn't little, but Selene had no more argument in her now. She wanted to stay right here, resting against Nicholas' chest, forever.

He seemed no more inclined to move than she.

When his hands pulled her closer, though, she yelped.

Nicholas stilled. "I hurt you."

"I'm sure it is just a bruise."

"And I'm a damn fool. I should have made sure you were not injured before I put you in that damn carriage. You can tell I am no soldier. Madame, will you be all right standing so that I can free you from this gown?"

"That is the first time I have heard you swear. Are these the sort of outbursts of emotion I can expect from you now?"

His smothered snort reassured her. It was still Nicholas. He was still the same. "If you can tease me, you can stand. Turn around, my duchess."

It was his calling her that which made her tremble more.

But she could do it. It was not so much to do. And she was an old married lady now. Married almost a week.

Turning in his arms, she brushed the hair that had fallen from its moorings up to bare her neck. "I ought to have finished taking my hair down as soon as I returned. Truthfully I did not think of it."

For some reason, Nicholas did not move for what seemed long moments.

Selene half-turned her head. "Nicholas?"

"Right now you had better just call me Your Grace." His voice was rough, a little tattered.

But his hands were gentle as he slipped each tiny button free of its binding.

When he said "There," Selene let go her hair to grab the gown before it slipped off her shoulders.

Was this what she had done to him? Made him show himself? Because it felt vulnerable and, truth be told, a little frightening too.

But his hands were on her again. She could feel every whorl of his fingertips, it seemed, as he ran them gently across the skin between her shoulderblades.

"A bruise indeed," he murmured, and she heard something else in his voice besides calm.

"Are you worried?"

"I am furious."

Ah, the truth. She knew it when she heard it, and she welcomed it. But he said no more.

Selene bit her lip. "Do you… can you untie the stays as well?"

Nicholas drew no closer, but the sound of his voice worked on her as if it was right in her ear. "You haven't taken the gown off yet."

"Of course." Still she didn't move.

Then mentally Selene gave herself a little shake. They were *married*. This ought to be a perfectly normal, reasonable thing to do.

Like fighting, for soldiers, surely it felt more normal with practice.

"I—I suppose you must play the part of my lady's maid, sir. Will you take the gown off over my head, or should I let it fall?"

"By all means, let it fall."

There was a purring, feral undercurrent to the way he said that, that made her skin burn hot. How could words be so intimate?

She let the gown puddle at her feet.

She knew he was still right there, she heard him make some sort of noise. But Nicholas still didn't move, so she did not. "I cannot step free of it without your help."

He took in a breath and let it out slowly. "You were right before, madame, I am a terrible chess player."

But he placed one of her hands on his shoulder so that she might balance against him as he knelt and gently removed her feet from the gown, one after the other.

"And the stays?" Her voice was almost too quiet to hear.

Nicholas mumbled another curse as he stood again behind her. His fingers were quick to undo the ties and pull them free. "And I am a terrible physician. I ought to search everywhere else to make sure you are not injured but…"

He let the sentence trail off.

Selene didn't know what *he* was thinking, but she would die of embarrassment if he went much farther.

And he ought to search everywhere? Heavens. Kisses were the gate to a very far country, it seemed.

Perhaps it would shorten his search if she helped. "My wrists sting a little and there is another ache in—in the small of my back."

"Of course there is." The way he muttered it, that sounded like a curse as well. "Selene, I am not a perfect man, I'm not even a good man. But I will tell you now, I am only going to look under your chemise to see the injury there and then I will not touch you again unless you ask me. Does that make you feel better?"

"I am not alarmed, sir."

"Yes you are. I can see you trembling and I know perfectly well you have never known a man's touch this intimately before."

"I am fine."

"Selene," his voice was low, and amused, and something else new to her, "this isn't a competition."

Her arms came around and she hugged herself tightly; then she laughed. How could she not laugh? He was funny.

"Very well, Nicholas, I will not be any *more* alarmed. I trust you."

* * *

HOW COULD SHE SAY THAT?

Nicholas did not consider himself particularly worthy of trust.

But somehow, because she said it, it made it true.

Kneeling again he put both hands under the hem of her chemise, and lifted it. He wanted to get one good look and he would leave her alone.

The slightly golden shimmer of her thigh almost undid all his good intentions.

But no. He could do this. She was trusting him. And she was his, she was already his, if he could keep her. With a little restraint he might have so much more than this.

But the muscle of her thigh was right *there*, so close he could bite it…

Gently, of course.

Maybe gently.

He groaned.

Selene half-turned. "Are you well?"

No he wasn't well. This was torture.

Never mind. Never mind. He had endured far worse.

Pulling the chemise up the rest of the way all at once ought to have made it quick.

Instead time seemed to stop.

He wanted to tell her about the beauty of her. The way her body swelled and ebbed and that no Greek sculptor could do it justice. How he longed to spread his hands, his kisses over all of her and make her completely his.

But some part of the back of his brain kept reminding him. She trusted him, and those were not the rules of this game.

The slightly blue mottled mark was smaller than the one between her shoulderblades, but darker. Nicholas kept his eyes fixed on it. The surrounding skin still called out for him to bite it—gently—but… "A deep bruise, madame, but no worse. Hopefully it will not pain you as it heals."

"I am sure not."

Remembering that he ought to have cared for her better, that she should never have been injured at all, cooled parts of Nicholas more but heated others. He could feel one of his hands making a fist.

"I will be fine, sir," said Selene, reminding him that he was still kneeling behind her with her chemise dragged up to her waist.

He let it fall.

They just stood there, too far apart for his taste, for moments longer until he said, "Shall I call your maid?"

"No, oh no."

"But you must go to bed, madame. You don't want to sleep in those sharp rocks, do you?"

That made her shake her head a little and smile. That was what she needed, to smile, and perhaps to rest.

After all, wasn't that what she had said to him?

Nicholas' eyes ran over the tangled mess of her hair. "Do you need my help with your hair?"

"Oh, I—I can do it, of course I can." Moving to her dressing table, Selene began quickly to pull the pins here and there.

Of course she had no idea that him standing there watching her brush her hair was at least as intimate as him doing it for her. Perhaps more so.

One part of Nicholas' brain made note of the way she separated the thick fall into sections and attacked them with the brush until they fell like smooth gleaming rivers over the thin chemise.

Another part of him, a wordless part, howled with restlessness and the urge to pick her up, lie back in that bed, and let that hair spill all over him.

"Nicholas."

He came back to the moment to see her standing right in front of him. When had she moved?

She said, "I would—prefer it if you would sleep in here this evening."

"Not much evening left, madame, the sun will be up in an hour or so."

"I would prefer it."

It occurred to him that this was her way of slowly killing him.

But another part of him melted for her.

She needed something and she had asked him for it.

If he had ever been able to do that, with anyone, might he have been different?

He was *becoming* different. Things were moving, shifting inside him, because of her. Selene made him different.

Perhaps things could be different for his sons.

Perhaps things could be different *for* him.

Perhaps he could yet win his wife.

"Nicholas?"

She was waiting for his answer. She was *asking.*

"Madame has only to ask." He attributed his ability to sound calm in this moment to decades of practice.

When Selene moved over to the bed, she paused with her hand on the bedpost.

"You can always change your mind," he reminded her softly. "Capricious, right?"

She smiled a little and shook her head. She was the farthest thing from capricious. She had been steadfastly on his side—well, since the moment he met her, really.

"I was just thinking. I do tend to... sprawl over the entire bed."

He laughed. Oh, he laughed. A deep, belly laugh.

"Of course you do. Well, I will fight for my half, never fear."

"Oh you..." But she slipped under the coverlet and curled herself into a small ball.

She looked so tiny there.

Mindful that no one else would be coming in to bother them, Nicolas made sure to check the fireplace and snuff out the candles. He'd stay dressed.

I should have checked the window fastenings, he thought as he slid into the bed on its opposite side, but didn't stop himself to go check. No one would pry his duchess from his arms tonight.

And he had to have some faith in Mr. Lyall and the rest of his people.

Rolling towards his wife, he pulled her back against him. She made a huffing noise. "Too much?"

"No, just—a surprise."

"Are you cold?"

"Not now. My heavens, you are like a furnace."

Perhaps he could convince her he had many useful qualities.

But not now. This one was enough for now.

"Then relax and sleep."

Lying there required that he exercise all his iron control to tamp down the parts of him that wanted much more. She *needed* to sleep, and he could give her that.

Settling the curve of her rear against his thighs and flattening his chest against her back, Nicholas could drape an arm over her waist and get much closer than he had ever been before. The scent of her hair, warmed by her brushing, tickled his nose.

It was heaven.

He could feel her relax against him, bit by bit, and he could hear when her breath changed and she had fallen asleep. In his arms.

No one had ever fallen asleep in his arms before.

No, that wasn't true. Thomas had, of course. And he remembered now, Edward falling to sleep in his arms as a baby. Very tiny. Much less trouble.

She had a habit of reminding him of good things he'd forgotten.

And talking. He'd survived it. Maybe he'd get better at it.

Maybe he'd find a way to soothe Edward's feelings without telling him that he did miss the boy's mother, knew Edward missed her more, and would give up everything he had to have her back just for his sake if he could. Though he couldn't.

And one didn't tell one's children that one would rather have fifteen minutes a night with Selene than eighteen years of polite and distant friendship.

Talbourne House had too many entrances and exits, too many people going in and out everywhere.

Very high walls, that was what he needed. Something in the country, far away. He did, far to the north, own a medieval keep with walls that were still solid. And the house in Scotland, as well as the primary residence in Talbourne itself.

If he left London, he would abandon a great deal of work half-done.

And admit defeat, of a sort.

He could do it, though. Take his sons and Selene to a country castle he could lock up tight...

And her mother, of course. And those two young ladies Selene had recruited and seemed so attached to already. And if Mr. Lyall did not come with him, he would lose touch with most of his holdings.

And, and, and...

Tactically, it called to him. Strategically, it was not feasible.

And he'd sworn he'd never pen her in.

Lying next to the woman who was his wife, Nicholas had plenty of time to think.

She seemed so small lying next to him, when in his mind she was an entire universe.

Behind the desire to carry her off and keep her safe there was something else, some stirring more of wonder than greed, more hope than want.

If he lost her, he wouldn't just lose the woman that he wanted. He would lose everything she brought to him, everything she *could* be.

He would lose his future.

He wasn't able to put it into words any better than that. It was a new idea, just hatching in the back of his mind, and he had to give it more thought.

There was something between them even more surprising than desire.

Nicholas watched the sky lighten with the colors of roses and lilies, since he'd been thinking quite hard about flowers lately, and guarded her himself.

Under the silken coverlet, together they were warmer than she was likely used to being. As she rolled in her sleep Nicholas had to let her go or possibly wake her. And she needed to sleep.

Even in her sleep Selene pushed, winding up half-lying across him and using him to support her back. Nicholas chuckled silently.

It occurred to him, in the dim light just past dawn, that his wife was a very good chess player.

And her first move had been to recruit allies.

Perhaps he could do that. Yes, he thought perhaps she had shown him how.

Turning again in her sleep, his wife flung her arm out and half jabbed her elbow into his chest.

Trying not to laugh, he absorbed the push but didn't give up his spot.

He would hold his ground.

CROSSING BORDERS

*S*elene woke when Martha bustled in and drew the curtains back from her bed.

She woke horrified, in a foggy thought that Martha was about to surprise His Grace in her bed.

But then she felt around. No, he wasn't there.

Of course he wasn't there.

If last night had demonstrated anything, it was that at crucial moments, her husband would not be there.

Someone that sounded like Martha was moving around the room. What must her scattered clothes and jewels and hairpins look like?

Then she shook herself. Was she worried her maid would think she had slept with her *husband?*

Martha clucked. "So late you were retiring, Your Grace, you ought to have let me attend you."

Didn't she realize her husband had stayed to undress her?

Oh my goodness. Her *husband* had stayed to *undress* her.

Selene wished she might close the curtains around her bed and just stay there and think. Possibly for several hours. This roll and tumble road that was her life needed a course.

It had been a huge miscalculation to assume that because Nicholas cheerfully offered to stay away from her bed, he didn't want her.

He wanted her.

He *was* the squirrel-island murderer. Just, without the murdering.

Because she wanted *him*.

This was where fairy tales grew unnerving. When people drew too close who ought not, they paid some price. Last night Nicholas had been very close. *Very* close. And if she brought him closer, there would be no distance at all.

She wouldn't be Lady Selene or Selene the housemaid or the Duchess of Talbourne either. She'd be… what?

There were a few things Selene knew for sure. She was a grown woman. She did not want to die a virgin. And now she knew two more things: another man's touch did not appeal to her.

And Nicholas' touch very much did.

She had only to ask, and his restraint would be gone. And hers as well, it seemed like. So she had to be very, very sure. She'd been thinking about armor just last night. To be naked with him would be the definition of *vulnerable*.

Nor was it clear that pushing for what *she* wanted was a good idea. Last night had felt… raw. Rough. She'd had to force him to show cards he had been hiding, so to speak. Yet she'd still failed to learn why he had left her so abruptly.

His mind still, sometimes, seemed to be elsewhere.

Though not, she admitted, when he kissed her.

If Selene could trust what she was beginning to understand of him, she could trust how she was beginning to feel about him.

Nicholas had a boundless ability to feel others' pain. She knew that now. His generosity could not be untangled from his sympathy with others' suffering. The same generosity stopped at the line where anyone asked him to give away his thoughts. Knowing a little of why he was like that didn't change it.

Cold logic about his secretly warm heart said that he may have indeed married her, just as he'd originally said, because her situation required it and he could.

Was it his fault if that was no longer enough for her?

Was it anyone's?

Her mother had never mentioned this. They didn't speak of things like this. People talked of dancing and fairytale flowers and no one said that marriages were consummated with hands and mouths along with... everything else. No one talked about how it invaded one's usual borders. The absolute intimacy of someone touching her anywhere, everywhere, frankly shocked her. *She* didn't even touch herself that way.

Nicholas made her want to walk straight into the parts of the story that were left out, and discover them for herself. She could *ask* him to shock her. And he would.

If she wasn't careful, this could end very, very badly. A version of murder on Squirrel Island that could indeed destroy her. She wasn't even sure how, but she felt it.

Actually, she knew quite well how, at least one answer. She'd warned him *he* ought to consider that one day he might fall in love, but like a fool ignored that she was in danger of the same thing.

This kind of danger required slow reconnaissance and careful strategy. And most of all it required that she know what she wanted to have happen. Wars might begin or end depending on whether all parties to a treaty table felt fairly treated and satisfied.

She was curious about what would satisfy him, but desperate to know what would satisfy her.

But she wouldn't know that unless she took the risk.

"This is too hard," Selene muttered to herself, half into her arms.

"What's that, ma'am?" Martha stopped by the bed.

"Mmph," was all Selene answered.

When had he left? Was he smarting after all she'd dragged out of him last night?

She knew better than to go blundering through a room full of delicate china, and a silent man's past was likely to be just that.

She'd had to do it. But as with all large and sudden movements in delicate places, there would be associated damage.

"Martha?" But Martha had gone.

Selene would tackle something manageable. The housekeeper.

But just as she was sliding her legs free of the covers, she heard, "Selene—are you awake?"

"Virginia! Of course, do come."

"I did not want to bother you but I am worried. Viola seems to have fallen ill. Her maid says she has not risen."

"Well, neither have I!" Selene swung her feet to the floor.

"I think something's wrong. Either she is ill or—perhaps she really does dislike me?"

"No, I don't think that's so." It was chilly. Selene felt around with a toe for some sort of slipper but suspected there was none.

"She was so stern last night, and then once we had seen Lady Redbeck to her chambers, she just… slipped away into her room and did not speak to me."

"I am sorry to hear it. I'm sure she intended no slight."

"Are you sure? The evening was… It was very odd, being in a room with so many men and having them all look at me. I was enjoying it, and then all at once I wasn't. It felt so peculiar that I began not to approve of myself. I cannot blame Lady Viola for disapproving of me as well."

"Never say so!" Selene gave up looking for a shoe and reached out her hands. "I feel guilty. You were on display to be kind to me." People had feelings where chess pieces didn't. Selene's slight misgiving grew into an actual regret. "I was and am grateful. We need never do it again! I fully expect Lady Viola to say the same."

"I hope she will. I have not been out in society enough to make friends with many other young ladies, and Viola is so clever; I fear I have been excessively silly just to be contrary."

Martha tapped at the door. "Your Grace, Lord Thomas wishes to see you. His nurse says he is most adamant."

Selene blew out a breath. "He is always *adamant*. Very well, I will see to Lady Viola first and then I shall see his lordship. Oh, and let us dress quickly, Martha. Virginia, please do not worry."

And *then* the housekeeper situation.

Anything to put off deciding what she should say now to Nicholas.

* * *

"Go away."

It was clear that Viola *was* ill. Viola was the sort of person who would say "Go away *please*."

"Are you suffering, Viola?" Selene said softly, feeling her way around the edge of Viola's unfamiliar room. "I can send for a physician directly."

There was a pause, and then Viola gave away the location of the bed when she said, "I am not in pain if that is what you mean."

"If you are suffering at all, surely a physician should be summoned?"

The breath that Viola slowly expelled sounded tired. "I have already seen far too many physicians."

"Really?" Viola had seemed hale and hearty enough to Selene—had she missed something? "Good ones?"

"Good ones, bad ones, cruel ones, kind ones—the old-fashioned ones who believe they can cure me by dunking me in water, and the fashionable ones who say that my illness is inherited and incurable and that I should be locked up in an institution."

"Never say so!" Moving forward as quickly as she could, Selene sat on the edge of the bed, feeling for Viola's forehead. There was no fever.

Viola sighed again. "Please. Let me be. My maid will leave the draperies closed so I can sleep."

"So you have had these spells before?" Still feeling a bit shy from pushing Nicholas so far last night, Selene couldn't ignore that here was her friend lying abed. "Do they pass quickly?"

The silence seemed long before Viola murmured, "I feel like they never leave me."

"Oh Viola." She wanted to send for Dr. Burke—after all, he was Viola's brother, he would want to know that she was ill—but hated the idea of forcing more attention on Viola if she truly did not want it. Perhaps to start smaller. "Virginia is so worried that she has offended you. May she visit you later?"

"If she likes." And that was Selene's final indication that her friend was indeed ill. Usually, if Viola was conscious, she had opinions.

"We shall visit you later and see if you feel up to strategizing about the knitting affair. Shall we?"

A noncommittal noise was all the response she got.

* * *

NICHOLAS WAS REALIZING that if he wanted Sir Malcolm's help, he would have to say something. He wasn't going to be able to convey what he wanted in grunts.

Atlas whumped down on the floor at his feet, settling in as if she expected Nicholas to have a long conversation. The heavy sound of her breathing seemed to highlight Nicholas' lack of talking.

"What is it, lad? Have I been too hard on the sherry supply?"

The older man's tone was light, but he cast his eyes down as if ashamed, and that was the last thing Nicholas wanted.

"I'd gladly provide you barrels of sherry to swim in, sir, but then I fear we would all lose you, and for what?"

The Scot's beetling brows drew together. "You'd no miss me."

"I would. The world has too few kind people in it."

Sir Malcolm only shook his head, looking away, mostly likely to hide the emotion in his eyes.

Nicholas carefully leaned down to rub Atlas' head so as not to be staring.

When the man looked back at Nicholas, he had a gleam of something in his eyes that made Nicholas wish he talked to Sir Malcolm more often. Maybe the old man needed more than a roof over his head.

"Then what can I do for you, son?"

The word *son* had a peculiar effect on Nicholas, who couldn't remember anyone ever calling him that before.

He couldn't put words to it, but whatever the peculiar effect was, it made it easier for his own words to come out.

"Do you know what is eating Edward? The boy—his lordship, I

should say—cannot speak to me without the most astonishing venom."

"Besides you marrying someone he'd never met, out of the blue, you mean?"

"Yes, besides that." Nicholas waved a hand as if brushing aside a cobweb.

Sir Malcolm narrowed his eyes. "Children don't understand that they can be your whole life, and you can yet love someone else too. And he's still a boy. He's got his head so turned around over a girl, he barely knows what he's about, and he's taking some of that out on you, too."

"He is?" Nicholas' gut rejection of the word *love* was swamped by this most astonishing news. "What girl?"

Atlas' ears perked up too.

"You surprised him with a new duchess—I'll let him keep his privacy and he can surprise you back at some future time."

This was a whole basket of worms that Nicholas felt was not a parallel for his own marriage *at all*, but he would have to leave it for the time being. "I want to ask you, as a favor, just to talk to him for me a bit. Find out what's bothering him."

"Eighteen and you want to mend fences before they get worse?"

Nicholas had to make a split decision. He decided he need to try a new strategy. He would trust this man. "I fear someone may want my new duchess dead."

"What??" Sir Malcolm reared up in his seat. "Are you melancholy because you have too much time on your hands, or is there some reason to fear it?"

"There's reason."

"You don't think—"

"I don't think. But Edward is so angry, and if he has some part in it, I must know. I want you to make sure—make sure someone isn't whispering in my boy's ear and leading him astray."

Sir Malcolm rocked back and forth in his seat a little. His eyes were still narrow, but not focused on Nicholas.

When his eyes focused again he said, "You've always been a

sensible lad. Not your fault you never hugged those boys. Look at the example you had."

The man's words made something prickle at the back of Nicholas' eyeballs. Most uncomfortable. He hoped the sensation would stop. "I hug Thomas."

"Smart lad." Sir Malcolm pushed himself up out of the chair. "Aye, I'll talk to the boy and soon. Suit you?"

"I am already grateful, sir," and clasped his guest's hand like he meant it.

* * *

"I *WON'T!*"

"Lord Thomas!" Selene swept into the nursery, making sure with her walking stick that nothing was in her path. "This is not like you!"

"You don't know me!" And in the next instant the boy burst into tears.

Selene didn't know much about little boys—or big ones—but it was her newfound conviction that hugs never hurt.

Falling on her knees next to the boy, she swept him up in her arms, hoping in some distant part of her mind that he didn't have too much jam on him today. She liked this dress.

The nurse seemed as much distraught over Selene's sudden appearance as by Thomas' tears. She was stammering apologies but Selene just shook her head. "Has something happened?"

"He refused to sleep last night and he's been a right bear this morning, I'll tell you." Once over her apologies, Nurse Carter had some frank things to say for herself.

"That would follow. Thomas. Shh, shh. I'm sorry you are so unhappy. Shall we sit here and be unhappy together?"

Surprisingly, he hiccuped and stopped. "Would you?"

"Of course I would, if you liked! Sometimes misery just wants some company, don't you think?"

"I don't like it in here today! And Edward won't take me anywhere because he says he is busy, and the rain is awfully cold, and Atlas went with His Grace and not me."

"Oh dear." Selene had not considered that a dog for his father might make the boy jealous. She was reluctant to fill Talbourne House with puppies without consulting Nicholas first. And she was still hoping to put off talking to Nicholas until sometime after the end of time.

Settling herself further on to the floor, Selene awkwardly arranged her legs next to her so that she could haul the little boy on to her lap. "You sound bereft."

"I don't know what that means." Cranky and angry and sad, Thomas still sounded like himself. "Nothing is nice today."

"Some days are like that. Tomorrow could be better."

He seemed to consider that.

"Tomorrow would be better if Edward or Atlas would play with me." The rain seemed to be a secondary consideration.

"There, you see? Bereft is when you have nothing and no one. But you have me, and you have nurse, and I would wager Lady Redbeck would love to see you today."

The little boy's sigh was long-suffering, just this side of dramatic. Selene suppressed a smile.

"Big people are *not* so much fun. You ought to bring me a little brother. Edward got one."

Oh heavens. Oh God in heaven.

Swallowing to suppress the roiling set of emotions his words had set off inside her, Selene murmured into the little boy's hair. "Edward had to wait years and years before he got one. And some people never get any at all. I didn't. You have a big brother, which Edward doesn't have."

This seemed to be worth considering for quite a long time as she rocked him.

Selene thought it best to distract him before this became a much more detailed discussion that she was *not* going to have. "Where do you like to run in the house?"

"We don't run in the house, do we, Lord Thomas?" Nurse Carter said, modeling virtue, just as Thomas said, "The long gallery."

Selene hoped the nurse could see her mouth *I'm sorry* over Thomas' head. "Why don't you ask Lady Redbeck if she is willing to watch you practice running as if on a cricket pitch. Do you like cricket?"

"No."

"Then why do you sound interested?"

"I like running."

"Fair enough. Nurse Carter, would you mind terribly taking Lord Thomas to visit my mother? I hope it won't inconvenience her. Please tell her I will see her later as well."

"Oh, well... I suppose if you wish it so, ma'am..."

If anyone did *not* want Thomas running in the long gallery, Selene would deal with that later.

"What about you?" Thomas piped up.

Selene was startled. "What *about* me?"

"Won't you come run in the long gallery too? Isn't that where ladies walk?"

She'd offered herself as company and he wanted to take her up on it. She was *honored*.

How hard were you allowed to hug little boys? Selene wondered as she wrapped her arms about the wiggling little boy and crushed him to her.

"I am so honored by the invitation. I am a terrible runner, but one of these days we will try together. I am not abandoning you. If you will be well for a little while, I have a few other things to attend to. I thought you might enjoy the running, and I have a suspicion that afterwards, you might want a nap."

"Really?" This suspicion startled Thomas in turn. "Not for sure, but maybe. I'll let you know."

"You do that."

* * *

FROM THE DOOR Nicholas watched Selene cuddle and comfort his younger child, and all the shifting pieces in him went flying.

She had only offered his son a little company in his misery, and yet Nicholas was floored.

Where had she learned to do that? Why couldn't he do that? What if he tried?

What if *he* was bereft? What amusements would she suggest for him?

Of course, he knew. She *had*.

Sympathy. Kindness. Solving the boy's problems, and when she couldn't, soothing his tears. Sharing his sorrow.

Was that why he had kept her in one part of his mind and his children in another, and hesitated to mix them? Because he'd wanted that and inwardly feared she would spend those riches on someone besides him?

It was just what his beloved small child deserved.

And what Selene deserved herself.

Maybe even Nicholas.

For the first time since he had decided to carry the girl off to his palace, for the first time since he had married her, Nicholas considered that perhaps love was only mysterious, not nonexistent.

Probably even more difficult for him than chess, though.

AFTER SHE'D CUDDLED Thomas a little more and promised to see him later, Selene found her way out and shut the door. Someone's footsteps were just fading away down the nursery corridor; she waited until they were out of earshot.

"Jonathan."

"Your Grace."

"Oh, don't sound so skittish. I am not going to interrogate you on where you went off to with my husband last night. I need to see Mr. Lyall but I want it to seem like a casual encounter, not like I am looking for him. Can you help me with that?"

He was surprised. "Yes, ma'am, I can. Let me find out where he is and we can make a most casual stroll past him."

"Thank you. And Jonathan."

"Ma'am?"

"If it was somewhere where His Grace felt he needed your protection more than I needed it, I am glad you were there with him."

"…Thank you, ma'am. I hope to prove worthy of that faith."

"Never you mind about last night. You and I have both learned that ladies' lounges are dangerous places." As she set off down the hallway, sweeping the light walking stick ahead of her to check her path, Jonathan fell in behind her. She muttered, only half to him, "I suppose if I had had a season, I would already have known that."

* * *

THE LAWNS of Talbourne House were large, and Nicholas was pacing across them more times than anyone had ever seen him do.

It felt unnatural, and dangerous, even to think the word *love*.

Yet at the same time he knew already that he loved his children. Loved them more than he loved his duty to Talbourne, if the truth were known.

Nicholas had not had options regarding having an heir, and yet he had been so delighted when the child arrived. Edward had been a handsome babe, far more handsome than he himself had ever been. If the child had felt as though it belonged more to Alicia, and in some twisted way to the father who had ordered him to have it, that was never the child's fault. He'd never blamed him.

And when Edward had fallen ill with the children's paralysis, the then-Duke had lost interest in the boy—and Nicholas had had more chance to spend time with him.

He would have continued to love his son whether he had ever walked again or not.

It was entirely Edward's determination to walk that had driven the boy, especially once a physician had let slip in his hearing that if his legs wasted away, his chances to walk again would be gone. Only a boy, Edward had gritted his teeth and worked harder day and night to recover the use of his legs than Nicholas had ever seen a grown man work.

His child had been one of the lucky ones; he'd been able to recover. But he'd also simply been dogged.

They had that in common.

When had they drifted apart? Had it truly been when he had become fascinated by the housemaid in the inventor's house and invented excuse after excuse to go see her?

No. It had been before that. When his mother had died, most likely. The boy's grief had been great, as how could it not be? Nicholas, never expecting to lose his wife so young, had been in a fog of confusion and sorrow himself. He had not taken the time then to guide his older boy through the trial. Perhaps he had not known how.

His own mother had said little to him on the occasion of his father's death except "You are Talbourne now." That had been his only model and even he knew it was a bad one.

Yes, he had failed there. Unable to talk about his wife's death himself, he had not talked to Edward about it either.

He would. If they could bridge the gap between them, he would.

Nicholas found himself standing in the gazebo where Selene had gone the night of their wedding. Not his finest hour either. He had made sure of his own goals but what of hers? She had needed to make an impression upon London and he had not understood it thoroughly. It had never occurred to him until too late, for instance, that others would notice that he had not given her a wedding gift.

He couldn't be expected to think of everything.

But also, he realized, it had partly been that some piece of him wanted to give her something different from what the world expected. He wanted to give her everything that he *wanted* her to care about. He wanted to give her himself. She hadn't been ready for that.

Perhaps she still wasn't.

But perhaps he was just figuring out what it meant himself.

Eyes drawn by the swoop of the falcons as they sank and rose, soaring past the ponds and the Queen Anne's garden to alight again on their masters' gloves, Nicholas saw something in his own lawns, and realized that he needed to look up every once in a while.

And he smiled.

* * *

Selene managed to sound surprised. "Oh, Mr. Lyall, imagine running into you here. It is you, is it not?"

"Your Grace." The gravelly voice of the man traveled as he bowed.

"I must trouble you with one or two small things in which I need your help. Can you send someone to do some shopping for me? I would like a set of dominoes to be ready for His Grace to enjoy this evening. Nothing extravagant, but nicer than one might find in a public house."

"Of course, madame. Something so small is no trouble at all."

"I am so glad to hear you say that!" Selene remembered that Jonathan at least, whom she considered an ally, was only a few steps away. It wasn't that she was cowed, it was only that Mr. Lyall sounded so... intimidating.

"I do have another small matter that I need attended to today. I am in need of a lady's maid, one suitable for the station."

"...I see. I will inform Mrs. Wilkes."

She couldn't flirt with Mr. Lyall. It would be like flirting with a brick wall. But it couldn't hurt to seem charming? She smiled her best "can't you help me please?" smile and tried to sound a little lost. Hating herself a little as she did it.

"Oh dear. It's just... Mrs. Wilkes has been *so* helpful, but we have just been unable to find a suitable lady's maid between us, and it *has* been quite some time now. Talbourne House is full of so many excellent young women, I know she had faith that one of them would turn out to have the knowledge of ladies' fashions, and the requirements of the position, that I need. But sadly it has not proven to be the case."

Mrs. Wilkes could never be described as helpful or having faith in their staff. There was no way, *no way* that Mr. Lyall did not know that.

As often worked best, Selene just paused, and let the other person arrive at their own conclusions which also happened to be hers.

"I see." The way he said it made it clear that he did. Selene silently breathed her relief. "London is large, Your Grace, and the reputation of Talbourne House is of utmost importance to all of us. Can you tell me what sort of qualities it has been hard to find in a lady's maid?"

"I can. I need someone who is up to date on London's fashions, and more, is passionate about them. Driven by them, if you see what I mean. I need someone who has done the work of managing a large wardrobe, is trustworthy enough to keep my jewels for me, and has enough of an artistic eye to do something original, if it can be found. And though it might seem odd, I would like someone who has already had some knowledge of other ladies' households. Someone with friends who do the same type of work." A spy, in other words, though only for fashion. Maybe only for fashion. Selene hoped the man understood.

He did seem to understand. "I will speak to Mrs. Wilkes today. I am sure we will find someone who suits you, ma'am."

"Thank you." She hoped he realized how sincere were her thanks. "I am so glad to know I can have the same faith in you that His Grace does."

"You can." And he said it as though he meant it.

Selene continued on her way—where had she been pretending to go? Oh yes, the south parlor—even though what she suddenly felt like doing was sinking down in a chair and just breathing in relief.

She had hoped to make an ally of Mrs. Wilkes, but if the woman had no interest in the wishes of her duchess, it was the right and proper thing to do to let the steward do his job and oversee the housekeeper.

Selene wondered if it was this touchy a thing to try to lead those newly united colonies.

* * *

"Your Grace."

Atlas' tail thumped against the ground at the steward's voice.

"Ah, Mr. Lyall. Nothing urgent, I hope." Nicholas was still outside, though a spring rain had come and gone and dampened his hat, his coat and his boots. He felt as though he hadn't seen Talbourne House properly since he was a boy.

He had pulled a carrot from the kitchen garden and intended to wash and eat it.

His steward pointedly did not ask about the dirt-covered carrot in Nicholas' hand. "I believe our counterfeit maid has been spotted."

Carrot forgotten, Nicholas now paid very close attention to every word.

Mr. Lyall kept it brief. "One of my men believes he saw her go into a Covent Garden house."

The houses where the prostitutes practiced their trade. It was what he expected, given the Frenchman's information. Of course, the Frenchman could have lied, but he wasn't an idiot, and that maid had been the worst spy in the history of history. One didn't succeed at spying by arguing with one's employer, then flouncing off.

One had to be particularly stupid to choose a spy that bad.

Stupid could still be very, very dangerous.

"I need to know which house."

"I will have it for you today, sir."

"Mr. Lyall," Nicholas said as the steward looked like he would withdraw. "I am grateful for everything you do here."

Taken aback, Mr. Lyall's sleepy eyes blinked, and blinked again. "If anything I do does not suit you, sir, just tell me so that I can make it right."

"I will. I always do."

The surprise on Mr. Lyall's face stayed with Nicholas even after the man had gone. Nicholas kicked a bit with his toe at the hump of dirt where he had pulled up the carrot. It smelled of earth and green.

Atlas decided to sniff it too.

These little experiments in talking to people were going well so far.

He wondered what would happen if he kept talking with his wife.

* * *

"This cannot be something that people do often."

Virginia had a ball of yarn on the settee next to her and was attempting to knit. Selene was attempting to teach her.

Selene would rather do anything than talk to Nicholas right now, and as long as Thomas was napping as was reported, Selene might rightfully hide in here.

"I wish I could remember when I learned how to do this." Selene felt the position of her friend's hands on the needles for the dozenth time. "We may have to ask my mother for help."

"Let me practice a bit." Virginia persisted, trying to fit the needle through the yarn loops but in the right way. "Though this must be boring for you. It makes no noise."

"I could well use some silence today," Selene assured her.

The butler's starched figure appeared in the door. "Lord Callendar for the Duchess of Talbourne, ma'am."

Virginia saw Selene's eyes drift closed and what little animation had been there drained away. "He cannot be serious," Selene muttered.

Virginia nodded to the butler. "Please show him to the north drawing room and Her Grace will decide whether or not to see him."

"People send cards. Unexpected calls are so rude." Selene had rested her head against the high back of the curved settee.

"You need a bit more sleep and less of that man dogging your steps." Virginia used the tip of the needle to pull through a loop. It did not look like the correct loop. "Shall I send him away?"

"You just sent him to the north drawing room."

"Waiting may do a man good. You have time to decide."

"Virginia. In my constant praise of Viola I have spent too little time praising you."

"I hope I do not need constant praise, Selene. Viola may need it more."

Selene contemplated that for a moment. "I believe her rearing didn't include much praise."

"Whereas I have been lucky in so many ways, one of them to be the only grandchild of an adoring grandfather."

"So then it was your choice not to have a season?"

"Oh, absolutely my choice. Your British games are amusing, but I felt no need to play."

The same starched butler, Mr. Collins, appeared again. "A Mr. David Castle for Her Grace, ma'am."

"I do not know a man named Castle, I won't see him today." Selene stayed slumped right where she was.

"Yes ma'am. He brings you greetings from Mr. Anthony Hastings. Shall I ask him to call again on another day?"

"Mr. Hastings!" She shot upright. "Oh no, Mr. Collins, show him straight in!"

"Shall I go?" Virginia sounded as if she'd rather stay.

"No no! Unless you will not be interested."

"Oh, I am interested."

* * *

Virginia kept her knitting on her lap as if she cared about it as their visitor was ushered in.

David Castle looked as though he were a fairy king escaped from the spring celebration last night. Golden and slightly built but with a definite angle to his jaw.

He was also young, younger than Virginia herself, she thought, and either very accustomed to grand surroundings or genuinely not impressed by them.

"Your Grace," he said, and his accent revealed that he was likely *not* accustomed to such surroundings. Unimpressed, then.

Someone had clearly described the duchess to him, as he went straight to her, a smile on his face that showed pleasure in meeting her even though she would not see it. "You are too kind to see me so quickly, too kind."

"Not at all, Mr. Castle, please come sit. It is you who is kind to visit if you bring word from our mutual friend Mr. Hastings. Is he well?"

"I believe he is quite well, madame."

"You believe? You do not know? When did you see him last?"

The young man looked uncomfortable. "Only yesterday, I assure you. We had only a brief conversation. We're not... usually friendly."

"Really?" Selene was leaning towards him now.

"Rest easy, madame, I doubt he would have sent me if he did not at least trust me that far."

"I'm sorry to hear he thinks he cannot trust you completely."

"As am I, and yet these are things that happen occasionally with men who have secrets, is it not?"

"Is it? I suppose so." Selene's voice was soft, and the habitual smile that lurked in the corner of her eyes was not there. "I have little knowledge of men, as I've learned, and less knowledge of secrets."

Mr. Castle settled into a chair nearby, nodding companionably to Virginia as he sat. He was perhaps too familiar, but Virginia found him reassuring after being leered at so incessantly last night.

"All I know is that I have been sent to give you whatever assistance I can render regarding the Duke of Talbourne's Parliamentary work."

"So generous."

"Your cousin Cass has been a great friend to me, and I am happy to do anything I can for you for her sake, regardless of Mr. Hastings."

"Oh, I hope not." Selene gripped the settee's arm. "That is how you and poor Miss Díaz and Lady Viola become so inconvenienced. I am making everyone's lives topsy-turvy."

"No, madame, that is *not* true." Virginia was much more sure of that, than of her knitting. "I did not come because Lady Grantley forced me; she suggested that if I visit her friend, I might have an entertaining visit, as well as give a good lady my support. And I hope I have."

"And I know Cass well enough to know that she suggested Lady Viola visit as much to give her a change of scenery as to provide any help for you," Mr. Castle added.

"And you, Mr. Castle, are surely upending your day at the very least in order to do a favor for me, but it is truly for the sake of Cass. Or Mr. Hastings, perhaps. I have asked too much of the few people I should have treasured rather than taken from." Selene had leaned on the settee's arm now and propped her head against her fist. She looked like her head ached.

Mr. Castle shifted a bit, uncomfortably. "I for one have no objection to being needed *or* useful. But whether I am conscripted or volunteered, I will admit to some slight curiosity that I would enjoy for you to satisfy, if you would."

"Of course, Mr. Castle, in any way I can."

"*Why* are you so interested in the Duke of Talbourne's work?"

"Oh, well, but…" She shifted more upright. "Any wife would be."

"I have little knowledge of the peerage, madame, but no, they wouldn't. My understanding from Cass is that many ladies have only to luncheon, and talk, and plan and attend parties. Perhaps do a good deed now and then. But you tell me. Cass' impressions may be spotty given her family history, and I have no first-hand knowledge at all."

"Your description sounds correct to me," Virginia put in, twisting her row backwards preparatory to knitting back the other way.

"So then?" He looked at Selene expectantly.

She seemed flustered. "Well, I… My father loved Britain. And government. He was always studying how they worked. I grew up with him explaining them to me, and I always wanted to learn more, hear more, find out more. His Grace's… marriage proposal seemed to me the right way—or rather the only way—to do as I had always hoped."

"Follow your father's example."

"I suppose so." Selene looked unsatisfied with her own answer. Slowly she added, "There is so much that should be done, and someone must do it."

"And your mother?"

"What about her, sir?"

Mr. Castle's voice was gentle. "I only wondered if she had the same interest in government, or if she busied herself in other ways such that you don't care to follow in her footsteps."

"Well, I…" Selene seemed genuinely taken aback by the thought. "I don't… I adore my mother."

"Of course!"

Virginia also leapt in to reassure her. "I know you do!"

"Mr. Castle, I can only tell you that this is who I am and what ignites a fire in me. Being who I am, I want to do what I can."

"Of course, of course," he said again. "As I said, madame, idle curiosity on my part. You must forgive it since, as I say, I have little direct experience of the peerage, and it hasn't been flattering, at least not overall. I have never had an interest in why this rich fellow in a year's-salary jacket does this but not that, and why the next one does something the same or different. I say this only so that you understand what I may or may not be able to accomplish for you."

"I will be grateful for anything you bring me. Someone else may read me a newspaper, but I need the information that is so boring that it never is written about in the newspaper. Think of it, if you will, as gossip. The small details of which peers are friends, which are related by marriage or by business, these are the things that drive decisions in Parliament."

"But they shouldn't," Mr. Castle objected, "as those decisions affect us all."

"But they do. And I am very skilled at making do with what exists. I have made tea from the same leaves four times and that is an act of perseverance as well as necessity. I am not giving up."

"Bravo, madame! *That* is a view I understand. My relationship to tea is much the same."

Virginia looked up from her knitting. David Castle had a smile that was worth painting—perhaps sculpting in marble. And because they both knew Selene could not see it, Virginia counted it genuine.

Selene was smiling back, because that was her habitual reaction to someone delighting her. "Then let us formalize our relationship, sir. I will gladly pay you for your time, and relieve myself of the guilt of imposing on you. And if you find the work to your liking, perhaps you will consider becoming part of the staff here. With me."

"Pay me with your husband's money?" The man's laugh was like silver bells. How did someone so clearly masculine make Virginia think of words like *delicacy* and *beauty*? "Let us see how the task suits me."

"Anything you like, Mr. Castle. Please. I will let the staff know that they should admit you to me at any time. And with my thanks for your forgiveness for the oddity of my interests."

"Oh, I'm not one to tell anyone *else* that they are odd!"

"Do you have a wife?" Selene was clearly wondering how such a lady might keep herself busy.

"I have a mother, madame, which suits me far better."

"And she has no interest in politics or government?"

"Can't afford to, madame. She is a washerwoman."

"I see. A washerwoman with a remarkable son. How lucky she is."

"I'm the lucky one, madame. A lucky fellow who is just what she raised me to be, that rare duck in London: someone who has been to more places than the one where he was born."

"Another thing we have in common then, Mr. Castle. Thank you."

He rose. "Thank *you*, madame. Miss Díaz." Once again he proved that he had not forgotten her, just not focused on her, as he bowed to Virginia before leaving, just as he had bowed to Selene, even though she could not see it.

"I like him," Virginia said quietly as the door closed behind him.

"I do too," Selene agreed. "I hope whatever drove Mr. Hastings away does not do the same to him."

Politely, neither of them mentioned that it had surely been her husband.

It was only minutes before her mother was rolled in, her chair pushed not by footmen but by Sir Malcolm.

"The rain has let up and the gardens are simply glorious." Lady Redbeck was practically bursting with pleasure and health, Selene could hear it.

"I am so glad to see you, madame! I had wished for a few minutes alone with you before we attend Lord Thomas, whose situation is dire. I am hoping he will be quite refreshed after a nap. But may I keep you for a moment?"

"Of course, darling!"

"Perhaps Sir Malcolm will join me in a stroll upstairs. I am off to visit Viola," Virginia brushed off her skirts as she stood.

"Happy to," said the good gentleman, leaving Selene alone with her mother just as she had wished; Virginia seemed to have divined her thoughts.

"You sound so cheerful, Mama! Is it rest, the fresh air, or the new nurse pushing your chair?"

Selene had only meant to tease, but when her mother paused before speaking, Selene wondered if she had said something too true to be teasing.

But her mother only said, "All of them are lovely. I feel so much better, and Dr. Billingsley suggested that if I wished, I may take more exercise and try to improve my health still further."

The panic that hit Selene was reflexive and instant. "But the risk!"

Again her mother paused in a way that made Selene think that she was being very deliberate in what she was about to say. "It is my risk to take or not take, my darling, and I believe I am ready to take it."

"But..." *But what if I am not?* Selene wanted to cry, but she had already had her lesson this morning about being perhaps too selfish. If her mother wished to try... "I cannot stop you, Mama, and of course I want you to feel better..."

"I am too young to spend the rest of my life in bed," Lady Redbeck said with the kind of energy she had not displayed in years. "And I don't wish to. There are new excitements yet to found in living, even at my age."

"Of course! You are not old." She reached out to find her mother's hand, and her mother took it just like always. Selene fought to keep her voice calm. "Just remember... remember that I love you, please. And I need you with me."

"You will be fine no matter what happens to me, dear." Her mother sounded so sure.

"I need you whether or not I have married a duke, Mama. I need you because I need you."

"Oh I know, dear," and her mother seemed to be waving her other hand dismissively. "That is not what I meant. I am glad that you will be, not just fine, but safe and happy too. But you were always going to be fine. You have always been that kind of child."

"Really?" Selene tugged just gently and her mother's chair rolled forward until Selene could feel her mother's toes in her slippers bump into Selene's shins. "I am glad you think so. But I have always been the kind of child who has an excellent mother, so you cannot assume that I would continue to be one without the other."

"See? There you have it. Arguing like a judge." Her mother's other hand, still feeling to Selene very thin and dry, came around and patted Selene's hand where it clasped her own. "You have always been like that. Just like your father."

"And you… aren't, Mama, are you? You aren't like father and me."

"Oh no. But then why would I be?" Selene could feel her mother moving, suspected it was a shrug. "The world is full of so many people we must expect each one to be much that no one else is. It's rather beautiful, isn't it?"

"Yes, Mama, it is." It was easy to agree because, Selene realized, she had heard her mother say so many similar things over the years. The sentiments were familiar, natural.

Her father had given her his love of the workings of governments, but her mother had perhaps given her a greater gift: this type of empathy, unconditional love of people themselves. As she had always loved her daughter.

Then thinking of her two beloved parents together, Selene smiled and reminded herself: it wasn't a competition between them.

"You must miss him so much."

"Now that you are married, darling, you may begin to imagine how much." Lady Redbeck's voice was full of unshed tears.

Taken aback by the comparison between her relationship with Nicholas and that between her father and mother, Selene almost blurted that she hadn't yet slept with her husband, knew now that she wanted to, and yet was frightened of what might happen if she did.

But she couldn't do that. If she could only survive one tough conversation with her mother today, she had to ask about her father's heir. Whatever Nicholas was pursuing with that man, Lady Redbeck ought to hear of it from Selene first.

And it would be so much easier to handle if Selene understood what the problem had been in the first place.

"Mama," Selene asked, squeezing her mother's hands gently, "are you feeling well enough now to tell me why you did not go to court to petition for your share of father's estate?"

"That is not a matter of feeling well enough." Her mother dropped their clasped hands and a little forbidding chill came into her voice.

"I don't wish to upset you, truly I don't. But I must know."

"What, the way you *must know* what the Duke and I talked about before we came here? No you didn't. You resolved it all on your own."

Her mother was just being obstinate now. It made a flash of answering stubbornness rise up in Selene. That, too, she had honestly inherited, and her mother was reminding her of its source.

"I am not at all sure that it is *all resolved*, as you say. But I won't let you distract me. That topic can be for another day. I am asking you to trust me and tell me why."

Her mother was silent a long, long while.

"It is not a matter of trusting you," she finally said.

"What can be the matter, then?" Selene was *not* going to let go of the topic. As with Nicholas, smashed china or not, it was better to break out than keep travelling in circles.

"Oh… As you are married now yourself, you must understand it. I would not let your father's name be batted around among solicitors in courts like a badminton shuttlecock."

Her mother seemed to be under the impression that Selene now magically understood a great deal more about marriage than she did. But what she did know was that her father had loved them both. "He would not have wanted us to live the way we lived, Mama. He would not have wanted you to suffer so. You *know* he would not."

"But he was gone, Selene, he was gone and my part was to protect him and there was only one way left to do it!" Her mother gasped in air as if it had been wrung out of her.

Selene started to reach out and comfort her, but held back. If she waited just another moment. Something seemed to have broken free in her mother and Selene needed to hear the rest.

And indeed after another great inhalation, and a third, Lady Redbeck went on of her own accord. "I was never clever like the two of you but I was loyal. And I still am. Death cannot part a husband and wife like we were, not like that. He hated that he was so poor with money, hated that he could not find a way to pay the servants, hated asking the tenants for rents; he hated everything to do with money. When we were young, I begged him to find someone to handle the finances of Redbeck for him, but he felt so inadequate—he could not even oversee such a person, and knew no one he could trust that far. If Redbeck were to be run into the ground, at least it was him doing it."

"Oh no."

"Don't think badly of him, Selene, never that. He loved you so, was always so proud of you. He never wanted to worry you. Neither did I."

"Mama, I..." She what? She still did not know what Nicholas wanted with her father's heir. Perhaps it was something relatively innocuous, such as to buy the house at Redbeck. But the Redbeck house was entailed; Nicholas could not simply buy it. No, her mother had done what she could for her father as she understood it. Selene wouldn't alarm her any further about it until she knew what was going on.

But at least she understood that her father had bankrupted Redbeck. So she might be more inclined to be less angry toward the heir who had done nothing for them.

Maybe.

Maybe not. It was worth thinking about.

Her mother had gone on. "It's over. I never told anyone, and if that man hasn't broadcast it far and wide by now I don't know why he ever would. We have survived, Selene, we are still alive, and you are a duchess and His Grace has been so good to us both! It is so lucky, darling, that he has had such an interest in you."

The thought of *how* she interested Nicholas sparked something in the back of her mind. "My heavens, I've left Lord Callendar waiting for nearly an hour!"

"What on earth can Lord Callendar want? He does not reside here, yet he is at dinner every night. If I—" Her mother's voice grew sharper. "Selene, what *could* Lord Callendar want?"

"I don't know, madame, I have left him waiting in a drawing room for the past hour, as I've just said."

"Selene, don't you be one of those women who takes marriage as an opportunity to indulge themselves in wicked ways. I have not raised you that way. And His Grace does *not* deserve that."

"Wicked? What is wicked, Mama? Some would say it is wicked to pauper your family."

Lady Redbeck's gasp told Selene the barb had hit home.

"Never mind, Mama." Selene immediately felt bad for it. "You have always trusted me? Trust me now. I am not encouraging Lord Callendar; indeed I don't know what he wants. But I did not intend to leave him waiting this long. If he is still here, I must see him. Please forgive my leaving."

"Of course," her mother said, but with a good deal less animation than the conversation had begun.

FOREIGN AMBASSADORS

"*L*ord Callendar. I must apologize for keeping you waiting."

Jonas jumped to his feet as Selene came in on the footman's arm.

He felt that leap of excitement, just upon seeing her, that he had so hoped he would not feel.

Yes, he had fallen.

"No apologies necessary, Your Grace, as long as you were not avoiding me."

"Never say so. Jonathan, would you send for my things? I think a walk in the fresh air would do me good, and Lord Callendar must wish to accompany me, he has been waiting so long."

"Truly? It was pouring when I arrived."

"Just another measure of how long I have kept you waiting. Have you your hat, sir? Or ought we to fetch it?"

"I have it at hand, as befits a man who may be turned out into the street at any moment."

He noticed that Selene was keeping her distance from him, remaining near the door as if she might run away.

Yet she said, "I hope you do not suspect that I would turn you out into the street. If you are a friend who behaves as a friend, I would have no reason to do so, would I?"

Jonas just couldn't think of what to say. He didn't want to be a friend, he was sure of that now, but he wanted a few more moments to speak with her before she threw him out. As he strongly suspected she would.

When he stayed silent, Selene made a frustrated noise. Which she then covered with pretend pleasure as she said "Ah, here they are," at the arrival of her bonnet, shawl, gloves, and walking stick.

They were both out on Talbourne's lawns, the spring breeze loosening just a few of the well-tamed hairs on the back of her neck, before Jonas leaned toward her to say, "I am pleased to see you using the walking stick I gave you."

Selene made the frustrated noise again. "It is unfortunate, I suppose, that it is the most useful wedding gift I have received."

"Most useful. Not your favorite."

"No. *Not* my favorite." Their feet swished through the grass. "My shoes may well be ruined. Again."

"Ah. A happy memory, at least for me. May I escort you to the same gazebo to which you fled on your wedding night?"

"We may as well," sighed Selene. "And I didn't flee."

"Madame, you fled."

"And you were a kind friend that night. I hope you will continue to be one."

Jonas looked around. "Do you realize there are three footmen following us?"

Selene just waved a hand. Two of the footmen fell back; one stayed within a few paces of them.

Jonas helped her up the steps to the gazebo.

She stood in its center, the lively spring breeze playing with the ends of the ribbons on her dress and bonnet.

He stepped close. "You don't make it easy for a fellow to say things that you don't wish to hear."

"Surely the definition of a friend is someone who does not *tell* you things you don't wish to hear." She had not moved closer to him, but she had not moved away either.

"I'm not sure that's true. You would wish for a friend to tell you things that you *ought* to hear. Don't step in that gopher hole. There is salad in your teeth."

When Selene laughed, just a little, he bent his head close to hers. "My heart is yours."

"Lord Callendar." Now she *did* move away. Just a step. And kept her voice low, no doubt so that that last footman might not hear. "I have not asked for it."

"One doesn't."

"What can be your *purpose* in making love to a married woman?" She was shaking her head.

It was discouraging that she did not seem the least bit pleased. Jonas nodded to himself, and moved to sit on one of the gazebo's benches, feeling like he was carrying his heart in his hand.

Trying not to sulk, he said, "There is a purpose to money, to politics, to barter and to work. There is a purpose to procreation, but I'm not sure there is a purpose to love."

Selene used her stick to find her way to the bench not too far from him. Clearly she did not want his words to travel. Jonas himself felt quite blasé about it. If she did not want to hear it—if she did not want him—whether the servants knew about his rejected heart was immaterial.

She leaned toward him but apparently just to keep the bite in her words between themselves. "You don't love me, Jonas, you don't even know me."

"Do I not? Poets write of love that happens in an instant."

"That is *not* how love happens. It happens over time, as people get to know one another. Slowly, with conversation."

"Is it? And that is how you fell in love with your husband?"

Selene did not answer.

"You forget I *saw* you, madame. I saw you arrive at Talbourne House. You did not arrive looking like a woman in love."

"Is that your goal? To blackmail me? I know exactly what I looked like, sir. I looked like *a servant*."

"I did not intend it that way."

"But I did. I looked like what I was. Just as I do now. I won't be blackmailed, sir, as I have nothing to be ashamed of. If your intention is to push me with shame, it won't work."

"Madame, you mistake me entirely." His body thrumming too anxiously to even pretend to be calm, he moved to her side the next instant. "You are the loveliest, kindest woman I have ever met—"

"—untrue, though kind of you to say—"

"—Selene, when you come into a room my heart leaps and I am happy. I am happy just because you are there. That's all."

Selene seemed to be thinking this over. One of her thumbs was rubbing over her fingers, wrapped as they were around the walking stick.

Wryly Jonas pointed out, "I gave you that walking stick. Not because it is beautiful, but because it might be useful. Perhaps you could employ me in some way, too. Not because I am beautiful, but just because I might be useful."

"Oh, I won't even ask you if you are beautiful. You are fishing for compliments even as you are vexing me entirely. What on earth am I supposed to do with you? Being happy to see me is not being in love."

"Isn't it?" Jonas reached to take one of her hands. "You are so eager to explain how love works to me, madame. Please, explain it."

But Selene did not let him have her hand. "If I am not mistaken, I am even younger than you are. I'm not about to lecture you on the workings of love. In fact I suspect you would only like it."

"That's true, I would."

"*Lord Callendar.*" She stood back up, so he did as well. "What I have been is friendless. You have been a friend since the day I arrived. Indeed, I suspect you may have saved my life. That is more than a little chivalry, sir. But it does not mean that there is anything between us but a debt."

"Perhaps a little more than a debt? As you have not yet thrown me out in the street." Heedless of the footman watching—a footman who looked as though he could easily throw Jonas and four of his friends out into the street, any street—Jonas leaned close just one more time. "Perhaps a little more than a friend? Just a little?"

"Not one tiny bit more than a friend. Not one. And not that unless you can keep yourself restrained on the topic of how you feel. I do not welcome these advances of yours, and I cannot ever welcome them. It is bad behavior on your part, and furthermore behavior I have not asked for nor encouraged. I've said clearly that I wish we were friends. But if we cannot be, then so be it and farewell."

"Ah." Jonas stepped back. The step hurt. As if his heart was under his boot. "My apologies, for you are nothing but correct, madame, and the fault is wholly mine, I do admit it."

"Sir," Selene said gently, "are you listening? For that is what I have just said."

He had to laugh, even a hollow laugh. "I understand. I will not importune you further, and as you said last night, I may contemplate further what a friend can be. I have much to learn, even if you will not teach me."

From the corner of his eye, Jonas saw a figure moving towards them over the wide open expanse of green lawn.

He knew it was His Grace without even being able to see the man's face. He recognized the man's shape, accompanied by a big loping dog like half the god of war—or the lord of hell. He knew Talbourne would be out here to protect his claim on his wife, even if he was never there at any other time.

A burst of anger flared in his gut.

But he could know one thing right now.

"I think being happy to see someone is a great deal of being in love," he told her, leaning slightly close again but not touching her. "That feeling where your insides are light and happy just because the person you love has walked into the room. Such a powerful feeling that one will mope around the doors for days hoping to feel it again. Do you not agree at all? Or do you think that it's only me who feels that way?"

"Of course not. Being in love is… is a long history of shared goals and time spent together, history, purpose. It is—"

"It is being desperately happy when the person comes near. I will prove it. For here is His Grace the Duke of Talbourne."

Jonas only caught sight of the expression on Selene's face for an instant as she turned towards the gazebo's entrance. One of her hands automatically flew to check that her hair was in place, as if she had forgotten she was wearing a bonnet, and her smile had a light behind it that had not been there for him.

"See what I mean?" was all he said, in a slightly bitter tone he could not prevent, as he drew back and Talbourne's boots sounded on the boards of the gazebo's steps.

"Oh, I—" Selene faltered a little as she realized what he meant. She must know she was nearly glowing in anticipation of Talbourne's arrival. She must know she was turning inevitably back to the gazebo's entrance, awaiting him, even as Jonas stood right by her side. She must know she could not help herself, even as she started to speak to Jonas but immediately addressed Talbourne instead. "But—Your Grace, have you come to see me or Lord Callendar on this beautiful day?"

"All respect to Lord Callendar, there is no comparison," Nicholas said easily as he drew close and took her hand, tucking it in the crook of his elbow as he preferred to do. "If you are not otherwise engaged, Your Grace, I had hoped for a minute of your time."

The man had all her time, and did not deserve it, as far as Jonas could tell, but his bitterness was his own to take home and see if he could drink away, perhaps. Or quash in some other, more productive way. It was perhaps time to stop playing childish games, as this love was in a fair way to do him some serious damage and would have to be taken seriously.

"Oh, of course. I am free," said Selene, still with that easy uplifted light about her face, and Jonas' heart, which had indeed fallen under his boot at some point, was crushed a little more.

She was good enough to add, "I mean, if Lord Callendar will excuse me."

"Of course, of course. I must be going, after all."

And he watched Talbourne walk away across the soft rolling lawns with his greatest treasure beside him, and Jonas learned a capacity for sins like envy that he had never known in himself before.

The dog and the footmen fell into step behind the Duke and Duchess, leaving Jonas quite alone.

* * *

SELENE FORGOT Jonas the second he was behind her.

And forgot how desperate she had been to put off talking to Nicholas.

"I never expect to see you during the day, sir, has something happened?"

"Yes and no. I have a carrot in my pocket. It's been rather an unexpected sort of day." Over his shoulder, he said, "Jonathan, I will look after Her Grace."

"Sir," and Selene heard them all leave through the swishing grass.

"Truly?" Selene wasn't sure what she was supposed to say to this. Nicholas did not exactly sound like himself. "Ah... did you *intend* to have a carrot in your pocket?"

"Truly, it just sort of happened."

He was steering her around a hedge of roses, past the kitchen garden; she smelled the freshly turned earth and the herbs. "Did you want *more* carrots?"

"Actually, what I wanted was to give you a wedding present. One that I think you will like."

"You already did give me a wedding present. Several."

"But this one is not for anyone to see, necessarily. This one is just for you."

"I would have thought it was too early for carrots."

"Selene. Forget the carrot."

"Never say so. As your wife, it is my carrot too."

They stopped. Atlas' panting seemed to give away her excitement. Nicholas took one of Selene's hands, and laid it flat.

Against a wall that rose in front of them, smooth and hard, impossibly smooth … made of glass?

"Nicholas. This isn't…?"

"Talbourne's greenhouse, my… madame."

Had she imagined that he had been about to say something else?

He went on. "It's a large greenhouse. Quite a good one." Again he took her hand and rubbed his thumb over the back of it, just for a second, before placing it against the handle of the door. "Atlas, you stay out here. Your Grace, would you like to open your wedding present?"

"Oh. Oh my." Selene's fingers curled around the door handle. His fingers curled around hers.

Joined at their hands, he helped her open the door.

The warm, humid air seemed to wash over her as Selene measured the width of her path with her walking stick. She could hear the rustling of leaves in an enclosed space, and smell distant traces of tobacco and earth… and overall the scent of orange blossoms.

The scent of her wedding day.

"I should have thought of it earlier. For a woman who wants to drip with flowers, and likes them better than jewels… have you raised them before?"

"A bit. Redbeck had a conservatory. Nothing this grand. My heavens, Nicholas, how far does it extend?"

His grin almost hurt his face, it was so broad. He'd been right. This was a good idea. And it had been right in front of him all the time, he just hadn't seen it.

"I can give you a bit of a tour but I admit I know little about it. One of the gardeners will have to teach you. Perhaps teach both of us."

"Oh, and Thomas."

"If he can be trusted not to have a tantrum and break any of the panes."

"He's too old for that! And perhaps… Edward? Does he come here?"

Nicholas cleared his throat. "Edward did come a bit, as a boy, especially to get some air that was warm, while he was still recovering."

"I cannot imagine a lovelier idea. Nicholas."

She turned to him so easily. And fit against him so easily too.

"Yes?" He leaned his cheek against her hair, just for a moment.

It was glorious and not enough.

"Is this where you found the blossoms for my... for our wedding day?"

"It is."

"And you let me think you had purchased them."

"I did purchase them; it was just a long time ago. All these citrus trees have been laid in since I have had Talbourne. My father considered them too impractical, I think. Or perhaps he simply did not like the things."

"Are there lemons too?"

"Yes, and I admit I like the scent even better."

* * *

"Lemons and rosemary. On your handkerchief," Selene said quietly, as if to herself.

"You surprise me. You never said you noticed that."

Selene just shook her head. She could not explain what that scent had meant to her on one of the darkest nights of her life, and how much she looked for it since. It always lifted her spirits, always.

Oh dear. Perhaps Jonas was right.

Perhaps that feeling was...

Turning her face into the front of his jacket as she had done the night before, Selene breathed deep the scent of him—wool and lemons and rosemary, earth, glass, and metal.

Her greenhouse.

"What grows here?"

Nicholas heard her despite the way her face was buried in his jacket.

Slowly, perhaps not to startle her, his arms came up around her. "Lemon-scented geraniums. Myrtle, and oleander; can you smell them?"

"Yes."

* * *

"JASMINE AND LAUREL; HYDRANGEA…" His voice was growing rougher, deeper, he couldn't control it. "Passion flower, when it's in season."

Selene leaned up on her tiptoe, tucked the tip of her nose behind his ear.

He swallowed. "Hyacinths."

"Apples?"

"I believe that is the moss rose."

"Smells delicious," she whispered into the hollow of his ear, and he turned his head and kissed her.

Just as she had wanted him to do.

* * *

IT WAS ONLY their third kiss, Nicholas managed to think as his mouth and hers fit together so perfectly.

He hoped they would fit together this perfectly every time.

He would never be able to smell flowers without thinking of her lips, he realized, or the fresh sweet taste of her.

He was losing things, and gaining things too.

When Selene leaned close against him, his arms came around her of their own accord, wrapping her in his touch, and her arms slid around him too.

Then his thoughts fled and his eyes closed and they kissed together in a fairyland made of the scents of spring and each other's touches.

Time kindly slowed for them and it seemed hours, maybe days, before their lips parted, reluctantly, slowly, and the breeze began playing with them again.

It felt as though Nicholas' heart beat hard, slowly, deep in his chest. Could she feel it?

Selene was swaying just a little in his arms, as if the breeze was blowing her back and forth just like one of the flowers.

He had no intention of letting her go. Of ever letting her go.

A lock of her hair had loosened a little, somewhere during that kiss. Nicholas smoothed it back into place with his fingers.

"I want more," Selene said, in a deep, sleepy voice that made him throb.

"Good."

"I am not even entirely sure what more I want but I suspect you know."

"Ah. Yes and no."

"How so?"

If she had pulled away from him then, he might not have simply told her. Instead she snuggled closer into his arms. He told her.

"I'm not a man who lusts after women, Selene. I mean, I never have. Before you."

Her arms tightened around his waist. "I don't understand."

Nicholas let his cheek fall to her hair. "Perhaps I don't either. I simply don't."

If she knew anything of the world, she would ask if he lusted after men instead.

She didn't. "But... your wife?"

"Eventually, when we knew each other well, we had an amiable relationship. But when we met, nothing."

"That makes sense." Was she *cuddling* him? Standing up, in a greenhouse full of fruit trees? She didn't sound concerned. "Of course you would feel more for her as time passed. And after your father—"

"No, you don't quite understand." Did it matter? Probably not. But Nicholas wanted her to understand. He wanted her to understand *him*. "Other men seem to burn for pretty girls they just met in the street. I don't. Ever."

"Not ever? Forgive me, sir, but that seems like an admirable quality in a husband."

"I'm not trying to be virtuous. I simply have no interest. Where looks inflame other men, I feel nothing."

"You may not realize this, but I could say the same."

He smiled into her hair. She didn't seem to care. He felt lighter—not because it had been a secret he needed to keep, only because it had been something he had not been able to share with anyone before.

But Selene grasped that this was important to him. "Has it been a burden?"

"No." It was a relief simply to tell the truth. "It has been more convenient than not, as my—as Alicia did not really care for sharing my bed. Perhaps she felt the same way. And so many men are brought low by their difficulties with women; I have never wished to be other than I am."

Selene's hand seemed to be running up and down his arm of its own accord. He liked it. But she was still listening, she still sounded thoughtful as she said, "I was just reminded today that everyone has a great deal to them that makes them unique. And though it may not be good logic, I find you more unique than most. It is what you are that appeals to me, Nicholas, not what you are not."

He appealed to her. He was massively grateful that this... whatever it was, was not only one-sided. He had been pulled forward and forward and forward by his peculiar feelings about her for so long... "Please tell me you think of me sometimes in the way I think of you."

"If you recall, sir, you have told me nothing of the way you think of me, only that you think of me."

"I think of you like—" It was easiest to explain by pulling her up against him and kissing her again.

So he did.

A long time later Selene murmured against his lips, "You still have explained nothing."

"I rather think I did."

She sighed. Half-frustrated with him, perhaps, but half something else. "Shall we... wait until this evening to discuss this?"

Oh no. There was no reason to wait one more minute than was absolutely necessary. But how to phrase that so she would agree? Without coercing her?

"Nicholas?"

"Truly, Selene, I would say we could discuss it right here in this greenhouse as completely as you like and as long. But I *have* tried to be a gentleman and still will, for I meant what I said when you accepted me. We ought to have a long relationship and I mean for us to get along comfortably for a long time."

She stood still, apparently thinking.

"What?"

"It is better than a useful coal bucket," she said, and he could make no heads or tails out of that remark.

"Selene, what would you like?" Whatever it was, it was hers.

"I think I'd like you, Nicholas, and I don't want to wait until late tonight, truth be told."

Just his thought.

"Then why don't I meet you in your room. Your territory, is it not? I'll take Atlas to play with Thomas for a while and then I will be all yours."

"Will you?" She didn't sound as happy as he'd hoped, but he would take this one step at a time. "I hope so."

* * *

I MEAN *for us to get along comfortably.* The words didn't match at all what Selene was feeling. Among other things, this wasn't comfortable.

She was hot and restless in her skin, felt awkward waiting for Nicholas, guilty for sending Atlas as a replacement for herself even though Thomas would probably like that better, and nervous that Martha would know that her husband would be in her bed.

"Martha, I won't need you till tonight."

"Very good, ma'am," and Martha just left. No questioning or wondering or anything else that Selene had imagined would make her even more self-conscious and nervous.

She should have had Martha help her undress. But how to explain that she wanted to undress in the afternoon?

This was impossible to explain to anyone.

Perhaps even to Nicholas. Which was ridiculous since he was the other person most concerned.

When he knocked, she jumped. Which was also ridiculous. She

knew it was him.

It had to be him.

He was the one she was waiting for.

"May I come in?" His voice seemed to fill all the space between them and touch her before he was even in the room.

And then he shut the door behind him.

Selene was suddenly so flustered. "Should I have—I waited for you. Ought I to be—" She couldn't finish a sentence.

Nicholas' silence in response lasted several moments longer than she wished it would.

Then he said, "You're nervous."

"You're *not?*" Of course he wasn't. He'd done this before.

"Of course I am nervous. I have imagined this moment for what feels like forever."

Oh.

He went on, "But I am nothing if not patient. If you don't wish to do this, why rush?"

Some spark of her usual self scratched at those words that were still bothering her. That he *meant for them to get along comfortably.*

"Well, you are eligible," Selene said, moving across the carpet to rest her hands on one of the posts of her bed. The duchess' bed.

"Eligible." He took another step into the room.

"And really, I admire your interest in the welfare of the public."

Perhaps he didn't like those words coming back to him right at this moment, but still he advanced. "Public service."

"Well, I would add that you ought to know you'd be doing me a favor, as I am not warm or easy to get along with, but I don't think those things are true, do you?" She wasn't trying to get away from him, she truly wasn't, she just felt more comfortable keeping the bedpost between the two of them.

"That's more for me to say, not you." Nicholas had stopped and was just standing there, probably looking at her, and she thought he was smiling.

She took a slightly deeper breath. "Your opinion about whether I am easy to get along with isn't wanted, sir."

"Very well." His boot made no sound on the carpet as he took a step closer, then another. His voice, that purring earthy velvet voice, seemed very close. "Then I won't offer it. Though I do think that you are warm."

She had been warm, in his arms in the greenhouse not that long ago. He'd made her warm. How did he do that? She felt warm now, her arms prickling with heat that felt like it was radiating from her and a heavy pool of something inside making her clothing feel unnecessary.

"Selene, just tell me what you want."

Hadn't she been asking *him* the same question since she arrived in Talbourne House?

"I want you to answer some questions for me."

Was he bracing himself? He didn't answer, of course, of *course* he didn't answer, but he didn't leave either and that would be her permission. She would take it.

Selene asked, "Have you been hoping for this the whole time we've been married?"

"This whole week?" He was here. He was right next to her, and he brushed his cheek against her hair, so gently. She loved that. His voice was so quiet. "This whole very, very long week when you have been right here in my house, just yards away from where I lie in bed thinking of you every night and every morning and most of the minutes in between? No."

"No?" He was so confusing and the sensation of his cheek now brushing just the edge of her ear didn't help.

"No. Not this week. For months, Selene. I've been hoping for this for months. All the time imagining it, longing for it, and plotting how to make it happen."

"My heavens." There was definitely something intoxicating about his nearness; he made her feel even more light-headed than wine did. "That seems quite a while. How can anything live up to all that?"

"By being real."

His hands felt big, they felt *hot*, like they might burn her through her clothes. They spread around her waist. She knew he was going to kiss her again. She was thrumming with nerves waiting for him to kiss her.

But he didn't.

"I so need it to be real that I can wait even longer if I must," said Nicholas from only an inch away.

"I want you to kiss me."

That was all she needed to say, apparently. His arms came around her, his mouth found hers and she might have been dancing, it felt so much like spinning.

Maybe that was just the earth turning. It certainly felt as though he made the world hers.

When Selene felt the world come back and found herself still standing on it, her arms were around his neck and the taste of his lips was on hers. "I am losing my nervousness."

"*Good.*"

Selene thought of herself as of sound build, and Nicholas was not a very large man, but he seemed to be able to move her so easily that she wondered if he could change the world's gravity with only his will. Before she knew it, she found herself seated at the edge of her bed while he drew off her walking boots.

It was only a foot away but with room to breathe, some of her doubts came creeping back.

"Nicholas, truly. If I am not what you imagine me to be—"

"You are Selene. I know who you are."

"But this is a—I have never done this."

"I know. I will be careful."

"I wasn't worrying about that," though now she was. *Careful?* She knew the theory of what they were going to do and hadn't even imagined it could be dangerous; now she worried about that too. "I mean, what if I don't like it?"

"*That* is what worries me. I have no especial talent for pleasing ladies, in my limited knowledge, and I find myself quite worried you will hate something I long for."

"Oh." Oddly, Selene felt lighter. "If we are both worried, this will be so much easier, don't you think?"

"No. If we're both worried, it is likely to be a disaster."

"No no." Grasping his hands, Selene pressed her palm to his, threading their fingers through each other. "If neither of us knows what we are doing, then neither of us can win while the other loses."

"Honestly, Selene, it isn't a competition."

"It *can't* be. I don't know the rules and neither do you. We are going to have to teach them to each other, aren't we?"

Nicholas sighed. "You are going to want to talk the entire time, aren't you?"

"You say that as if it is a bad thing."

"My duchess, may I help you out of that gown?"

"Ah… Yes? If I may help you out of your clothes too?"

"Be my guest, madame." He drew her up to her feet, but without stepping back.

So that she found herself pressed full length against him. "You are already cheating."

"No, I think this is within the rules."

* * *

NICHOLAS HAD ALREADY DISROBED her torturously slowly the night before. He couldn't do it again.

The gown she was wearing, something sweet and blue and besprigged with flowers and he didn't care about it at all, had some odd under-apron part that tied with strings as well as an over-layer with buttons. He had it all undone in seconds and eased it all away, congratulating himself for not ripping through it.

He wanted her because she was *Selene*. Anything she was would have drawn him. The gentle curves of her body, just as playful and elegant as she was, showed here and there through the chemise in ways that were revealing and mysterious at the same time.

"I'd so like to see all of you."

But Selene frowned. "This isn't fair. You can see me but I cannot see you. I want an even playing field."

"It's not a—" But wasn't it a game, of sorts? Hadn't he been playing

299

to win her all along?

Nicholas finished unlacing her stays, and Selene impatiently stepped out of them before drawing her chemise up and over her head.

Nicholas' mouth watered. She was magnificent, all lightly golden skin with a rosy flush on the peaks of her breasts that matched her lips, and coppery curls at the apex of her thighs even redder than the curls that tumbled down her back as she hastily pulled out masses of hairpins.

He hated to remind her, but he was a fair man. "Selene. I can see you."

"Are you still clothed?"

He by God wouldn't be.

Taking his cue from her, he stripped off everything in seconds flat. "Your playing field?"

"Yes indeed." Pulling the coverlets back Selene scooted up the bed to lean on the headboard. She smiled a wicked little smile and gave him a *come here* crook of her finger, and if he'd had a way to capture how she looked right then, he could have revolutionized the art world. "Now. You get on the bed too, and close the curtains."

Nicholas smiled, and rolled his eyes, but did as she asked.

He loved her games.

It was really quite dark inside the bed with its curtains drawn. He noticed the cool texture of the linen sheets, and the way the outside world was far away and silent.

"Now what?" he asked his duchess.

"Now each of us must... make a move, and the other person must say how they liked it."

Nicholas crawled up closer. "You are torture, madame."

"Well how else will I know how to please you, Nicholas?"

Those words from her mouth almost undid him right there. The very idea of her *wanting* to please him slid the last moving pieces inside him into place. He was built anew. He had no idea what luck had brought him to this moment, but if all his bad luck was payment to get him this, he was glad to have paid it.

There was a rustling as if she were wiggling in the pillows. "You... ought to make a move first."

Oh, he could do that.

* * *

WHATEVER SELENE WAS EXPECTING, it wasn't for Nicholas to find her hand and place just one of her fingertips between his teeth, biting it a little.

She laughed.

"You think that's funny?"

She could tell he was smiling. "I did not expect that, sir."

"I cannot amuse you if I am predictable."

The very idea of Nicholas amusing her, or for that matter being predictable, made Selene laugh again.

But he had already moved on, kissing the inside of the wrist he had captured.

The tingling warmth that spread up her arm made Selene gasp, not laugh.

But she managed to say, "It was my turn."

"Oh, my apologies."

When Selene reached out again, her hand met the solid, warm wall of his chest.

And the curly hair on that chest.

"My heavens." It was a startling sensation. She would never have expected it. "Do you have this much hair everywhere?"

"Why answer that question? As you are about to find out for yourself."

Even as she inwardly cursed him for being an uncooperative devil, not answering her questions even now, about *this*, she brought her other hand to comb through the curls there too. Flat nipples quite unlike her own here hidden there, in what she silently felt was mostly like fur.

"I forgot to ask you! Did you like that?"

"Yes," and he managed to make that one word hilariously funny, implying both that the answer was obvious and that she had been foolish to ask at the same time.

"Oh!" She tried to slap at him, but he was too... well, *naked* for her to feel wholehearted about it.

"My turn."

Both of his hands stroked down the back of her head and brought her hair forward, smoothing it over her shoulders. His palms caressed her hair, her shoulders, her skin, all at once.

Astonished, Selene just froze, mouth open. It had been such a quick, graceful, sensuous gesture, and again nothing like she expected.

"Did you like that?" Nicholas asked into the palm of her hand, which he had again turned over and kissed, reminding her of that other kiss in the alcove at the Gravenshire ball, and something hot bloomed low in her belly.

"You took two turns." Selene was surprised at how husky her own voice was. "Really, you can't expect me to overlook all this egregious cheating."

"You can't expect me not to cheat when I never agreed to your rules."

"What—where should I touch you now?" She didn't want to sound young and unsure, but there was only so much she could do about that; it's what she was.

"Anywhere you like."

"Oh, you—" Reaching out to touch him, or possibly throttle him, Selene felt him catch her hands and begin to draw her forward. "I'm choosing where to touch you," she reminded him a little peevishly.

"And I'm helping."

Her small snort said she'd believe that if and when it actually happened. But she let him draw her closer, till she had to walk her knees over to where he sat on the fluffy overstuffed mattress. "Where did you go?"

"I'm leaning comfortably against this bedpost. You should join me."

"What do you mean?"

Nicholas reached and put his *hand* under her *knee*—what a personal place to touch—and pulled her leg over his *lap*. Selene found herself sitting on his crossed legs, her own legs splayed inelegantly on either side of his hips.

She felt vulnerable and very, very exposed.

"I'm just making it easier for you to take your turn." Nicholas sounded very well pleased by this new arrangement. In fact the noise he made as his hands settled around her waist was halfway between a growl and a purr, and pulling her closer he nuzzled the spot where her neck met the bone of her shoulder.

Then he *bit* it.

"Nicholas!" Selene felt her whole body jerk with the shock of it. The slight sharpness of his teeth, the hot pressure punctuated by a swipe from the tip of his tongue as he pulled back—it was more than startling. She couldn't even begin to describe how startling.

It made her ache, too, in places inside, and the core of her felt swollen. It made her want to touch herself, more than she had ever wanted to touch herself. And it made her want to touch *him*.

"Tell me you liked that." There was a pleading note to his voice she'd never heard before.

"It would be difficult to explain just how much." And it would. She didn't have words for the hot liquid feelings that made her boneless and restless all at the same time.

Her hands slid over his shoulders, which seemed much larger bare than they ever had in a wool coat.

She reminded him a little breathlessly, "After all, you are my only model on how to converse in this situation…"

He made another of those growling noises, deep in the back of his throat

Selene didn't consciously give up her nervousness, it just melted. She wrapped her legs around his waist and pressed herself against the furred warmth of his chest, and the sound he made then was incredible. She couldn't resist rubbing herself back and forth a little; the hairs on his chest tickled her breasts and made her moan a tiny little moan herself.

He took the motion for her move. "My turn," and his hands came up under her rear end, raising and pressing her against him. Yet he dropped her almost immediately to slide his hands up over her ribs to cup the weight of her breasts, one in each of his hands. How could a shiver be *hot?*

"No," Selene insisted, "that wasn't my touch. I had planned to try this." Hitching herself just those few inches closer, Selene felt a hard, long heat where she trapped the most sensitive part of him between their bellies, then nuzzled his ear for a moment before delicately tracing the edge of it with her tongue. "That's my touch," she said in a most self-satisfied way when she was done. "Did you like that?"

"Selene," and Nicholas sounded a little as though he were choking on something, "can we just state for the record that you are winning, and set me free?"

"Free of what?"

"Of holding still."

"Well if you don't want to hold still, Nicholas, then don't."

* * *

HE MAY HAVE GROWLED something about this woman killing him as he surged forward, kissing her with all the hunger he'd been holding back, letting his hands touch her, cradle her, hold her, *everywhere* he'd been longing to touch for so long.

It was so much better than he'd imagined.

The smooth swells of her body fascinated him. He could feel the dip in the small of her back as he stroked his hand up from the gentle rounds of her hips to the strong muscles of her back. He could feel the delicacy of her shoulderblades between his hands, then around and up under her armpits—she gasped a startled laugh! He'd tickled her—to settle her more closely against him.

Nicholas couldn't help rocking his hips a little. In this position it only slightly squeezed the hardness of him trapped between them. But it was good, so good, a thousand times better than his imagination had been, his lonely, lonely imagination.

And she was kissing him back.

Selene was kissing him back.

He *did* have luck.

He cradled her head between his hands, tilting her just a little to stroke her tongue with his, fitting together the silky surfaces inside their mouths in ways that were so new he was ready to spend a lifetime figuring them out.

"I want to give you pleasure before I even risk hurting you at all," he whispered into her ear and felt her shiver.

"You are, you are," she assured him, tangling her fingers in his hair and keeping him close when he started to pull away.

"No, I mean this."

Lifting her bodily with his hands around her ribs—he could only do this for a moment but it would be worth it—he closed his lips around one of her stiffening nipples.

She cried out—surely he would hear that sound forever—and grabbed his head, holding him closer.

He chuckled against her breast. "So… you liked that?"

"Again, please, again," and she sounded utterly different and yet so entirely herself.

He obliged.

In a few seconds he had to put her down, and she whimpered.

In one lunge he pushed both of them away from the bedpost and into the bed, lying her down and resting his body between her legs so he could cradle first one breast then the other, teasing the peaks with the tip of his tongue.

Then he closed his lips over one, and sucked.

Her little wailing cry made him feel ten feet tall.

He slid a little lower.

"When I enter you here, it might hurt," Nicholas told her, resting his face against the soft swell of her belly and cupping the center of her with one hand. "I can stop, always. I don't ever want it to hurt, but it might the first time. Shall I?"

He couldn't see her in the dark little cave they'd made for each other, and he wanted to. But she was clutching at him in a way that spoke of nothing but urgency and wanting him.

"Oh yes," breathed his duchess. "Please."

Nicholas had never wanted so much to be careful, and gentle, and inside her all at the same time.

"Let me touch you a little and see if you stretch."

"What stretches?" Selene sat up on her elbows as if to discuss it further and at great length.

He'd never thought that she really knew nothing at all about how this would work. "There is a barrier, well, a sliver of one, and if you have never had anything inside you—"

"Of course not!"

"—it may need to stretch. Or even tear. I'm hoping it doesn't."

"Well can we get it over with? Because it sounds like something to put behind us."

"My darling, I will do my best," Nicholas swore as if taking an oath, and stretched up to suck on her nipple even as his fingers swept through her curls to explore.

He could spend days exploring the folds and all the tiny little specific shapes of her here, and here, and here—

But when he stroked over a swollen, throbbing little nub just within those shapes, she shuddered, and dug her nails into his back. "Again!"

So, obligingly, he did it again.

"Again!"

And he did it again, and again, and gave the tiniest nip, he couldn't resist, to the pebbled nipple he was worrying with his teeth and his lips, and when she cried out again, he did it once more, a little harder.

And she shuddered in his arms so hard, shaking all over, grabbing at his shoulders, his neck, making sounds that weren't quite words but that he wanted to hear more anyway, until falling limply back against the bed, still with his hand pressed to her.

"That was amazing," and she pressed hot, fast little kisses to his lips, his cheeks, his brows, his eyelids. "*You* are amazing. I see now why princesses want to escape their towers."

Half-drunk on his own smug accomplishment, he just kissed her throat, and her lips. "Shall I try?"

"What, there's *more?*"

He laughed. He would never get tired of her making him laugh, never. "I have not yet even been inside you, you satisfied woman."

"Oh no. No, that won't do. And I'm sure you want to."

He rocked the hot hardness of his length against her leg. "I want to. But I can spend happily right here, right now, next to you, and still be happier than I have ever been in a woman's arms."

"My heavens." Then she sounded suspicious. "Wait, are you saying that only so that I won't feel that I've lost?"

"Oh no, my darling." Nicholas slid next to her, pulling her to sprawl on top of him. He liked it; it reminded him of the way she took up most of the bed. "I have definitely already won."

* * *

SHE PINCHED HIS ARM, just a little. He was so damnably *smug*. "But you have not had that pleasure yet, have you?"

"Not yet."

"So do it."

"The pleasure and the being inside you needn't happen together. Or aren't you listening?"

Oh, Selene was listening. She had heard those *my darlings* and was already treasuring them away for much, much future consideration. "I don't want to wait. And my heavens. If it will feel for you anything like what you just did felt for me…"

"If we do it right, I think it will feel good for you too. Perhaps not the first time."

"Nicholas, *please*."

He wrapped his arms around her and pulled her against him so tightly she had to breathe differently. "Don't say please to me like that unless you mean it."

"I won't." She pushed up, just a little, and wiggled back till she could feel him trapped underneath where she was slick and tender. *"Please."*

"If you—if you want to raise up a little, you can control how quickly or slowly it happens."

Yes, she realized what he meant. He was so close to where he ought to be able to slide inside her already; she could feel the slickness there, waiting for him.

"You seem so reluctant," she said even as she felt between them to grip his hardness. She had thought touching him everywhere would seem strange, but it didn't; it was a part of him and she loved it, loved touching all of him.

Nicholas groaned, so deep and loud that she worried that she was doing something wrong. But when she loosened her grip and stroked him more gently, he still groaned that way.

"In all truth, Selene," he almost panted, his breath was coming so hard, "I am more than a little frightened of hurting you."

"I see. So then. We will do this together."

"And you—if it hurts, stop."

"I understand." And just like that, she'd wiggled herself back up, flexing on her knees splayed on either side of him to position him at her entrance.

"My *God.*"

"Was that too quick?" She started to settle down over him, his tip stretching her just as he'd said. "I should have warned you, once I have decided not to be afraid, I am not."

"God, this isn't entirely bad," and she could feel the muscles in his arms locking with the effort he made not to pull her entirely down onto him.

"It does stretch." And stretched more, so hard she felt a pinch. "Ouch."

"Then stop there. You can stop."

"Did you hear a word I said?" Without waiting at all, Selene sat up higher, settling into his lap by using her weight to push past the resistance.

Which wasn't bad, really. There was an even sharper sensation, and Selene felt sure that something might have torn, just a little. And it ached, not the way she ached inside, but like she'd cut a finger. It was certainly not worth *stopping*.

Relaxing enough to lay full-length against Nicholas again—her husband, her *lover*—Selene felt his heartbeat against her cheek. It pounded so strong and steady, and in this moment, it was everything —*he* was everything—she'd never known to dream about but always wanted.

"Thank you," she whispered against his skin, kissing his breastbone, curly hair and all.

"Thank *you*, my precious," said Nicholas, his arms wrapping around her and holding her safe, so safe.

And then after a moment, she said, "Don't you want to move at all?"

"Yes and no. Mostly yes."

"Then please."

"Don't say it unless you—"

"Nicholas. *Please.*"

And when he rolled them both over, it was like setting a thunderstorm free.

She shook and held on as he plunged into her again and again, kissing her everywhere he could reach, making half-growling and half-pleading sounds that might have been words but that were unrecognizable, caught as they were in the storm.

When she felt that swelling pleasure again, all she could think of to say was "Nicholas!" And he answered with that feral satisfied purr, into her breasts, her throat, her hair, nuzzling her ears and biting her earlobes ever so gently and all the while things tumbling out of him that sounded like "*mine*, mine, mine."

"Yes, yours," Selene whispered back, rocking herself against him as hard as she could, seeking that pleasure again and then finding it, a gunpowder blast that shook her even as he sucked hard at the base of her throat where her pulse was pounding and said one more muffled "mine" against her skin, and then he broke.

Still throbbing herself, Selene still noticed that she could feel *him* throbbing too, the liquid heat of his pleasure inside her, and it was a whole new type of shocking intimacy, just one more astonishment in the massive collection of astonishments they'd amassed in the last hour. Or however long they'd been locked in here together.

He was breathing hard as he rolled to her side, pulling her along with him to keep her nestled in his arms. As if he would never let her go.

"My darling," he kissed into her skin, and Selene felt his words sink into her and nestle inside.

"Hello, Nicholas." She pillowed her head on his shoulder.

He chuckled into her hair. "Here is the bad news. I have a terrible urge now to fall asleep."

"So, sleep."

"Thank you, Your Grace." He sounded like he meant it.

"What is the good news?"

His hand splayed across her back, holding her firmly in place. "I can still hold you while I sleep."

"Then sleep, sweetheart," Selene told him, and held him just as tight.

It astonished her that he did.

And then, limp and radiating all the heat they had generated between them, she fell asleep too.

* * *

WHEN NICHOLAS AWOKE, he was in the dark.

With Selene in his arms.

In her bed.

Which was warm and full of the scent of his favorite new game.

He had no idea what time of the day it was. How long had they slept? She'd fallen asleep too. Tired, most likely.

Only the night before he'd laid here and held her and felt that his dreams were close.

And now here they were.

As carefully as possible, sliding first one arm and then the other away, Nicholas managed to part the curtains and make it out of the bed while still leaving Selene sleeping.

Sliding the topmost coverlet off the bed as well, Nicholas wrapped it around his waist.

Thinking of the night before, Nicholas rubbed a knuckle along his lower lip, which was just as slightly sore as one would expect if it had been bitten.

He wasn't so sure any more that his wife's sensibilities were all that delicate.

It only took a moment to thrust his head out the door. Jonathan, of course, was on duty. "What is the time?"

"It is eight o'clock in the evening, sir." The bodyguard addressed His Grace just as if he weren't wearing a quilt in the hallway. And handed him a slip of paper. "Mr. Lyall wanted me to give you this at the soonest possible moment, sir."

"Have some food brought up immediately, would you, for Her Grace and also something for me."

And Nicholas closed the door.

He knew what was on the slip of paper. It had to be the address where he would find the French maid who had threatened Selene right here in his house.

It had to be dealt with. And as quickly as possible.

But frankly, it wasn't as important as Selene herself.

He stuffed the paper in the pocket of his coat before turning back to the bed and looping back its curtain.

It was a shame that his knee on the mattress shifted her and woke her. On the other hand, he got the reward of watching her blink sleepily, the curves of her breasts and hips outlined in the linen sheets as she rolled over, frowning.

"I apologize for waking you, Your Grace." His hand found its way to stroking her hair back from her face of its own accord.

"I'm starving."

"I'm clever, then, for I have asked for some food to be brought up here directly."

"For me, I suppose, while you run off to take care of some *errand.*"

She curled herself into a ball beneath the sheets and Nicholas' chest ached. He had never heard Selene sound bitter before coming to Talbourne House.

"I was planning to get back in bed with you, but if you insist—"

He pretended playfulness so well that by the time she had reached out to yank him back into the bed, he *was* playful.

* * *

"THIS IS BETTER THAN EATING," she murmured as he fitted himself next to her, pulling her into his arms again as he slid under the sheet to join her. "Oh. Did people notice that we did not dine in company?"

"Of course they did. Do you think they will have any reason to start up new gossip? Newlyweds fail to dress and appear to dinner. Special edition required of all the news gazettes."

Rolling just a little to find the curve of the muscle of his chest within striking distance, she bit it.

He made that growling, purring noise again.

"I was not giving you *carte blanche* for sarcasm, sir. I am new to being watched every minute of every day. And my latest experiences have gone poorly. Agh, that public departure from Gravenshire's ball, was that truly only last evening? What a horrifying impression I am leaving on all of London society, wearing a girl's gown to my own ball and then leaving the Duke of Gravenshire's looking as if I had been tumbling around on the floor." She shuddered. "Not to mention the nightmare of encountering that man. I am terrified my mother will want to know why he had business with you anyway."

"It isn't business, strictly. The man has to be held accountable for his own responsibilities and there is no one but me to do it. She ought to have brought the lawsuit herself."

"But Nicholas." Selene felt a little cold. She pulled the covers closer to her chin. "She did not *want* to do it."

"I understand. But the law is larger than her, and larger than your father, I'm sorry to say. Though you might not realize it, if a precedent is set that an heir can get away without giving a widow her portion, others may follow suit, and I do not want to see that happen. Other widows may not have a convenient son-in-law to enforce their rights."

"But she didn't want it." She knew he understood, but also it seemed that he didn't. "How can I explain when she has given everything she has, everything she is to protect my father's memory? It is her dearest wish, perhaps her only one."

"Don't tell her," Nicholas said with the same breezy ease with which he'd said just a few days before, *It is only getting married, after all.*

"I don't—" The unease that had been gathering like a cloud settled in her bones. Chilly and vibrating with nerves at the same time. She couldn't put her finger on exactly how she felt about him saying that, but she knew it wasn't good.

"In any event," he added, "the whole thing may never reach the courts. Often people do the right thing when pushed."

"Do they?" Selene felt her voice was a bit faint, but she didn't want to speak up. She wanted to shake this uneasy feeling and go back to being the Selene who woke up in bed with a Nicholas actually, miraculously *here*, a much more married and desired Selene, one who knew a great deal more about a great many things hidden in the undiscovered country, including how much she wanted her husband—and how much he wanted her.

"I don't like that, Nicholas, I don't like it and I don't like the way you say it. I thought we were—"

But how could she ask him if he had felt as she had, as if she'd found the other half of herself and could never be lonely again?

What if those feelings had only been because of the heat of the moment?

What if they had only been hers?

He was waiting for her to finish her thought. She felt as though she had to get this right, and she didn't want to flay his feelings again as she'd done just the night before.

"I don't want to struggle all the time," she told him slowly, feeling for her words. "I felt... like we were together, earlier, perhaps really together for the first time. Not your aims and my aims, but our aims. I *liked* feeling like that, Nicholas, I loved it. I can't lose it already. And we cannot make love every waking hour."

His arms tightened reflexively. She wasn't even sure he knew he did it, this holding on so tight. It had to mean that he felt something of what she felt, didn't it?

"Then be patient with me, for silence is a habit that is hard to break," he finally said, and the relief she felt at that was like a warm summer rain. "It hasn't served me well with my son, and it hasn't served me well in the Lords. But I am trying. It isn't even going well. But I am trying."

Selene rolled over and shoved an arm beneath his head to wrap her arms around his neck and still stay tight against him. "Why do you not let me *help*?"

Was that a sigh? Nicholas never sighed.

But finally he said, "You are extraordinarily wise, madame, but you are good-hearted. You dislike the idea of thinking ill of someone. On delicate matters, I don't know what you may let slip only from your general good regard for people, which they sometimes don't deserve. And wherever we may speak, I cannot be sure that no one else is listening."

Selene could feel herself trying to make a fist behind his head, to rub her thumb over her fingers. She ought to try to stop that, it was a bad habit. If she could learn to turn her head towards people who were talking, she could learn not to give her own thoughts away.

"No one can hear us in here, can they?"

His arms tightened around her again. "They would have to be just outside these curtains. I believe we are safe in here. But madame, we have never been here before."

"But we are here now, are we not? And like crossing the Rubicon, we only need to take a step once into a new world to make it ours."

"Indeed, Caesar." He was kissing her nose. Touching his lips to hers. His tongue to hers. "Then I may come back here?"

That made her feel a little shy, and as if he were encroaching a little on her hard-earned territory, all at the same time. "Yes. Though I am reluctant to go so far as to give you *carte blanche*, allowing you to do as you wish at any time."

"No?" He'd moved on to nuzzling her earlobe.

She honestly didn't think he was doing it on purpose to distract her. But then, she'd recently been informed she was too inclined to give people the benefit of the doubt.

"No. In fact you still haven't told me anything, only told me why you don't want to tell me things. Lord Callendar told me more."

That noise that he made was really quite alarming when he made it right up against her ear. "Told you what?"

"My heavens, Nicholas, you can't be jealous of the man while you are literally holding me in your arms. Told me you were planning a vote with Gravenshire and were recruiting Morgame to help sway people your way, but he didn't know what it was."

"I can most definitely be jealous while I am holding you in my arms; it is no doubting of your loyalty, but he is a sneak and an opportunist and I am *not* inclined to generally think well of people."

"Just tell me what the vote is. Perhaps I can help."

"I want a man to speak to us all about how the East India Company affects India. It may be time that Parliament put some limits on the power the East India Company has amassed. The reauthorization of their charter comes only every twenty years, and it ought to be fairly examined. So many of the men in the Lords are happy as long as money flows through the Company to Britain and to them. But other merchants are complaining that the Company's stranglehold on trade with India shut them out unfairly."

"So you want more open trade."

"Perhaps. The Company's men are at least bound by the Company's oversight. I don't know how fair that is, but the rules for it exist. We have no means of seeing what other merchants may do there. And what's more, I worry that we are bleeding India to death. Too many of my fellow peers feel that India will be an endless source of wealth forever. They have never seen a stream run dry. No supply is endless. And what of the effects of the Company besides money? What other effects are we having there that we ought to be discussing before we let the Company run as it wishes again for another twenty years?"

"Thank you." It felt intimate and exhilarating and whole, just as when she finally had him inside her the night before. "Thank you for telling me." Her mind was already working, pulling apart the various threads of what he'd said and seeing how they tangled together. "Your goal is quite delicate and complex, but votes are swayed on simpler ideas."

"I can't believe how much I wanted you just because... And you were the perfect choice to be a duchess after all."

Why hadn't he finished his thought?

And what he *had* said felt a bit wrong to Selene somehow too, but he had already given her so much, last night *and* today, that she was unwilling to worry at it.

"You said you just happened to think of it. And that you were not warm." Selene snuggled even closer, still surprised and entranced by the feel of his furred chest against hers. He was definitely warm.

"I did not want to give my plans away."

Selene yawned and squished her face against his chest. She could figure the rest out later. And how to help him. She was sure she could.

Of course he noticed the yawn. "You need to sleep more, you know. And eat. We will eat first."

"Eat first. I never dreamed that Talbourne House would be so exhausting."

"Eating first. And then as it is early evening, I will let you, my lady, dictate how we should spend our evening together."

"I had dominoes for us to try. Oddly, I've lost interest in them now."

"I am quite amenable to changing our agreement." His voice played a tune like serene string instruments, but she knew that purring feral sound was just below the surface. "I doubt either of us ever really wanted only fifteen minutes."

WHEN SELENE WOKE, she had that disorienting sensation that one has when one goes to bed far too early, or far too late.

She stretched and smiled a secret smile, just to herself. She had discovered so many things the night before.

She could get drunk on such rich attention. No wonder lovers were dangerous.

Finding the bell pull with her fingers, she rang and waited for Martha to appear.

Of course her husband was gone. She expected nothing else. Of course it hurt. She had expected that too.

It didn't change the hurt, but she had expected it.

It was still a momentous morning, after what had been a momentous night.

Though she was also discovering that it was hard to hold on to excitement when one was excited alone.

"Your Grace?" came Martha at the door.

"Let us begin the day as if it is ours to conquer, Martha," Selene said.

* * *

EVEN RISING as early as she did, she wasn't surprised that Nicholas had gone out. If he had still been in Talbourne House, she flattered herself, he would have been with her.

She *was* surprised that Jonathan was with her, in Talbourne House, and claimed not to know His Grace's whereabouts.

And she was surprised hours later when Nicholas wasn't there to luncheon with her and the guests as usual.

Though she was more surprised that Edward *was*.

"We got away with some claret last night, didn't we, boy?" Sir Malcolm chortled as he came in, and astonishingly, Edward answered him, almost as amused.

"A bit too much, and a poor mix with pistols."

"Pistols and claret? Do tell, gentlemen." Selene didn't want to upset the delicate moment, but they had put out conversational bait she could not resist.

Edward sounded a little chagrined as he seated himself to the right of his father's empty chair. "I don't think we broke anything important."

"I don't *think* we did," Sir Malcolm confirmed, if shakily, and

317

Selene resolved to find out if anything large around Talbourne House had been broken by any pistol shot last night.

She also wondered if having Edward spending his evenings with Sir Malcolm was very wise. Much as she liked the baronet, she did not want to see Edward picking up his drinking habits.

She'd have to discuss it with Nicholas.

When she saw him again.

Virginia's arrival kept her from feeling melancholy. "I hope you are well today, Your Grace."

"Miss Díaz. Do tell me if you have slept well. And if there is news of Lady Viola."

* * *

THE NEWS of Lady Viola was that Dr. Burke had come to visit his sister, and stayed with her well through luncheon.

When he finally arrived in the blue drawing room where Selene and Virginia were still attempting to knit, he was subdued.

"I am so sorry for the inconvenience of this illness striking right now, Your Grace."

"Don't be absurd. The inconvenience isn't the issue. What can we *do* for her?"

Dr. Burke sighed as he settled himself across from the ladies. "Viola would not want me to tell you much. It comes and goes, it has for a long time. My patients tend to be rich older ladies or soldiers with limbs off, so I have little experience of whatever ails her except inasmuch as I am her brother and have grown up with her, and that sort of experience tends to cloud medical diagnoses more than clarify them. My parents, though, have sought every kind of physician to view her and make their prescriptions, and I cannot applaud their efforts for little has helped."

"How shall we help her? Is it good to leave her to her own devices, shut up in her room, as we have been doing?"

"I think it's as good as anything, honestly." Dr. Burke sounded more hopeless than Selene ever remembered hearing him before.

But, she reminded herself, as he said, he was Viola's brother and had grown up with her. Some fresh medical opinion may yet help her; for now, the illness had only kept her abed for a few days.

"Shall we try to persuade her to attend Lady Winpole's musicale this evening?" Virginia too sounded subdued. Selene knew how she felt. Viola, in her odd way, was an engine of energy that kept the three of them spinning evenly. Without her they both felt like parts of a broken wagon wheel, bumping along and not whole.

"It is entirely up to her. I daresay she sounded as if she wished to go, and that is as good a sign as any. Wanting anything while in the grip of one of these spells is usually the sign that it will soon be over."

"Nothing to worry about, then." Selene folded her hands together, holding her hope tight inside of them. "She will be perfectly fine soon enough."

* * *

As THE DAY GREW LONG, Selene's hope shrank.

Where was Nicholas?

It brought back unpleasant memories of her wedding day, memories she still didn't even understand, of his room-filling presence disappearing and leaving her alone.

Alone to figure out how to handle all of London who decided to attend, and how to be a duchess.

As she was alone now, wondering again if she had done anything wrong.

No. She hadn't done anything wrong on her wedding day, and she hadn't done anything wrong last night, either. It had been too perfect. He had been perfect. They had been everything to each other, that was how it had felt to her. Games aside—or perhaps games *included*.

It wasn't just everything that he had said, though she still had those brief *my darlings* clutched secretly to her heart. They had been better than any fairytale princess' dancing or flowers or jewels, and of that she was certain.

It was also everything he had not said, but told her with his touches.

But where was he?

Even with all her past experience to the contrary, she hadn't imagined that he would only say it all *once*.

Clearly, she *was* too inclined to think well of people.

As the time approached for her to dress for the Winpole evening, Selene found herself sitting in her chair in her chamber, at the table where the dominoes game still awaited his attention, with her knee bouncing up and down uncontrollably along with the thumb running back and forth across her fingers.

She must breathe. She would be a ball of nerves and nothing else before the night was over if she did not think this through.

This was *not* her wedding day. She knew him now.

She at least knew more about him.

Nicholas would have a reason. It might not be a reason she liked, but it would be a reason.

She still knew so little about what he did in the time he spent working on issues for Parliament. But she had the feeling nothing about Parliament would be able to keep him away from her this entire day.

No, she believed that he did care about her. At least, she knew, feeling her cheeks grow hot from the memory, that he very much cared that she was *his*. He desired her, she knew that. And possession of her—at least as an eligible coal bucket, she thought acidly to herself —mattered to him.

Possibly she flattered herself, but she believed at this moment it mattered to him more than Parliament.

Both his sons were safe in this house. Only something about them or her would be preoccupying him right now.

And despite whatever mixup had occurred in the ladies' lounge at the Gravenshire ball, Selene had no reason to think that there had been any real danger.

The only thing that had really given Nicholas pause, was—

"Jonathan." She reached the door and threw it open in record time. "The silver closet, please."

* * *

THE RUSTLE OF MRS. WILKES' starched petticoats managed to sound resentful. "Your new maid should arrive this evening, ma'am."

Most likely well after Selene needed her help to dress for the musicale. It didn't matter. "Mrs. Wilkes, I declined to discuss with you a matter I now realize I ought to have pursued. My *first* ill-fated maid." From what seemed now like very long ago.

"Ma'am." Mrs. Wilkes volunteered nothing.

"I'm willing to wager that His Grace did not bring it up with you either." Because what people believed of others was what they knew of themselves. Nicholas thought her too trusting; that might well also be his blind spot.

And while he might somewhere inside him think that a maid could wander in to Talbourne House and find herself waiting on a guest, Selene would never believe that.

"No, ma'am."

"Of course." If Mr. Lyall had investigated and decided to leave Mrs. Wilkes alone, it was because Mrs. Wilkes was already in the group of people to whom Nicholas had extended clemency. And Mr. Lyall must have taken it upon himself not to bring Mrs. Wilkes to the Duke's attention for what he deemed an innocent mistake.

"Mrs. Wilkes, I'm sure you have some reason for being here in Talbourne House that makes the Duke very lenient with you. I would someday like to know it. Not now. I'm more interested in how the assignment of that maid came about, than in rectifying the situation."

"Oh. I must have misunderstood something. Mr. Lyall gave me the impression that finding you a new lady's maid was urgent. If I made a mistake—"

"Mrs. Wilkes." Selene felt her nerves were stretched already to their utmost and she had nothing left to give this woman, who must want to live in a silver closet for a reason, everyone had reasons for what they did, but she had no more patience and she had an urgent need for answers.

She took a breath and tried to stay calm. "You are quite free to dislike me; people do. But I wish I knew what was at the heart of your dislike. After all, you do not know me."

"Help don't know the gentry, madam." There was a twist in her voice, a twist of something full of hate that was so palpable that Selene could hear it.

"That's a rule," Selene said slowly, feeling along that twist of hate. "A rule everyone ought to follow."

"Without rules everyone follows, everything falls apart."

"What kinds of things would fall apart?" Selene's question was quiet.

"People wouldn't know who they were. *What* they were. We all get up and do as we should because we know who we are and what we are and what's required of us. When people throw that over—" The housekeeper's voice stopped as if it had been cut.

Selene thought she'd take a stab at finishing the thought. "When people like me throw over all the rules about where we should be, who we are, and what we should do, it's chaos, isn't it? How would we know what to do? What could we expect? You don't want to live in a world that's all topsy-turvy and confusing where anything could happen to you, do you?"

"No one wants that really." It came out all in a rush, like Mrs. Wilkes hadn't intended it to come out at all. "Chaos makes everyone nervous, ma'am."

Especially, Selene thought, people who live in closets.

"And who told you that I had worked as a servant?"

The question took Mrs. Wilkes so off guard that she answered it. "Lord Burden mentioned it." She left off the *ma'am*.

"I see. In what context were you even having a conversation with Lord Burden?"

Mrs. Wilkes seemed to realize that she was trapped. Not in a closet, but in a truth. When had a servant like her had a conversation with an earl? Talk about not following the rules.

"He'd been exploring and come down here. I asked him what he wanted and we got to chattin'." Something had happened to Mrs. Wilkes' accent as she spoke. "We were just… talking. He mentioned it."

"He wanted to tell you."

"It didn't seem like that, ma'am. He was friendly enough, and I was interested."

Meaning they were gossiping.

The housekeeper rushed to explain. "He and I were of a like mind and it was just friendly conversation."

"He listened to your problems. Offered you solutions."

"He was a friendly ear."

"He suggested a maid you might take on. And perhaps even assign to me."

Mrs. Wilkes' voice was as dry as her starched petticoats. "He might have, ma'am."

That maid *had* been intended for Selene. Though how *very* bitter she was toward duchesses might have been accidental.

Perhaps, Selene thought, Lord Burden hadn't really spoken to the woman in great detail.

"And did it make you angrier, Mrs. Wilkes, that I made the maid you assigned leave?"

"I never cared, ma'am, I—" The sound of her teeth nearly slamming shut over the rest of the thought was audible.

"Please do finish the thought."

"Servant girls shouldn't play at being duchess."

"Oh. I see." As with some of the people she'd met in those moldy cold rooms, people who had a burning need to shout at her just because they could, the palpable hatred of someone she didn't even know felt almost like a blow.

She steadied herself with a hand on the table, wishing it were Nicholas' arm, and then drew herself up to her full height, drawing her shoulders back and turning her face toward someone who thought that servant girls shouldn't play at being duchess.

But Selene wasn't playing.

* * *

"GENTLEMEN, I ASSURE YOU." Nicholas' voice cut right through the cacophony of arguments flying around the room in French. Everyone quieted so that Nicholas could say, "My patience has limits."

He could practically feel the moments of the day sliding away like sand in an hourglass. He shouldn't *be* here. He should be at Talbourne House with his lady.

He could feel it like he'd felt that pull towards her under his skin all these months. But now the pull seemed to come from right down in his core.

It had taken precious time to convince the girl to leave with him, that she'd be safe. Nicholas could certainly understand why she might think that Nicholas wanted to kill her. But since he didn't, he had to talk instead.

Even if he hadn't been in a hurry, his first visit to a bawdy house made it clear in minutes that there was no reason to linger. It did not look as interesting inside as he had expected. Nor did the young women who plied their trade there seem at all alluring, but then for Nicholas, that was expected.

Of course the place had water leaks at the window frames and cracked floorboards. He'd expected that from a place under Burden's care too. Why were men who were convinced they could do anything, so unwilling to actually do something?

Going in, he passed two men coming out that he knew from the Lords. Apparently the water leaks didn't affect business.

Nicholas nodded as they passed and told the first person who crossed his path, quietly, that he needed to see whoever managed the place.

As a prison, it must have been unpleasant.

And still it had taken ages to convince this Céline woman to leave under his protection.

Then yet another trip across London, which had included a stop at a public house to feed her, as the girl was hungry enough to say so, making it clear that Burden didn't believe in providing food to those in his care either.

And now more time was ticking away while the French revolutionaries were arguing, in this dingy room under a stone bridge.

He couldn't let them start up again; he wouldn't be able to stand it.

"I appreciate that often we must listen to our own arguments three and four times before we persuade ourselves of them." Everyone glared warily at him. At least he had their attention. "However, I have given all the time I can give today to the rehearsal of others' arguments. Sir, your countrywoman will be left in your care or the jailer's. I brought her here as a courtesy to both her and you. For masquerading as a maid in my house and giving me reason to fear for the safety of my wife, I cannot have her roaming London unchecked. Nor does she deserve to be held for the foreseeable future in a locked room by Lord Burden for *his* purposes, nor, to the best of my knowledge, does she deserve to go to an English jail for the crime of being French during wartime." He did not add that if she went to jail, she would likely hang or be sent around the world to a penal colony; he didn't have to.

"I don't even *know* the girl!" The leader of the anti-imperial conspirators seemed affronted that Nicholas implied that he did.

Céline clearly did not appreciate his tone, and had words to say, all of them in French, about her countryman's education, his breeding, and if Nicholas understood the language correctly, his rear end.

Nicholas fixed the leader again with just his eyes, reminding the man that he could be as cold as he had to be, and said, "You aspire to lead a new country. Yet you cannot find an escape for your countrywoman. How much faith should Frenchmen have in you, do you think?"

Though Céline had not had much interest in being attached to this motley band of men, she seemed to agree with this argument. Her eyes flashed disdain at him as she kept her mouth shut. She'd taken a chance to leave with Nicholas, knowing she risked her life. Nicholas rather admired her for it.

Peter Lyall, once more guarding the door, looked ready to take the rest of the day if necessary to let these people work it out. Nicholas found it incredibly hard to appear as calm.

His new insides needed Selene more than ever.

And he found himself glad.

Selene was waiting for him, he knew she was. He shifted his walking stick from one hand to the other, just to remind the fellow it was there.

"All right." The decision sort of half-exploded out of him. "All right, we will take her and find a way for her."

"Out of Britain, by tomorrow, or I will be back to ask why not."

"Yes, yes."

"I'll assign a man to keep watch and see her board that ship. Or boat. I don't care if it's driftwood as long as she's on it and leaving Britain's coast."

"I will see to it."

Céline had a fresh burst of adjectives to say about that, apparently most of them aimed at Nicholas.

"Young woman," Nicholas said, fixing her with the same eye he'd used on the conspirator, "you agreed to come with me of your own free will because your alternative was to stay a prisoner in a brothel. I did not promise you the chance to wander over Britain as you please. As much as it is vile to me to force anyone to do anything, right or wrong, I cannot have you roaming London."

"You just want a leg up on your Lord Burden," Céline spat the name.

"All in all, aren't you glad that it is him I am pursuing further, and not you?"

* * *

"Lord Burden will know who released the girl from his house," Peter Lyall pointed out as they climbed back into the carriage.

"And what of it?"

"Should I... How do you wish to ensure that he won't seek retribution?"

Nicholas sighed. He was tired of games with stupid people, and Burden was one of the stupidest people he'd ever met. "Mr. Lyall, idiots like that shoot themselves in the foot if you just let them play long enough with a loaded gun."

"Or he might accidentally shoot you, sir. Stranger things have happened."

"I'll deal with Burden." Looking at the sleepy-eyed, broad-shouldered man sitting opposite, Nicholas smiled an uncharacteristic and genuine smile, one that reached the corners of his eyes. "We'll deal with Burden. I have no more stomach for this today. My duchess is waiting for me, and I want to see my sons before we must go to this musicale this evening."

And though it was even more uncharacteristic on Lyall than on himself, his steward's face managed a smile. "Of course, sir. I hear the pianist who will be playing tonight is quite good."

"Thank heavens for that." Though Nicholas still smiled as he looked out of one of the carriage windows, watching the wood and stone walls of the crowded part of old London roll past. He'd be home soon, with her. "Perhaps Her Grace will enjoy that."

* * *

"I DON'T UNDERSTAND why the ducks can't have all the bread they want."

"I'm not certain myself, but I believe there is a reason." Selene searched her mind for everything she knew about ducks and found it was nearly nothing. "Perhaps it would be like you eating cake all the time."

"I'd love to eat cake all the time." Thomas was building something out of rocks lifted out of the pond's border, but the gardener Selene had spoken to had said it would be all right, and Selene was grateful he had something to do besides run.

She heard Atlas come nosing around her skirts, panting like a big dog on a sunny day, which she was, and Selene patted the dog's head. Atlas seemed to enjoy going back and forth between Selene and Thomas and keeping a close eye on both.

"Eating cake *all* the time would make you quite ill, I promise," Lady

Redbeck said in her sensible way, her knitting needles softly clicking in her lap. She had promised Selene to help with the planning of the knitting affair for London ladies. She was reacquainting herself with yarn.

"I could try it," Thomas said gamely, ready to sacrifice his health for the pursuit of experimental knowledge.

"So many boys have tried it so many times over so many years, that to repeat the trial is foolish. And you are not foolish, Lord Thomas."

Thomas seemed to be thinking over if he was willing to be considered foolish for the sake of unlimited cake, when Lady Redbeck added, "And here is your father."

The leap in Selene's chest might have carried her practically to the sun, it seemed so high. She heard Thomas splash halfway through the shallow end of the pond, probably ruining his shoes, as he ran to greet his father, but Selene knew exactly how he felt. Atlas, too, bounded toward His Grace.

Selene just stood, trying to surreptitiously brush away any dirt that might be clinging to her skirts, and smiled.

"Your Grace," she said as he approached, with a small curtsey.

"Please do not rise, Lady Redbeck. Your Grace, how radiant you look this morning." And he took her hand, and he tucked it into the crook of his own elbow just as he always did. But it felt like more now. It felt like he was holding on to her, only her, and would never let her go.

"We have discovered where the ducks live." Selene sounded breathless. She *was* breathless. His silence today seemed warming and all-encompassing, like the way the sun had dried the grounds and brought everything bursting out with youth and life. "There is even a peacock."

"There are a few, if I recall correctly." He leaned a little closer. The sound of his voice, the sensation of his breath on her skin made her shiver, thinking of the night before, and he chuckled as if he knew what she was thinking about. "I don't recall whether or not the peacocks like me or dislike me."

"Ask them to marry you, and find out," Selene murmured back.

That made Nicholas laugh out loud. Right out loud, where everyone could hear him—his son, her mother, the footmen, everyone.

She'd never felt more accomplished in her life.

She wanted to ask him if they might go in to rest before they had to prepare for the Winpole musicale. She wanted to ask him to come in to her room again. She wanted to ask him if he knew how to get her out of this dress, and what he thought of seeing her without the dress even in the daylight.

But this was one of the memories, she knew, that she would treasure forever; she could feel it. Her mother being there, whole and alive, made it perfect. Thomas, and even Atlas, made it, made *her* glow with a warmth she wished would last forever.

And Nicholas made it hers.

Sliding her hand down his arm, she intertwined her fingers with his, unwilling to make a more public gesture of everything she was feeling and hoping he understood.

He squeezed her hand back. Perhaps he did.

"Eh, the ground is too wet for games out here. Lady Redbeck, how did you get this chair all the way out here?" Sir Malcolm's voice accompanied the slight squish of yet more shoes by the pond, where it was still a bit wet from yesterday's heavy rain.

And then a miracle occurred, for Edward answered him. "You know perfectly well there are four stalwart footmen over there who carried her out here light as a feather. As if we are all going to be tasked with hauling her back like a snow barge in Sweden full of timber."

"What's a snow barge?" Thomas sounded genuinely interested, and Selene sent her currently favorite Scotsman a silent thought that she hoped he could hear. Because he had made everything better.

Not even another social failure tonight could mar Selene's joy today. For what was the disapproval of London in the face of such real riches?

TREATIES AND CONTRACTS
RECONSIDERED

*S*he managed to keep a hand on Nicholas, on his arm or coat, nearly every step of the way back to Talbourne House itself.

"You must have had a long and tiring day."

"It was," he agreed without embellishing on that.

They had things to discuss, including Mrs. Wilkes and what she knew now about Lord Burden. But Selene felt that whatever he'd been doing all day, she could trust that he would not have left her if she were not safe. They would talk. There would be time. Surely there would be a moment in the hallway, or at her door, to ask if he would like to come in and rest with her.

They might not rest.

Which might be even better.

But as he opened the door to her chambers, she heard someone leap to their feet and come forward smartly, curtseying just inside the door.

"Good evening, Your Grace. Your Grace," and she curtseyed again. "Mrs. Wilkes has sent me up for you to try as a lady's maid, ma'am. And I'm to tell you that Mr. Lyall says I have the qualities you're looking for, ma'am."

"Do you?" Selene was far more interested in the scent of Nicholas' wool coat, warmed by the sun, and so firmly filled with the form of her husband, and she wanted to have a good long quiet conversation with him. "I am so very grateful. I will want to hear more about your experience later."

"Yes, ma'am. I've worked for a viscountess and a countess, and Mr. Lyall has promised me a quite good salary change whether I suit you or not, so I don't mind when you want to discuss it, ma'am," said the good woman, diving into her background when Selene had just asked her to wait. "I've got a good eye for draping, as everyone says, and I don't mind telling you I will be delighted to help dress you, ma'am. I like a fresh look, and there's no one in London with as much hair as you have who isn't wearing it powdered."

"Really?" Despite herself, Selene was interested.

"Really. And that sort of warm gold. Touch of sunset, that's what I call it, and we can find some lovely colors to go with it. I dressed Lady Overburg that night she ended up in the number of Stake's Gazette that sold out twice last year, and I bet I could do a lot more with you."

The little maid—for her voice came from below even Selene's shoulder—sounded as though she were rubbing her hands with glee. "Though of course I aim to please, ma'am, with whatever it is you want to wear. Martha's been showing me some of your wardrobe, but if I had a better idea what you like, we could make some nice picks for this evening on what to wear, and do your hair up right to go along with it."

The calm that had settled into her as soon as Nicholas was back with her spread right down to her toes. This was finally going to work. All that she had tried to put in place was falling right where it should be. She'd be the duchess that Nicholas had asked for, that Talbourne needed. That she *wanted* to be.

"What is your name, please?"

"Oh, Betty, ma'am, I beg your pardon, I should have said so."

"Please do not worry about it." Betty sounded as though she had come from somewhere in London where keeping jewels safe wasn't usually a problem because no one had any. But Selene had the utmost faith in Mr. Lyall. Betty was no doubt exactly what she had asked for.

And she found herself itching to see what a difference it made to have a lady's maid as a duchess ought.

She could hear the warm indulgence in Nicholas' tone as he bent over her knuckles. "I'll be accompanying you to the musicale, my lady. No need to fear that we won't have our fifteen minutes this evening. In the carriage, at least."

"Oh, you…" But she couldn't be scolding—*or* formal—when she felt his lips brush her knuckles. So softly, yet the sensation made her feel as though her knees might buckle out from under her.

And then he kept on walking towards his chambers.

And Selene could not resist.

"Betty, how much time would it take for you to tell me what you know about what other duchesses are wearing to the events this season?"

Betty seemed a good planner as well as well informed as she said, "Given where the sun is now, ma'am, we don't have enough time before you must be dressed to go. But trust me, I can tell you quite a bit while we organize all your hair."

"*All* my hair?" Selene asked, drawing back a little, a bit nervous from precedent.

"*All* your hair," Betty said firmly, leading her inside.

* * *

RUTHLESSLY LEAVING her mother and Virginia to share the deep back seat with Sir Malcolm, Selene slipped into the rear-facing seat, where Nicholas had to join her.

"What an underhanded maneuver for a duchess," Nicholas murmured for her ear alone once they were seated and the carriage was rolling over the flagstones.

In the space where his cape happened to fall over the side of her dress, his hand captured hers.

"I don't know what you mean, and besides, you know by now how I don't like to lose." Selene told herself she needn't feel the least bit self conscious about him taking her hand, or hiding it. It was a reasonable thing for newlyweds, surely. *She* certainly didn't want the others to know how desperately she wanted to touch him after being away from him all day.

"No one is playing," Nicholas purred as he settled back, happening to press his body against hers.

It wasn't just to brace her against the jolting. She was sure of that.

* * *

"Oh, there is Lady Grantley just at the door! How fortuitous."

Selene smiled at Virginia's excitement. "And Sir Michael? Is her husband with her?"

The mention of her friend's husband made Virginia laugh. "Oh no. He has stopped shaving, and Letty won't let him out of the house."

"Never say so!"

"Eh, shaving must wear on a man. The problem is that his beard is massive and grows straight out. He looks like a circus bear-wrangler. And he hates to put on his false leg but won't go out in company without it."

Her mother said, "Your Grace, don't gape."

Selene closed her mouth and tried not to think less of Lady Grantley for having such a peculiar husband. "How lucky she is that she has a brother willing to escort her to social functions."

"Indeed, madame." Nicholas sounded grave. "Never fear for your lack of a brother. I do not mind shaving at all."

* * *

"What sort of entertainment do you plan for the season, Your Grace?"

"I don't have much of a clever mind for devising entertainments. What do you think London is lacking?"

Lady Morgame talked of nothing but recipes for punch and other people's marriages. Selene hoped she would take the conversational bait and talk with Letty about parties and leave Selene to strain her ears for stray words from Lord Morgame's conversation.

Lady Morgame was not, however, stupid.

"Are you truly as enamoured of politics as you seem?"

The lady's abrupt question focused Selene's attention, fast.

"Your father loved politics, did he not?" Letty interjected quickly.

Smart woman. "I have long been a follower of politics," was all Selene would admit without knowing Lady Morgame better. "Yes, from my father's love for it."

"That makes sense. I'm glad to know it, as otherwise it might appear that you had an unseemly interest in other women's husbands."

"What a horrible impression to make, especially when I am genuinely interested in your ideas for entertainments." And she *was*. The easiest way to lie, Selene knew, was to tell the truth, simply about something else.

"Hmph," sniffed Lady Morgame, and, despairing of hearing anything really useful for at least a quarter of an hour, Selene gave the lady her complete attention and did not just leave her to Letty.

It would be well enough. The Prince was at another affair and everyone knew it, so tongues were wagging freely all over the room. There was not, as far as Selene knew, another duchess there. Or duke. People would want to talk.

She just needed a little time.

* * *

"Your Grace."

Nicholas was enjoying the event more than most. He couldn't keep his hands on his wife every second, as he longed to do, but he could raise his eyes and lay those on her at any moment.

Interruptions, therefore, weren't wanted.

Knowing that Jonathan wouldn't have interrupted him if it weren't necessary, Nicholas just inclined his head.

"You asked me to tell you if any of... certain parties left the room. They've all just gone, sir."

"Where?"

"Out and up the staircase to the right, as far as I know, sir."

Nicholas just nodded.

Jonathan, he knew, would stay here and guard Selene with his life. Which was good, as Nicholas could see Lord Burden watching her with the sad, stupid eyes of a cowardly dog. She would be safe in here, as the crowd was large, Virginia was near her, and, though he hated to admit it, the damn Callendar boy was staying within a few steps of her too.

He didn't trust the man any farther than he could throw him, but he knew Callendar wouldn't let any actual danger befall Selene.

Nicholas slipped out the carved double doors and headed for the staircase.

* * *

SELENE STOOD ALONE for just a moment, waiting for one of her friends to come back, knowing she was quite safe and wondering who around her might be useful for Nicholas' vote.

She was eavesdropping, in other words, when she heard them.

"The stamina of these younger men. Do you know, we saw Talbourne heading into the riding shop as we were heading out!"

"Don't tell me. Not stiff-neck Talbourne. You never leave the place before dawn. Or had you worn yourself out with the notches there before the night was done?"

"It *was* past dawn, and the fellow tipped his hat as cool as you please before heading inside. I bet he kept it on while he tupped whatever girl he picked."

"I don't believe it. Never saw Talbourne in one of those places before."

"No man looks that calm on his first trip to the nugging-house. Cold as ice, just like he looks in the Lords. Though he looks too stiff to lie down. Probably picked a girl by measuring her height against his—"

"Selene, what's wrong?"

Selene realized she was holding herself up with a hand against the wall. "Why," she said, trying to make her voice sound normal, "do I look as though something was wrong?"

"Yes," Virginia whispered, "your face is practically blue, as if you'd just dropped dead. Had we better go and sit down?"

Selene forced herself to take a deep breath. The men's voices had moved out of earshot. She hadn't recognized them. She was glad for that.

There would be no fainting lounge today.

"Are—"

Selene just put her hand up. She had to think for a moment. Yes. She had to think.

Nicholas had left their bed—their newlywed bed—and gone to a brothel.

He had a reason. He must have had a reason. Maybe not even the obvious one.

She didn't care.

The roiling, sick sensation in her stomach was made up of many things. Embarrassment, humiliation, shock.

She'd gambled that she knew him, and she'd been wrong.

He was willing to sleep in her bed, but not to tell her his business, or his secrets. She might pry some out of him, but he would never simply share them.

The problem with the lover who turned to murder, Selene realized, wasn't the murder. It was the shock from someone you trusted.

Those shocks would just keep on coming. That was who he was. A man who could make love to her like that, then go off to a brothel. Who could have secret meetings with the one person she hated, the person who had ruined her life. Then toss off that uncaring *don't tell her.*

The more she thought about it, the more she realized she had always been on the path that ended here. That *don't tell her* was the real him, a Nicholas she hadn't wanted to see. The man who would tell her he worried about his reputation one day and then tell her it didn't matter the next. There were reasons, always reasons, but she wasn't to know them.

She wasn't a part of him. They were not part of each other. She was *a duchess*, not the duchess, not *his* duchess, and to him she was just some sort of happy accident.

There was no sharing to this life. They weren't partners. Their dances had misled her, their night together had misled her.

The way she'd felt joined to him? She was wrong.

Slowly the voices in the room came back to her. There were dozens of women there. How many of them had felt this way? Where were the wives of the men she'd just heard talking?

Did all of them find the job of being married so lonely?

She couldn't do this.

She *wouldn't* do this.

There was *no* role in which she would ever be pathetic.

She wasn't unsteady now. Now she felt as solid as a rock.

And she had to think. She had to *think*.

Her friends would help her, if she could just think of what to do. She might spend forever lonely for a man who had only existed in her daydreams, but she wasn't utterly alone.

Selene forced herself to take one more deep breath. "Do I look better now?"

"A bit." Virginia still didn't sound sure.

When in danger, move. "Is Lord Callendar about?"

"He is. Why? I thought Lord Callendar had displeased you?"

"It's not a question of pleased or displeased, it's a question of—" Moving the pieces she had around the board. She must formulate a new strategy. "I will be damned if I leave this party in disgrace again, but we're going to go as soon as we can. Let Sir Malcolm know that he should be ready to collect my mother, will you? And tell Lord Callendar that I wish to speak with him."

She didn't ask if Nicholas was in the room.

He never was.

* * *

Nicholas didn't have to see a clock to know that they were into the second hour of rehearsing all the same arguments he had heard before.

He didn't *want* this. He didn't want to sit listening to these men circle ever closer to something they could agree on. They were just like the party leaders, no different. And it took too much time.

He wanted his wife.

But if there was anyone who could understand how important this effort was to him, it was Selene. This was the only thing he wanted, besides Selene.

Well, he hadn't got his wife by hoping for her.

He had seized opportunity, more than once.

And look what he had gained.

If he had learned anything, it was that one could have what one wanted, but only if one took the risk.

Selene had insisted he talk.

Perhaps he could continue to practice.

"Gentlemen. What exactly is it that you fear?"

Around the table, they sputtered in their tight coats. "We're not *afraid*, sir."

"Then what is the concern? Because my proposal is a simple one. I have not proposed that we keep or change the charter for the East India Company. I have only proposed that we listen to the one man in Britain who knows more about its effect than any other. If the Commons calls him, the Lords will hear him too. You are making complicated something that is really very simple."

"It isn't at all simple. The embarrassment—"

Nicholas fixed the blustering fellow with both eyes. "If you believed then that you took the correct action in spending *seven years* investigating his actions, if you did the best you could knowing what you knew, in all honesty and without malice, then you have no reason to be embarrassed now. Nor have your colleagues."

They may well have had malice, or gone too far; or perhaps they

WHAT A DUCHESS DOES

hadn't gone far enough. But they wouldn't admit it now, and trying to keep their faults hidden was costing them all too much.

Nicholas pressed on. "You do realize, surely, that the hours we are spending discussing whether or not to ask Mr. Hastings to speak only add to the public perception that we have something to hide in regard to the gentleman."

"*What* public perception?" another man burst out, and Nicholas shrugged.

Let them imagine that there was gossip in the streets. He would *create* gossip in the streets if he had to.

"The stalwart men of Parliament can withstand a little embarrassment if it gets us the information we need."

"But why do we—?"

Nicholas had run out of patience for the repetitious questions. "None of us have been to those lands, gentlemen. Yet Britain wants to steer her fate. Will we do it based only on our imagination? Or do we have the foresight, the *wisdom*, to listen to a voice close at hand and well-stocked with the knowledge we need?" He wouldn't go so far as to suggest that they listen to someone who was actually *from India*; these men would bolt. He hoped he lived to see that day come.

"The Company men will riot if we change their system."

And there it was. Nicholas looked closely at that man; he'd make sure to remember him. He silently thanked the fellow for giving him the opening that he needed. "Does Parliament take orders from the Company, or is it yet the other way around?"

That would prick their pride. That was the real question on the table. It wasn't at all clear that the Company took orders from Parliament—and that was what made Nicholas most uncomfortable of all. He had been raised to remember always that a capricious King could take anything of his at any moment. But the King's power was at least limited a little by laws. If Parliament did not direct the Companies, then who limited the Companies' power?

"We are responsible for what the Company does, gentlemen. If we allow other British traders in, we will be responsible too for what those men do. We cannot hide from that, we cannot debate it away.

It's a company charter, not one of the laws of God. At this moment we have the chance to change it, and if we waste the chance, we won't even know what we wasted."

Nicholas stood. "There isn't anything more I can say."

The party man sitting opposite him was watching him. That was the man who would make the final call. He'd heard everything Nicholas had to say, over and over again.

Nicholas didn't expect him to say anything, and he certainly didn't expect what the man said next.

"What drives you, Your Grace?"

"What do you mean, sir?"

The fellow shrugged. "You are probably the richest man in the room. Yet as far as I know, you have no business with the Company yourself. Why? What do you know that we don't?" His eyes were dark and glittered in the candlelight. "What do *you* fear, sir?"

Slowly, Nicholas sat back down.

They wanted just what Selene was always asking him.

They wanted to know what he was thinking. They wanted to know his goals. They wanted to know *why* he did what he did.

This was a game he hadn't expected.

He looked evenly across the table at the man. If he got up and left right now, they wouldn't trust him. But he was not going to spill all his inner hopes and dreams. If he wouldn't to his wife, he certainly wouldn't to them.

But perhaps it was a game he could play.

"Your Grace, we can all tell that something has happened. You might as well tell us what."

Selene sat with her hands folded tightly in her lap. If she set her hands free, she couldn't tell where they might fly to. "I am grateful for the loan of your carriage, Lord Callendar."

"Madame." Jonas was clearly having trouble staying as formal as he should. Fine. "If you are not ill and no one has approached you with any ill will—"

Her mouth dropped open a little as some of her tumbling thoughts connected. "Have you been keeping Lord Burden away from me?"

Jonas stayed silent. Her mother said, "Selene—"

"Lady Redbeck, I assure you *and* Lord Callendar, I am quite unharmed."

"Then why do you look that way?" Virginia's voice was subdued, but she did not stay silent. "We left earlier than planned and we asked Lord Callendar to take us back to Talbourne House. That is not nothing. Something has happened."

"You can't expect us to act stupid." Sir Malcolm sounded almost sorry as he said it.

Selene's mind felt like it was made up of circles within circles within circles, all spinning madly in opposite directions and yet producing thoughts that were so clear, so oddly clear. Free of daydreams about fairy tales, the world was really very simple.

She could tell them something true without telling them the truth.

Without feeling it, she sighed. "His Grace is suing the current Lord Redbeck for my mother's share of the estate."

The sound her mother made was more than a gasp. It was nearly a shriek.

Selene twisted to put her arms around her mother in the seat. "I'm sorry. I'm so sorry."

"*Why?* Why would he do such a thing? When it was all I asked him not to do?" Her mother's voice sounded choked, as if she were swallowing the sobs she would not let out.

"You asked him?"

"When he asked about marrying you. He asked why you had not married, why you had no dowry. I told him. He told me I ought to go to the law, but I said no. I said never."

He'd known. He'd known all along that it was what her mother had not wanted. And she could still hear the easy way he'd said, *Don't tell her.*

"He doesn't think it will become common knowledge, Mama,"

Selene murmured into her mother's hair. "Please don't cry. Not yet. We'll cry later."

Jonas was subdued. "Will you be well, madame, discussing it with him when he gets home tonight?"

Blessing him silently for saying just the line she wanted him to say, Selene didn't have to work hard to sound shaken. "I don't wish to, Lord Callendar. In fact, I had hoped to impose on you for yet another favor."

"Anything," he said quietly.

And she felt something, ouch, that stabbed somewhere inside, knowing she was taking advantage of his feelings when she didn't want them. But the spinning circles in her mind demanded a solution, and she would find one.

"Stay with us for a moment when the carriage reaches Talbourne House, would you? It will only take me a few minutes to speak with Mr. Lyall."

* * *

PETER LYALL KNEW PERFECTLY WELL that he was looking at the end of his life as he knew it.

It was playing out about as he had expected.

"I need to know where I can take my mother and my friends *tonight*, Mr. Lyall. It can't wait for the Duke; it can't wait another minute."

He looked back and forth between her face, which was pointed toward some far horizon even as her words stabbed straight at him, and Lord Callendar's face. The young man looked older tonight, with creases in his brow, but he was clearly here to back the orders of the Duchess.

Which was odd at least and dangerous at worst.

But the Duke had been clear from the first day she'd arrived. Let her go wherever she wanted to go. And Lord Callendar had been given the hospitality of the house, albeit with a grudgingness that fit awkwardly with it.

"If His Grace returns within—"

"*Right* now, Mr. Lyall. Or I shall take my family to Lord Callendar's residence."

Peter Lyall wondered if he might be as strong as he felt and still have a seizure of the heart. For all His Grace didn't seem to care about gossip when it came to his wife, having her decamp to another man's house would be disastrous.

He'd tried to warn His Grace that this day would come. He could serve the interests of His Grace, or he could do as Her Grace commanded.

He closed his eyes and wished he were in Scotland or anyplace equally far away.

"The Dowager Duchess is in residence at her townhouse in the City, and there are many unused rooms." Maybe he could make it to a ship heading around the horn of Africa.

"Brilliant. Have you anything left in the carriage house that can carry luggage? Have it hitched and brought round, would you please?" And she turned to Jonas. "Will you help me?"

That man seemed just as helpless as Lyall felt. "Of course."

"I will need help to bring Viola down. Mr. Lyall, do ask Sir Malcolm if he wishes to go with us. Please, Lord Callendar, help me find my chambers."

* * *

PETER LYALL WATCHED as Her Grace entered the house on Lord Callendar's arm.

Jonathan stood by the carriage.

"Jonathan—"

"Just so we're clear, Mr. Lyall, I won't be leaving her unprotected, you know that. But I'll take my orders from her now."

Yes. Quite clear. And also what he'd expected.

* * *

THE NEW MAID Betty started bustling before the door was even open. She seemed ready to disregard Jonas' presence, which seemed an admirable quality to Selene right then.

Right away she wanted to take charge. "Now then—"

"We're packing, Betty, use any wrapping you can and bring whatever we've got."

"No problem at all, ma'am," said the lady's maid as though this happened to her all the time.

* * *

WHEN NICHOLAS finally left the self-important gentlemen in tight coats, he felt lighter. Things he had never thought possible, were possible.

It was sheerly amazing, he thought, how Selene changed everything.

He was so lost in thought, in fact, that he nearly ran into Lady Grantley at the bottom of the stairs. Had she been waiting there?

"Is the Duchess quite well?"

Was she? Nicholas surveyed the room. He could find her anywhere. She wasn't here. "Is she in the ladies' lounge?"

"She left, earlier than we'd expected, and she said she was fine but she looked odd."

"Ill? Worried? Frightened?"

"No, just... odd."

"I'm sorry to hear that; I didn't know. I must return home myself, my lady, I apologize. And Mr. Hastings." He looked over the tiny woman's shoulder to Anthony. "I apologize to you, too. I was perhaps abrupt when we spoke last."

"*Abrupt.*" The man seemed to decide to embrace manners rather than resolution. "Very well, sir. I accept."

"Please excuse me."

What had happened? He looked around the room for Burden as he left, but couldn't see the little pinched man with the pinched face anywhere. He had better not have done anything to Selene.

He couldn't see Callendar either, and he shoved down his roaring, raging jealousy to remind himself as calmly as he could that Jonas wouldn't have done anything to harm Selene.

And she'd left Jonas over and over again, for Nicholas.

* * *

"Tell me about the townhouse, Sir Malcolm, is it quite comfortable? And have you met the Dowager Duchess?"

Sir Malcolm just sounded sad. He'd decided to come with them, solidifying Selene's suspicion that he had developed a *tendresse* for her mother. But all he said was, "Edward and Thomas will wonder where we are."

She knew. She already knew. She'd been thinking for hours of the little boy she'd fallen in love with, and her husband's angry, difficult, stubborn, and secretly gentle older son. "They will certainly visit us tomorrow. I gave Mr. Lyall strict instructions. I think Thomas will find it a treat. And Edward had planned to make an extended visit to his grandmother anyway."

But as the miles grew longer and the wheels kept turning, leaving behind that jam-stained little boy, Selene came closer than she had yet to wavering.

But no, she wasn't leaving Thomas. She was giving herself some room to breathe. She had to figure out what she wanted to do next. Not for her mother or for Nicholas or even for Thomas, but for herself.

She would see him tomorrow.

She meant Thomas, not Nicholas.

As long as she kept reminding herself of that, she could manage not to cry.

* * *

The butler of the Talbourne townhouse was as circumspect and unflappable as she expected from any member of a Talbourne household.

His certainty that the Dowager Duchess would not want to be disturbed, however, did surprise Selene.

Nonetheless, as long as they stayed to the servant staircases so as not to wake Her Grace the Dowager Duchess, the fellow was perfectly willing to have fires laid and dust coverings removed in a suite of rooms at the back of the house. The house was tiny compared to Talbourne House, of course, but large for a townhouse—two or three of Cass' house would fit inside, Selene thought. Maybe four.

Every available footman was needed to move Lady Redbeck to her room. Jonas had carried Viola, wrapped in a rug, down the stairs at Talbourne House, and he carried her up the stairs in the townhouse without a protest.

Selene waited for him at the foot of those stairs till he came down, standing by the china cupboards and thinking that something about this felt familiar.

His voice, when it came, was the wrong one.

"It is uncomfortable, to just leave you here."

It's still my husband's house, she thought, but it seemed awkward to say it.

"We will all be fine."

Jonas was shuffling a little restlessly. "Don't let Lord Burden in the house, you know."

"I know, sir. I mean, I know he sent that maid to spy on me."

Jonas made a frustrated noise. "And you were pushed near those stairs, and someone attacked you right in the Gravenshire house—you must realize that you are in danger, Selene."

"Not much, I think, since I seem to have many brave knights guarding me. Knights and—" Why wasn't there a chess piece representing a duke? "You don't think the man means to kill me? What would he gain by that?"

"He needn't have a reason."

"People always have a reason for the things they do."

Another frustrated noise. "Not always they don't. The staircase may have been just an accident."

"Yes, I think it was." But then, she had been told recently she was inclined to think well of people. "If it was, then the maid was really only to spy on me and just couldn't hold her temper. And at the Gravenshire ball, I would have been—"

"You would have been kidnapped."

Selene shrugged. Nothing seemed to matter much right now, anyway. "That doesn't sound that dangerous."

"You foolhardy beautiful woman. And where do you suppose Lord Burden would keep you, his house?"

"He seems foolish enough. Why, where do *you* suppose Lord Burden would keep me?"

"Do you not know how Burden makes his money?"

"Unfortunately, I cannot even express to you how little my parents cared about anyone's money."

"His father left him a great many brothels, madame."

"Oh. Heavens." Even with surprise dulled as all her feelings felt dulled right now, that *was* surprising. "I can't imagine that priggish little man doing business in… that." A thought struck her. "Do you suppose those ladies *want* to be there?"

"Only you would ask that question. Some do, some don't. The ones that don't generally haven't anywhere else to go. But the places aren't set up for anyone to sneak away. They don't want any customers coming and going where they can't see."

"I see. It would be an unpleasant prison, but—"

But her discomfort wouldn't be all the harm.

His Grace might be able to arrange to shrug off having a wife who was a housemaid, since she *had* been in Cass' house, after all, a place where no one came and went, where Cass had had a well-known chaperone until she was married (for all anyone knew), where no one had *seen* her.

If members of the ton traipsed in and out as often as those awful men had said, she'd be seen. He'd make sure she was seen. The very thought made her shudder. Even if she wasn't physically harmed, it wasn't a place a woman left with her reputation intact. And they talked about it. That talk would *definitely* travel.

"Why bother, though, Jonas?" His name just slipped out while Selene was clearly thinking hard, her thumb rubbing her fingers till her knuckles grew red. "Why all that bother for *me?*"

"Capture the queen, the king is vulnerable, Selene. And he would have been. He would do anything to keep you safe. Vote any way they wanted." Jonas' disgust was obvious.

"That is absurd."

"Vicious and vile, yes. Absurd, no. Kidnapping hasn't been a political tool in England for a hundred years. But someone convinced Burden to revive it."

"*Convinced* him?"

"Oh yes. He isn't clever enough to think of it himself."

Well, she'd still be as safe tonight sleeping under a roof that belonged to Nicholas and with his men stationed all around. "I ought to be safe enough here, and so will all my family. Jonathan will stay with me, I'm sure. Mr. Lyall has done me a good turn, thinking to send me here." She reached out, her fingers bumping a little awkwardly against his chest so she could find his arm and pat it. "And you have done me a good turn bringing us here. I am so grateful to you, Jonas."

"I wish I could do more."

Selene squeezed his arm in its coat-sleeve and, moving carefully so as to hit the right target, leaned close and up on tip-toes, to find his cheek with her other hand so she could kiss it, just once.

"Just… thank you."

She left him there, trusting him to go.

And as she trailed up the back staircase so as not to disturb the sleep of a Dowager Duchess she hadn't yet met, step after step up to the third floor, Selene thought about how far she had come from her role as a housemaid, and how far she had not come at all.

* * *

JONAS ADORED ALL the little maneuvers of politics, he mused as his carriage rattled away from the Talbourne townhouse in the night, but this was a game with way too much risk.

Putting aside what Nicholas would do—which was a very big danger in and of itself—he couldn't keep visiting the newly-married, now-decamped Duchess of Talbourne without people noticing.

He winced to himself. Nicholas would notice first.

It could be easily solved by *not* visiting her, but Jonas didn't have any illusions about his self-control. He couldn't stay away from sweet politics, he definitely wouldn't be able to stay from her.

He wasn't even sure how far he was willing to take this game. He wasn't the type of fellow who stole other men's wives.

Well, he *hadn't* been that type of fellow.

The Duke hadn't become someone different in the space of an hour. He'd done something to drive his duchess away. He might be able to fix it.

Jonas would sleep on this tonight, but by morning he'd better decide if he wanted to go to all-out war with the Duke of Talbourne for his lady, or find some way to help the idiot for Selene's sake.

The sky wouldn't even begin to lighten for a few hours yet. He had till morning to decide what sort of man he was.

IT WORRIED Nicholas that Selene had asked Callendar to take her back to Talbourne House. He inspected every inch of the Talbourne carriage that he could without crawling underneath. It seemed fine. Why hadn't she taken it? Or more reasonably, why hadn't she waited for him?

He told the driver to take him home.

It was a long drive and Nicholas had plenty of time to worry. He'd spent a great deal of the evening in that upper room with the men in tight suits, but the Talbourne party had intended to stay for the entire musicale, and these things usually lasted till the wee hours.

As he stepped down from the carriage at his own threshold, from inside the huge doors he heard the strains of a light, plaintive flute.

Some guest of his was having music.

Nicholas had had quite enough of company for the evening, and he did not like disturbing the pleasures of his guests anyway.

As he set off to walk around the family wing, woodwinds joined the flute and their intertwining notes floated out on the night air. Maybe Selene would be waiting.

* * *

HE OUGHT to walk around outside Talbourne House more. He'd already found some paving stones that needed to be reset, and some ugly topiary he thought Selene might prefer to replace with flowers. Maybe a lilac bush.

The grass was high and the ground wet. Perhaps he needed to speak with the gardeners. Talbourne House had never had grounds that stayed wet before. Mr. Lyall ought to tell him if they had changed something about the water drainage.

Nicholas was still looking at the wet grass stuck to his boots as he came around the corner to the lower door that led straight up to the family rooms. The one with a little paved nook.

The one with a man hiding by it.

Someone had given the fellow some clothes, but they were still rougher than a Talbourne servant would wear, and certainly far from that of the people who came and went as guests. And his head was sunk in his shoulders a little as if he already felt guilty.

He scrambled to his feet as soon as he caught sight of Nicholas. The look of wide-eyed shock on his face gave away that he hadn't expected to see the Duke of Talbourne.

But Nicholas knew that. He knew every face of every person who lived or worked in his home, and this man ought not to be here.

"You ought not to be here," he said as calm as ever.

Panic seemed to flood through the man, moving from his face down to his fist, which he tried to swing at Nicholas.

Controlling the man from the head like a snake, Nicholas instantly cuffed the man about the neck and, going with the energy of that motion, let him overbalance himself down to the paving.

Rather than go down with him Nicholas transferred his walking stick to his right hand and used it to press down between the man's shoulderblades. He stepped on an elbow and used his weight to keep the man down and disinclined to try to get up.

"You can be sensible, or you can be broken into pieces right here on these stones. You choose."

The gurgling half-squeal the man let out was untranslatable, but the way he spread his hands on the floor and stayed down was clear enough.

Looking at the man spread out on his paving stones, the man who would have tried to carry Selene away, Nicholas was surprised at the fountain of rage that burst up through his chest and made him want to beat the man senseless.

It made sense to feel angry. This man was in his home, attempting to kidnap his *wife*.

But this angry? He shied away from the images in his head, relaxed the hands that were shaking with the need to inflict far more damage than the man had tried to inflict on him.

But no, it wasn't. Because this man had been sent to take away his heart.

"I don't like you and you are in *my* home. You're going to cooperate."

The man could tell it wasn't a question. He nodded so vigorously that he accidentally thumped his own head on the stones.

"Get up."

* * *

NICHOLAS KEPT hold of the ruffian by the collar of his coat.

"Get Mr. Lyall," he told the first footman he saw, and the young man ran.

When they reached the grand foyer, Nicholas let go of the man's collar just as Atlas came bounding up to greet him.

He'd need to spend some time training the dog, Nicholas realized. An animal that large needed to charge carefully.

But he managed to keep his feet as Atlas pressed against him with her huge shaggy body, panting with excitement.

He pointed at the man he'd collared. "Kill," he said to Atlas.

The man whimpered, but Atlas just panted and continued to wiggle against Nicholas, halfway to the goal of pushing his knees till they bent backward, he thought.

He ought to have hidden the fact that his dog didn't have any attack instinct at all as far as he knew.

But it had kept the man frozen to the spot for just a minute longer, and here came Mr. Lyall, and Nicholas decided to forgive himself for giving something away for once.

"Mr. Lyall, I—"

What was it he saw in the man's face? He didn't recognize it at all.

"Your Grace."

"What has happened?" Something had happened, he knew that much. And it wasn't him catching this cut-rate cutpurse out the back door. "Are there more of these men? Are they in the house? Do you—"

"Her Grace," said Mr. Lyall, stopping him instantly, stopping his very breath, but then the man didn't finish the sentence.

"What *is* it?" A black, deep hole opened up somewhere inside him. All his childhood panic about never showing how much he wanted something was waiting right there to swallow him up.

Nicholas both wanted the man to say it, and wanted him never to say it. Even the man he'd apprehended didn't move.

"Her Grace… has left."

There was a long, bleak, silent moment.

"Is she all right?" That was the voice Nicholas never intended to use where anyone could hear it.

Mr. Lyall showed no surprise. Maybe he had always expected that a voice like that lived inside the Duke.

"She is well. She insisted that I provide her with other lodgings, and I sent her to the townhouse. I thought you would want that. I hope it does not anger the Dowager Duchess, but…"

"You did right." She wasn't here. *She had gone.* "Thomas—"

"His lordship does not know, sir; he is in the nursery. Lord Fettanby is out."

"He went with her?"

"He took the gig, sir, and left quite early. I do not know when to expect him home."

She'd gone.

Mr. Lyall cleared his throat. "Her Grace was accompanied by Lady Viola and Miss Díaz, sir, as well as Lady Redbeck. Sir Malcolm escorted them."

Nicholas felt his jaw clenching and his upper lip twitching as if to show his teeth. "And Lord Callendar, I suppose."

His steward only nodded.

That screaming storm of anger and fear that he'd never entirely managed to suppress was waiting inside him. He would never unleash it. But it might swallow him whole.

Talk about failing. He'd been playing entirely the wrong game. Because it wasn't Burden who had taken her after all.

"Send all but four of the footmen to the townhouse." Nicholas tilted his head in the direction of the man he'd captured. "Find out whatever he knows about whoever hired him. I trust you will make sure he gets to the custody of the correct sheriff."

"Of course, sir." Peter Lyall waved to the two footmen who were standing at attention down the hallway beyond the ballroom; they leaped forward and seized the offender on both sides, taking him away. "And the footmen at the townhouse are to…?"

"Watch the entrances and exits, Lyall." There was a heavy tiredness to Nicholas' tone, a bend to his neck as if bowing to the inevitable. "Make sure she is safe, whether she stays there or goes—or goes anywhere else."

"Of course, sir," his man said again.

Atlas sat down with a whump at his feet, the slow sweep of her tail shooshing back and forth across his boots and the inlaid pattern in the floor.

Nicholas just laid his hand on her head. The openly loving life of her soothed that place in him that was raw and dark.

"Did she—did she leave for good, Lyall?"

He looked up to look into the drooping, too-knowledgeable eyes of his steward.

"I don't know, sir. I wish I could tell you."

"I do too."

Leaving the details to Lyall's capable hands, Nicholas moved slowly to the bottom of the stairs. Atlas heaved herself to her feet and followed him.

The shallow, carpeted stairs looked endless, leading upward to the empty void. It didn't matter how long it took him to climb them, because she wasn't up there.

He'd lost.

She was gone.

* * *

"I AM SO sorry to intrude on you this way." Selene sipped her tea.

She could have tea anywhere and any time she liked.

"There is no apology necessary." The Dowager Duchess sounded like she might have expected Nicholas' mother to sound: she had a lovely voice and didn't seem to care about anything at all. Certainly not little details about who owned what and waking to find her house filled with strangers.

Selene no longer trusted that impression.

"Nonetheless, this is a difficult circumstance. I wish we had met before. I am sorry that we did not at least meet at the wedding."

Her Grace's teacup made the faintest of all possible sounds as she set it back into its saucer. "I had made plans, and I am not in the habit of changing my plans due to a last-minute invitation."

Not even to her son's wedding?

Well, that explained a great deal about Nicholas' childhood.

In the next moment Selene felt a tiny pinprick of sympathy. If the lady preferred to make plans, having Nicholas for a child must have been difficult.

But she didn't say anything about that, or that based on her limited knowledge, the Dowager Duchess ought to have done far more to care for Nicholas as a child. Instead she said, "My friends and I decided to stay a little closer to the city as the season comes into its own. We are so excited for the Ayles ball this coming week-end."

That wasn't at all why they were there, but Her Grace didn't have to know that. *Don't tell her,* a voice mocked her from the back of her own head.

"Are you? I was asked to sponsor that but could not find the time."

"There must be many demands upon your time."

Perhaps Her Grace suspected that Selene was prodding for details. If so, she gave no hint of it. She simply provided them. "I have a charity I visit on Mondays and Fridays. My friends have a sewing circle that meets once a week to sew for them. I take tea on Tuesdays with some young ladies I am helping to sponsor for the season. And my friends and I trade calls on a reasonable schedule."

"Yes. How reasonable that sounds." If one said *reasonable* instead of *rote.* "So many things requiring your attention."

"Enough."

Well, she was no more of a talker than her son. But Selene had developed some recent ability to keep this sort of person talking. "What interested you about this particular charity, madame?"

It was only easy to get to the heart of people with a few questions if they allowed it. Nicholas' mother paused for just a brief moment. Then she allowed it. "Orphan children, madame. I have a soft spot for them."

"Truly?" This woman had no soft spots. Selene could easily imagine how she herself would lose hers, over time. "If you enjoy children, it is a shame you did not have more."

Chancy business, thought Selene, venturing into sensitive territory, but then she was feeling more reckless these days.

The Dowager didn't seem to take offense. "Just as well in its own way," she said, drinking from her teacup again. "I don't have a knack for them."

* * *

"OH MY GOD." Selene did not like to swear but at this moment she felt it.

"Was she awful?" Virginia was sitting alongside her, in chairs by Viola's bed. Viola hadn't said three words, taking the switch from Talbourne House to the Dowager townhouse without any interest at all.

But Viola was there, and she was sitting up, and that would have to be the prize for today.

"She was perfectly fine. I don't think it would even be right to call her cold. It is like talking to a piece of paper." Selene wondered if she had always been like that, or if her emotionlessness was the result of marrying the man she'd married. It was a chilling thought.

"Well, but His Grace is something like that."

Not alone with her. He hadn't been, anyway. "To some."

Virginia was not dissuaded. "If he was around her much as a child he must have learned that from her."

To which Viola said, "One needn't be like one's parents. Or like one's parents want one to be."

Virginia took a big breath, clearly wanting to make a fuss over her friend for talking, but then, perhaps following Selene and Viola's examples, decided to be more calm. "No, one need *not*. But a parent's example is what a child sees."

"The Dowager Duchess' example would be appalling whether one can see or not," murmured Selene.

But Virginia was right. That woman had been Nicholas' main example growing up of how *not* to be like his father.

It certainly wasn't hard to see why Nicholas didn't say how he felt.

But that woman truly seemed to feel nothing at all.

Whereas Nicholas felt things, she was sure of that. It was just that no one would ever know what they were.

A DOG TONGUE woke him up.

"Atlas. No."

Atlas paid absolutely no attention, licking Nicholas' face with abandon as though Nicholas were wearing a cologne made of steak.

Probably the tears, Nicholas thought, and that made him remember.

She'd gone.

The exhaustion of last night washed over him again as well, though the sun was high enough to tell him the day was half gone. Apparently part of him would rather sleep than wake up and remember she was gone. How *much* he'd lost.

He'd *really* lost.

Oh, God. He couldn't fix this. Primarily because he didn't know what he'd done.

How was he supposed to figure out what particular thing had driven her away? She had deserved better than him from the start.

Atlas went back to licking his face.

"Your Grace."

Nicholas craned his head. There was Thomas standing in his half-open door, with his nurse lurking behind him and primly avoiding catching a glimpse of the Duke in bed.

He stretched out a hand.

Thomas ran in and climbed up on the tall bed, wiggling down under the covers and pulling it up over both their heads. Fortunately, Thomas was too young to care why Nicholas was lying mostly clothed in bed until the sun was high. He had his own agenda, as everyone did.

"Papa, I have something to tell you."

Had *he* taught Thomas this? To hide under the covers to tell him secrets, and call him by the title he liked best?

Selene had done nearly the same thing.

Was *he* the one making his family this way?

His father was dead, the Prince Regent paid him no attention. Did he really need to be so quiet?

"Papa, I'm squished."

Nicholas stopped squeezing his little boy quite so hard. It was difficult, though, letting him go even an inch farther away. In fact,

357

Nicholas was inclined to get the dog to climb into the bed as well and perhaps they'd all stay there for the rest of the day.

"I have something to *say.*"

"Yes. I am listening."

"Papa, where is Her Grace?"

In the tiny circle of what I most fear to lose, thought Nicholas. *You, and Edward, and her.*

Thomas was in terrible danger of another very tight hug.

"She is visiting Grandmama in town. Would you like to visit her?"

"Oh, yes!" The little boy bounced up and down and his father realized that a few more like that might break his ribs. The child was getting bigger. That was what happened, they got bigger and went off and found love and never told him about it and left him all alone.

As Edward was doing.

As his duchess had done.

He was in a fair way to lose more than his father ever had, with no more idea of what to do about it.

At least Thomas wasn't upset. The relief on the little boy's face was obvious. "I thought something was wrong."

Just me, Nicholas didn't want to tell him. *Just me, I've done something to foul up the only chance at love I've ever had.*

Love?

Yes. Selene had been his only chance at the love of a partner, his other half in every way.

At least Thomas loved him.

Nicholas was pretty sure.

Could one be sure, without asking? Asking seemed risky.

He'd ask.

Perhaps. In a roundabout way.

"Will you be well here, with only me?" He wouldn't mention Edward.

Thomas was surprised. "And nurse, and the cooks, and all the footmen and Simon in the garden—"

Dear God, his son wouldn't grow up thinking the gardener loved him more than his father did.

"I love you, you know, Thomas. I love you so very much."

And Thomas smiled a little-boy smile, a fearless one. "Oh, I know, Papa. I love you too."

One more engulfing hug wouldn't hurt him. "For sure?"

"For *sure* for sure."

It hadn't hurt at all to say.

He'd say it to Edward. He should have—

He should have said it to Selene.

He loved her, he by God loved her right down to the core of his being, and he had been afraid to admit it even to himself. When he ought to have known it, ought to have told her.

No wonder she'd left. Something had made her doubt him, and he'd let it happen, because he hadn't given her that certainty to hold on to.

Why *wouldn't* she think it was all a game to him? Even that night. Nicholas had let their spectacular game speak for him. But without words, one couldn't be sure.

Just as one couldn't assume a draw, one had to offer—

He sat up, dumping a laughing Thomas into his lap.

No. He hadn't agreed to a draw. *She hadn't offered one.*

Selene was scrupulous about following the rules. She said what must be said.

If Selene were sure that she wanted him to concede this marriage, she would've done him the courtesy of telling him so.

Philip was bringing in a vase of flowers. Roses. Forced early in the greenhouse, perhaps; it was too early in the year for roses.

"How does one force roses, Philip?"

The fastidious fellow was straightening their leaves the way he did coat lapels. "I don't know much about it, sir. Feed them, keep them warm, sunlight. Whatever makes roses happy, I suppose."

Happy. Not just safe, but happy.

Nicholas would never force anyone to do anything. But what if he could persuade? One couldn't really *make* roses bloom, but with enough care, apparently they could be coaxed.

Playing—and losing—all those games was only valuable if he learned something from it.

No, that wasn't true. It had been valuable in that it was time spent with her.

Still, Selene had taught him something about strategy and how to play.

And how to laugh. And how to hope.

His teacher of games. His duchess. His everything.

She'd made him hope, in that little room in the Winpole house with the men in tight suits who wanted him to tell them who he was, what he wanted to persuade them to do.

That, he'd done.

She'd made it possible for him to do that. Not every crack in the wall would let everything in him come howling out. His insides were different now. He was different now.

There was a real point at which the game was over. No one knew that better than Selene. And she hadn't left him a message, nothing. And she'd been—well, if she didn't love him, she had been very well disposed toward him when he'd left her. Something had happened, but was it likely she would swing all the way to hating him in the space of a few hours and never swing back?

Maybe she'd just needed time. Maybe the game wasn't over.

Nicholas looked over to where Thomas was wrestling with Atlas on the floor. "I needn't warn you not to trip Philip?"

"Of course not," the small boy said in disdainful tones that Nicholas was all too afraid he'd learned very close to home.

"Lord Thomas, when you visit Her Grace today, will you take her some flowers from me?"

"Of course," the boy said immediately, sitting up in astonishment that his father had asked anything of him before being bowled over again by the dog.

He'd better have someone else try to train that dog better, Nicholas realized. He himself couldn't even bring himself to do that, his aversion to making anyone do anything was so ingrained in him.

But as with the men in tight coats, perhaps he could persuade...?

He would need a new plan.

One of his failings, he realized, was that he had never really finished the first one.

* * *

SELENE HAD NEEDED TIME. That had been her first instinct, to find a place for her and hers where she could have a little time.

And she'd discovered that she did have a temper. It burned far colder than she had ever expected.

Of course, no one had to know that she was secretly enjoying contemplating revenge. Or if not revenge, at least something that had *nothing to do with what Nicholas wanted.*

The war council was down to Virginia and her mother.

Selene thought she could take half of Britain with less.

"These are the ladies you want." Lady Redbeck sounded very sure. "Of course, my knowledge of who is influential in the Lords is six years old."

"We will work with what we have, madame, and be grateful for it."

Virginia sounded worried that she might have to write every invitation. "Do we have to have the invitations go out today?"

"Absolutely today. No late invitations, no shocking surprises. We are going to have a social gathering according to *all* the rules."

Left to her own devices Selene was *not* unpredictable, and it wasn't as though it was difficult to follow the rules of propriety. It required only taking others into account a bit, and talking to people.

Selene insisted, "This event is going to be positively boring."

"Well," her mother sniffed, "you won't like the way people talk about you afterwards if it's *boring.*"

"It will involve knitting. And cakes. And gossip, about ribbons until I fall down dead on the floor if that is what my guests wish to talk about. I am *not* the Duke's discarded paramour and I am *not* the secret daughter of Catherine the Great. I am Her Grace the Duchess of Talbourne and I will by God be known and remembered as such."

"My goodness, darling, you speak as if you are marching off to die on a battlefield. You needn't *swear*. Take a breath, dear. It will be fine."

Selene considered asking her mother never to call her *darling* again.

"It *will* be fine. We must give Betty something to work with. We never decided whether London should think I am fashionable, or sober, or a bluestocking—"

"Oh no, darling, not a bluestocking," Lady Redbeck said with dismay.

"Mysterious."

Selene heard everybody turn. But she knew the voice. "Lady Viola! You are feeling better?"

"I'm up," Viola said shortly. "You must aim for mysterious because you have no other choice. There have been too many odd things that you aren't going to explain. You will be the mysterious Duchess of Talbourne because you have no other option."

"Oh dear," said her mother.

Virginia, however, found the excitement in the thought, as always. "That is *enchanting*. No one can resist mystery. You will have so many chances not to explain yourself! And lovers will fall at your feet."

If they did, she'd step on them. No more lovers. There was a limit to how many times she could become someone new, and Selene had passed it. She was making a stand right here.

"How does one dress mysteriously, though?" mused Lady Redbeck.

"Betty will know."

"Lord Callendar and Lord Thomas Hayden for Your Grace, ma'am." The butler stood just inside the door.

There was a mixed blessing. Selene felt rather abashed at the way she'd been so familiar with Jonas last night. Too familiar. "Thank you, Mr. Hoyland."

"His lordship apparently decided to pay a call just as I did." Jonas was shoved aside, apparently, as Thomas thundered in. Where had he gotten such heavy shoes?

Not that it mattered. In the next moment he'd launched himself at her and she braced for what suspected would be a small boy impact.

Laughing, she hugged him as hard as she dared.

Had it really only been yesterday that she'd thought she had everything?

She laid her cheek on his hair and willed herself not to cry.

"I brought you a *biiiiiig* bouquet from His Grace and a message."

She didn't want a message from him, she told her heart sternly, feeling it leap in her chest.

But she ought to have told Virginia, because Virginia was the one who asked, "Do tell, what is the message, Lord Thomas?"

"He said to tell you the flowers were all already yours. I don't know what that means. What does it mean?"

Selene put him down before he felt the pounding of her heart. Someone must have brought the bouquet in; she could smell rosemary, and moss rose, and the orange blossoms, oh heavens no, not orange blossoms.

"I couldn't say," she managed to tell Thomas. Which was in its way true.

Jonas cleared his throat, bringing her back to the present. "There's a card here you must not miss. Mr. Lyall must have sent it along with Lord Thomas. An urgent note, from your cousin. Dr. Burke's father has collapsed and they've gone to attend him."

"Are you reading my messages?" It was too familiar a tone, but he'd surprised her.

"Yes," he said without apology.

She ought to have realized Jonas would come back. It had just felt like she was ending everything, last night. She ought to have realized that he hadn't agreed to end anything.

Men were just an astonishing amount of trouble.

But here was another crisis. Dr. Burke's father. "Well, we must see if there is anything we can do for the household. Send someone to ask Mr. Adams there—No, wait! Viola! That is *your* father!"

"I am so sorry, Lady Viola, I should not have broken the news that way. I forgot your relationship with Dr. Burke." Jonas was truly abashed. "Can I help you arrange travel? You will need an escort."

"I am *not* going to Morland."

Selene was surprised; Viola was never this vehement about

anything, and certainly not since she had been ill.

"Lord Thomas, would you like to see my room?"

"I'm sure I've seen it before."

Of course, this was his grandmama's house. Her mind balked at the idea of Thomas and the Dowager Duchess in the same room together.

"Then you can show it to me. I will see you there as soon as I speak with Lady Viola."

Apparently an hour in a coach had made the boy ready to do anything that wasn't sitting still. He thundered out just as he had thundered in.

When the child was out of earshot, Selene was ready to reassure Viola in any way. "You needn't go to Morland, Viola, of course not!"

"I'll send a note to my brother Victor here in the city and see if he is going. Oliver will take care of anything that needs attention. I won't go back there."

Selene decided to ask the delicate question that was hovering unasked in the room. "And your mother?"

Viola's voice was as cold as Selene had ever heard it. "Oliver will handle anything that needs to be handled."

"Of course." Viola didn't sound as though she wanted comforting. Families could be awful, Selene well knew now that she knew a little more about Nicholas'. "I am glad that you and I are family now, of a distant sort, with your brother married to my cousin."

"More importantly we are friends, and that is more than family often manages to be."

Selene couldn't argue with that. "Would you—would it be more seemly for us to cancel our social affair?"

"Not at all." There was the old decisive Viola. "Oliver will let us know if the worst happens, or whatever has happened. Till then I needn't do anything differently, and I won't."

"Is that for—" Viola's certainty didn't seem to have anything to do with Selene, yet Selene was grateful. "Thank you for it, in any event."

"I would rather be here with you than with my mother on any day," Viola assured her.

"Is it—she must be...?" Selene couldn't think of a polite way to finish.

"She had four children to love and squandered the love of every one of them. She could have seen herself clearly at any time and changed the course for all of us. She didn't."

Selene nodded, slowly. "I have been thinking very ill of the Dowager Duchess, Viola. She... when His Grace was young and should have had a champion, she was not there. But she seems to recognize that."

"Personally, I feel differently about those who hurt people through inaction, and those who hurt people through action. I would leave it to the Duke to sort out, as you leave Edward to him too. Unless he removes her from his life, he is choosing to deal with her, and you can respect his choice."

"But he doesn't deal with her. Nor she with him. They live a handful of miles apart and never see each other, for all they are cordial and the children too."

"Perhaps that is what works for them." Had that been a shrug? "Knowing my own family's failings all too well, I wouldn't presume to judge."

Selene felt a need to hug her mother. "I'm glad you will stay."

"Let us get those invitations out, those hats will not knit themselves and London must be won."

"If we do this, there must be shopping." Virginia was firm. "You may need something for your own affair, and the Ayles' evening is the very next night."

Selene entertained herself for a moment with thoughts of what would happen if Betty were loose in the shops.

"I must give Betty and Martha to sort through what we brought with us." She didn't mention that they might need more time given how it had all been bundled up and moved here in the middle of the night. "Mr. Hoyland, have them bring the bouquet to my room."

"The bouquet is downstairs, ma'am, the housekeeper is arranging it in our largest vase. It will be brought to you directly."

"But I thought—" She'd smelled it, she was sure she had. "Yes, please do."

Jonas said quietly as she passed, "I don't suppose you'll have any time to speak with me."

She owed him a debt, her life was too complicated right now, and others could hear. "Has your position changed on anything?"

"Not in the slightest."

Wonderful. "I certainly owe you for your assistance last night, Lord Callendar, though it has not changed my position either. We will speak again."

She could smell orange blossoms everywhere, and lemon and rosemary cologne, and she wanted time to cry, by herself, alone somewhere, perhaps for a year or two.

But then she felt again that yawning sense of betrayal, and her back straightened. "Good afternoon."

* * *

"SAY THAT AGAIN, MR. COLLINS?" Nicholas couldn't believe his ears.

"Lord Callendar for you, sir. I put him in the blue vase room."

At the sight of Nicholas' face, Mr. Collins seemed to reconsider putting the guest in a room full of fragile porcelain. "Shall I send him away, sir?"

"No, I will go right now, myself."

* * *

WHEN HE CAUGHT sight of Nicholas, Jonas set down his hat. He'd been keeping hold of it in case he was shown the door.

"Your Grace."

Nicholas didn't even pretend to be polite. "Is she all right?"

"Yes, certainly."

"Then why are you here?"

"Your wife berated me just two days ago for attempting to seduce her." Jonas flicked an eye towards Talbourne. "Which I wouldn't have said out loud, had I thought it would put my life in *immediate* danger.

Which I see it has. Dammit, Talbourne, you would be so much easier to like if you didn't go straight to making a fellow feel his death was near."

"Callendar, since you address me so informally, surely it must occur to you that your wisest course is to leave this room right now. And possibly London."

Jonas refused to move any muscle that might give away how those words settled in the pit of his stomach like a cold stone. He'd decided he was the sort of man who wasn't ready to give up the fight, but who still fired a warning shot over the bow of an honorable opponent.

"Two days ago she had no interest in me at all. Last night she asked me for several favors, and she told me openly that she was grateful I was there." Jonas rubbed his cheek. "She was grateful."

"I do wonder what your plan of retreat is from this conversation."

"Any sensible man would have the same question I have. What did you do?"

"I… have only been myself." Nicholas didn't move, but something gave Jonas the impression that what had been incandescent rage the moment before had collapsed into despair.

At that Jonas turned and faced the man head-on. He looked straight into Nicholas' face, searchingly and long.

"Do you know," he said as casually as if they were simply crossing paths in a ballroom, "I think I hear what she hears. Under the cool music there is a man screaming to get out."

"Lord Callendar," Nicholas bowed formally and turned on his heel to walk out.

"I thought you liked the truth."

The man kept walking.

"Isn't that what you wanted Parliament to hear? Just the truth? No one's plan to get richer, no one's plan to seize land, just a little truth on which to be a little wiser?"

That made His Grace pause. "I have a great deal of respect for the truth."

"Will you hear it?"

Nicholas turned and fixed him with just one eye.

Jonas spread his hands, displaying his lack of a weapon. Still his words cut. "I think I may be in love with your duchess. But she would not hear me say one word of that."

"I don't doubt that."

"I know. You are angry with me for daring to want her, not with her. Never with her. Because you know you can trust her, not just with me, but you can trust how loyal she is to you."

The Duke said nothing.

"Two days ago I was in an agony of disappointment because she so clearly did not care for me. One day ago, I told myself to stop being a child, that I was despondent only because she was the first thing I've ever wanted that I couldn't have. But last night she told me she was grateful to me, and I realized I had two choices: encourage her to lean more upon me until she needs me wholly, or listen to her words and consider what a friend could be."

"A friend." The word was cold granite, the way Nicholas said it.

"A friend. It is a difficult idea, sir, and one I have been thinking hard about, as you may imagine. I originally came to Talbourne House to befriend you, perhaps offer you my support on a vote I'd heard rumored you wanted. One on which I happen to agree with you. For many reasons, most of which I won't bore you with, but partly because you have never asked anything of me. And that intrigued me. Almost everyone in London has asked something of me at one time or another."

"Including Her Grace, now." Nicholas' voice was too emotionless to be called sarcastic. Instead it was bleak. "You have earned all the friends you wanted, then."

"No no, you misunderstand. I misunderstood too. I was foolish. She wanted a true friend. Someone with her best interests at heart. I thought from our first meeting that you could use a friend too, but I thought I had nothing to offer you that would make that happen. I like helping people, you didn't need my help, and that was that. Now I realize, friendship isn't traded like that. Either I simply am your friend, or I am not."

"Lord Callendar…" Now there was gravel in Nicholas' voice, and it was sharp. "I do not want to be your friend."

"Don't worry, you're not. But you still could be. Perhaps because of your goals, or the company you keep—which I very much admire—or perhaps because of your duchess, whom I admire even more.

"So I'm here to tell you what you don't deserve to know." Jonas shrugged. "That I only want Selene to be happy. And what she wants is you. No accounting for tastes, but I know it for certain. As do you. You have the power to give her what she wants. I don't. Not yet."

"You told her that I was a cold fish and that she deserved better."

Jonas grinned, an honest grin that reached his eyes and made them dance. "I know how many listeners there are in a duke's residence, sir. I stand by the statement, though it wasn't intended for your ears. Do you disagree with it? You *are* cold, and she *does* deserve more than that."

Nicholas' hands closed into fists.

It was the most involuntary gesture Jonas had ever seen from Nicholas.

Jonas ignored it. "But you were cold when she met you, and still she lights up for you. Before you let that die you had better be sure you can live without it."

"If it is already dead?"

"Well, I came to tell you it isn't." Jonas put his hat back on, and pulled on a glove preparatory to his departure. "It's the most noble thing I've ever done, and I don't mind telling you, I may not have another big gesture like this in me. If you can't figure out how to repair things with your duchess, I won't feel bad at all about convincing her that I am a far better choice."

"I thought you wanted to be my *friend*." *Now* Nicholas gave the word quite a bit of sarcasm.

Jonas only grinned again. "And you said you didn't wish to be mine. If you insist on being a swine, I won't continue to cast pearls before you, I assure you. I'm not stupid. And I *can* win. But only if you quit the field."

Not waiting to be dismissed by the Duke, Jonas tipped his hat. "Good day, sir." And left Nicholas standing alone.

THE GRAND ARMIES

"Ugh, cards are coming back by the same messenger with regrets for the knitting affair." Virginia tossed the little pile on the silver platter before them.

"Well, I may be out of London society already, then." Selene's voice had a careless tone that she did not feel. The urge for revenge was fading. Now she just wanted to make some kind of place for herself.

Though it would be nice to gain those votes and give them to *anyone* who wasn't Nicholas.

"London society is a changeable thing." Viola didn't sound as though she'd lost hope yet. "Do you know anyone who can help persuade ladies to attend?"

Her mother, whose social persuasion they had already tapped. Dr. Billingsley was with her now. Her health had improved to the point that she felt a bit acid about old friends who had never come to see her while ill (and *poor*), but she was willing to have them for Selene's sake, and Selene would take it.

Cass' husband might know a few ladies to persuade, if Selene understood some things she'd overheard correctly, but he wasn't available now. And that would be scraping the bottom of the barrel.

Selene snapped her fingers.

"Yes I do. Lady Donnatella owes me a favor. Will you send her a message?"

* * *

EVEN THE BIRDS on the blue parlor wallpaper seemed to be mocking him.

But Nicholas was going to do this anyway.

Mr. Lyall had been dispatched to London with all haste to see if there was any news of what the icy Duke of Talbourne had done to his lady. There was gossip, but no credible version. The truth didn't always surface quickly.

The worst had happened, and he had survived. The yawning abyss inside him hadn't swallowed everything up. He'd lived to play another day.

And now that Nicholas was resolved to properly *finish* his plan, he had no time to waste.

"My friends," he said, shocking them all from the start, "I need a favor."

They could not have looked more surprised had he pulled out a knife and started shaving his head.

Lady Hadleigh and Lady Fawcett both had eyebrows climbing sky-high, and even peaceful Lord Halworth was blinking.

But Halworth spoke first. "Your Grace, we all owe you more than we can ever say. You have only to ask."

Nicholas felt his throat get a little thick. So easily. He might have had such consideration at any time just by asking for it.

"Obviously Her Grace has decamped for the town house in the city, and who could blame her. I might get on anyone's nerves, and marriage has its ups and downs, doesn't it."

Both ladies started in with a chorus of *oh no's*, but Nicholas just shook his head. "No one could blame her, I assure you."

That made them subside.

"But I suspect you already know how attached I am to my duchess, and... ah..." He couldn't do it.

He *had* to do it.

"If you learn what I did to send her packing, I would be grateful to know it."

Well. The eyebrows had nearly reached the ceiling. The maids would be scraping them off.

"Not what I expected," Lord Halworth admitted.

"More importantly, she will be attending, and holding, social affairs. It's extremely important that Lord Burden be kept away from her."

He'd always have servants watching. But servants couldn't always be in the room.

And he couldn't rely for something this important on that damn Callendar.

"I never liked him," Lady Hadleigh said immediately. She didn't mean Callendar, she meant Burden, realized Nicholas.

"Don't be silly, *no* one likes him," Lady Fawcett piped up. "This isn't just about disliking him, is it, Your Grace?"

"No, it isn't. And be careful—don't put yourselves in any danger. Just, keep an eye on Burden and make sure he stays away from the Duchess of Talbourne. He's both stupid and dangerous and that is a terrible combination."

Nicholas' eyes fell on Lord Halworth. "Not that you should put yourself through the effort of traveling all the way to London. I did not want to make you feel left out."

Halworth's steady eyes just smiled a little as he nodded with his head resting on his fingertips. He understood.

"Speaking of leaving out," the gentleman said, "I suppose this is not an invitation you're extending to the other frequent occupants of Talbourne House."

"You suppose correctly. In fact, Lady Hadleigh, Lady Fawcett, I would be deeply beholden if you might give me a few ideas on how to suggest to some of our other guests that they have worn out their welcome."

"Like, for instance, the Raffington sisters?" Lady Hadleigh gave him a smile and a wink. "I have a thought for that. Plus I think I have a friend who is about to send Lady Villeneuve an extended invitation, too."

And tiny Lady Fawcett burst out in a voice that was almost blood-thirsty, "Oh, let me send that Withers on her way, please, I would love to!"

She startled a laugh out of Nicholas, a real laugh. "Do exactly as you please, madame."

If the rest of the guests went away, people would notice who stayed. Remember their stories. But they knew that. If they were willing for people to start to talk again about them, Nicholas would do everything he could for them, forever. Them and Sir Malcolm.

He did have friends, he'd just convinced himself not to see them.

"Will she come back, do you think, Talbourne?" Lord Halworth asked him quietly.

Nicholas felt his insides sink, slowly, as he shook his head. "I have to hope so."

* * *

THE TOWNHOUSE DIDN'T SUIT Lord Thomas; neither did his grand-mama, who watched her grandson tear up and down the multiple staircases with a sort of bewildered horror. Two days and Thomas hadn't lost his passion for that.

But if Nicholas didn't stop her, Selene would have Mr. Lyall bring him every day. And Nicholas *didn't* stop her.

He was always willing for her to do as she pleased, she thought to herself with a sort of tired sadness, alone in the drawing room.

What she pleased—she missed *touching* him. She missed his hands, his voice, his laugh, and the scent of orange blossoms seemed to follow her everywhere.

Speaking of following her everywhere.

"The Right Honorable Baron Callendar," Mr. Hoyland announced, and Selene just wanted to melt between the floorboards and disappear.

"Jonas, *what?*" She couldn't fake sounding gracious any more.

"So charming." He came into the drawing room and pulled a chair close to where she stayed leaning against the settee's arm.

She felt like she needed it to hold her up.

"Are you going to visit *every* day?"

"Yes."

"You aren't going to tell me anything else about your feelings, are you?"

"No. Christ, you're hard on a man's ego, Selene."

"Then why? Why do you come here and make me have to think of something to say to you that won't embarrass either of us?"

Jonas was silent long enough to let Selene breathe, in, out, again, and hope that maybe he would just go away.

"Shall I call him out?"

Selene *screamed* and clutched at him.

She had his coat lapel in her fist when Virginia ran in. "Are you all right? What is it?"

She had to think.

She could pretend lightness. She could do that. She laughed. "Nothing, I only thought I heard some insect buzzing in here that might bite me!"

"Oh!" Virginia looked at her fist clenched on Jonas' coat. "Shall I—?"

"I'm quite well, really, I'll be along in a moment. Thomas is in the garden."

As soon as she had gone, Selene hissed at Jonas, "Don't you dare. Don't you *dare*. That is the *last* thing I want. Do you *hear* me?"

She wanted Jonas' agreement. She wanted Jonas to say *fine*. But Jonas said, "Whatever he did to hurt you—he ought to pay for it."

She let go her grip.

Nicholas didn't—she was sure he hadn't done anything really wrong. She might be too trusting, but he had given her that, truth about who he was. Given who he was, she didn't really believe he had gone straight from their bed to that of a paid woman in Covent Garden.

But it still hurt that those men believed it.

The humiliation hurt, and that he had left her open to it, without even *telling* her, and most of all, that he'd left her alone. Again.

Shut out.

Keeping his secrets even from her.

That breezy *Don't tell her* haunted Selene as much as the scent of orange blossoms.

She'd known that night he must have had an explanation. She hadn't wanted to hear it. Because the world was bigger than just the two of them. He didn't have a care for how she appeared. She had agreed to be his duchess; she hadn't agreed to be a target for all of London's gossip forever.

And she couldn't *trust* a man who was never there.

Except he'd been there when her mother collapsed. He'd been there when she really needed him.

But that had just been luck.

"I knew my mother would be upset at my husband dealing with Lord Redbeck, I told you so. I'm only giving her a little space to recover."

"Bollocks."

Selene shifted away from him. "People don't talk that way to me, sir."

"I backed away too quickly, before. I should have realized it would only be a matter of time before he let you down once too often."

Yes, he had. But she wouldn't admit that. "He didn't, Jonas, he really didn't." When had she become the sort of woman who used a man's given name in private? Since she'd got married, she supposed. And Jonas felt like an oddly close sort of friend, even given how much trouble his supposed adoration was for her.

"You look like hell. You have circles under your eyes, you're not sleeping. You aren't even sitting up straight. For you that is nearly catastrophic. If he didn't do this, who did?"

Well, she *had* agreed to marry him. Agreed knowing he didn't love her. She had given herself to him completely knowing that he didn't love her, only *hoping* that her most secret dreams could still come true. One couldn't be a duchess on luck and hope. Maybe that's—

Maybe that's what she got for falling in love all by herself.

She wasn't going to talk to Jonas about their fifteen minutes a night, who was good at winning and who was good at losing, or kissing Nicholas among lilac petals, orange blossoms, or the curtains of her bed.

A real duchess, Selene suspected, could cut ties with a man she loved but who didn't love her, and still stay under his roof.

But she couldn't.

"I can't explain it and if I could, I wouldn't to you."

"Thanks for that."

"Leave him alone, Jonas, please. I am *begging* you. Please."

"I won't touch him. But how can I help? There must be a way to help. Give me something to do for you."

"Unless you know ladies of the *ton* willing to come socialize with me and knit, there's nothing."

LADY JULIA HARRELL brought the card with her back to the Gravenshire townhouse. "Are you responsible for the Duchess of Talbourne inviting me to this knitting affair?"

Tella sighed and closed her eyes. She put on a bright smile for her friend. "I am!"

"You don't knit."

"The point is to learn, I believe. Lady Ayles will be there, and she is bringing Lady Gadbury. You enjoy Lady Ayles' company."

"You've never done anything domestic in your *entire* life."

"Oh pish, Julia, I still have time to learn. Not everyone can already be as engaged as you are. And I'm not dead yet."

MR. COLLINS BROUGHT Lady Fawcett a card at the dining table.

Nicholas hoped it was about Edward first. The boy had come home but refused to leave his rooms, and Nicholas was worried.

After that he hoped it was something good about Selene.

Lady Fawcett examined it. "The Duchess is holding a knitting affair Thursday."

"Are you invited?" Now that the dinner party was smaller, they were grouped around Nicholas at the end of the long formal table. He appreciated it. It made him feel less lonely.

"Of course not. But I know when it is."

"So?" The stock of liquor was also holding steady without Sir Malcolm in the house. Nicholas wondered if he ought to send some over to the townhouse. He decided to let it be. Sending the flowers was enough for now. He'd sent some every day.

She hadn't sent them back.

She probably threw them out.

"So, I shall simply attend." Lady Fawcett looked massively pleased with herself. Clearly she was enjoying having little missions of her own. Lady Withers had departed that morning after a full half a year's "visit" and Nicholas was glad no one had told him any details of that.

Nicholas appreciated the efforts of his friends more than he could say.

He still had no news that would help him directly, no news of any specific thing that had upset Selene. But he was starting to realize that he could work with only the pattern. When she was hurt she wanted him there, and she must have been hurt somehow and he was not there.

He could work with that. He couldn't fix the past or make promises about the future she would believe. He would have to wait again for the right moment, another opportunity.

Or he'd have to arrange one.

If that Callendar boy was there, he might get shot, but he was willing to risk it.

* * *

"I'll show you the garden, darling."

Selene had visited the garden several times already, as had her mother. Sir Malcolm had walked with Lady Redbeck through the tiny box garden a few times, Selene thought. Her mother's walking was getting steadier. Especially in Sir Malcolm's company.

But the baronet was nowhere around, so Selene assumed her mother wanted to talk.

She let her mother work up her courage while she poked the edges of the borders with her walking stick.

Surely the tiny paths weren't as boring as they seemed. She'd only been at Talbourne House for a little more than a week. And Thomas visited every day. She couldn't possibly really miss the grounds that much.

No, it wasn't the grounds that she missed most.

"Selene, Lord Redbeck came to see me this morning."

"No!" She reached out for her mother's hand. It had always been to reassure both of them, she knew now. "Are you quite all right?"

"I am fine. I thought I had better see him, since you had warned me His Grace was pressuring him for my share. Better for me to see him, I thought, before anything public happens."

"But what did he say?"

"He said he would pay it."

"*What?*"

"He said he couldn't see his way to paying solicitors to pursue it when the Duke was right and would undoubtedly win. He apologized, Selene, it felt quite odd. He asked if there was a man of business to whom he might direct the funds."

"*Apologized?* You nearly died! He ought to be horsewhipped."

Lady Redbeck, however, was uncharacteristically calm. "And I wish you had not had to go through all that either. Years of wondering how we would eat—I am so sorry, Selene, so sorry."

Selene stopped and pulled her mother into a hug. "I understand."

"Do you? I barely understand myself. I felt so lost and alone and in such a fog, and after keeping secrets for your father for so long I couldn't bear the idea of letting him down. But I wasn't thinking of you, darling, and I wasn't thinking of myself." Her mother squeezed her a little again, let her go but stayed close. "I think it hadn't really sunk in that he was gone but I was still here. We were, both of us."

"I won't forgive that man."

"You needn't, darling. Just understand if I do. I might."

"I won't."

Her mother seemed to be thinking about what to say next. "May I give you my arm, dear?"

Selene took it.

They walked another half-round in the little garden.

Lady Redbeck quietly said, "I think I owe the Duke some thanks for nudging the whole dreadful affair in the right direction."

"Just because he was right doesn't mean he should have done it without your knowledge, Mama. And your agreement. It is your life, not his."

"I felt the same way when you told me, but now I feel differently. Rather amazed that he was willing to take it on. I always imagined you would marry brilliantly. I never thought about what it would be like to have a son-in-law."

Selene had no idea what to say to that.

After a moment her mother added, "Perhaps I should ask him to manage the funds for me."

"If I am not mistaken, Cass has a brother-in-law who is a man of finance, Mama. Let's keep it in the family for now, shall we?"

"Yes, dear, that's what I'm saying."

Well. Selene hadn't picked up *all* her conversational maneuvers from her father.

"I would not feel... quite ready to call His Grace that."

"Well." Her mother patted her hand. "I'll leave that up to you, you're the one who married him."

After all that wrangling with her mother over what she'd said to Nicholas. The truth came to Selene in a flash. One good reason her mother had for not telling her anything, was that she wouldn't have to accept any blame if it did not work out.

"*Mother—*"

"Young man, can we help you?"

379

"Indeed, madame." It was Mr. Castle. "I asked at the door and the butler sent me round here."

Selene was *not* going to forget this conversation. But for now... "Mr. Castle, this is a pleasure."

"Shall I walk with you, Your Grace?"

Her mother seemed finished with the conversation. "Take a few more turns, do. I have things to attend to in the house."

Selene listened to her mother go with a newfound respect for—and suspicion of—her cleverness in handling people.

Once they were alone, she got right to the question. "I hope you have news."

"You must understand I am only carrying news from Mr. Hastings."

"He might as well visit. The Duke of Talbourne is not here."

"You do know there are four footmen in front *and* in back of this house, do you not?"

She hadn't. Well, it meant nothing. Nicholas had never counted guarding her as forcing her to do anything. And this was just another one of his houses.

Mr. Castle did not press the issue. "We don't know what the Duke is proposing to the Lords."

That she didn't need to know; *Nicholas* had told her what he was proposing. It had felt like it had taken months to get it out of him but it had only been that same extended week.

Time was playing tricks on her. It felt like a year since she'd heard those men's voices.

"But I do have some of that other news, gossip like you said, if you are interested."

"Please go on, Mr. Castle, I am *sure* that it will help."

"I've got to recite it quickly, it's the only way I can recall it all."

Surprised, Selene asked, "Did you not write yourself a list or a note?"

"No. This is how I must do it. Are you ready?"

"I am listening carefully, sir."

David Castle began to recite.

* * *

"THESE LOOK DEAD."

The gardener, Simon, just chuckled. "I only just cut them back, sir. They'll be as bushy as you please in a month, maybe two. No, definitely a month in here."

Nicholas had taken to visiting the greenhouse in the mornings. What he was learning would, he hoped, be interesting to Selene if they ever got to walk there together again.

And he liked it. He liked the growing things, he liked the thorny roses that grew back better after being so ruthlessly cut down.

Looking at the roses, even as a cluster of bare stems, helped him think.

Of course now he had the rest of the day to fill.

He tucked a sprig of rosemary behind his lapel and took off walking back toward Talbourne House, with Atlas trotting beside him.

He wasn't too old to learn. He was making better plans than he used to make. Still, plans took time. One had to wait for that fortuitous moment. And it was damned hard to wait.

The curtains were pulled back from some windows. Windows in Edward's rooms.

The boy seemed to want some air and sunlight, but still hadn't come out.

Surely the Duke had waited long enough for *that*.

Nicholas would never have walked up to his door and knocked, demanded, or even asked to come in. A duke's presence was an intrusion. *His* presence was an intrusion. He hated making others feel as, well, as his father had made him feel.

He could not make himself known, however, without speaking.

He surveyed the glass with his measuring eye.

Nicholas didn't want to knock on his son's door, but he bet he could throw a pebble that far.

It took him some time to find some pebbles. The greens were immaculate.

Still, once he did, he found to his great satisfaction that yes, he could throw a pebble that far.

Even down on the ground he could hear the *tink* when they hit the glass, a sound drowned out immediately by Atlas' deep, ringing bark as she leaped about, looking for whatever it was he'd thrown that she couldn't see.

Edward didn't come to the window immediately. *Tink.* Woof!

He'd need to find more pebbles if he ran out.

Finally the window swung open and his older son stood looking out.

They looked at each other.

"Did you *mean* to throw a rock at my window, Your Grace?" his son finally shouted down.

"Well, it doesn't happen by accident," Nicholas shouted back.

Edward seemed to need to think about that for a moment.

"Is there something I can do for you, sir?" he finally responded.

"Will you walk with me?" Nicholas' invitation was punctuated by another bark from Atlas.

How dire could it be to take a walk?

His son's window closed. Nicholas decided to be patient. He'd wait a few moments to see what happened. After all, when the boy didn't speak, he was only taking after his father.

Still, he was surprised at how quickly Edward appeared at the door. And stopped.

Nicholas walked over to the flagstones where he'd apprehended that would-be intruder.

"You look well enough, sir." Edward stayed standing by the door. "I thought you'd—I thought you were distraught at Her Grace's absence."

Bereft, gutted. "Parents needn't burden their children with every little up and down in life. Certainly not so much that you should avoid walking with me."

"But aren't you—don't you want her back?"

More than he could say. "Edward," Nicholas murmured in

complete honesty, "it was you I thought it would be pleasant to walk with."

The young man didn't seem to have anything to say about that, and they were all the way through the Queen Anne's garden and on their way out toward the far distant trees before Edward said, "I've been unforgivably rude to Her Grace about your marriage."

"Then you should tell her so when you see her again," Nicholas said mildly. Even if Selene never spoke to him again, he was sure she would not refuse his sons anything.

"I didn't—I had come to think of you as different from other men's fathers, you see. You don't do—you don't say the things they—I had no idea you had ever had a mistress."

Well. "I never did," Nicholas went on just as mildly.

"But *surely.*" If Edward didn't just spit it out this stuttering might go on forever. Still, Nicholas was determined to let the boy speak. "Men do not just meet a girl and marry them."

"Of course, they *do.* I think it a bad plan."

"But then what...?"

Nicholas didn't feel he owed his son all the details of his personal life. But his boy perhaps needed to hear the things he didn't feel inclined to say. As unpleasant as it was, this talking to people thing had benefits and seemed called for now.

"I knew Miss de Gauer for some time, son. I had thought about marrying her for some time. I didn't tell you about it." He fixed his son with one eye. "But then we don't always tell our family our personal involvements, do we?"

Edward shrugged off that insinuation a little uncomfortably. They would have to talk another time of the boy's love interests. "I realized, of course, that you had known her for some time. I just wish..." This time Edward trailed off and didn't continue.

"You wish I had not betrayed your mother. I didn't. Your mother and I—" Nicholas stopped walking and turned to face his son. His beautiful, dogged son who had reached an age where he wanted to know about his family. "Your mother and I made a good pair in our own way. We cared about each other. And we cared about you, very much. And Thomas. This isn't—this hasn't been a marvelous family in which to see caring, but it has always been there."

"Thank you, sir, I do know that." Edward seemed to have calmed a little. "And I don't blame you for wanting—well, something different for a second marriage. Something more... carnal."

"Son, don't think that. I hope you wait to marry the woman who feels like you've always known her, the other half of you you didn't know you missed until you met her."

"Surely you don't mean Miss de Gauer. I mean, the Duchess."

"I mean only her."

They walked on. The chief falconer was just ahead, with a beautiful red hawk on the leather cuff on his arm.

"I didn't know you—" Something was wrong with Edward now. He *wasn't* calm. "I didn't know you felt like that!"

The boy's head was down and there was something wrong with his breathing.

He was *crying.*

Quickly Nicholas pulled him aside, behind a large tree. Boys might not mind crying in public, but men didn't generally want it seen. His son was still somewhere in between.

Had he said too much about the boy's mother?

He gave Edward his handkerchief.

"Edward, please, it's fine, it will be fine."

"No, don't you see, this is what I couldn't own up to, though Sir Malcolm told me I ought to do it and do it quick. I couldn't even do that right! I never thought that she meant so much—"

"Edward, my wife is fine and I am fine and so are you and Thomas. Even Grandmama is fine, though I imagine Thomas is driving her round the twist. What ails you, son?"

"Lord Burden, he—he said something to me that day and I didn't think it was true, I wanted to talk to her myself, and she didn't seem like a serving girl *or* a lightskirt and I told him so. I went to tell him, left her standing on the stairs when I saw him waving to me, knew she wouldn't know. I went to tell him so but then I couldn't, because I couldn't be *sure.* Maybe you weren't the man I always thought I knew.

When I couldn't say anything he just left me there. But I couldn't face her again and anyway by the time I went back to look you and Lord Callendar were talking with her and I wasn't about to look. And then you *married* her, you went and married her straight away and I knew he'd been telling me the truth! But—"

If he didn't cut Edward off sometime, this could go on for quite a while. "But it's hard to believe anything Lord Burden says," Nicholas supplied himself.

"*Yes*. He's such a pusillanimous little man."

"He is that. Edward. You didn't push Miss de Gauer down those stairs, did you?"

"What? Of course not!"

"And you didn't plot with him to kidnap her later, did you?"

"Are you *mad*? I would never!"

"No. Of course you would never." Nicholas pushed Edward's hair back from his eyes the way he'd done when he was a little boy. "I never thought you had. See, I know you, don't I? And you know me. You know my head's not turned by pretty girls, and you're right. Miss de Gauer—the Duchess is special to me. So special I didn't want to miss my chance. Can you understand that?"

Edward thought this over for a moment.

And displayed some of his father's calculation when he smiled through the tracks of tears. "You wanted to secure her hand before any of those other men like Lord Callendar could snap her up."

"It's not a crazy strategy, son."

"I'll remember it."

"Yes, if you're thirty-eight. In almost every other circumstance, there's time." He squeezed Edward's shoulder a little. "Do you hear me? No need to rush at your age."

And Edward laughed, just a little. "I hear you. Don't do as you do, do as you say."

"And now I am a hypocrite. Just as well."

He stepped back onto the path, and after a second Edward followed him. He'd stolen his father's handkerchief.

"I haven't hunted with the falcons in ages."

"You didn't need to." Edward nodded toward the low buildings. "My mother came out here and did almost all the hunting with them anyone could want. We ate all the food she hunted. Did you really not know?"

"I didn't." It was all too easy for paths never to cross in a place as large as Talbourne House. His and Alicia's had seldom crossed. For some reason that made Nicholas miss Alicia, not as his wife, but as his son's mother. "I'm glad you're here to tell me these things."

The falconer saw them coming, bobbed his head at them and waved his cap.

Before they got within his hearing, Edward said, "You're not just giving up on her, are you?"

"Your mother?"

"Your wife."

"Oh no, son. I am in no way giving up."

Edward looked pleased, but then worried. "But how will you—you would never force her to come back. What will you do?"

"Same as the first time. Give the lady a choice. Perhaps a slightly clearer one this time."

* * *

THAT NIGHT in her bed Selene reminded herself it had only been days since she'd come here, though it felt like years. It had only been days, time that might easily be counted in hours, and the spinning wheels in her head did count them.

Certainly long enough to think.

And what she thought was that she could spend forever in a push and pull between her mother listing Nicholas' good qualities and Jonas listing his bad ones.

It was what she felt that mattered.

She'd had time for the hurt and humiliation to fade a little. The abandonment hadn't.

She'd slept in his arms thinking of them as two parts of the same whole, and he hadn't felt the same way.

It would have been so easy for him just to share what he was thinking.

But then no, it wasn't. He wasn't like that. She couldn't change it.

Selene did not want him to be other than he was. For that wasn't love. At least, not in her limited understanding. Her mother had adored her father, she hadn't tried to change him.

Though it might have been better for them all if she'd managed to influence him a little more.

No, she did not want to change him; she just needed to feel like she was part of something bigger than just herself. A two. A partnership. She'd thought him a sturdy pillar on which to lean, that she could make him less lonely. That was the foundation on which she'd trusted him with her body, and her heart.

She was very much afraid that her faith had been more in daydreams and fairy tales than reality.

Selene wanted to be greedy for once. She wanted to *be* loved, not just to love. Not just hidden hands underneath capes on a carriage seat and kisses behind curtains.

She wanted it *known* that she was loved. Across the kingdom. That was what the wedding at the end of the fairy tale was *for*.

She wanted to know that she was loved.

But this kingdom was quite real, people could marry for plenty of other reasons, and her wedding had been at the beginning, not the end.

Not that the wedding had really been the beginning. He'd already been everywhere in her thoughts before she came to Talbourne House. Already enchanting, with his magic potion of lemon and rosemary and suppressed laughter. She just hadn't recognized the feeling.

She'd thought she'd known him. That she had been in the right place with the right person. In danger of losing her mother, she'd thought the wedding would save her.

That she wouldn't be alone again.

Well, people panicked when they were frightened.

Selene knew now that her mother was right, understood what she'd meant. She was going to be fine; she always would have been, and she still would. Housemaid or duchess, she would make something of her life, and she needn't be alone unless, like Nicholas, she made herself so. There were so many people in her life who cared for her whether her toss-and-tumble life was rolling upwards, or rolling down.

She'd certainly learned to tell the difference.

And she loved those people just as they were, she did. She loved *Nicholas* just as he was. She didn't *blame* him for not feeling more for her than what they'd felt in that bed. (Thank heaven she didn't have to *sleep* in that bed right now.) It was just that her daydreaming self, deep inside, wished that he loved her too.

That was why princesses kept breaking the rules.

But he didn't love her. She couldn't keep chasing him constantly only to be locked out. She couldn't bear it. It was him that was in the tower and she couldn't get in.

He did *think* of her; he'd said so, and he'd explained it with kisses. She suspected her silent man really did like her. If he couldn't put it into words, was that his fault?

Yes and no, she decided. After all, just like the night her mother had been so ill, people didn't think straight when they were frightened. And Nicholas was frightened all the time.

That thought hit her like the gong of a church bell. *Nicholas was frightened all the time.* And he had been ever since he was tiny, going by his report of his horrific father. No wonder it had taken him ten years to work up the courage to try to speak up in Parliament.

Maybe *she* would have to find a way to tell him how much he meant to her. Maybe he needed the example.

But she had tried, she'd tried since the very beginning. She'd told him how she wanted to help him, how she wished he would laugh. She'd taught him to play games, and to lose, and she'd given him a *dog*. She could be saucy, but she couldn't be much more forward. What kind of message could she send that he would hear?

Maybe the out-loud kind, a part of her spinning-wheel mind whispered nastily, but Selene shook her head even though the thought was hers. She wasn't ready to do it. She'd put herself *naked* in his arms, and woke up the next day to find him gone again. *Off to a brothel*, a *different* mean little inside voice said, and Selene squashed it very firmly silent.

She really did not think he'd left their bed to find some other woman's.

But she wanted his reassurances. That felt weak. But she did want them. Not after she heard something in public. She wanted to know she didn't have to wonder.

But if she asked for those, she'd risk hearing a *no* she couldn't take. And knowing for sure that she'd been too ready to give the benefit of the doubt to someone who didn't deserve it.

She still had moves to play. She had not turned on her mother in difficult times, and she didn't want to turn on Nicholas either. But she didn't have to make a final decision on that now. She wanted those votes for herself. She wanted the luxury of deciding what to do with them, all by herself.

She was a duchess. Even if the territory she could call her own was very small. It would be peopled by loyal friends.

She wasn't giving up on that.

* * *

Burden had certainly planned to give up.

One brief meeting with an impatient business partner convinced him how unwise that would be.

Not that anyone would actually harm him. *Surely not*, those voices from history seemed to say.

Still, it wouldn't hurt to keep going. He'd always known that, once he attempted to seize the Duchess of Talbourne, he could not stop till the Duke of Talbourne was brought to heel.

He still had a few moves to play.

"Lady Burden," he addressed his mother as she wandered through, porcelain bowl in hand, probably about to dress some flowers. "We need to pay a call on an old friend of yours."

* * *

"YOUR GRACE, YOU HAVE AN UNEXPECTED VISITOR."

So? Mr. Collins usually escorted in anyone Mr. Lyall chose to admit. People came and went all the time. "What is the problem, Mr. Lyall?"

"Says he's a baronet, but looks like an ocean castaway. Beard out to here, sir."

That description could only fit one person.

"Show him in, please."

In just a few minutes, there the gentleman was, framed in his doorway. He was rangy and tall, with a cane, his reddish beard was indeed bushy, and he wore an old-fashioned rose-embroidered waist-coat under his coat.

Nicholas had become rather partial to roses.

"Sir Michael Grantley, sir."

"Thank you, Mr. Lyall. Sir Michael. Do come in."

The man stood in his door, as if assessing the threat before he entered. "Your Grace."

Nicholas shrugged and instead of returning to his place behind his vast desk, took a chair. "You're welcome to sit. Is your leg bothering you?"

"Not much. Quite a drive."

"You came alone?"

"Yes, my wife said I should come."

"Of course, I remember your wife. I regret she is not with you, but then I regret Her Grace is not here to entertain her either."

"Well, we both know that, don't we?"

The young man seemed to decide something, came and sat after all. Seated, the straps and buckles of his artificial leg showed just a little under the drape of his unfashionably full trousers.

The Duke thought he'd better wait to see what the man had gone to all this effort to say.

Left to silence, what the man had to say was, "You've put my household into rather a tizzy, sir."

"I didn't know that."

"Did you not?" The baronet fixed Nicholas with a pair of unwavering eyes that were currently as cool and hard as moss-covered stone. "My—Anthony isn't spooked by anyone, but he's spooked by you. And my wife is half-convinced that you've threatened either to kill Her Grace, or to lock her away in a castle somewhere. She sent me to find out."

"Ah. No plans for murder or imprisonment, I'm happy to say."

Sir Michael did not relax or nod. "You're lucky Dr. Burke has been pulled out of London by a family emergency, sir. He's a gentle soul and an idiot in some ways but he loves his wife, and she loves her cousin. And you might not know this about him, but he's a very good shot."

"And why would he now want to shoot me, sir?"

Sir Michael was still holding his cane. It occurred to Nicholas that he wished his walking stick were a little closer.

"I'm a little confused myself. I have a business partner in the city, you see, someone who knows you, though only by reputation. Everyone hears gossip about a duke."

Nicholas only inclined his head.

Sir Michael took it as permission to continue. "Now my friend says that the bets on you were always that you were the type who... doesn't care for women much. If you know what I mean."

Nicholas didn't even blink. This was a type of poker he'd learned how to play long ago. He'd graduated to tougher games.

"But Anthony says that he heard some story at the Winpole affair the other night that you'd been seen going into a whorehouse in the city. Which doesn't really square with what I know, if you follow me."

That story. *That was it.* Nicholas could have kissed him, this stranger who'd walked in his door with exactly what he needed.

He didn't bat an eyelash but at this moment he was ready to crown Sir Michael king.

"What horrendous gossip. What can I do for you, then, Sir Michael?"

"You can tell me what to tell my wife."

Nicholas had to figure out what to tell *his* wife. "You don't discuss this sort of thing with Lady Grantley, surely."

Michael just shook his head. "You prove that you have never really met my wife, sir. There's nothing she won't discuss, I assure you."

"Even so, I can't answer your effrontery in coming here with such wild accusations by explaining myself to *you*."

"Beyond inappropriate, I know. But I gave up on being appropriate some time ago and I assure you I am better off for it. Lady Grantley is very fond of Miss Cull—Mrs.—She's fond of Cass. In that lady's absence, she has taken an interest in Her Grace. And I can promise you, sir, as surely as I sit here, if Lady Grantley comes out here to interrogate you, you'll be worse for the wear."

Nicholas decided he quite liked Letty Grantley, too.

He smiled.

He smiled at a man he didn't even know, leaned back in his gilt chair, and just waved a hand as if to invite Sir Michael to help himself to anything he liked. "Is Lady Grantley attending Her Grace's knitting affair?"

"No. She's terrible at it." Michael didn't take the conversational bait. "So, did someone tell Her Grace a little too late that she'd married a molly? Or were you actually buying the wares of the ladies as reputed?"

Nicholas was enjoying himself. "Now why would I admit to being a molly when it could get me pilloried in the street, or even hung?"

"Because you don't care. You pulled a housemaid out of Dr. Burke's house and married her. Reputation can't be your top worry. And if it were, you could have married any number of more convenient women."

"I married my wife because I wanted to marry my wife, sir, as you may well imagine without even asking me." Nicholas' tone was the careless assurance of the very highly placed. Who could make a duke do what he did not want to do?

"The very reason why I suspect you are not of the man-loving persuasion. But I wanted to be sure. Lady Grantley wasn't sure of my guess."

"Good God, man, you discuss such things with your wife?"

Michael shrugged. "I was in the Navy. So then you did visit the

Garden house to sample some wares?" Far more than the other possibility, that made Sir Michael look disgusted.

"I didn't. I had some business to conduct there."

Michael still looked puzzled. "But—"

"I have been *extraordinarily* forthcoming, sir. You cannot imagine that I will allow you to take this line of questioning further."

He didn't owe anyone any explanations of his inner life.

And he didn't care to discuss it, except with Selene.

"Sir Michael, I'm extremely grateful that you have traveled all the way out here to visit me today."

"You are?"

Nicholas would have to work on his welcoming voice. "I am. I am in your debt, sir. If you will excuse me, I have some rather pressing matters to attend to." Armed with this, he could go into battle tomorrow night and actually win. Maybe. With some luck. And a wife with a very forgiving heart.

"You are?" Whatever Sir Michael had expected from coming all the way out here to ask the Duke of Talbourne if he loved men or frequented prostitutes, it hadn't been the promise of a favor.

"I am. I hope we meet again, sir. Under more fortuitous circumstances."

Nicholas stood, indicating that the interview was over, and leaving Michael without much to do besides stand as well, unless the man were prepared to browbeat a duke.

Nicholas waited till Sir Michael had a firm footing, then bowed. "And I'm almost afraid to suggest it, sir, but perhaps when we meet again I'll have more occasion to speak with your wife."

* * *

"SELENE!" Virginia was hissing.

"Don't hiss in the hall. Do come in."

Virginia was at Selene's side with speed, as Betty placed the last few hairpins.

Selene was nearly as nervous as she had been for her wedding. "What on earth is the matter?"

"*Lady Fawcett* is here!"

"Never tell me so!" Selene's smile, no, it was a grin, spread so widely across all her features that Virginia was astonished.

"Shall I send her away?"

"What? Of course not! I like Lady Fawcett. And oh, Virginia, he sent me a *spy*!"

"He sends bouquets every day as well, you don't get this excited."

"Don't you see? This is something important, something that would need his attention!"

"You two are both very odd." Virginia leaned a little closer. "So do I understand that you consider this a show of affection? Does this mean we are favoring the Duke today?"

Jonas had been back, good as his word, just to ask for errands, every day; Selene always saw him and sent him directly away.

He wasn't Nicholas.

She liked Jonas, she did, and he had been an extraordinary friend.

He might even be, someday, the sort of gentleman who would send a lady a spy.

But Nicholas was that sort right now.

Other women didn't see the charms of her husband. Surely that was lucky.

If she got her feet under her doing the duchess work, she'd face him again and figure out how, or if, she might have everything she craved of him.

SELENE WASN'T GIVING UP, but this wasn't easy.

"It is so hard to be away from one's husband so soon after marriage, isn't it?"

Yes. It *was*. This was the half-dozenth veiled barb that had come her way as all the ladies sat around the warm, cozy drawing room filled with the smell of fresh-cut spring flowers.

It was the first one she felt immediately she could answer.

But she wouldn't. She had strict instructions from Viola not to answer anything directly unless it was whether she wanted another cake. She was to be *mysterious*, and mysterious people didn't answer questions.

Presumably Betty's work, hiding one of her ruby combs discreetly in her hair and draping filmy chiffon around her décolletage, made her seem more mysterious too.

Instead she just gave a not-quite-smile that Viola had insisted would be mysterious too, and let Virginia steer the conversation away in that adroit way she had.

"There are too many social events to be bored or lonely at this time of year in London," Virginia asserted quite firmly, and murmurs of assent went round.

"Though one gets tired of one's husband away every evening, with Parliament in session," a voice Selene didn't recognize half-whined.

"Wednesdays and Saturdays are quite enough of my husband's company for me," another lady answered, and there were answering giggles.

"I think it exciting, with the new Parliament in session. It began so early, and there is so much for it to do."

Selene *knew* that voice. She just had to place it. Not her father's, no, Talbourne House. Not her wedding... *Yes!* That was Lady Ayles! She remembered, after all the discussion of whether or not to wake them up on her first morning as a duchess! She'd bid them farewell. Had not had time to speak more.

Well, she wanted to talk to Lady Ayles more *now*.

But she couldn't. She had to follow the rules and be mysterious. For the moment.

"Exciting is *not* the word. Nothing ever changes," someone else contradicted Selene's new best friend.

"Not at all. Parliament is designed to change slowly and to change things slowly, though things can change in a moment as well. The Earl of Rawleigh is quite ill, I believe. We may have a new one at any moment."

This observation by Lady Ayles sobered the group. "I don't believe I've met his heir," someone said.

"I believe you may have," another lady answered. Lady Gadbury, that was who that was. Lady Ayles had brought her.

"Oh, do you know him, Lady Gadbury?"

"We've met."

"And will he be another eligible bachelor for the London social scene?"

"No." Lady Gadbury was curt. "He's married."

Lady Ayles didn't seem at all interested in the new Earl's marital status. "Once the Crown calls him to sit, if he serves, he may do great things in the Lords yet. He is quite young, I believe."

"Nonsense," said the lady who felt nothing ever changed. "Why, the Duke of Talbourne took his seat quite young and he attends assiduously, yet I've never heard any great change coming from it."

Selene firmly stifled the instinct to defend Nicholas.

"Well, he's not that young any more." The lady who was happy to have her husband gone most nights was speaking again. "Maybe at his age one's energy has run out. Lord Callendar, for instance, is far younger and more energetic. Don't you agree, Your Grace?"

It was a trap.

They wanted gossip, some of them, and they wanted gossip about her and Jonas. That was why they had come.

She couldn't be mysterious and answer them, but she couldn't say nothing. Defending herself, or Jonas, would be disastrous. Not answering them would be even worse.

These women didn't know her. They respected her title a little, but if they could make a meal of her reputation, the title wouldn't mean much.

And there was no one to outrank them.

Well, maybe one.

Maybe two, she thought as Lady Donnatella stepped into the breach. "Really, Lady Worringlen, I don't know why you bring up Lord Callendar. He does not sit in the Lords and I hope it may be some time before he does. He is too busy socializing with all of London to attend to any serious business."

Under cover of Tella's voice, Selene leaned close to her mother, whom she had seated at her side for just such an emergency. "We need the Dowager Duchess. *Now.*"

For once her mother didn't argue or avoid.

Her mother put down her knitting and silently left.

Lady Ayles, who was sitting in the next chair over, made a joke of it. "I cannot blame Lady Redbeck for retreating. I thought I knew how to knit but these needles are proving me wrong."

"Really, Marjorie, this isn't hard," sniffed Lady Gadbury on her other side. "I haven't done it since I was a child but the memory of one's hands comes right back."

"My hands have no memory. But it is good to do something that will produce some results. These are for some children, you said, Your Grace?"

But Lady Worringlen hadn't retreated. "Do tell us, madame, what children do you have hidden away that need so many mittens and hats?"

There was a rustle of skirts at the door. "They are not hers, they are mine."

Smothered gasps went all around the room, followed by the *pluff* sounds of soft balls of yarn hitting the floor as the ladies all stood. Then the rustling of curtseying skirts. "Your Grace," said Lady Worringlen. "I had no idea."

"Really? I have long been a patroness of the New Road orphanage, Lady Worringlen. I would have thought you knew." With the perfect carelessness of one who had spent a lifetime telling people nothing, because they ought to already know everything about her that mattered.

"Duchess," said Selene, making it crystal clear that there were only two in the room, and that she was the only one with the rank to address her mother-in-law as such. "Do join us."

"I will not, but thank you. Lady Redbeck was only seeing me to the door. I have a schedule to maintain, as you know."

"We do know. This is the season when everyone in London is so busy." Lady Redbeck sounded innocently agreeable. "Some of the ladies were just saying how astonishing it is that Lord Callendar, who has such a full schedule, still finds the time to visit us daily here."

"Not so surprising. He only stays a handful of minutes each time. I believe he is a friend of my son's, is he not, Duchess?"

Bless her bless her bless her. Though that was a question Selene would *not* answer, the Dowager Duchess' good work had already been done. *Her* reputation was unimpeachable.

A few more decades of help like that and Selene might consider forgiving her for not doing better by her son when he was small.

"I would never speak for the Duke on who is his friend and who is not," Selene murmured with what she hoped was the appropriate amount of deference, either to the question or to her husband's rank.

"One of those men who thinks that by turning up unexpectedly, he is being helpful," said the Dowager Duchess without genuine interest. "Good afternoon, Your Grace. Ladies."

The murmurs and rustling that went round the room were better than music, as far as Selene was concerned.

* * *

SELENE DIDN'T HAVE a move to make here.

She had at least five, each one with a number of possible consequences, both good and bad, that would shape the rest of her play, possibly for the rest of her life.

Because people's memories were long. And now was when she truly would create an impression of herself that would stay with them. *Mysterious* would do, at a distance, but what people talked about behind closed doors would be the person she chose to show them now.

It had to be really who she was; otherwise it wouldn't last, wouldn't stick. It had to be something that she truly believed.

And she believed that no woman deserved to die on a desert island because she had dared to venture out of her tower and speak.

Being mean to Lady Worringlen now would only be fun for people Selene didn't wish to please.

Being kind would be both more strategically useful, and more who she was.

"It really isn't possible to remember every interest of every duchess, surely," she murmured to the room, giving everyone a chance to join in soothing Lady Worringlen's feelings.

The general murmur of assent told her that her war council had picked the right people.

"Thank you for saying it," said one very young voice, a lady just married out of her first season, if Selene remembered correctly. "I was just sitting here terrified of what I ought to know about Her Grace *and* you!"

That made everyone laugh.

"I mean—your pardon, Your Grace."

"No pardon needed. I am not terribly formal. Her Grace's age has its privileges, surely."

"Nonsense, darling," said her mother, being her wonderful, usual self. "You have never been terribly formal, which I am privileged to say because I have known you all your life. I imagine Her Grace was far more formal than you when she was three."

"I fully intend to go the other way, becoming less and less formal as I grow older," Lady Ayles put in cheerfully.

"That is because you spend all your time reading all the papers, and gossiping about it all with your husband like a schoolgirl," said Lady Gadbury, sounding both very fond and a bit jealous.

Bull's eye. Lord Ayles, Selene recalled, had stood for his seat in the House of Commons not just because his father had funded it, but because he was passionate about it.

So passionate, apparently, that he had married a woman with the same interests.

"I cannot imagine who would not find the new Parliamentary session fascinating," and the general well-broad groans and slight scoffs around the room said that Lady Ayles' passion was well known and not generally shared.

Well, Selene shared it. She would make sure Lady Ayles stayed after the others had gone.

She reached out to pat the arm of Viola, whom she had seated on her other side. Viola patted it back. Yes, Lady Ayles would be a brilliant new ally.

"I for one am grateful you give me direction, madame, for without it I would not even understand the dozen words a week I do hear from my husband." Lady Gadbury was definitely a bit sad, and jealous of Lady Ayles' marriage, but fond of her friend.

"And I am grateful you do not speak of it further, Lady Gadbury, or our bridge games would be the last stone on my coffin," said the lady who was bored with London life. They laughed.

"I am glad you, at least, do not repeat all the legislative gossip, Lady Alland." Everyone fell silent. It was a bold move of Lady Worringlen, venturing back into the conversation after her set-down. "It is all petty, shopkeepers counting windows when they ought to be worried about the larger world."

The ladies all nearly held their breath, waiting to see what Selene would say. It was her party, and she was the one who had returned Lady Worringlen's sly sharpness with graciousness.

Lady Worringlen apparently had some bad feelings to work out. That was fine. She was here because her husband was both a frequent attender to sessions in the Lords, which was rare, but also one of the main parties to the Talbourne proposal to carry a canal to the sea.

"It does seem bizarre, doesn't it, to count windows and tax us upon how many we have," murmured Selene. "But then just as foolish to brick up windows, as people do, just to avoid the tax. Not that darkened windows bother *me*," she added, to see if her guests were relaxed enough now for her to make a joke. Some laughed. Good enough. "It seems that everyone wants to argue about windows without asking the larger question of what Britain's money buys for Britain, and why we need to tax windows."

There. All the necessary pieces were in play now, surely. Selene would have Lady Ayles, Lady Gadbury, and Lady Worringlen stay to dine. Viola and Virginia and her mother would ensure it. Lady

Gadbury would be bored with actual political talk, so Selene would have to find a way to amuse her if the conversation lasted long. But Lady Worringlen and Lady Ayles would care, and Selene was sure that if she played the game right, she would have not one vote but three that she could practically give as a gift to Nicholas... or whomever else Selene decided to favor.

It might spoil Nicholas' chances for that canal.

But if he would not talk to her, he must know that she would decide these things for herself.

* * *

"I CAN'T THINK of a thing that would interest you, Your Grace." Lady Fawcett was brimming with apologies. "I tried to remember every word on the drive home, but it was really so much about knitting."

Nicholas was willing to bet heavy money most of it wasn't truly about knitting. And he still wasn't a gambler.

"Perhaps not the topic, Lady Fawcett, but the people you might recall." The downside of having insides all mushed up and mixed with feelings, like hope. He had hoped for something from Lady Fawcett's adventure.

"Well, the Dowager Duchess did pop in, and that was almost too exciting, I assure you. Lady Worringlen got quite a set-down, and your Duchess was very nice about it."

Worringlen? Interesting.

"Did the Duchess speak to no one else?"

"She spoke to many of us, of course. There *was* a bit about taxes." Fragile little Lady Fawcett was almost wringing her hands. "I do wish I had more to tell you, sir."

"Never you mind." Spying wasn't a task that could be learned all in a moment, realized Nicholas; then he wondered how long it had taken Selene to train those two stalwarts of hers.

"She hugged me before I left."

"Did she?" Surely that was good news? "I did wonder how Her Grace would take your uninvited visit."

"Yes, I thought she might say more, but then she didn't."

If Selene didn't even care to take note of Lady Fawcett's visit from Talbourne House, had she truly washed her hands of him? Nicholas felt the idea gnawing at his insides.

He wouldn't know if she had any more to say until he spoke with her himself.

* * *

"LADY BURDEN, you know I cannot promise anything, but I *can* say that the Countess does expect to be there."

Angels were singing for Alistair; this was the sort of conversation that he loved. No need to say *what* Countess. It would be *the* Countess, as everyone called her, the right one, because that was how these sorts of things worked out for him.

"*You* won't need to invite her, surely." Lady Burden sat still long enough to keep her eyes fixed on her friend.

"No no, I believe she's already been invited; of course she is invited to everything. It's more a question of assuring that she attend."

This was how Alistair should have tackled the problem from the beginning. A refined solution, not clumsy spies and clumsier kidnappers.

He was *so* delighted, in fact, that he let it pass that the medallions on the wall were merely painted, and let his mother enjoy three full cups of tea before insisting that they leave their hostess to her day.

She was so lucky to have her son to look after her, he thought.

* * *

AFTER THEY'D GONE, the lady pulled out a piece of very plain notepaper she kept in the back of her drawer, and composed a very short note.

IN CHESS AND IN STORYBOOKS, moves are constrained. It is difficult to simply throw the pages on the floor, or shake all the pieces into new positions.

In life, however, it happens all the time, and whether such shocks are intended to be for good or for ill, one can't always predict what will happen.

* * *

THE NIGHT OF THE AYLES' ball, Nicholas took off his gloves, ready to put his plan into motion, and was approaching the garden gate of the Ayles townhouse when Mr. Lyall came flying around the corner of the garden wall at a dead run.

He'd only just left Mr. Lyall seconds before.

"His Highness is coming," Mr. Lyall panted, hands on knees. The man wasn't a runner. "He is expected within the hour. They're keeping a spot for his carriages in the lane."

Well. That changed things.

Nicholas' instantly revised what he had thought would be a well-planned playing field. "Jonathan is with Her Grace?"

"I haven't heard different, sir."

"And... the Countess?"

Mr. Lyall just looked grimmer than usual. "If his Highness will be here..."

Yes. Of course she would. The Prince's former mistress would undoubtedly be here. "I hope not the Marchioness as well."

Having the Prince's *current* mistress there would make the mix explosive.

Thank goodness there was no danger of the Prince's wife attending; that would presage the apocalypse. Fortunately, she hated her husband.

Mr. Lyall just looked as helpless as Nicholas had ever seen him. "I had no idea this would happen, Your Grace. I can only apologize."

"Not at all, Mr. Lyall, no battle plan survives contact with the enemy. I thank you for even the small warning."

In an instant all Nicholas' intentions changed but one.

He could lose anything but her.

* * *

NICHOLAS SAW HER COHORTS, as he thought of them, as soon as he was inside the door. Lady Viola appeared to be in better health, he thought, in something pale green, and Miss Díaz de la Peña next to her looked splendid as always in pink.

Nicholas walked straight up to them, so quickly and directly that they both drew back.

"My apologies for abruptness, ladies, but if Lord Callendar is here, he must be kept away from Her Grace tonight."

Virginia's dark eyes narrowed. "See here, you don't get to choose—"

"So true, miss, but the Prince Regent will be here tonight."

He heard Viola draw in a quick breath. But Virginia didn't waver. "We are Her Grace's friends, not yours. We are—"

"Lady Viola, I trust that you will explain to your friend in language appropriate to a drawing room that the Prince favors mistresses who are married women, and that as far as anyone knows neither his current favorite nor her husband could persuade him to take his interest elsewhere."

"Oh *no*." Miss Díaz sounded suitably horrified *now*.

"Indeed. One drawback of our government. No one gainsays a duke—except a prince." *Or the King, and now this Prince had taken on that mantle as well*, thought Nicholas.

"Is there any real danger?" Lady Viola's eyes stayed calm, her voice low.

"Madame, I do not know. Better safe than sorry. He likes women who are pretty and fascinating—that doesn't set him apart from most men, I know, but there are few women who meet that measure."

Nicholas took a quick look around. The guests had largely arrived; he had intended to make a dramatic entrance. Clearly, His Highness intended to make one even more dramatic, but he would likely be there any moment. Callendar was nowhere in sight. "See here, ladies, His Highness tends to gravitate toward women that he thinks are... not particularly attached to their husbands. Say what you like about me, we can fight that battle another day, but keep Lord Callendar away from her. It is not about my reputation or hers. It is about this one large, dangerous, sharply toothed trap."

"We will." Virginia didn't argue any more. "Someone *laid* this trap?"

"Oh yes. Someone due for a reckoning." Nicholas didn't mind letting his anger bleed a little into his voice.

"Not Lord Callendar!" Viola seemed scandalized by her own thought.

"Oh no. Not Lord Callendar, I'm sure of that."

* * *

HE HAD SAVED what he really wanted for last.

He had saved what frightened him most for last.

He knew where she was, had known where she was from the moment he walked in the room.

Lady Redbeck drew back in her rolling chair, looking mostly astonished as Nicholas bore down on them both from out of nowhere.

"Your Grace," and he put every ounce of feeling he could into calling her that, "if I may."

* * *

NICHOLAS? What was he doing here? Had her mother known he would be here? From the way she sounded like she was fidgeting in her chair, it would appear not.

From the moment Selene realized that he was *here*, he was here and he was coming over, right now, no more time to think, Selene's mind emptied of thoughts of what her mother was doing, where Virginia and Viola were, how she'd planned to tell him how she'd gotten those votes for herself.

All she could think was that he was here, and she had never been so happy in her life.

He leaned close, the way he could when he had something to say only they would hear, and his words came quick.

"You are in some danger. It will not look obvious. Will you trust me enough to follow my lead?"

"Why?" He was a smart man. He knew she wasn't asking him for the whole story. She was asking him for the stakes. If he couldn't tell her that, he wouldn't be telling her anything.

"Because I love you and I cannot bear to lose you," he murmured just by her ear.

Worth playing for, though she doubted he meant what she wished him to mean. "Yes," said Selene.

"May I?" he murmured before he took her hand, just the way he did, as if he were about to tuck it into his elbow, as though he intended to keep it, as though it was his.

As though it had been no time at all since he had touched her last.

But his hand didn't tuck hers safely away. Instead his fingers slid between hers, his hand folding around hers until their hands melded together, an interlocking whole of flesh, blood, and bone that seemed shockingly intimate in public.

It would have seemed shockingly intimate anywhere.

* * *

NICHOLAS' calm was real as he took Selene's hand for the first time in forever and for once allowed their hands, their fingers to wrap around one another right out in public. She was here, and he was with her. They would come through this together.

He moved into the spot next to her that was his.

"I had many things to tell you, madame, and I only fear that you won't give me the time as this is not the place to say all of them."

"Can you say any?"

He could, yes he could. He would rather have kissed her. He had prepared a whole speech, in fact, and it wasn't important at all.

Her face had the thoughtful look it sometimes did, expression looking away into the distance, and there were no smiles in the corners of her eyes.

He wanted her to smile even more than he wanted to kiss her. Which was staggering, given how badly every part of him wanted to kiss her.

"No one else here will understand the way that you do that I never wanted to marry you to help your mother." He heard Lady Redbeck make some noise; he knew Lady Redbeck could hear him. There would be a lot more in a minute. He ignored her. "I did not need a duchess until I met you. I never realized how much my life was lacking until you filled all the empty spaces in it and gave my heart a reason to beat."

People around him could *hear* him. They were growing quiet.

As they grew quiet, his voice traveled farther. And more people grew still, till his voice was coming back to him from the far walls of the room, as if the hundreds of people around them were not there.

As if it were just the two of them.

* * *

THAT WAS NICHOLAS' silver honey voice, going on and on, saying daydream things in *public*.

And it didn't grow louder, or only a little. Instead, everyone around him grew quiet.

In the same way that he had caused the crowd to part before him that night at the Gravenshire's ball—had it been with a look? A gesture?—people around him turned to him, listened to what he had to say.

And the amazing things he was saying—no one around them would understand all the nuance of what he was saying. But Selene did.

"It was never because you were eligible, or willing to put up with me. Though I thank you for it. Not because I deserve you, I know I don't, but I want you, madame, and only you. And I do not mind saying it, since surely it is a virtue for a man to be in love with his wife."

Some tiny part of Selene's brain ticked over wrongly and she realized that was him saying it *twice*.

He said he was in *love* with her.

"Say that again."

* * *

THERE WAS HIS SELENE, his bold, brilliant queen, come out to play. Nicholas smiled, and the effect on the room was rather like his words. Another wave of murmuring swept the place. London would soon be flattened with astonishment.

"I am so sorry that this little separation has driven me to making these sorts of newlywed statements in public. But then again, why should I be? London's bachelors must be afire with jealousy of men as happily married as I am."

Nicholas did not look over to where he was sure Callendar was standing. He didn't know if the fellow was watching or not. In a way it wasn't important.

The unworthy little part of him that felt that it *was* important couldn't be allowed to make the rules.

"I am not a man of sonnets, Your Grace, though you well deserve them. Might you be willing to dance with me, even poor in words as I am?"

* * *

"I DO LOVE TO DANCE," and Selene's voice sounded thin to her after her husband's rich voice. But the murmurs that broke out around the room said that their sudden audience was satisfied, and people seemed to pretend at least to stop paying such close attention. Sir Malcolm was saying something to her mother.

Selene had a hard time hearing anything but Nicholas' voice. "Will there be a waltz?"

"There will now," and Nicholas seemed to nod at someone over her shoulder, and then lead her through the crowd. People made way for the Duke and Duchess.

As they had done before, at the Gravenshire's, at their own wedding, Selene knew she could take these moments for some small conversation if she kept her voice pitched to share only between them. She leaned toward him a little as he led her toward the music.

"Are you quite well?"

She expected a *yes* or a *no*. Instead he said, "Better than I have been for some days, except for my near-terror that His Highness will take a fancy to you."

She didn't ask if that was really such a dire thing. She well knew the stories of His Highness' *affaires*, as did everyone in this room.

"Yes, Lady Ayles told me so when we arrived. It was all she could talk about. I think you are overstating my charms more than a little. Certainly the situation is not so dire that you need to claim you love me before all these people."

Nicholas stopped, and drew her into his arms. Right there, in front of all these people. Pitched for her ears, but still very clearly, he said, "I only said I love you because I do. It is as much a fact as the world turning on its axis every day causing the sun to come up. People needn't test the question, it is simply true; the evidence is before them."

The music started.

Selene's heart began to pound. He was serious.

He was always serious, she remembered, except when he wasn't.

"If you are teasing—"

"Shall I place an advertisement in Bridle's Daily Gazette?"

"What are you *doing*?" It was distractingly delicious, being held in his arms this way and being swirled to the music. It was much closer to the reality of their games in her bed, than to her daydreams. Selene fought the urge to let her arms drift upwards and tangle about his neck and pull him close.

She would not fall for that game again.

"I am dancing with my wife. It is a waltz," he reminded her.

"I meant just before now."

"I was explaining how I love my wife."

He said it so easily, so smoothly, and yet it wasn't the way he usually said things at all. It wasn't in that emotionless voice that had kept his insides hidden for so long. It was what she'd always heard on the inside, but out where everyone could hear.

She couldn't—she didn't—she didn't want—

Then she threw those thoughts away. She could, she did, and she did want. She wanted him. She wanted to feel him, his sturdy, strong self, against her, every day.

It was a horrifying weakness to discover at this stage of the game.

"I've discovered I have a temper after all," she murmured to Nicholas as he danced her around the room.

"Hardly surprising; I've inspired others the same way."

Selene thought of asking if he meant Jonas, but then she thought it might be better if she didn't.

"Have you given our hostess a fit of apoplexy? An unplanned Prince coming to her party has given her enough problems."

Nicholas was apparently looking about the room. "Lady Ayles? She does look pale."

"Let us hope she makes it through the night. She has promised that her husband will take my advice in the vote on the Hastings speech. Her friend Lady Gadbury too. That ought to be enough to start them moving—"

"Selene," Nicholas said, low, against her ear, causing her to shiver, "if you don't stop I'm going to kiss you in front of all these people."

"That doesn't sound like you, I must say."

"It does not, and yet you can change my reputation just that quickly." His voice grew serious and his arms tightened a little. "Truly, we must get through this evening without the Prince Regent taking an untoward notice of you."

"Oh." Her stomach fell. "That is why—"

"*Every single word* I've said is true." His sudden vehemence surprised her. "If you doubt it, I have done a poor job of being a married man after all. No wonder you took that rumor amiss."

"How did you know what rumor I took amiss?"

"Your Grace," Nicholas murmured, "if you keep asking things and I keep answering, London will learn a great deal on topics about which we've been silent, won't it?"

"I have not been silent. I have been quite clear about what I thought and felt every day." Selene tossed her head, feeling that some gesture of defiance, no matter how small, was called for. Truly she *had* been quite open with him.

"Oh? So you have told me every detail about what that bastard Callendar means to you, then?"

"*Nicholas!*" Oh, she must *not*. Hissing carried.

"And have you told me every time I made you feel small or alone when I should have been by your side? Don't misunderstand, I blame only myself. But I need your help, madame. I need to know."

"But that's not the most impo—" Selene bit her own lip.

Nicholas' arms pulled her scandalously close. "It is *incredibly* important, to me."

For some reason that made her eyes prickle as though she might cry. She *hated* that. Why couldn't tears save themselves for private moments only?

Nicholas didn't push. "Let us survive the evening. I have a miscreant with whom I must settle accounts. I hope to do it before the evening ends but after His Highness leaves."

"Quite. I understand." Selene straightened her spine. "If you must go away, I'll look forward to when you come back."

"Duchess, I will not be leaving your side for a moment. Certainly not for the rest of this evening. Hopefully, not for the rest of our lives. I hope to discuss it with you in great detail later."

My heavens. Selene tried to make light of the way his words made her insides feel warm and heavy and the way she wanted to lean her head on his chest. "Well, *some* moments. I doubt you want to help me wash my hair."

That made Nicholas make that little purring, growling sound. Very softly, only she could hear it. "I would love to help you wash your hair."

She shivered again. He had to feel that. "We have to stop talking and dance."

"Quite so, madame. Not dripping with jewels and flowers, but I hope you like the waltz."

He sounded like—"Did you *plan* this?"

"I arranged a number of little surprises before the Prince's arrival forced my schedule."

"Had you planned to say all those things you just said?"

She felt his shoulders shrug beneath his coat. "Primarily only the part where I said I love you."

VIOLA STOOD at Lord Callendar's elbow as both of them watched the Duke and Duchess of Talbourne dance by.

There were a few other couples on the floor, but most people seemed leery of joining, as if it would take them too close to the icy Duke.

Lord Callendar's eyes, however, followed them very, very closely.

"What were you even planning to do?" Viola's voice was quiet, and curious. "Had you hoped she would be willing to seek a divorce?"

"People do. That Hastings fellow he's so keen to have Parliament hear married a divorced woman."

It took Viola a moment to place that he meant the Indian governor, not Anthony. "That took years, did it not? Or were you simply going to carry her off to the forests of America?"

"Or Russia, or China," Jonas said absently. "People do."

"No, they don't," Viola said in her practical way. "And you love London, and London loves you. You have a political future here, Lord Callendar. You must have thought that through."

JONAS WAS WATCHING his dreams drift away, the merest smoke on the wind, as Nicholas' head bent so close to Selene's. Even with a wary look on her face, she lit up for him in a way that she never did for Jonas.

"Not everything people do is so carefully thought through, Lady Viola," Jonas said over the sound of his crushed heart breaking, quite finally, in two.

When the clamor came of His Highness' arrival, Jonas turned to watch the Prince's party spilling into the already tightly-packed room. He very well understood the danger of continuing to show an undue interest in the Duchess in front of the Prince, and he wouldn't do that to Selene. She didn't love him, but he thought she still counted him as a friend, and he would do as friends ought and keep her best interests in mind.

* * *

WHEN THE MOMENT CAME, waiting to be presented to the Prince, Selene did feel her nerves making her wobble a little.

But it didn't matter because Nicholas was there keeping her hand on his arm and holding her up.

"This isn't a game," she heard his voice, urgent, focusing her attention. "This is deadly dangerous for both of us. Because I won't let him take you from me, Selene. Please, I'm begging you, do not be adorable."

"You've never told me I was adorable before, how am I supposed to stop it now?" Selene murmured through her teeth.

"Don't be saucy, or witty, or even listen all too closely. He loves people who listen to him. For once in your life be stiff and cold and off-putting."

Selene wanted to ask Nicholas to very quickly give her lessons, but then it was time, and she tried to be as stiff and off-putting as possible while still curtseying.

She hoped Betty's interpretation of "mysterious" this evening, with a tulle overlay on her dark blue gown embroidered with silver stars, wasn't as fetching as she had planned it would be.

"Charming," said the Prince as the introductions were carried out, and Selene stopped herself from biting her lip. *I am* not *charming,* she thought hard in his direction.

She knew the story of his following the Marchioness to Ireland, and could guess how Nicholas felt about *that.* The lady hadn't been given a choice in becoming the Prince's new mistress; neither had her husband.

She hadn't heard that the Prince was interested in yet another new mistress, but maybe one didn't until it was too late.

She kept her head down, did not turn toward the Prince, kept her hands still, and the smile off her face.

And she let Nicholas do the talking.

Apparently he could talk marvelously long about nothing when he really had to do it.

After some discussion of horses that was easy for Selene to ignore, she and Nicholas politely moved on and let His Highness be adored by other people in the room.

She leaned close. "Are you quite well?" He sounded fine, and his arm was steady; but something made her ask.

"This is the most dangerous party I have ever attended," Nicholas said, low, not pitching his voice to travel.

"Not really."

"Madame, you have no idea how far I would go to keep you safe. Even leave you alone when I most want to be with you."

"*That* was why you went to the brothel?"

"That is a longer story, one that I must tell you more about later. As to rumors about my visiting a house of such ill repute," and now his voice was carrying a little, and people near them were quieting so they could hear, and Selene realized he meant to do that, "I would never ask any gentlemen to say where they had heard such scurrilous trash, as that would be to imply that the gentlemen who said they saw me had themselves visited the place. That is how society races to the bottom of the barrel, madame. Such gossip serves no one."

"So you didn't go to a brothel?" Selene asked it much more quietly.

And just as quietly, he answered. For her ears only. "I did, but I need to explain. Which I won't do fully here. It has to do with your silver-chased wedding gift."

Silver-chased—the walking stick Lord Burden had given her, the one she never used because it was so stupidly, ostentatiously heavy?

Lord Burden, who *owned brothels?*

She must have been tired that night, not to make that connection. Not that it would have mattered; she hadn't wanted to guess what Nicholas had done, she'd wanted to *know,* because he had *told* her.

She still did.

And he *was* telling her things. "Is our friend here?"

"Oh, he's here, and I will certainly find the time to speak to him before this night is over." If Nicholas was trying to sound other than grim, he was failing.

"Oughtn't you get it over with now?"

"I am not leaving your side for an instant while His Highness is here, not to mention the Countess who controls his social schedule and picks out new mistresses for him."

"My heavens," Selene said faintly. "They must know each other well for her to... do such things for him."

"She is a past mistress of his."

"Never say so." Even fainter still.

* * *

NICHOLAS SMOTHERED an urge to bury his face in her beautifully arranged hair and mess it all up.

Instead he led her to a reasonably defensible corner, wishing for some sturdy stone slabs that would provide better cover.

"It must be quite shocking, being an old married lady and learning so much about affairs that I would bet your father talked about as entirely political."

"It is educational every day," she agreed. "But Nicholas, is the danger so very much?"

"Madame, in this case I am more grateful than I can say that you were willing to follow my advice without time to consider and even though we parted on such… difficult terms."

"You asked. And you answered my question."

"You make the game sound simple. When I could have lost." Nicholas squeezed her hand when he wanted to kiss it. "I still might."

"Not such a simple game, when we have both been playing it so badly. Have you met him before?"

"Oh yes. If he is bored—and he is often bored, he has no gift for governing and is too lazy to ride the horses he so adores—he tries to soothe his lonely feelings with a fascinating *married* woman who makes him happier."

That Selene considered, as if acknowledging that there was some small danger of her being willing to make people happier.

But she said, "I don't concern myself too greatly with making people happier. Perhaps I should."

"No, you concern yourself with making *me* happier. And greedy as I am for it, I don't think him smart enough to know whether that can be transferred to him." Nicholas made sure all the people he was watching were still where he expected. "Or perhaps he is smart enough for that. As he picks women who have become unattached to their husbands, or never were, who want someone to appreciate their fascination and who are willing to give him the endless attention he craves in exchange."

"But that isn't *me*."

"Tonight it will not even be the *appearance* of you. Callendar is on the other side of the room and not even *looking* at you, and I would bet a thousand pounds that he is smart enough to stay there. You have your mother here, and a husband who is nearly unhinged in his adoration of you, and you are being suitably uninteresting. That is our safety tonight."

"I wish I had known. I would not have asked Betty to try for *mysterious*."

Nicholas surveyed her gown. He hadn't even noticed it. "Ah, is this the dazzling Betty's work? It is a pretty frame, madame, but one most sees the artwork, and as you apparently don't feel at all mysterious right now, you don't appear mysterious either."

"I could learn to be mysterious," Selene insisted. But quietly.

"You could learn to be anything, madame, I am positive of it. I only want to make sure we are free for you to do that, and not traveling the globe escaping the grasp of a—" Best not to say that thought out loud. Not even in a defensible corner.

It wasn't easy, judging how far to let his feelings have free rein in public. He also had to keep in check his hope that they would have some time alone together, later, when he could let the storms loose and show her how wildly he wanted her.

It was one thing for her to let him rescue her. It was another for her to love him back.

* * *

HER PARENTS HAD NEVER EXPLAINED this side of London, and the spinning circles in Selene's mind, had given rise to new spinning circles to incorporate all this new information.

She would need a *lot* of time to understand all the nuances of all this.

She knew everything known to London society about the Prince's true love, as far as anyone knew, the woman who was twice widowed and the wrong religion for a Prince to wed. She was older than he, and perhaps gave him the type of attention the Prince must have craved, growing up the way children did in these castles where family members might go weeks or months without seeing one another.

Even without knowing any more about him, Selene felt a little sorry for him, loving someone who made him less lonely, but not being able to have her because he was a prince.

"I think we need to go home and give the children hugs," she murmured to Nicholas.

One of his arms came around her waist. Most inappropriate when they were not dancing, but the crowd was thick enough that perhaps no one would even see. "Does that mean you will come home, Your Grace?" His voice got rougher. "What if I said *please*?"

Heavens. Just the sound of his voice made her straighten her spine to hide the way it made her hot and liquid inside, her knees weaker and her lips startled open.

She hoped it didn't show, but it must have, because then Nicholas' voice was rougher *closer*, right against the shell of her ear where it gave her shivers she couldn't control. "For the love of God, don't look like that."

"For the love of God stop *doing* that, then." She meant her hand to push him away, but it just rested against his chest, where she could feel his heartbeat through all his clothes; and she wondered if he could feel hers too, because it was all she could hear. "We will sort all that out later."

"At home?"

Wanting him this desperately was dangerous for her, too, if he would disappear again the next time it was tactically called for.

Ah. But she perceived it now from a different perspective. These roles they filled, they had constraints. Other forces had a disproportionate effect on their personal lives. The Prince couldn't have the woman he loved, so he took ones he could take.

Thank heavens Nicholas had not faced that type of constraint. But he still had to balance what he wanted with what his responsibilities required.

Like eating nasty fish.

She'd known that, of course, known it since she was a child, but still had not truly realized its possible effect. On her own life. On him. And on her.

It came to Selene in a building wave, like a roll of thunder, that he was *exactly* the person she had always supposed him to be. She *could* rely on him. He would take action in a crisis to protect her, and her happiness. He could put what *he* wanted aside in an instant to do something for her.

He was a peculiar sort of reliable.

"Will you be honest with me? That means being direct."

Nicholas' breathing was a little ragged. "I think you left me because you weren't sure of my feelings, weren't sure of *me*. But I have always been honest, madame. Not, perhaps, forthcoming."

Perhaps? "I found my breaking point. It broke."

"Surely we can mend it?"

Selene felt tears pricking behind her eyes. The ability to suppress tears, she thought, had turned out to be useful in the life of a duchess —or perhaps just in the life of Nicholas' duchess—and that seemed a miserable basis on which to build a life.

"I tried so hard to be everything you needed, and you kept brushing me away—" Oh, those tears were going to make an appearance if she did not keep tight hold of herself.

A little wildly she wondered if the Prince Regent was particularly attracted to tears.

"The mistake was all mine. I thought I only wanted you for my bed. That alone was earth-shattering. I never suspected there was more. It was bad enough to want you, to *need* you, likely far more than you needed me."

"Hah." Her half-laugh almost choked her. "That a housemaid could give—"

"Far more than a duke. That was the case. *Nicholas* needed *Selene*. And still does."

Selene regarded the tiny whisper of hope that flared up inside her as suspicious. "I am too trusting."

"Only I would say something like that just in time for you to use it against me."

"You said I was an eligible coal bucket peacock."

"You said half those things yourself."

"Yes, that's the way to play this, Nicholas, that's going to turn out very well for you."

Nicholas made a noise that must have been his teeth grinding together. "Give me a little *time*, madame. It has been less than a fortnight. Even at my most pessimistic I thought it would be at least a month before you left me forever."

"Perhaps." They couldn't keep standing here in a crowded ballroom whispering to each other while her hand rested on his chest where anyone could see. "How *boring* it will be for you to reassure me."

"I could do with a bit of boring. I haven't even told you yet about the kidnapper I apprehended outside our door."

"*What?*"

Selene's voice *was* loud, and it carried.

Nicholas hoped that loudness didn't remind the Prince of the music halls he liked. "I am only saying that we have quite a bit to talk about." He was still conscious of the way they were in public, always in public, but his arm around her tightened a little. "Give me a quiet place and a little time."

Selene opened her fan and fanned herself. "This isn't quiet."

"Yes. Elsewhere. But this crush won't last. His Highness' friends are not here. This isn't his usual crowd."

Selene stopped herself from rubbing her fingers with her thumb, instead clasped her hands most appropriately by her waist. "Someone invited him here specifically."

"Oh, you know who that was."

She'd never heard him sound so openly disgusted. But then, there was someone here more rotten even than old, salty fish.

"I wish I could be in the room when you speak with him."

"It will be easier for me if you are not."

* * *

Viola and Virginia convened by Lady Redbeck's chair, which Sir Malcolm was managing for her.

"This is an extraordinary affair." Virginia was wearing Selene's pearls woven through her hair and she looked like a goddess. Good enough reason to be wary at a party like this. "Am I correct in understanding that unmarried ladies are safe from His Highness' attentions?"

"As much as anyone can be." Lady Redbeck was unexpectedly tart.

Virginia ducked her head a little to catch the lady's eye. "And widows?"

"I think he's had his fill of widows, too."

"The more fool he. I've quite come to like them." Sir Malcolm patted Lady Redbeck's shoulder, just once.

Virginia caught Viola's eye.

"How are you feeling, Viola?" Virginia kept her voice low.

"As well as ever. Tired. Which happens often, but I am well enough." Viola nodded to where Lord Callendar stood alone, watching the dancing with an uncharacteristically somber expression. "He isn't terribly well."

Virginia patted Lady Redbeck's shoulder too, then moved around the chair to draw Viola aside and regard the forlorn fellow. "This is an experience that will be good for him," Virginia said in her decided voice. "He needed to be thwarted a little. He can't have everything he wants."

"When one has never had any exposure to it, the first dose of reality can be quite a shock to one's system," muttered Viola.

"Young, healthy—he will survive." Virginia dismissed Callendar with a flick of her fan. "What of you, Viola?"

"I have a note from Oliver; my father is declining. I wish he and I had more to say to each other." Viola's eyes picked out Selene and Nicholas where they stood. "People say His Grace is cold. They have never met someone who is truly cold. It takes a certain type of person to freeze out their children."

Virginia contemplated the Duke and Duchess. His Grace's muted dark and silver hair seemed a perfect complement to Her Grace's bright head. They seemed to say little to each other but to be hearing each other perfectly. She wanted that, someday. Perhaps. "No, he isn't that cold. He reminds me of one of those steam engines, you know, the new ones, with so much pressure built up inside that one is in constant danger of explosion."

"No, he isn't. Selene wouldn't care for being constantly in danger of an explosion."

"That's what I mean." Virginia tapped her fan against her skirt thoughtfully. "When he is near her, he isn't."

LADY AYLES WAS DEFINITELY REGRETTING HOSTING a party by the time the Prince departed.

"You can actually hear the nervous excitement calming down, can't you? I so regret not attending you more, Your Grace."

"Please don't apologize, Lady Ayles; I promise you I feel nothing but sympathy. Into every life some trouble must fall, and if a Prince at your party is the worst that befalls you, you will be doing quite well." Which was only true. Selene could not imagine the horror if the Prince decided to attend a party of hers.

"Who would ever have thought that His Highness would accept my invitation? He never does. One sends them, you know, so as not to offend him."

"Lady Ayles," Nicholas interjected, "are you more free of responsibility now? I would be so grateful if you would keep my wife company until I return. I must take care of a little business matter."

"I salute you, sir, I have nothing left in me. But my husk will be glad to entertain the Duchess. Please, madame, there is a comfortable settee on that wall and we can find a cool spot to sip some punch and plot for Britain."

"You are truly a woman after my own heart, Lady Ayles. Your Grace—" Selene waited till Nicholas bent his head a little closer. "Be careful."

"Always, my lady, never more than when I know you are waiting for me."

"He is charmingly romantic," sighed Lady Ayles as Nicholas walked away.

"He can be," and Lady Ayles had no idea why Selene's tone was so dry.

BURDEN WAS HELPING himself to someone else's claret.

"I thought you might be more willing now to talk about some of the ways in which I will be needing you to vote," he said as poured.

"I'm not," was all Nicholas said from where he had closed the door behind him.

Burden rolled his eyes. "You do not seem to grasp the position you are in, Your Grace."

"I have many faults but I always know exactly what position I am in, Lord Burden."

"No no," and now Burden smiled because he was enjoying himself. The light glinted off the ruby liquid in the crystal glass he held, and it nearly matched the light glinting off his teeth, his grin was so wide. "I have been waiting to explain it to you. I have arranged things such that you need to acquiesce to my requests."

"No."

Talbourne's near silent immobility drained the pleasure out of the moment for Burden. Drained the pleasure out of the claret, even. He set the glass down.

"Your Grace," Burden said with exaggerated correctness, "you don't seem to understand. I know your wife has left you, hell, all of London knows. But I know more. I know that you rescued her from a life of servitude—I wish I'd seen that, a de Gauer washing laundry, that would have been delightful. After the looks her father used to give me. And I know that you only did it because of a mad passion for her."

Talbourne still stood exactly where he was, his tiny shrug only emphasizing that he wasn't frozen, but ready to strike.

Burden wasn't worried—though he also did not go closer. Eyeing Talbourne from his safe distance, he went on. "An unfortunate mad passion, given that the woman has so soundly rejected you. *So* soundly, in fact, that I have arranged for His Highness to meet her this evening. I don't think your wife will find it hard to give up that puppy-eyed baron who is following her around for a prince."

"The Prince Regent."

The wariness in Talbourne's tone was like honey to Burden. Now the man knew with whom he was dealing. Burden had made arrangements with the Countess who kept His Highness' social calendar. He'd just shown he had the woman's ear. It was a significant power.

If he could read anything from Talbourne's face, it was that Talbourne did not like it.

"The same. He likes his women tall, but he also likes them witty, and your wife will suit him there." Burden felt so exultant he wanted to crow like a rooster. This was it, he was *winning*, and against the icy Duke so many in London were too timid to cross. "She may not appeal to him at all. Perhaps she will only want an audience with him to petition him for a divorce."

"She may." More than anything else Burden had said, that seemed to weigh on the man he was attempting to bring to heel. His shoulders hunched a little and the words were slow and heavy. "I hope she does not."

"I suspected as much. You have a *tendresse* for her, which I suppose I can understand given that the girl is pretty and she cannot see you to be bored with you."

Talbourne fixed him with an eye.

The duke didn't seem to realize that he ought to look defeated. It was unnerving. Burden had to remind him who had the upper hand. "Make no mistake, divorced or not, if you do not vote the way I wish, I will spirit your wife away to some place where you will never find her."

"No, you won't." The Duke turned and walked along the wall, pausing to admire a particularly deftly painted *trompe l'oeil* medallion featured on it. "What you mean is that you will kidnap her and stash her away in one of the many brothels that you own in London—or perhaps Bristol. But you won't."

Burden's smile didn't move when Talbourne mentioned *brothels*; after all, Talbourne had simply walked in and taken that French girl out of Burden's pocket. He did, however, falter when Talbourne mentioned *Bristol*. But he rallied. "So you have learned some secrets of mine as well. Regardless. If a threat of hiding her there has no teeth for you, then a threat of employing her there may have some weight.

Even a few gentlemen seeing her there, dressed the part, would destroy her for society, wouldn't it? How many men do you think it would take?"

Talbourne just shook his head. His eyes glittered like cold metal as they lit on Burden. And he kept strolling, closer to the table where Burden had set his claret down.

It occurred to Burden that he might want to examine the portrait on the opposite wall, just to keep his distance. He moved that way.

"You are unimaginative, Lord Burden. Well, perhaps so am I. But you also stupid. And you are cruel. Kidnapping has not been used for political purposes in Britain for more than a century, and you decide to revive it. Foolish."

"It works because people like you still have things they hold dear."

"I know." Talbourne paused in his stroll across the room and stared at his feet. "Oh, I know."

"In your case, a wife you have already badly used. All of London knows she has left you; despite your little performance, no one in London will question if she disappears. In fact, unwittingly you have put me in the best possible position to carry out this plan."

"You?" Talbourne had reached the table, but did not even put out a hand to touch the crystal decanter Burden had already breached. "You are in no position any more."

"Talbourne, you are ignoring me. I warn you, do not." Anger made Burden pull himself up. He was explaining exactly how he had the upper hand. "I have the resolution to do as I say."

"Do you?" Again those cold eyes raked him up and down. "I doubt it. You could have pushed just a little harder when you ran past her at the top of those stairs and she would have tumbled over, wouldn't she? You could even have ordered that spy you planted as a maid in my house to slit her throat, and she would have."

"I could have, but I couldn't use her against you if she were dead. It was a mistake. I was standing too close to her and moved too quickly."

"Something startled you, and you ran like a rabbit. You thought my son was returning, perhaps. You are made of the same stuff as the person you employed to capture her at the Gravenshire ball, just as willing to run."

Burden just shrugged. "And Céline is no killer."

"Are you sure? I interviewed her extensively and she has a steel in her that you lack entirely."

"You—where is Céline now?" Burden knew he still had the upper hand, but losing possession of Céline hadn't helped his plan.

"She is on her way out of England right now, as the man to whom I entrusted her care does not want to cross me."

That was unfortunate. The small part inside of him that was nearly screaming with alarm was growing. But Burden held on to his confidence. "The Frenchwoman was not your vulnerability. Your wife is."

"My wife? The Duchess of Talbourne? Whom you have not so much as spoken to since I learned of your plot? You will never have the chance to get within an arm's breadth of her again."

That sounded ominous. Even the dimmer parts of the back of Burden's brain were alarmed now. In fact there was a chorus of shouting voices inside him and they were all shouting *run, run, run*.

But the Duke was just a man. Just standing there. Nothing to fear. He had not even brandished a weapon.

Burden managed to scrape up one more dollop of courage from somewhere. "You cannot be everywhere all the time. I may yet get close."

"You would be surprised at how many places I can be. Aside from a personal skill for doggedness, I have two things you lack. Willing staff, and at least a few friends."

"She has been friendly to me in the past. She will receive me."

"Because you gave her a present? No. She won't." Talbourne's voice was quiet, still filling the room, disgusted and menacing and still somehow patient. "My dog has better sense than to be bought off with something from you. You have to bribe people with things they actually want. As I have done with a few of your people. They are disappearing from you, rather more than usual, are they not? And you cannot kidnap enough to replace them. Because your places are watched by my men."

Burden's bluster was trickling away. "It is a legal business."

"That does many illegal things. I know all your so-called *company* tricks, I know where you go to take unsuspecting girls from the streets or even from their homes—" here Talbourne's lip curled, as if even he could not stop it—"and I have the means to follow those men and foil their attempts, I promise you, to the end of time."

"A crusading moralist? I never expected it of you. You cannot stop every brothel in London."

"I can stop you."

That was a blow. Burden felt it as such, right under his ribs, chopping at his breath. For the first time he realized that the parts of his brain that were trying to tell him he was in danger might be right. "And me?"

"What about you?" Talbourne sounded as if nothing interested him less.

"You can't do anything to me." His over-welling confidence came to his rescue again. "Brothels aren't illegal. And if you have known for some time, you must obviously realize that there is nothing you can do to me."

Talbourne nodded. "Every action carries its own risk. Inaction is always safest. But there comes a time when one must act and know that one is ready to take the consequences."

The duke backed away from the candles on the table, till his voice issued from the shadows. "You are right. I cannot bring any legal question to bear on you. But you overlook the dangers of justice as we carry it out. You are more likely to be convicted of practically anything simply because no one likes you. I understate the case, actually. No one likes *me*. But *you* are positively despised. Partly because you lack the intelligence you profess to have. You are so lacking in intelligence, in fact, that you have handed me the very weapon with which to end you."

"Meaning?" There was nothing between him and the door. If Talbourne lunged for him, he ought to make it.

Though it was Talbourne's very stillness that made him seem so deadly. He stood there, a gray outline of a man, on the far side of the room and never drew closer, leaving Burden the path to the door.

But he did still speak.

"His Highness has a *soft* spot for women, you fool, one of the many things that you lack. You think he spent all those years pursuing a *Catholic* woman from a Protestant throne just out of stubbornness? His feelings rise and fall more often than the tides, as does his bank account. But he does have feelings. He likes to be advised by women, and the women who advise him? *Those* women do not like procurers.

"I might never have crossed paths with the same Countess you threaten me with, but that you brought her here tonight. Here, where I can arrange far more than you can imagine. You are right in the smaller way. *I* cannot do anything to you. But the Prince Regent can. And he is going to hear some very unsavory things about you tonight. I would not be surprised to find you banned from court. Who knows? He may decide that you disgrace your title and find another use for it."

And then Talbourne's voice grew icy. "And though you belittle my steadfast inhabitance of middle ground, I assure you it is an excellent position from which to persuade those on all sides of me that despising *you* is something on which we can easily agree. You no longer have a political future. And I suggest you leave London."

Rather than stepping towards him, Talbourne stepped back, completely into the dark. "There are people who would prefer to see me beat you in the street with my fists. They like punishment to be immediate, visible, and violent. They don't understand that all I had to do was keep my own protected till one of your wilder swings carried you to the ground. I kept you watched, and protected my own, and let you destroy yourself. Even had you waged an all-out war against me, it was always going to end this way."

Burden was feeling ill. The claret was giving his mouth a bad taste. "And if I waged war on you now?"

The Duke of Talbourne seemed to fill the room though he remained in the dark and had not moved a muscle. "So lucky for you, if you don't."

* * *

NICHOLAS WAS tired and he wanted to take Selene home. It would take more than an hour to get there.

They ought to go to the townhouse. It was so much closer.

He didn't have to make decisions alone any more.

"Shall we aim for Talbourne House, my duchess, or leave it for the morning?"

"Will Thomas be quite well alone?"

"Hardly alone, madame, as the residence is filled with people to care for him including Edward, but if we leave early, we will see him in time for a walk in the morning." He lifted her hand and kissed it. "I left Atlas with him."

"Which reminds me, we must discuss puppies."

"Really? How many puppies?" He caught sight of Callendar, looking rather lifeless but keeping his distance even after the Prince had departed. Nicholas nodded, just once. Callendar nodded back.

"I suppose that is one thing we must discuss. The townhouse ought to do." Selene seemed to think of something else. "Your mother is also a fascinating topic of conversation."

"I doubt it. What of *your* mother?"

"I think she wishes to stay until the smaller hours of the morning and flirt with Sir Malcolm. It is shocking behavior."

"Devastating," said Nicholas in his emotionless voice. "Does it upset you, madame?"

"No. She still misses my father more than she can say. But one can lose one's other half and still find a way to go on. You know that yourself."

Nicholas hadn't found his other half till a housemaid nearly tripped over him. He'd find a way to tell her that, too. She could know how he felt and still honor the memory of the mother of his boys. They both could. And Edward seemed to understand, which would make it easier for Thomas.

"I am more worried that I think she has decided to exert herself more so that she can walk again, and I hope that is not for Sir Malcolm's sake."

"Everyone must decide for themselves how much to gamble in life, madame. Everyone must decide for themselves when the risk matches the possible reward."

* * *

THEY FOUND themselves standing awkwardly by the Talbourne carriage, horses shifting and shuffling and Mr. Lyall and the footmen awaiting the order.

"Did we decide where to go?" Was Nicholas just *asking* her?

"I thought you had decided, sir."

"I wanted the destination to suit you, madame."

"Is this how we are going to do everything from now on? Because this is going to take a lot of time."

* * *

NICHOLAS COULDN'T STOP the laugh, it built up in him and just came out, till he found himself leaning back against the carriage, in danger of being crushed by the wheels, he supposed, laughing a deep, resonant belly laugh, arms folded across his chest and looking at his duchess.

* * *

SELENE COULDN'T RESIST *THAT*. What a devastating weapon. How unfair of him to choose to deploy it. She had to hide her smile.

"Mr. Lyall, take us to the townhouse, please."

"Ma'am."

Selene put out her hand. "You may hand me up, sir."

"Your Grace," said Nicholas most properly but, after putting her hand on the door frame so that she could find her way, lifting her by the waist to find the step.

* * *

SHE SETTLED herself in the middle of the deep, wide upholstered seat, but as soon as he entered the carriage Nicholas seated himself in the corner and pulled her against him.

The carriage rattled on its way.

Selene tried very hard not to be distracted by the feel of his lips against her hair or his arm holding her against him. "So. Is there a real version of any of that story that you just said?"

He froze.

Then he said, "A long time ago, in a tiny castle not very far from here, a maid nearly tripped over a duke. Rather than let either of them fall, the duke said, 'Miss, would it be better for both of us if I moved to another chair?' This was a charming and flirty little maid—really, inappropriate—for what she should have said was simply *yes*. Instead she began talking about all sorts of things—"

"What? I cannot believe you recall that." Selene felt her face growing warm. "You needn't just repeat everything over again."

"Apparently I do. I thought fashioning it into a story would make it less boring. The duke had been asleep, in a way, for a long, long time."

Selene relaxed. She snuggled down into the warm hardness of his arm holding her close. Perhaps he had meant it, meant every word.

She might have to hear the story a few more times to decide for sure.

Nicholas continued. "Now it may well be that many saucy house-maids in the kingdom had the power to wake the duke from his sleep, but we will never know, because this one captured all his attention."

"Wait. *Many* housemaids?"

"Well, if I must know them to find them pretty, one supposes that other housemaids—or ladies of any sort, presumably—might eventu-ally have awakened my ardor. But it was you."

"If you must know a lady before you find her pretty, you would have to talk with her, and you were in no danger of that."

* * *

SHE HAD HIM THERE. Nicholas supposed he ought to be careful with this new habit of telling her things. "True enough, I suppose, madame."

Selene rested her head back against him. Some hairpin began to dig a divot into his skin. Nicholas began removing them and placing them carefully in his pocket. He did the same, too, with her ruby comb. She didn't stop him.

She had taken the story in rather a new direction. "I really did think that you wouldn't go to a brothel, for just that reason. How would that even work? Would you pick a lady and talk with her for a few hours before..." She turned a little in his arms. "Is that how such places work?"

Nicholas didn't see the point of expounding on just how little such places suited the way he was made. "I think you were afraid of it, even just a little. Or you might have stayed to talk to me about it."

"I did think... perhaps that... that after we..."

"You thought that after I had been primed, I might be ready to fire even on an unfamiliar target?"

"Heavens." She had twisted in his arms enough to press her face into his shirt. "I suppose that's one way of putting it."

"I suppose that is no more unreasonable a supposition than that I had gone to find the company of some young man instead of a woman."

"Oh my. Oh hea—Does that—*Do* people? I mean, men?"

"Absolutely."

Selene seemed to need much more time to think about that. "People never do stop surprising me."

"I'm glad it doesn't seem to worry you, madame, since your friend Mr. Castle is rather obviously of that persuasion."

"Is he? That is *amazing*, that you know that only from looking at him. Is it something I can learn to discern, do you think?"

"In regards to some. Certainly not others. Mr. Castle is Mr. Castle, after all, not an entire class of person."

Selene's arms slipped around Nicholas' waist, and his eyes closed. This was all he had ever wanted.

She sighed. "I know you said we are on the same footing in playing that type of game, sir, but it seems to me I am at such a disadvantage. You know so much more about the entire matter."

"There is no one but you in the entire world who knows anything about how to play that game with *me*." All her hair fastenings were now safely in his pocket. Keeping her safely tucked against him with one arm, he sank his other hand into the tumbling locks of shining hair, breathing in the scent of roses and happiness and peace. "Do you not hear how holding you makes my heart beat faster?"

"I can *feel* it," Selene murmured. "I didn't know that was only for me."

"Only for you."

"I could listen to that for a very long time."

"Shall I ask the coachmen to take us to Talbourne House instead?"

* * *

THE IDEA of waking up in her own bed—or his—in Talbourne House, and breakfasting there, and walking with Thomas and Edward and Atlas, was irresistible.

The only thing she wanted more was to sleep in Nicholas' arms.

But Selene had the suspicion that she could have that anywhere she liked.

"Yes, I'm capricious, you know," she yawned. "Why don't we."

"I couldn't agree more. I myself am in the mood for a drive that will take longer than fifteen minutes."

* * *

As SHE SETTLED into his arms she let out a pleased little moan that made him hard in an instant. "If you keep making sounds like that," he murmured into her hair, "...well, it will take longer than fifteen minutes to show you what will happen if you keep making sounds like that."

"In a *carriage?*"

"Oh yes."

"Heavens." Selene seemed to consider this. "I think I would like to save that game for a drive when we are really in need of it and less tired."

"As my wife commands. I'll pick up my story again, then, shall I? Just in case there are parts of it that you do not know."

"You did not really think someone had tried to push me on those stairs, did you?"

"Since the assassination this time last year, all of London is nervous. Your friend Callendar thought the same thing."

"Really? He did not say so."

Nicholas wasn't going to discuss Callendar's good points. "I'm sure he thought as I did, that it was best not to frighten you."

"You do not truly want all the details of the French insurgents who are trying to overthrow Napoleon, do you?"

"You think I will think well of someone, and say too much."

"You cannot say what you do not know, madame."

"You would be amazed at what I have managed never to tell anyone."

"Amaze me."

Selene snuggled closer, then reached up to pull his head down so she could place her lips close to his ear. As if they were in a crowded room, or their bed. "I love you."

"I am amazed." He pulled her so close that the shape they made together rocked as one in the dark. "You win."

OCCUPYING THE THRONE

*W*hen Selene awoke in the curtained bed of a duchess, the first thing she thought of wasn't her gown tossed across the dressing table bench, or her friends and lady's maids and mother abandoned in a London townhouse, or even the large arm tossed across her as she slept.

"Nicholas, I forgot to tell you about the votes!"

The arm tightened. "You have many brilliant qualities, madame. Votes are but one."

"Yes, yes, I know. A suitable duchess."

"For *me*. Just for me, please."

That made Selene smile. "What should *I* do if *you* say please?"

"I think you know the rules of that game."

The purring, growling sound of his voice, so close, so unguarded, made Selene's very *bones* feel warmed. "It won't even last fifteen minutes if I do not fight back."

"It will last a great deal longer than fifteen minutes whether you fight back or not, I assure you."

Selene reached back to stroke his hair, loosened with sleep, as he pulled her against him and kissed her bare shoulder. "Not just Ayles and Gadbury, but Worringlen. Lady Worringlen promised."

"Worringlen."

"Yes. You… you won't get the canal you had hoped for, to connect Talbourne lands to the ocean."

Nicholas stayed so still that Selene began to truly worry. Of course, the whole point was that she had arranged things to suit herself. She *could*, very well. If he regretted it, he could blame himself for not joining forces when he should have done.

"Oh my *God*," said Nicholas in rich, dramatic tones, rolling heavily over on her as if in a dead faint. "Whatever will we *do* without that canal?"

"Heavens above, get *off*. Very well, you are teasing, I understand."

"I would gladly have traded that canal for this vote if only for the number of lives affected." Nicholas rolled a little, thoughtfully, as if he quite enjoyed squashing her into the mattress. "Though eventually we may need something like it, if we build the manufactories in Talbourne that I hope we do."

"Get *off*."

There was shifting, and rolling, and some mutual elbow poking before they settled down in a much more comfortable position.

"Hmm." Nicholas' hand, large and warm, stroked down her hip. "And Gadbury too, did you say? That *is* odd. Gadbury seldom attends."

"Lady Gadbury said she owed Dr. Burke a favor? But that made no sense to me."

"Some people's reasons are not discoverable."

* * *

FLIPPING HER IN HIS ARMS, Nicholas was able to reach the base of her throat with his kisses. Selene's hands slid down the curve of his spine.

Selene murmured, "If Lord Morgame is not brave enough to back you and the Duke of Gravenshire together, he certainly ought to do it if you have two others on your side as well. Rather, three."

"Certainly." Congratulating himself on being the model of restraint, Nicholas finally settled his mouth on the soft curve of his wife's breast.

"Oh my *G—!*"

Nicholas decided he quite liked the choked sound of her voice when he did that.

"Are you going to do that to the other as well?"

"Unless you don't wish me to."

"I *do* wish you to."

As he was obliging her, she went on. Her words were becoming more halting as she went. He could win this, he thought.

"I think… Lord Morgame… is actually persuaded by your position, he just doesn't wish to appear to be entirely in your pocket."

"I always knew that would be likely," Nicholas admitted, nuzzling his way across her soft stomach to the nest of curls where he most wanted to be.

"If you—*Nicholas!*"

The only worthwhile part of visiting a whorehouse, he thought, was that there *was* some educational artwork.

He'd been wondering for days if he might be able to be good at this. Judging from Selene's gasps and the choked words she managed to put together—he thought she might be saying something about Parliament's funding—he had some talent.

The particular way she writhed for him, so torn between abandoning herself to the pleasure he was giving her and still trying to put a coherent thought together, just confirmed all that he had ever suspected. She *was* perfect for him, he would *always* want her this much, and he had apparently been saving up all the luck due him in this lifetime to be here, with her, like this.

When he decided to let her catch her breath, Selene gasped, "I hope you haven't forgotten that turnabout is fair play. Always."

The very thought nearly pushed him over the edge. "Madame, you'll unman me."

She grinned, her eyes crinkling and her hair falling all around her as he rolled over and pulled her atop him. "Then I would win."

"Not everything is a game, my duchess."

Nicholas held his breath as she arranged herself to capture him, which, as far as *he* was concerned, would count as *him* winning. But he wouldn't tell her that.

"You needn't always be so serious, either," Selene told him with the utmost seriousness as she slid herself around him, making him so hard it was almost painful, and making him groan. "Though I do love that side of you too. Someday I hope you trust me enough to tell me what made you change your silence."

"Besides you?"

"Yes, besides me," and she smiled as she rocked back and forth a little, bringing the sun and the stars close enough to touch. "You think things you have never told me. You left those French revolutionaries alone, and left Burden cooling his heels too."

"You won't be seeing him again. I hope you do that more."

She did. "I mean, you are a man of such selective action. I wish I understood you better."

"I am a duke. You are a duchess, and I think you feel somewhat the same. I think we have that in common."

She laid herself against his chest. "How do I know if you don't tell me?"

Was this really the time for inconvenient logic?

"Is this really the time, Selene? But then as I hear myself say it I know I must practice telling you what I think. Let me try. I am a little distracted."

His very favorite and far more naughty than one would suspect duchess rocked again. "Only if you wish to."

Growling deep in his throat, Nicholas wrapped his arms around her and rolled them both over.

"More than most of her people, Britain is what *we* make it. And that's wrong." He had laid her out before him like a feast, but his body only made small, teasing strokes into hers. Selene wished she had let this topic wait.

But then he started talking.

And as had happened the night before, when Nicholas started talking, his voice demanded attention. And he had a lot to say.

"We all agree, we men of former crowns, we agree to be bound by the same laws only if they apply to all of us, together. If one of us reneges on that agreement, the law should rebuke us. The law ought to make us more equal, not less. If I had killed Burden, a jury of my peers would likely have let me go because they care more about preserving their privilege than justice. The same peers let men die for petty crimes, or for being poor. That makes everyone in the kingdom less free, for if men are subject to law depending only on how they are born, we must stay in our places like cages until we die."

Slowly he relaxed into her, the two of them holding each other. "Are you sure you wish me to tell you all this?"

"I do, Nicholas," she breathed. "I do."

"You see, if Parliament is no check on the King, or the corporations, then the people are subject to power unchecked, and what kind of justice is that? No people will stand for that forever, not here, or in India, or anywhere. Government ought to let everyone live free from fear that someone with more power will take away what they have. If it cannot do that, for *everyone*, then frightened people will overthrow it."

His arms tightened around her.

"The French did just that, then fell in love with beheading. They worshipped force, and that force put their entire country back into the hands of a king. A king who used that love of force to stretch his hand across the entire Continent."

He buried his face in the crook of her neck. "There are things we mustn't say out where people can hear."

"Then how lucky it is we have in each other someone we can trust with our thoughts," Selene murmured in between kisses on his cheek, her hands smoothing down his hair and then tangling it up again.

"Selene, Britain is holding on to her possessions tooth and claw to fund this war because we must win it. But Britain has also fallen in love, with the steady stream of money. If our government does not do more than keep money flowing into the coffers of rich men, then it will fail. Our people are tired of fear and the whims of rich men too."

She slid her hand around his neck. He was right, she did feel that too. And they did know that about each other.

He took a deep breath. "We men in these seats have the luxury of moving slowly. I know all too well how many lives are being crushed in the machinery of Britain's wealth. I wasted a decade through being unsure that I could help. I finally knew I had to try."

"Nicholas." She slid her arms around his chest, rocking herself up into him and biting his earlobe lightly, then whispered into his ear as if she were telling him a secret. "Do you realize that you are every dream I have ever had?"

"It is lucky, my darling, as I waited a lifetime to find you."

"Lucky for Britain that we have decided to be on the same side." Her tightened arms urged him to keep moving. Perhaps he could feel her crisis growing closer. The warmth inside her grew as much from his words, and his willingness to share them, as from his body loving hers. But she wouldn't tell him that.

At least not today.

"On the same side when facing the rest of the world. In here, perhaps not."

"Oh yes," Selene gasped, "what awful competition."

* * *

NICHOLAS FELT that he was missing something important as he settled into his seat in the strangers' gallery of the House of Commons. Of course he was missing something: his wife.

"This bill is for the reauthorization of this company's charter, originally granted in 1600; it is presented and ordered to be printed." The bored voice of people everywhere whose primary job was moving pieces of paper from one point to another. "This bill is referred to committee."

Lord Ayles looked up towards where Nicholas sat, and nodded.

Lord Ayles would shepherd the thing through committee, and the committee would have far more weight than the debate on the floor of the Lords, which Nicholas and Gravenshire would get. With the unexpected addition of support from Lord Worringlen, and a rare show of interest from Lord Gadbury, Morgame's vote would come along, and the far more popular man would bring a number of his friends with him. Since the Lords were funding nearly everyone who occupied a seat in the Commons, Nicholas would get his public debate, and he would get Warren Hastings to inform it.

It was a horrible system, one that Nicholas regarded as only marginally better than having a despotic King rule everyone to benefit his own personal interests.

There was plenty of room to make it better, and Nicholas had time. If his votes would no longer have the benefit of being a surprise to all sides, they would still be *his* votes, and he would not waste them.

* * *

"YOU MIGHT HAVE VISITED THE LADIES' gallery."

Selene scoffed. "In the attic. With ladies all around me peeping through a hole in the floor. Imagine how interested I would be in *that*. I ought to be able to visit the strangers' gallery just as you can."

"You ought to be able to occupy a seat of your own."

Selene loved when he said this, because she knew he meant it. "In the Commons, or the Lords?"

"Surely, wherever you like, madame."

Selene rubbed her head against his cheek, knowing he would respond by kissing her temple. He did.

There were types of predictability that she just adored.

"Nicholas!" Her spine straightened as a thought struck her. "What if I have children?"

"You have two," her husband pointed out without inflection. "I presume you mean if you have more."

She hugged *that* to her heart. "Thank you for that. Truly, my favorite of all my wedding presents. I meant to say, Edward has no interest in Parliament, and I am all too afraid Thomas *will* have. But what if we have a *girl?*"

"Not impossible, madame."

"She really ought to be able to serve if she likes, Nicholas, don't you think so?"

"I do."

Selene's thumb was rubbing her fingers, which she had gotten quite good at not doing in public. "We ought to start with a vote for her, sir."

* * *

THEY OUGHT to start with a vote for his *wife*, Nicholas thought, but of course she thought first of someone she loved. Even when it was someone who didn't exist yet. They ought to start with a *seat* in Parliament for his wife.

Something worth speaking up for.

"Yes," Nicholas said in that way he had, where only she could hear how the idea excited him. "Let us work on that."

EPILOGUE

"*H*ow many Talbourne coaches did you say were coming?"

"Three, sir, and a cart that's keepin' up with 'em well, full a' trunks and such."

"Great balls of fire. Last year it was on'y His Grace and them boys. What's happenin'?"

The stableboy pointed toward the long drive to the Scottish house of Talbourne, where the procession of vehicles was kicking up dust from the dry summer road. "Whatever it is, it's happenin' in three coaches, I'm tellin' ya."

"Take down Lady Redbeck's chair first, would you be so kind?"

"I can walk, Selene, you know," her mother said, a little testy after hours in the cramped carriage that was rather overfull with people.

"Let us not test that too much today. Mr. Lyall?"

"It's right here, Your Grace. I suppose Sir Malcolm wouldn't mind a little help pushing it up that hill."

"Let me push, sir."

"Oh, Jonathan, thank you. I don't want Sir Malcolm pushing it all that way."

"I'm not broken down, thank you very much. I've pushed that chair for miles and I'll push it miles more."

"But it needn't be today, surely?"

"Viola, do you see my knitting needle?"

"We'll find it once the carriage is empty, surely, Virginia."

"I believe I just stepped on it."

"Oh dear."

"I can replace it, Miss Díaz, with my apologies."

"Never say so, Lady Hadleigh, I'm sure it will be fine."

"Have a care for the *socks*, those are supposed to be mine!"

"This green wool is for Lady Fawcett—"

"Lord Halworth may have them!"

"—no need for noble sacrifice, madame, he is funning, I believe he is *wearing* the blue pair I made."

"Where on earth is Thomas?"

"Do not panic, Your Grace, he tumbled out the door and has already set off running across the green. I think Atlas is with him."

"How can you not *know*, Lord Fettanby?"

"Ahhh… Well, I cannot exactly see him."

"*Thomas!* Nurse Carter, can you see him?"

"…I *think* he went round the gate?"

"Nicholas!" Selene put out her hand. "Where is he?"

"He knows this place very well, my love. We come every summer." Nicholas tucked her hand in his elbow. "He will be fine. Everyone is fine. We should walk. I'd love to show you the house."

"I want to hear all about it."

"And I want to tell you everything."

* * *

Want more of Selene and Nicholas? Who doesn't?

They return in Book 4, **Crown of Hearts**

Anthony and David Castle take a trip across England.
They may kill each other—or they may fall in love.

And they return again in
The Caped Countess
befriending Tella, the hostess of that disastrous Gravenshire party!
Lady Donnatella's story begins a whole new series of
Regency action heroines in love.

SIGN up for exclusive insider news (and free advance peeks!) at judith-lynne.com, or see About the Author and find me on social media.
Keep these books coming - share a review at Amazon or Goodreads!

NEXT IN LORDS AND UNDEFEATED LADIES

A sneak peek from
Crown of Hearts...

His heart pounded far too hard for a simple walk down the lane.

Anthony had searched the woods all around the inn on the far side, wondering if Castle had stopped back where men went to relieve themselves and gotten... caught, somehow.

Hopefully, not propositioning anyone. There were no guarantees with that man.

There was no one hanging about the privies, and no sign of him along the lane, either.

Anthony could feel his footsteps hitting the dirt, one after the other. Just like he'd crossed England, staying north of London, heeding the advice of the prostitutes on the coast who'd warned him to avoid the city, avoid being pressed into their trade, and avoid being captured into a ship's crew.

He'd gotten good advice, but he'd also taken it. Had Castle ever taken good advice?

What the devil had happened to him?

Were there snakes in this part of the country? It was barely a few hours from London proper. People had lived here for thousands of years. There couldn't be any exotic traps, like dragons or quicksand or jealous gods, that would capture and kill a golden-haired little fairy-king by the side of a dirt road.

But there were always dangers of the human sort.

His steps grew a little faster as his heart pounded harder.

He could walk all the way back to London if he had to. David must be somewhere along the way. Even if someone had picked him up and forced him into a carriage. They'd only been on the road a few hours, and not at top speed. Anthony could catch up...

Out of the corner of his eye he caught sight of a space, a hollow, in the tall autumn grass.

He ran to it.

Yes, there was David Castle, stretched out in the arms of autumn itself. The grasses waved over him, curling around him, as if they were happy to cradle him there; their fat heads, full of seeds, bobbed over him, trying to outshine his hair and failing.

He'd pulled his hat down over his face, which was lucky, as it no doubt had saved him from unpleasant effects of the sun. His head rested on his bundle of clothes, and those square-tipped hands, small yet so masculine, were folded across his middle.

He was dead asleep.

This presented a veritable deluge of problems, but before he decided to start facing all those, Anthony stepped a little closer.

Mr. Castle was *very* asleep. He didn't move when Anthony quietly, with two hands, grasped the sides of his hat and lifted it from his face.

It would be quite a painting. His lashes, darker gold arcs, lay on cheeks flushed with warmth, his lips, unconsciously parted. His face was nothing feminine; it was just that men rarely displayed that kind of delicate perfection.

Despite himself, Anthony smiled.

He had no talent for painting or drawing. But he recognized when a moment called for it.

It reminded him of a moment in the story that had changed his life.

In which a man fought mightily to conquer his passion for a beautiful young Persian warrior.

David Castle, of course, was no Persian warrior.

Anthony kicked his boot.

And said, "You've lost us our seats in the carriage." Quite loudly.

* * *

Read *Crown of Hearts* now!

and turn the page for notes on this book...

AFTERWORD

Mr. Hastings—Warren Hastings, not our Anthony—was a real historical person, and his speech to Parliament in 1813 *was* unexpected because he had gone through seven years of impeachment hearings, and that speech had real consequences.

Like all real things, results were mixed. Trade *was* opened up to merchants other than those of the East India Company. Those merchants *did* cause much pain and suffering among the people of India, unmonitored and unregulated as they were. It was in many ways a widely recognized disaster.

The 1813 reauthorization of the Company also set aside 100,000 rupees, one *lakh*, for education in India, still regarded as one of if not the foundational event of a system of public education in India. The reauthorization called for "the revival and promotion of literature, and the encouragement of the learned natives of India", setting off decades of debate about whether that meant *only* Arabic and Sanskrit, as many assumed for a long time, or if it meant English too. It did not in itself reverse the goals of colonialism, in fact it aided them just as often. Nor did it magically preclude racism; Macaulay's 1835 Minute to Parliament, on the direction Indian education should take, is full of that. Rather, I believe it to be an interesting example of how government is a series of small decisions made up over time, each one of which could lead to many outcomes, depending on how they are guided by principle; in the end, the principles matter most.

I believe that decisions that lock more fairness into the system—like, for instance, providing more education—lay a foundation for more fairness to come, fairness like ending colonization. But of course, we can never be sure. Opposition never goes away, and we never know the final outcome of our decisions, as it is never the end of the story. I agree with Nicholas, that it is better to try, and encourage others to be fair, than to do nothing.

Selene and Nicholas' love story had to be more of a fairy tale than either *Not Like a Lady* or *The Countess Invention*. They had an innocence to them, a sweetness, that felt to me like a balance to their passion for politics, that dirty gritty business where no one wants to see the sausage get made but the sausage must be made nonetheless.

From the moment I began planning this series, too, I knew that I wanted to convey something of what it must have been to be one of Britain's less-than-two-dozen dukes. More power, more problems, and I knew nothing would be easy for my stone-cold duke and his flirty, devastatingly discerning duchess. That's why they needed so many friends.

And any duke would have been wary of the Prince Regent, whose actual history with women is unfortunately represented here quite fairly, I think.

Mr. Warren Hastings' impeachment itself is still fascinating more than 200 years later, and I'm indebted to John T. Noonan Jr. for his 1982 in-depth analysis of how the trial progressed. Most agreed that what Mr. Hastings did in accepting bribes and using his position for others' gain was wrong; it was, nonetheless, not illegal. It is a classic case in which we see that the law does not tell us what is right or wrong, only what can be prosecuted. (And not even that, when government is not self-consistent, as the case against Mr. Hastings progressed even though everyone tacitly agreed that he had most likely broken no law, primarily because everyone also agreed that he had *definitely* been unethical.)

The story is made even more complex by Mr. Hastings' personality, as he was apparently an intellectual fellow who desperately loved his divorcée wife and loved paying school fees for poor young British men to help them get ahead. He *did* spend a great deal of his time in India learning Indian languages, and collecting animals that he later tried to rear in England. The massive amount of money he made through blatant corruption while serving as *de facto* colonial head of India, he largely gave away to relatives, and people who claimed to be relatives. After seven years of legal costs, he was destitute. That is not to say he was an admirable person, and whole books have been, and still could be, written about that.

There was no denying, however, that he knew more about India and Britain's effect on it than any man alive *in Britain* in 1813. You can imagine my interest in the way morals, ethics, law and politics swirled around each other in such a case. A good backdrop for an icy duke who carts his unsuspecting maiden off to his castle to marry her before she can come to her senses and ask for a good lawyer.

Nicholas is his own kind of fair.

I have far more sympathy for Selene, whose father likely read her Mary Wollstonecraft's *A Vindication of the Rights of Women*; she would undoubtedly have arrived at the idea of votes, and seats, in Parliament for women, without Nicholas, but it is the two of them together that are unstoppable. It is the right time to start; in 1813, there are and soon will be children everywhere who will become the respected, and loud, voices of the 1840s. I so admire Selene's ability to remake herself in new circumstances, and I sympathize that she might have had very different adventures but for an unfortunate fascination with the scent of her secret suitor.

Jonas makes his own problems. (But I have a soft spot for him too.)

I hope the reader enjoyed seeing Virginia and Viola in this book, the one returning from *Not Like a Lady* and the other manifesting from her mysterious absence in *The Countess Invention*. While I like to think I plan well for a great many details from very far ahead, I wish that I had realized back when I could do something about it that I gave this dynamic duo, who had always been planned to be here, such similar names.

Plenty of childhood diseases did and still do cause blindness (particularly measles), with visible damage to the surface of the eye; but plenty of diseases that did and still do cause blindness, don't visibly damage the eye at all. My heroine survived a fever (meningitis) of the latter sort. I think she will forgive me, as she's a bit vain of her looks.

The white cane that we know to associate with blind people became widespread after World War I. But a cane is such a useful item for a blind person's independent mobility, and so omnipresent in Britain at the time (including the lightweight rattan type that Lord Callendar so wisely chose), that I have no difficulty giving one to Selene.

I am in awe of her ability to lose games gracefully, but then I admit that may be related to her ability to win as well. Even when she says that she is not much of a player. She may be right. Nicholas *is* extremely bad.

I hope we meet again in Anthony's book.

AND LEARN MORE ABOUT LADY DONNATELLA...

Get ready for an entirely new series!

The Caped Countess, available July 2021!
The first of the action-packed
Cloaks and Countesses

* * *

By day, Lady Donnatella seems like a duke's silly daughter.
So she can save London lives by night.

When she stumbles into something larger than a street fight, everything she's balancing may come crashing down...

It's another lonely season for Tella, dancing and gaming madly while keeping marriage away. She cannot tell her family or friends that her true self is the one battling danger in the city's dark streets. Nor will anyone guess; she's perfected her disguise.

Then her night-time alter ego is seen—just when she can no longer count on her best friend, or her beloved great-uncle. And the resulting fuss in the newspapers isn't making any of this easier. Nor is the reporter who saw her...

Henry Fitzwilliam, third son of a marquess, left London society to serve in the wars, and won't go back. He's devoted his life to telling the stories Britain needs to hear, and perhaps this Caped Count falls into that category. He can't be sure until he gets much, much closer.

Tella can handle a fight, but tracking a murderer makes for higher stakes. She might need someone at her back. Fitz might be the worst choice—or he might be more perfect than either of them suspects.

The Caped Countess

Available to order now

ACKNOWLEDGMENTS

One book is a happy thing, and two could be plain stubbornness, but three is an act of determination rivaling those of the Duke and Duchess of Talbourne, and I am so thrilled to be able to bring you their story.

As always, thanks to Holly for eagle-eyed editing and story advice born of thirty-mmph years of sharing each other's art. Nothing can replace the shorthand of having talked about writing together for this long and nothing works without her.

Thank you to Anne, who loved Nicholas and Selene as much as I did (perhaps more!), and who gave them, and me, the benefit of her gracious wisdom, her eye for detail, and her precious time.

And thank you to my husband, my inspiration, my rock and my kite string. Every day with him is an honor and a privilege and I can't thank him enough, ever.

Thank you to the people who pre-ordered this book and gave me hope in the darker days that it would find its readers. And most of all, thank you to the people who love these characters and tell me so in their reviews on Amazon and Goodreads, on Facebook, and on Twitter; this book is, as always, for you.

ABOUT THE AUTHOR

Judith Lynne writes rule-breaking romances with love around every corner. Her characters tend to have deep convictions, electric pleasures, and, sometimes, weaponry.

She loves to write stories where characters are shaken by life, shaken down to their core, put out their hand… and love is there.

A history nerd with too many degrees, Judith Lynne lives in New Jersey with a truly adorable spouse, an apartment-sized domestic jungle, and a misgendered turtle. Also an award-winning science fiction author and screenwriter, she writes passionate Regency romances with a rich sense of place and time.

Please sign up for the first information on new books from Judith Lynne, as well as sneak peeks and exclusive content on your favorite characters, at judithlynne.com!

ALSO BY JUDITH LYNNE

Lords and Undefeated Ladies

Not Like a Lady

The Countess Invention

What a Duchess Does

Crown of Hearts

He Stole the Lady (January 2022)

And stay tuned for *Cloaks and Countesses*!

The Caped Countess

The Clandestine Countess (July 2022)

CPSIA information can be obtained
at www.ICGtesting.com
Printed in the USA
LVHW061305030122
707736LV00021B/307